THE LAST DAYS OF THE

Midnight Ramblers

THE LAST DAYS OF THE
Midnight Ramblers

SARAH TOMLINSON

FLATIRON
BOOKS
NEW YORK

THE LAST DAYS OF THE MIDNIGHT RAMBLERS. Copyright © 2024 by As Is Enterprises, Inc. All rights reserved. Printed in the United States of America. For information, address Flatiron Books, 120 Broadway, New York, NY 10271.

www.flatironbooks.com

Designed by Jonathan Bennett

Library of Congress Cataloging-in-Publication Data

Names: Tomlinson, Sarah, 1976– author.
Title: The last days of the Midnight Ramblers / Sarah Tomlinson.
Description: First edition. | New York : Flatiron Books, 2024.
Identifiers: LCCN 2023025140 | ISBN 9781250890481 (hardcover) |
    ISBN 9781250890498 (ebook)
Subjects: LCGFT: Novels.
Classification: LCC PS3620.O5807 L37 2024 | DDC 813/.6—dc23/
    eng/20230606
LC record available at https://lccn.loc.gov/2023025140

Our books may be purchased in bulk for promotional, educational, or business use. Please contact your local bookseller or the Macmillan Corporate and Premium Sales Department at 1-800-221-7945, extension 5442, or by email at MacmillanSpecialMarkets@macmillan.com.

First Edition: 2024

10 9 8 7 6 5 4 3 2 1

For Kirby, my agent and my friend
Dude, we did it.

THE LAST DAYS OF THE

Midnight Ramblers

PROLOGUE:
HOW TO BE
A GHOST

Before the how is the why.

Ghosts do it for three reasons: money, access, praise.

Not public praise, of course, on a book jacket, for instance. But the more intimate nod promised in most contracts: the heartfelt note of gratitude, hidden in plain sight, on a star's acknowledgments page. That's right, ghosts are guaranteed such a mention in collaboration agreements, a sweetener to deals that, when they disintegrate, are settled via a "kill fee."

Sometimes a client forgets to mention you, the person who wrote their book. But this sting is private, and there's an easy fix. You are often the one to draft the thank-yous to the editorial team in the voice you have been occupying for months. Your editor, aware of all the reasons you deserve credit, contractual and otherwise, simply has you add your name to this list.

What you are celebrating is more than your mimicry. It's the infinite number of moments in which you've inferred just who and how to be. That's the secret to making it as a ghost. Most people think you have to be a great writer, but no one's claiming to be Chekhov. You don't need to be the person who best captures the celebrity's tone, either, although that's important. Really, it's about not judging your clients, whether they're reality TV divorcées on their way to rehab or the biggest rock stars with the deepest secrets, no matter how dark the memories they divulge or how badly they behave from the stress of deciding on deadline how candid to be; the bond is invisible, but ghosts must be capable of meeting their subjects, always, with unconditional love.

They do love you back. Sometimes. And always, it feels that way for a while, in the heady days just before and after submitting the book. Best is when they include their own, genuine and warm shoutout, mention a shared moment or joke, for which the most devoted superfan would line up overnight in the rain. Since ghosts must work in the shadows, and the job is hard and can fall apart even when you do your best, it's validating to see evidence of your accomplishments in print. As with any form of intimacy, you can't help but want an emotional souvenir, a way to capture what happened and carry it with you into the rest of your life.

There are other tricks to be mastered, as with any trade. Be patient, be attentive, be clever (be amusing, if possible), be comfortable being wrong (when some celebrities are ornery, they like a foil—those in their inner circle are easy targets). And maybe, just maybe, you'll maintain your place in the VIP lounge of life. For most ghosts, such perks are enough. They had always been plenty for this one. But that was before the project that almost cost everything, and gave just as much, by revealing another way to be: wake up and seize a life that's truly lived, which has deeper value than a spotlight, or a book credit, could ever come close to.

There's always a collaboration like no other. The one that teaches you whether you have what it takes or not. If you dare to step up, ghosting is far more than a job; it's a vocation. You must risk everything, maybe even your life, certainly your pride, your assumptions about yourself and others, and the stories you tell about who you are and why you matter. If you pull it off, you will know you are woven into every word on the page, even the consciousness of those you have occupied as a ghost. And yet you will still want, maybe even need, to be acknowledged—

It's proof you exist.

FIRST:
SEDUCE

Like an actor who cares about her craft, a ghost approaches each new role afresh, while building on the experience of her past books. Each assignment comes with its own gift bag of unique skills, and a deeper understanding of how to excel, not just at writing but at life. There are many entry points for getting to know someone well enough to become them. The first art is seduction; the trick isn't for you to be wanted by the celebrity, but to make her feel wanted, in just the right way, by discerning her deepest value system and assuring her that you see treasures not everyone can, and you will unearth them and make them shine on the page.

First, this ghostwriter must land the job. Mari Hawthorn was waiting in the Polo Lounge at the Beverly Hills Hotel on a Friday in mid-January. Beneath the distinctive green-and-white-striped ceiling, in a room with the posh intimacy of a cruise ship, silverware tinkled, and laughter rose up in waves. Perched on a deep banquette crowned by leafy plants, Mari (rhymes with "sorry," a joke her sister, Vivienne, loved to make) was starting to sweat. She tugged the wrists of her clearance rack J.Crew blazer, but couldn't remove it. Her nicest blouse had a tear in the armpit. Even business casual in LA required polish, and she'd splurged on a manicure and blowout. Her long brown hair was styled in loose curls, heavy on her neck. She ruffled her bangs, hoping for a little rock 'n' roll attitude, given whose table she was seated at.

She was about to meet Anke (rhymes with "Bianca"), infamous '60s rock consort and style setter who'd reinvented herself as a glam earth mama and luxe jewelry designer, adored by *Vogue*. Anke's staying power added to her mystique, as did her post–World War II evolution from Berlin shopgirl to international "it" girl. The first model to pose topless on the cover of a magazine, she had been a desirable companion for artists and rockers alike.

Anke's real claim to fame, though, was the love square she had formed with three founding members of the Midnight Ramblers, what many felt was the defining rock act of the twentieth century, as good as, or better than, the Beatles and the Rolling Stones. The Ramblers, too, were among the world's biggest rock stars, having provided a soundtrack of bohemian flair for three generations. They had the hit singles, going back to 1964, including "Bought on the Never Never," a youth anthem for the ages; the walls of platinum records; the handful of Grammys, even an Oscar. And they gilded their legend, still—somehow forever creating trends, launching the best new bands by giving them opening slots on their world tours, propelling the most interesting young designers out of obscurity by wearing their clothes. They seemed, always, to be one step ahead of where everyone else would want to be. With them coming up on fifty-five years since their debut, and still on top, they made it so: Rock 'n' roll was not just a young man's game. They were about to launch another worldwide tour, spanning all of 2019.

Mari's father enjoyed bragging about having booked one of their first US shows, without mentioning that he had flamed out as a rock promoter after he had gambled away the payouts of too many bands. She wasn't above telling this story at parties, without mentioning the fallout. Like many, she loved the Ramblers and had found an album for every stage of her life. Stop anyone on the street, and they could sing you the chorus of a Ramblers song. Each August, hundreds of fans offered up flowers, photos, and handmade tributes to mark the passing of the band's original leader, and most far-out genius, Mal Walker. He'd drowned at the band's LA rental house in 1969. When he was found to have been on Quaaludes, alcohol, marijuana, and acid, he had earned a place amid those iconic rockers who had lived too hard and died too young. The fact that the girl, Nancy, he'd taken up with not long before he died had been pregnant with his love child had added to the mood of romantic tragedy sur-rounding him.

A few months after Mal's death, the Ramblers' charismatic Ameri-can chauffeur, Syd, had lobbed a grenade at the band. In a *Daily Mail* interview, he alleged that Mal could handle his drugs and had met with foul play. A torn-from-the-headlines book followed: *The Last Days of the Midnight Ramblers*. The hefty payout Syd had received threw his accusations into question, and his bombastic title seemed silly as the band thrived. But ask anyone in the entertainment world: Allegations live on and retractions go unnoticed. Before the band could take Syd to court for slander, he overdosed on heroin. The events of that sum-mer had remained shrouded in mournful glamour, inspiring dozens of books and a biopic starring Jude Law as Mal. But until now, no one from the inner circle had been willing to step forward with their own memoir.

Anke would have plenty to reveal in hers. She had left Berlin with Mal and was married to him at the time of his death, even though he was also seeing Nancy. Her grief had led her to have a heartfelt love affair, and a son, with the Ramblers' lead guitarist, Dante Ash-combe, one of rock's uncontested talents and renegades. Although they got together immediately after Mal's death, the golden couple had been adored by the public. The fact that they had become a family so soon after Anke was widowed raised a few eyebrows, but there wasn't the same obsession with baby bumps as now, and the fans were almost all rooting for them. Everyone loved Dante. Not even heroin addiction, multiple tabloid-fodder divorces, or his 1980s reggae phase knocked him from his perch. He was *the* icon of cool and would be as long as rock lasted. And *then*, for five years in the early '70s, Anke had been with Jack, the Ramblers' sexy singer with the sultry moves, flash fashion, and head for business. He was the Swiss watch of the band, who had stepped in as leader after Mal died, overseeing the group's schedule, lineup, merch, and movements across the globe. Yet he appeared as free and fun as any iconoclast could be.

A longtime fan of the Ramblers, Mari felt a special connection to them thanks to her dad's dubious role in their early career, even though she knew better. She always did her research before an initial interview, and she had read all the articles, and skimmed all the non-fiction books about the band and Mal's death that she could order on her Kindle. Syd's book was long out of print, and the few copies online were selling for hundreds of dollars. So, she would only be able to justify, and afford, that expense if she landed the job.

Mari had, of course, read all the coverage of Anke in decades of fashion magazines and watched her interview in a recent documentary about Mal. Appearing regal and gorgeous, Anke spoke with dry wit about his talent and excess. But when the interviewer had tried to lead her toward revelations about his death, she had demurred. Then refused. Then left the set. She didn't give a fuck about setting the record straight. Or cultivating a likeable image. Noted.

This was where Anke would dodge her ghostwriter. It would require delicacy, but Mari would apply just the right finesse to unearth gems. Obviously Mal's death must be written with respect. And Jack and Dante were far more famous than Anke, so she must not appear to be trading on their names—any intimate stories, especially if they made the men look bad, must add up to a greater whole. For they had been Anke's love affairs, as much as theirs, and if she could own her recollections and be insightful in her observations, all could land perfectly on the page.

Mari had arrived early, a good offense. They would not begin on time—it would be off-putting for a celebrity to be punctual, like a serial killer who knits. Having attended meetings at many fashionable LA restaurants and hotels, Mari knew how to look—and even feel—like she belonged. But she never ordered before a prospective client arrived, so she waved off the server.

It had been nine months since Mari had been up for a job. She'd had a good run for a few years—learning the writing skills required to craft a memoir, and the diplomacy and stamina needed to finish a book. She had even carved out a niche for herself—"the divorcée whisperer," as her editors joked, because she had a way with the exes of famous men. They were a vulnerable but fiery bunch, and all seemed to know each other—word got around that she was like a therapist you could drink with who would hit the deadline no matter what.

But then her last client had gotten away from her, a fact her editor had deduced over a single lunch with the actress, although Mari had failed to put it together during many, many hours of conversation and writing. The diva, who had once been married to a famous boxer, had amended years of public tantrums and DUIs through sobriety and hard-won domestic stability with her third husband—the memoir's selling point. As the deadline had approached, Mari began noticing her client's suddenly erratic behavior, of course. But she had loyally accepted, and written, the actress's manicured version of events. After galleys had gone out to the press, TMZ exclusively reported the star was in a swanky rehab to avoid losing her kids in her latest marital breakup. They gleefully excerpted from her memoir, making her seem like a hypocrite and a fake. The editor blamed Mari for not having seen this nightmare unfolding in real time, and for allowing the old version of the story to be publicized via the galleys.

A more experienced ghost was brought in for a down-to-the wire revision, receiving the bestseller credit. But Mari's draft had circulated, and the discrepancy had blown up on social media, stimulating sales but further damaging the actress's reputation. Mari had technically written her first bestseller, but neither the acknowledgment—even a covert one—nor the full final payment had been hers. She was broke. And although she knew what a good ghost she could be, she still needed to prove it. This time, she had to write well and be infallible.

She had placed her cell phone beside her. The moment Anke arrived, she would surreptitiously turn it off. Until then, it must be kept on, in case Anke's assistant messaged with a change of plans. It buzzed. Mari looked down. Her agent, Ezra, was calling. She looked up. Half the people dining in the room were on their phones. Ducking her head, she answered.

"Hey, dude, when's your lunch with Anke?" he asked.

"Now."

"Oh, man, sorry, you didn't—?"

"Yeah, sure, I'll put you on speaker—"

He laughed, but it sounded forced. He was checking up on her. She needed to convince him a bit—that she could finesse this interview, and that she could handle a project this exclusive. They had worked together for three years, and he had never had to save her from disaster—no one blamed her for the actress's vodka-and-Xanax-fueled meltdown, although Mari should've known it was imminent; sometimes it took a new writer to save a project—but Mari had never given him bestseller bragging rights, either. Mari had written one book for Anke's publisher—a tell-all for a reality TV divorcée turned high-class escort. It had almost written itself. It had landed her, barely, in the publisher's stable of vetted ghostwriters. Normally, with a star as big as Anke, Mari would have had an initial interview with management, but Anke no longer had a team.

"David says she's really funny, if she lets her guard down," Ezra said.

Anke's editor, David, and Ezra were old friends, which was how Mari had been sent to meet Anke, even after her last snafu and wasteland of workfree months. Not only was she lucky to have this interview, but she needed to earn it in the room; this book's subject was of a higher caliber, and if Mari landed this ghosting job, she would prove herself to be higher caliber, too.

"Any other tips, coach?" she asked.

"You're a natural. But sometimes you try too hard. Don't let on how much you want it."

"Doesn't she want me to want it?"

"Sure, but you can't seem like you *need* it. Publishing is changing. It's no longer a sure thing that you'll ghost a book or two a year. You're the divorcée whisperer, but those memoirs don't sell like they used to. Not to mention the actress who shall not be named. It took a small miracle to bring this lunch about. And yet you've gotta act like none of that ever happened."

"And I was just worried about getting a piece of lettuce stuck in my front teeth."

They laughed. She liked that Ezra always told her the truth. It was rare in most businesses, and especially in Hollywood.

Twenty minutes past one, Anke took over the room. She received air-kisses from an aging film star, barely recognizable behind his face-lift and reading glasses, then posed for the selfie requested by a daytime TV host. Anke was seventy-one, but she was so slender and lithe, she appeared decades younger. She radiated the detachment of a young Nico, without heroin's aura-marring darkness—Anke had hung up that bad habit with her bell-bottoms.

At their booth, Anke glided to a stop. The air burst into bloom, warmed by the carnal aroma of tuberose and jasmine. As anyone who cared about such things knew, Anke's signature scent was Robert Piguet's Fracas. She was dressed in white—silk Balmain blazer, foamy scarf, skintight jeans—and enormous black sunglasses. Sliding her shades up onto her long blond hair, she revealed smoky cat-eye makeup. Mari beamed warmth toward her.

"Hallo," Anke said, her voice musky, slightly Old World. "You have found our table. I hope you don't mind my directness, but you are quite corporeal for a ghost."

"You should see my X-rays." Mari smiled.

She extended a sure hand, as polite and nonchalant as if Anke were her server at a four-star restaurant, and then shook with Anke's assistant. He stood close enough to Anke to be her shadow. Tall and yoga-lean, the man was of indeterminate age, but clearly much older than was suggested by his outfit—expensive head-to-toe black, including a vintage Neil Young T-shirt, accented with a few turquoise-beaded suede bracelets. His well-cut shaggy hair framed a handsome face—pale skin, switchblade cheekbones, a gap-toothed pout.

Anke rested her hand on the table. From afar, she stood erect, perfect model posture, easy yoga grace. Up close, Mari saw her fingers wrinkle the tablecloth, seeking support. Knowing better than to acknowledge any vulnerability so early in their relationship, Mari got up fast. She ceded the center seat to Anke. In a casual, choreographed motion, Anke's companion slid into the booth after her, blocking any errant admirers.

"This is Ody," Anke said. "My assistant."

Mari and Ody nodded to each other. He exuded ageless nonchalance, but up close, Mari clocked the fine lines around his eyes, the artificial darkness of his hair, dyed to cover the gray. LA was full of such gorgeous, stylish insiders who seemed too old to do such work. But by acting as devoted ladies-in-waiting to their celebrities, they enjoyed money, access, glamour.

The waiter fluttered back, asked about drinks. Anke smiled flirtatiously at him.

"I will take a dry martini," she said. "Gin. Francisco knows how I like. Light, light, light with the vermouth. An olive and a twist."

The waiter bowed to Anke, as if he were a knight dedicated to serving her, then looked to Mari.

"Earl Grey tea, please," Mari said. "Almond milk, steamed, on the side. And lemon for my water. Thank you."

Normally, Mari drank whatever her clients did. But no booze at an initial meeting before two p.m. Anke was Anke and could, and would, do as she pleased. Mari had to express distinct needs—they helped to establish her place at the table—but they couldn't take up too much space.

"How's your day been?" Mari asked.

Anke studied her. Ody watched, chaperoning.

"It could not be better," Anke said. "This is a most auspicious time."

Mari considered the contrasting realities of Anke's grand stroll through the dining room and her hidden grip on the table. She was acting. But her unique European-flavored English and extreme comfort in her surroundings made her appear utterly authentic.

Seemingly satisfied, Ody turned to his smartphone, began typing. Mari hesitated, weighing the task at hand. She needed to appear more accomplished and successful than she was. And to do that, Ezra was right—she had to seem like she didn't care about the job, or at least wasn't desperate to land it. As the waiter delivered their drinks, Anke sniffed her martini.

"This has vermouth," she said.

"Yes, but only—"

Anke held up her hand in the air.

The waiter was back with a fresh drink so soon it seemed physically impossible. Most celebrities wanted it known at restaurants around town that they had been nice and tipped well. Anke wanted what she wanted, no matter how it looked. As with the documentary. *Noted.*

Mari considered her opening move.

"Congratulations on your memoir. It's a great honor, the opportunity to tell your story."

"The memoir is good," Anke said. "Really it is one thing of many. A collaboration of my jewelry designs with the noble Cartier. European interview requests. The fiftieth anniversary approaches. There is much interest in Anke once again."

"Fifty years since Mal drowned, so young. That must bring up a great deal of emotion."

Anke appraised Mari, as if she had read about feelings once in a book.

"Such landmark events become a sort of touchstone, it seems." Mari threw herself into her pitch. Sensing Anke auditioning her, she doubled down. "When telling one's story, these are the alchemic moments—of transformation. In my experience, grief is the fiercest forge there is—it remakes us in its fire. That summer must have been hell. And like no other time in your life."

Mari could have felt foolish, speaking in such epigrams, but she never let herself get anywhere near her emotions at meetings, even when she alluded to the darker aspects of her own experience. It was her special technique, to create an air of supreme authority—she had lived many lives, and told many life stories, and she knew how it should be done. And yet it must be as if *this* celebrity were the only luminary with a story worth preserving in print.

"You are too young to know about grief," Anke said.

"You were even younger that summer," Mari said. "Grief follows its own clock."

Anke dipped her lovely face, communicating assent.

"Yes, that is how it feels," Anke said. "Like alchemy. Like there were many conversions in my life—grief sometimes. Others were gold. Perhaps we approach yet another moment now."

Looking up from his business, Ody studied Anke's face. She met his gaze but didn't acknowledge his apparent concern. She took a hummingbird sip of her martini. Her sheaf of bracelets wind-chimed down her arm—Cartier bands, Chanel, some with diamonds, some not, all gold, interspersed with the ruby-fanged serpentine bangles of her own design. Her other wrist was wreathed by an asymmetrical Bulgari watch from the '70s, also gold.

Ody remained silent.

"Can you sense such moments as they happen, or only after?" Mari asked.

There was an almost imperceptible shift, a deepening intimacy, like when the second round of drinks arrives.

"I am reminded of when I was with the boys in the Hollywood Hills," Anke said.

Mari smiled over the rim of her cup, encouraging Anke toward candor.

"We landed in Los Angeles from London," Anke said. She paused for another precise sip, then let her words go in a torrent. "This was in April. Mal was my old man. We were staying in a house built for Charlie Chaplin. No one was ready to relinquish the illusion that the band was still close, even though it was unraveling around us. Our first night, we had a small party. Rock stars. Naked wood nymphs with garlands of holly in their hair. Jim put LSD in the punch, always throwing open the doors of perception, and he was climbing on the roof in his black leather pants, ready to fly. Pamela cried below him, exhausted like a new mother. Dante found me by the pool. I rolled the best joints. He was all thumbs, except with guitars, and women, of course. I spread out a shawl on my lounge chair. I was throwing the I Ching—tossing the three coins that give you the lines to form the hexagram for your reading. As Dante lit the paper and inhaled the herb, I jangled them in my hands. 'That mad fucker Mal set his kaftan on fire,' Dante said. 'He's going to burn us all up in our sleep.' As he spoke, I released the coins."

Anke was introducing herself as prescient, in control, even amid the luminous frenzy of the greatest rock stars, including Jim Morrison, and Mal, who was crazy, drug-addled, out of control. With Dante as a bridge in between. Listening for what Anke was saying beneath her words, as well as what she was maybe avoiding, Mari wanted to question her without seeming to doubt her. Murder, even manslaughter, was a serious allegation, and yet everyone at the table knew it was on the periphery of their conversation. Ody stared into his phone, but he had stopped typing. Finally, Mari realized Anke was done speaking—that was all she cared to reveal.

"I read you predicted these events," Mari said. "I thought maybe that was hyperbole."

"Let me tell you something, Schatzi," Anke said, pulling her drink close. "There is a molecule of truth in everything you read."

"Yes, and there are many ways to write what's true and hide it at the same time."

Anke turned her jeweler's gaze on Mari, said nothing. The silence stretched and dragged. Mari sipped her tea, buying time as she formulated her response, which couldn't let on how incredible she had found Anke's tale, and how much higher-profile this gig was than any book she had written. Mari needed a job. This was way more than that. It was a ladder. And, somehow, Mari sensed that working with Anke would teach her the skills she needed to climb.

Mari had coaxed Anke to talk, but had she divulged anything? Why had Anke led with Dante, not Mal, and then not revealed her forecast? Why had Anke said she thought such a moment might approach again when she seemed triumphant, or was at least projecting triumph?

"So, the tiles foretold Mal's death," Mari said.

Anke didn't answer. She was no fool—she knew the men in her life were the draw for most readers—but they could not be the draw for her writer.

"What did you do?" Mari asked, keeping the focus on Anke.

"I saved myself," Anke said. "As I have always done."

"As you always will do," Ody said.

Mari was surprised by this assertion, which was rare for an assistant. She watched with curiosity as Anke bowed slightly in his direction, before turning back to Mari.

"For Bono's last birthday, he took his family and closest friends on an eco-safari to Africa," Anke said. "I had horrible jet lag. I went out to the fire in the main lodge at three in the morning. I found him awake. I asked him, 'How is it you have achieved massive success, telling truth? But you have not alienated yourself from your country, an ancient, conservative one?' He said, 'We may have told the truth, but we never left ourselves out of the reckoning. Let she who has no hypocrisy cast the first stone.' And then he quoted his own lyric: '*I must be an acrobat to talk like this and act like that.*' It has stayed with me. Just because someone has done wrong, there's no need to rub her face in it. To punish her without mercy. To expose her. We are all flawed."

The anecdote was high-profile, but might not make the book, if Mari couldn't finesse more significance out of it than Bono's perspective. Mari wondered why Anke was telling *this* story now, which "flawed women" she was alluding to, if not herself. Mari respected Anke for not airing old grievances. She hoped this meant Anke would be too classy to want to do so in print. Even when it came to the truth about Mal's death, which Mari needed to coax out of her, there was a way to name names while earning your right to use them. Anke seemed to infer this.

"What do you think?" Anke asked.

"You have many incredible stories to tell. The question is, what do you wish to say?"

"Please, my dear. What does anyone want me to say besides what happened to Mal?"

"Of course. But there are ways to make what they want and what you want the same."

"Ja, it is the only way to survive life with a certain kind of man." Anke almost smiled.

Mari's mind flashed to her father, the epitome of a certain kind of man. She, personally, hadn't had a man in her life for several years. But she knew this kind of girl talk went over well.

Mari laughed. "On behalf of women everywhere, I have questions for you about *that*."

"Perhaps the question is this. You were on the list of approved writers. But you have never written a bestseller. The other writers all have. What that is special do you offer us, then?"

Mari poured herself more tea, added almond milk. She leaned toward Anke, telegraphing earnest mastery. She hadn't only been listening to Anke; she had been reading her, a skill she had obtained in childhood, as many children of addicts learn to read those with power over them. It was obvious to Mari, from the seriousness with which Anke considered Mari's questions and the lyrical precision with which she remembered: Anke might not care about gossip, but she cared about how her words were received. Her Achilles' heel was her desire to be taken seriously, rather than being admired for—and trapped by—her beauty. And the men it attracted, who had created the shape of her life, with their presence and absence—even her child was a boy. With all this in mind, plus her genuine interest in Anke's subterranean stories of wooing and keeping the Ramblers, Mari conjured Anke's wisdom, seeking the entrée that would give her deeper access.

"Your book will be a bestseller, no matter who you hire," Mari said. "I respect you too much not to state the obvious. You were married to Mal when he died, which is one of pop culture's greatest mysteries.

There you have it: Thousands of books sold. But that marriage was only ten months of your life. Your book will be read because you know how to show others the greatness they, too, possess, how to move through a dark time with grace. You have told me provocative stories about Mal, Dante, and Bono, the happenings of Hollywood and the plains of Africa. This will be a memoir that illuminates, and improves the reader—what we all seek from the books we read. The memoir *not* of a groupie, but a teacher, an agent of insight and alchemy."

Anke winced at the word "groupie," even though Mari had enunciated the qualifying "not." She had kept her face placid at the mention of Mal's name—the mastery of decades of practice. There was power in acknowledging another's worst fears, but it could backfire. Anke tossed down her napkin. As Ody folded it, Anke leaned toward Mari, who exhaled.

It had worked. She had accomplished the central goal of an initial meeting; she had finessed her way inside—in this case, by admiring Anke's street smarts. Equating them with a kind of acuity others, even those far more educated and cultured, could only hope to achieve.

Anke laughed. "My mother, she thought I was good for nothing but a teacher or a secretary. I wonder how she would like it, to see me now, teaching in my own book."

Mommy issues, Mari noted to herself, maintaining her poker face.

Anke took a big swallow, finally enjoying her drink. Then she looked at Mari. Really looked at her. Mari felt happy, and flattered, but made herself shake it off. She was irked to find she wanted Anke to like her. What she needed was for Anke to trust her.

"I sat with my medium," Anke said. "She is the one everyone goes to, the one they based that TV program on. You know, the show with the Arquette girl."

Mari had no clue but nodded as if she did.

"She tells me, 'Anke, my dear Anke, rejoice, finally, your time has come to pass. My guides show me that your book will be an international bestseller. It will secure your legacy. And it will be associated, somehow, with the name Haw or Horn.' This is her insight for me."

"I'm Mari *Haw*-thorn," Mari said, lighting up. "Do you think she meant me?"

Embarrassed she had let herself go, Mari came back to the room, noticed the next table: Goldie Hawn, with her impish smile and pixie chin. The gods were never subtle, it seemed.

Anke followed Mari's glance, smiled as Goldie blew her a kiss; such was Anke's particular power, she had grown accustomed to it long ago. She finished her drink. "This is the way true connections occur in life," she said. There was a new warmth in her voice.

Mari flushed from excitement and her too-tight blazer. Euphoria filled her if a meeting went this well. She was superstitious about assuming anything, but she almost dared to hope.

As Mari drove home, she analyzed her situation. Editors and agents worked with the same ghosts again and again. Just when Mari was about to reach this insider status, she'd had her minor disaster. Yes, writers got replaced and still had careers. But they had to recover quickly, especially in a shrinking market for these types of memoirs, and at a time when celebrities had begun turning to non-ghostwriters with their own social media platforms. If Mari didn't get this job, and it was nine months before her next meeting, there would be no *next* job. Mari was supposed to phone Ezra. Suddenly, she didn't want to—the problem with someone who told the truth was that it was sometimes unbearable to hear. But Mari always did what was needed.

"Hey, dude, how'd it go?" Ezra asked.

When he had started using this term of endearment, she had been glad to have made her way into his inner stable of writers. Auditioning for each and every client, she clocked any stability as a prize.

Hearing him use it now made her feel like she still had him, still had a career.

"It went well," Mari said.

"Yeah? Then why do you sound like that?"

"I could only pretend I didn't care if I got the job ghosting a best-seller for Anke Berben for ninety-two minutes. And then my brain exploded. You're hearing the aftermath."

He laughed. "So, it did go well. What's she like?"

"Interesting. Articulate. Sure, she's the most famous groupie in the world. And Mal's death is the ultimate rock riddle. But she's more like—not to sound pretentious—a lady."

"Or a very gifted actress. I mean, somebody probably killed him, right?"

"Maybe—I don't know. She seems genuine. And smart. Or she fakes it well. I like her."

"Don't be a fangirl. Anke's one of the last white whales of '60s rock memoirs—this book could spring you from D-list purgatory. Make you a contender for bigger, higher-profile books."

He'd mentioned how Anke's editor helmed well-reviewed, culturally relevant memoirs.

"Yeah? My first jobs gave me chops—with a story like this, I can do some real writing."

"And real reporting. I told you David's verdict, when he won it at auction. With the fiftieth anniversary of Mal's death, everyone's going to be talking about this book. It's got to reveal something new. David had another writer in mind, but I told him you can do it. Can you?"

"Thank you, yeah, it's an amazing opportunity. I'm ready, coach."

"You are ready, dude. I wouldn't have fought so hard for you if I didn't think so."

Her call-waiting beeped. The screen read "Unknown ID."

"It's them!" she said.

"Okay, remove that exclamation point from your voice. And go. You got this."

She took a deep breath as she switched over.

"Hello, Mari. It's Ody. We called David, to hire you, and he said we couldn't."

Okay, this was unexpected. It took a beat to digest. "But I was on their list of writers."

"When pressed, he said you aren't experienced enough. You won't be able to pull it off."

Mari dismissed the snub. Even skilled ghosts labored under a barrage of criticism, about their writing, personality, or status on the team. Maybe David owed another agent a favor.

"Not to overstep, but the wisest move Anke can make is to hire *her* writer, not David's."

He didn't respond. If she tried to explain about her "bestseller," it would sound desperate.

"I can do it. I know I can. Anke knows I can. Even the psychic knows!"

"You don't understand how important this book is for Anke," Ody said. "It must be more than a bestseller. It must be her legacy. I'm sorry, but we can't risk it. Anke says 'Ciao.'"

SECOND:
INSINUATE

Deferential but normalizing. It's a skill. Wear flats, as the client is probably short. It's a rule. Especially when meeting a man. Always flirt as much or as little as they do. That goes for men and women. Be genial, but slightly less so, to the support staff. Ghosts aren't celebrities, but they aren't assistants, either. Remember names and use good manners, but don't run errands or place the order for lunch. Stand apart, proudly, in the unique space you occupy. You must be confident enough for both you and your celebrity on the days when their darkest stories make them doubt themselves.

Mari lurked in her fortress of solitude—her Honda Civic—the only place she was guaranteed privacy, since she'd had to give up her apartment. She couldn't bring herself to face whatever came next. Like telling Ezra. Or not. Until he heard from David and called her to see what had gone wrong. She had never not gotten a job before. Would he drop her? Or could she get him to help her save the situation, maybe make one last plea to David? No. He had already done so much. And she *had* landed it but also lost it. Better to go down with her pride intact.

She scanned the West Hollywood condo building in front of her. It had felt almost fated, in the bad way, when her sister, Vivienne, had blown back into town. Mari had recently accepted she could no longer afford her apartment but had nowhere to stay. Meanwhile, V's new music producer boyfriend was letting her use his condo during renovations—yet another of V's glamorous but bizarre setups. Building supplies filled one bedroom while a new contractor was found to replace the one who'd gone AWOL. The other bedroom was where her sister indulged in her ritualistic beauty routines and entertained her boyfriend. So Mari slept on the couch. Worked on the couch. Plotted and dreamed on the couch. Tried to be grateful for the couch.

Mari had been planning to stride in triumphantly, champagne bottle aloft. Now she didn't want to go in at all. Her sister possessed the same street smarts as Anke, and it made her equally adept at reading people in order to seduce them or turn their weaknesses to her advantage. As if she had been summoned, Vivienne texted: "Zip me up? I have a date."

Mari sighed, threw down her phone. "Not today, Satan."

Annoyed, she realized this was one of Vivienne's pet phrases.

A movement caught her eye from the balcony above. There was Vivienne: dramatic cat-eyes and plump dewdrop lips, waves of dark hair, all creating a visual umami. In what only her sister would think of as a low-key dinner-date outfit—a white Herve Leger bandage minidress.

"Why didn't you text back?" she called down. "Are you mad?"

"Vivienne, you *just* texted me," she yelled up as Vivienne buzzed her in.

When Mari exited the elevator, Vivienne gave her a sloppy kiss and launched into a detailed analysis of her upcoming night. Mari followed her sister, knowing if she tried to decompress on the couch, she'd draw the kind of attention she couldn't handle. She half listened, to keep up her side of the conversation, for the same reason. Lifting the wine bottle out of the ice bucket, she inferred it was expensive, took V's half-drunk glass, and topped it off. V always seemed to be fun buzzed but never got too drunk, especially before a date. Mari was usually too busy to get drunk but had nothing but time now. She watched Vivienne dust her yards of exposed skin with iridescent powder. She was gorgeous, but she looked thin, almost sickly. Mari wondered if she should ask her if she was okay. But she didn't have the energy. She didn't trust her sister to tell the truth anyway. V couldn't afford to not be okay. Neither could Mari.

Having basically ghosted even her closest friends in the writing community for the past two years, Mari hadn't felt like she could ask any of them for a place to stay. So, she had ended up on the couch of infamy. Without consciously making the choice to do so, Mari had put everything into these jobs of hers that remained invisible. Each project was tricky, each deadline punishing. But there was always the promise that the next one would be easier, would pay a little better, would be the smash success that made her career into a sure thing. Her rate had doubled since she'd started, but without a bestseller on her CV, it was still low.

After having to bow out of too many weekend beach trips and friends' book launches because of deadlines, she'd been dumped by her last boyfriend, a novelist. He had waited to break up with her until she had met her latest deadline, which said a lot, but it was already too late. Her ex was part of the local writing scene, and her grief, and fear of running into him, kept her home. It was a relief, really. She had grown tired of parsing how other writers employed air quotes when they asked: "What are you *writing* these days?" They were the first to gobble up celebrity anecdotes—even though she never divulged dirt that couldn't be found on her clients' Wikipedia pages. The other writers were charmed by her and her strange sparkly stories, but they didn't respect her. Not when they were all taking the risk of producing original novels, memoirs, and screenplays and launching them into the world under their own names.

Mari loved writing, and writers, and even though ghosting had its own baggage and rules, she was quite clear the four published books she'd toiled over did make her a writer. Still, her lack of stature stung sometimes. Thankfully, after her breakup, she'd had another deadline—the vodka divorcée. When she was sad, the hard, endless work of building a book was a balm and an excuse to cocoon. Let her celebrities go to the fancy book parties; at least when she was home writing, she knew she was actively helping herself to get somewhere better. But now there was nothing new to write, and the promise of somewhere better felt like a fantasy.

V finished powdering her cleavage and began using a curling wand on her hair, which looked perfect. Finally, she examined Mari in the mirror.

"What, does the book have a crazy deadline?" V asked. "So? You're a deadline ninja."

Mari smiled but couldn't fake the laugh.

"Even I know no one says yes at the meeting. They'll hire you on Monday."

Mari would sometimes bend her words to connect with a client, but she never lied. And she couldn't see any benefit in doing so now. She lived on V's couch. Clearly V would find out.

"I didn't get it."

"But you always get it."

"*Always is just a promise the joker hasn't broken yet.*"

"Um, no Ramblers lyrics right now. Fuck those guys. Fuck Anke."

"I liked Anke. And I think she liked me. But no bestseller. She didn't have a choice."

"Celebrities always have a choice. And they always get what they want."

V was probably right. But of course she didn't see why this was not a helpful observation. Which was weird, because she knew exactly where Mari's head had gone: money.

"Maybe you can borrow a little cash from Dad."

"Can I have some of whatever you're on?"

"Sometimes he wins, and when he does, he feels gen—"

She was cut off by Mari's arch expression.

"Sure, he's not usually winning. And clearly you can't handle a no, like at all. Maybe if you didn't expect so much, you guys would have a better relationship. Any relationship."

The sliver of truth in what V said made Mari hate it more. On the other hand, the level to which V had toughened herself, where their father and her boyfriends were concerned, made Mari want to land every job, get her and her skinny sister a real apartment. They both needed it.

Four hours later, Mari was collapsed across a lounger on the small balcony, listening to West Hollywood sprinkle its sparkle on Friday night—she heard Donna Summer feel love in her crystalline voice over a synthetic centipede beat; a group of young men cheer and shriek; a lone person sob and heave in the alley behind the condo.

Even five years ago, she would have been sucking the marrow out of Friday night. Before becoming a ghostwriter, she had been a rock critic and had enjoyed all the guest lists and open bars. But then her work for mainstream media outlets had dried up, and the online publications didn't pay enough for her to survive. She had been lucky to fall into ghosting through a friend of a friend. Once she had, she'd never looked back and lost all her PR contacts. She had $40 in cash and $100 on her last credit card. Loneliness was no reason to crack her emergency fund.

Mari nursed her wine and replayed her lunch. She had done everything right. She was sure of it. She'd demonstrated her capacity to hold all of Anke's fears, while making her feel appreciated for her true self, beneath her beauty and her Fracas. For once, Mari hadn't been pretending, either. Anke truly had lived a life worthy of a deep, insightful memoir that would be read by many. How much of this was even within her control? If Mari wasn't ever given the chance to publish her first acknowledged bestseller, how could she ever land a bestseller?

Mari's phone rang. Unknown ID. It was ten p.m. on Friday night. But what if?

"Hello, this is Mari Hawthorn."

"Mari, it's Ody. Anke called David and threatened to take her book to another publisher—"

Mari listened, too shell-shocked to even wish, grateful V had only left her with half a bottle of wine, so she wasn't more than lightly buzzed.

"Your agent and our lawyer stayed late tonight to get the paperwork done, and they've just finished. You must come to Anke's condo to sign. We have a check for the first half of your fee. And then we will leave for Anke's house in Palm Springs—"

"Thank you. I can be right over."

A glimmer of hope crested within Mari like placing the first, right words on a blank page. A low five figures, but five figures, would be in her hand in a few hours, in her bank account on Monday. It did feel weirdly fast, especially when Anke seemed so thoughtful and controlled. But in Mari's experience, celebrities always had at least five competing obligations, many of which she would never know about. Maybe this was just how it happened. The sacrifices had paid off, and maybe, just maybe, Mari was headed for her first sure thing.

"We fought for you," Ody said. "We told them you could write a bestseller. Anke has no time to waste. You must be sure you can do it. You must do it—"

"Yes," Mari said. Anxiety spiking, her throat almost closed around the word. And then a burst of adrenaline filled her with energy.

"This is going to change your life."

Mari had heard enough grand pronouncements about her fate from her celebrities and their handlers to take Ody's words in stride. But in this case, she knew he was right. A whisper of fear slithered down the back of Mari's neck. As they were signing off, Mari moved into the living room, where her life's essentials were stored in her suitcase by the couch. Riding her rush, she willed herself to exude confidence, to feel confidence—it was a leap forward, but Anke couldn't know just how much. Anke would have nobody but her. She was a real ghost after all.

Ody maneuvered them through Friday night traffic in Anke's classic white Mercedes 450SL sedan, thick with Anke's rose scent. Keeping one hand on her dachshund, Rimbaud, who was curled in her lap, Anke offered Mari a mint.

"Would you like one, sweetheart?" she then asked Ody.

"Thanks, Mutti," he said.

With curiosity, Mari tried to place the word, which sounded German.

"Mari, I am pleased to introduce you to my handsome son, Odin," Anke said.

Of course, that's why he had looked familiar. She had been thrown by his nickname.

"Nice to see you again," Mari said. "I caught your set at the Troubadour a while back."

"You were one of the few then," he said.

Ody had released several critically acclaimed folk-rock albums, but he had never achieved anything like his father's fame, and in the past decade, his output of new music had all but stopped. Mari might not have recognized him except for her former life as a music critic.

"People pry," Anke said. "It is easier to call him my assistant."

There was an obvious logic here that hid a deeper significance Mari couldn't track.

"You look nice," Anke said, gracing Mari with a smile. "I like your hair like that."

Mari grinned, losing her cool. Her hand flew to the messy bun, concealing that she hadn't had time to wash it. She knew she should be cautious. She had landed herself here, and she wasn't going to be derailed by the lack of a bestseller on her résumé or a naive devotion to her client. She blushed, tucked away the compliment. "Thank you."

Anke settled into her seat, Rimbaud snoring lightly. Before Mari could prompt her with a curated question, Anke began describing her new designs for Cartier. Mari knew this would receive only a few lines in the book, but she went with it, hoping to put Anke at ease.

The inside of the Mercedes was tranquil, even with tractor trailers and casino traffic barreling by them on both sides. The leather seat enveloped Mari like a caress. Before she knew it, they had reached the lunar landscape of the desert, alive with the eerie whoosh of two-story windmills. Silently, they did their work of generating power from the heavy gusting winds.

Mari took stock of her situation—not the possibility of the book, but the reality of pulling it off. There was no one except Vivienne to wonder where she was or when she would be back. It was lonely sometimes, but Mari knew her ability to immerse herself would serve her well now.

Her focus needed to be on Anke, who had been widowed young by a pop culture golden boy, avoided being taken down by the suspicion surrounding his death, and rebounded with two of his bandmates, who happened to be among rock's most legendary lovers. When she had returned to her first love in Germany, they'd had ten perfect years, and then he'd died. At best, the next seventy-two hours would be intense, requiring intellectual and emotional dexterity. At worst, if Anke clung to her secrets, Mari would have to deduce, on the spot, the perfect means of extracting them from her. Always, she would have to be analyzing what was revealed, making sure it was the real truth. Anke had fought for Mari and brought her close to help tell her story, so Mari didn't think she would be denied access. But still, it felt exhilarating, and high-stakes, to be accompanying this legendary femme fatale to her desert retreat in the middle of the night.

Mari dared to relax a little when they reached the condo complexes and vast hotels that announced Palm Springs. The presence of others at the many vibrant outdoor bars reminded her there was a whole world beyond this car, this book. She craned her neck for a better view.

"I haven't been here in years," she said.

"I come out when I need peace, several times a month," Anke replied. "It has changed a great deal, as you will notice—there are more gauche chain stores. Ody, take us down Palm Canyon Drive so Mari can see."

Nodding, he glided to a stop at a red light. Mari was fading fast, but she didn't dare let on. She dug her nails into her palms to stay awake.

"When did you first come to Palm Springs?" Mari asked, glad for a segue into the past.

"Look at that gorgeous armoire," Anke called out. "Pull over, Ody. Please."

Anke rolled down her window. A wash of cool dry air infiltrated the womb of the Mercedes. Anke leaned out to get a better look at the upscale vintage furniture store. "Call Dominique tomorrow. I know he covets that Eames chair in the den."

Ody nodded again. As if remembering Mari and the job at hand, Anke explained: "Every time I buy a new piece, I shed one as well. It is my attempt to maintain simplicity."

Mari nodded, picturing the "simplicity" of her couch-bed at V's borrowed condo.

Anke rolled up her window, dramatically, as she did everything. She fell into the major production of settling Rimbaud and straightening her scarf.

Mari considered repeating her dodged question, took a different approach.

"I think it can be helpful to remember our work together isn't a media interview," Mari said. "All the material we create is yours—you own it, control it. This is a safe place to say anything, to consider how you feel, figure out if it's true. My discretion is absolute. Together, we'll decide what belongs in your book. Yes, readers demand intimacy, but not everything is for public consumption. The truth is important, but so is a certain degree of privacy."

"You make it sound easy," Anke said. "We will unearth the secrets of half a century. Pick and choose which *truth* we wish to share. Whose truth? Mal's truth, I was another disposable wife? He was young, but he'd had two before me. Dante's truth, I was the mother who would give him an ideal love, better than drugs? Jack's truth, I had a perfect face and body, and to possess me would make him top gorilla?" She sounded tired, unguarded, and these were candid assessments of her relationships. Or was this just another facade? Mari couldn't tell yet. To make this book work, she'd have to learn fast. Ody looked over at Anke. Maybe concerned?

"Your truth, Anke," Mari said.

"And who can tell me what that is?"

As they turned onto a quiet residential street, Mari felt bolstered by the sudden darkness. Anke wasn't scary. She was fragile, hiding her age and pain, and maybe the story of a murder.

"I can—I mean, I can help you—find your truth—for yourself, of course."

She waited a beat.

"What is your truth, Anke?"

Anke began to cry. It was like seeing someone without their dentures, their cheeks cleaving to their empty skull. Mari's hand flew to Anke's arm—something a ghost never did, touch a celebrity, as if you were a fan seeking a photo and a hug. Like Anke, Mari had let emotion get the better of her, for once.

It was awkward, reaching around the seat to maintain contact, but

Mari had to see it through. She squeezed Anke's shoulder, then pulled her hand back, letting Anke right herself, if possible. Not speaking even as the quiet in the car grew sticky, Mari waited for what words the tears would spill. But Anke didn't speak. Mari wasn't feeling confident enough to keep pushing, especially when she couldn't read Anke's face in the dark. Mari exhaled. Let her silence fill the car, hoping it telegraphed respect. For the first time, she wondered why Anke was writing this book now and what secrets—her own and others'—she might finally be ready to reveal.

"Here we are," Ody said. He had stopped in front of a high stucco wall with an elaborate gold gate bearing a baroque *A*. They had driven through the city's downtown to its far edge. The mountains were close on their right, sheltering them from the desert's vastness.

Anke surprised Mari, once again, by pulling out a giant key ring. Carefully, like she was stepping onto the moon, she placed one foot onto the ground and pulled herself up, using the car's frame. Rimbaud was quick at her feet, eager to chase the night's smells. Without a word, Anke had ended their talk. She paused, glamorous in the headlights, as she worked the key into a heavy-duty padlock and swung the gate inward. Ody nosed the car up a circular driveway, edged by palms, banks of desert mallow with bold orange flowers.

"Shouldn't we wait for Anke?" Mari asked. She worried she'd missed an opportunity.

"Anke always walks the property when we arrive," Ody said. "Alone."

Mari would have to do better. She caught a view of the magnificent main house, Moroccan-influenced, and wrapped in vibrant pink bougainvillea. Then Ody parked and retrieved Mari's Diane von Furstenberg weekender, bought at Marshalls. Glancing in the trunk, she saw everyone else had Louis Vuitton luggage, including the dog. On the walk to the front door, the air smelled like Mexican jasmine, creosote, and, somehow, Anke's distinctive scent.

"Anke rises early for meditation, sun salutations, and a swim." Ody led Mari into her room. Dark beams sliced a white stucco ceiling, and the furniture was also antique wood, contrasted by white sheepskin rugs, white linens, and dozens of white throw pillows, flecked with rose and gold thread. "You will meet at eleven, in Anke's suite, to work. Rosenda will put out breakfast and tea. Anke noticed you prefer Earl Grey?"

"Yes, thank you," Mari said.

He nodded, placing her bag on the pink velvet bench that formed a footboard. She circled the mattress, set down her purse. By the bed was a pretty still life: a picture of a Hindu deity, a glass bottle of peacock feathers, a stack of books. Goldie Hawn gazed serenely from the top.

"Anke has Goldie's memoir," Mari said.

He turned to go, already working his phone. "Yes, they're old friends. Goldie sent over a copy when she heard about Anke's project. Anke thought it might be helpful for you."

Mari sensed the D-list receding—after how hard she had worked, the shift was sweet.

"I just texted my number. Good night. Sleep well. Anke is glad you are here."

Mari came to, already feeling behind. Her phone sounded nearby, and she pawed for her device. But she couldn't help but bask. The sheets were organic cotton, high thread count, the room dim and scented by cedar incense. Even a brief visit to the good life was delicious.

Sitting up, phone in hand, she panicked. The root concealer she'd used on her grays had rubbed into a pillow. She dabbed at it, reading Ody's text: "Anke wishes to start at ten. Thank you."

"Of course," Mari texted. Finding her glasses, she saw it was quarter to ten. *Fuck.* She had slept through two alarms, having vowed to make space for her own morning meditation, yoga in her room, note-taking over tea. She had learned the hard way how easy it was to be consumed by clients and their books, her mind dominated by the thoughts and needs of another. Her body grown pulpy and dull with disuse as the deadline pressed out all other requirements. But today would not be the day she came first.

THIRD:
COAX

Your client is famous, and so you probably know a great deal about them up front, but digging deeper into their real story is an art. You can't just ask them to open up, but you can make them feel safe enough to do so. A bold supposition can sometimes do this. Trust must be earned, and the more daring your deductions, the sooner that happens. Like any type of intimacy, a ghosting relationship is a form of seduction. You're trying to prove yourself worthy, as the object of their conquest—their original reader—while attempting to entice out all of their truth.

At two past ten, Mari ran her fingers through her hair before entering Anke's chamber. She wore her expensive kaftan, bought at a boho consignment store owned by a friend who gave her a discount. It was too short, and she was still carrying the ten pounds of deadline weight from her last book, so she wore it over black leggings, which countered the gauzy feel of the dress.

Mari was caught tugging the fabric down over her thighs when Ody swung the door inward and greeted her with an impassive nod. Nodding back, she strove to appear collected. This was it: Mari was here to get something out of Anke that would placate their editor, maybe solve one of pop culture's oldest mysteries, and save her ghosting career. But the trick was to act like they were already dear friends, the kind who casually told each other everything.

Holding a warm, easy smile on her face, Mari walked toward Anke, who was enthroned on a long, low daybed. To her right, a wall of sliding glass doors opened onto a courtyard. The extradimensional desert light turned a bank of Japanese oleander into a living painting. A fountain could be heard splashing, just out of sight.

Mari surveyed the room, assuming a journalist's impassive gaze. Want filled her. It was perfect. Luxurious but comfortable—throw pillows cascaded from the couch onto the sheepskin rugs, inviting one to peruse the chunky art books and elegant poetry volumes; there was a scent of sweet incense with a cedar undertone; two enormous vases held fragrant white lilies and roses. They had been here less than eight hours—where were the flowers from, and who had arranged them? Mari appreciated the aura of magic created by these invisible hands.

Anke sat cross-legged on the divan, Rimbaud beside her. She could have been a magazine photo of herself. Her raw silk dress was sheer enough to reveal her lean, tan torso. A pale pink cashmere throw covered her shoulders. Her hair, a little damp from her morning swim, made her appear youthful and fresh. She held a china cup and saucer.

"Guten Morgen," Anke said. "I trust you slept well."

Ody settled into a small desk in the corner. Anke smiled at Mari, a relief, since they had parted without a proper good night, in the wake of Anke's tears.

"I did—I was quite comfortable, thank you," Mari said. She sat on the couch a few feet from Anke. "Your home is very beautiful."

"Ja, it is a beautiful house." Anke paused, as if to say more, sipped her tea.

Mari opened her computer to her waiting Word doc, typed a note to herself: "Who owns the Palm Springs house?" Smiling at Anke, she let them acclimate for a beat, then dove in.

"I hope I didn't upset you last night," Mari said. "You can give me feedback, not just on my writing. There's nothing you could say that would hurt my feelings. Your book comes first."

Mari always gave this speech to her clients, although usually not so early in the process. Most people nodded, or said something like "It's helpful when you ask questions." They weren't used to the possibility of collaboration. They only cared that the writing sounded like them.

Anke poured tea, her face amused.

"There are many things I could say that would hurt your feelings," Anke said.

Mari didn't let herself consider the possibilities.

"Yes, I'm sure, you have a real way with words. Well, please tell me if you're ever uncomfortable with the direction I'm taking us, or with my approach."

"If we only write about the comfortable moments, it will be a very short book. People fear too much this idea of being uncomfortable. Sometimes, I cry."

"Because?"

"Because I am sad. Why do *you* cry?"

Mari didn't cry—she couldn't afford the luxury, but that seemed an intense thing to say. She wasn't here to confess. She was here to finesse candor, and maybe a confession.

"Because I miss people and moments that aren't coming back," Mari offered.

"Don't get old—you won't be able to bear it. Everything and everyone are gone."

"You grew up in Berlin after the war. From your earliest days, much was gone."

"Ja, no one who was not there can know that level of ruin, of being broken down, the fog of waking up from this terrible nightmare and taking the blame, being sick at ourselves."

Mari fumbled in her bag, as unobtrusively as possible, not wanting to interrupt. She only relaxed when, along with her typing, her recorder's red light reassured her that she was capturing the words she would need for the book. From interviews she had read, Mari understood Anke's allusions to all she'd been running from—the desolation and shame felt by the youth of Germany after World War II. She needed more personal stories about Anke's family and her first love, Fritz, whom she had thrown over for Mal, and then returned to after her years with the Ramblers.

"Did your father survive the war?"

"Ja. Long enough for me to be born."

Anke did not appear moved to say more.

"What was your mother like?" Mari asked.

"My mother," Anke said. She paused long enough that Mari debated the best follow-up question. "She tried. There is a right way. Even in the worst of times. A good lesson from her. Berlin recovered from the war, but we were still poor when I was a child. Anything we could find or barter—a cup and saucer," Anke said, examining the items she held, as if they were artifacts from her past, "you treasured. Even when I was older and stomped around our flat, I respected our few possessions. I have always been this way. Now I am surrounded by items from all my travels, all my lives. I save them, add them up, and create a home, an oasis in the desert, a sanctuary beyond time."

Anke's speech tapered off. Mari considered.

"You didn't like your mother," Mari said. She ducked her head, as if embarrassed by her intimate inference.

Anke didn't seem daunted. But she didn't answer. She bent over the antique tea set, resting on a teak tray. With careful movements, she prepared the perfect cup of tea. Mari considered how some beautiful women occupied space differently; they knew how to be, not just to talk. If Anke felt Mari's eyes, she didn't increase her pace or look up until Mari held her drink.

"Were you close with your mother?" Anke asked. "You have a knack for the girl talk. You must have been."

"Mostly," Mari said.

She wasn't being coy. She had been so startled by Anke's observation, she couldn't think what to say. She teetered on the edge of her temptation to draw Anke closer, and her need to maintain professional distance. And yet Mari had an implicit sense of fairness—if she was going to ask someone to strip bare, shouldn't she risk a little exposure?

"My mother was beautiful, without ever trying," Mari said. "She didn't wear makeup, and she cut her own hair. It was very long, the color of liquid amber. I used to love to brush it."

"You are pretty," Anke said.

Mari stared at her, trying to read her words. Anke smiled. A compliment, then.

"Thank you," Mari said. "But this was—real beauty. I think as much as we love our parents, we measure ourselves by them. Did you ever feel that with your mother?"

"I couldn't afford to think of my mother in those terms, of competition, or love, or beauty. From an early age, I was fighting for my life. You can say I am melodramatic, the war had ended, I know nothing of danger, per se." Anke hit the words a little harder, in the way nonnative speakers do when savoring a phrase they've mastered in a borrowed tongue. "But I knew I was different. Unique. People hated me for it. I heard their jeers: 'What, do you think you are so special?' Ja, I was. Not because I say so, but because my life shows me so."

Mari had learned from experience when to let her clients run. Ravenous, she reached for a piece of melon, trying to be as ladylike as Anke, or at least neat. Finally, Anke's story had reached the Ramblers, but Anke fell silent. Mal and Anke were married for ten months. Much had happened between the wedding and the funeral.

Much had been speculated about the death. Mari had been lulled into thinking Anke would just go there. Apparently not.

"You were a special young woman," Mari said. "Brave enough to choose freedom. From a new generation that was daring to remake the world their parents had destroyed in the war."

Anke met this compliment head-on. She didn't play at modesty, as others might.

"Ja, I was special. The ordinary life is not for me. My mother lacked the imagination to see this, so I have to leave Germany, to shake her off, so I do not suffocate."

"It sounds like Mal rescued you, from a life that was too small."

Even if Anke dodged and feinted, Mari had to start working her for info on Mal and the band. But it required finesse. Mari leaned away from Anke, savoring her tea.

"Tell me about Mal," Mari said. "I've read so many legends. But what was he like?"

"He was magic."

"When he was with the Ramblers, in particular? Your description of the band's summer in LA was so vivid, so thrilling, I felt like I was there. You're a natural storyteller."

Anke cocked her head, as if considering Mari's words. Mari had noticed this tendency over lunch. While it made her nervous, she appreciated Anke's care as to what she did and didn't believe. Most people take everything at face value. Not Anke.

"If I have a talent for anything, it must be natural, gifted by the fates," Anke said. "I never had the patience to learn from others. School?" She made a dismissive gesture. "Prison for children. I never make Ody go to school. On the boat, he study astronomy, geography, languages, and he read all of Shakespeare. What more can a person need to know?"

Math? Mari thought to herself, knowing this joke wouldn't land with Anke.

"There's no greater storyteller than Shakespeare," Mari said. "It's the details, don't you think? The subterranean patterns, how the reader is brought to an understanding, rather than told."

"Ja, I have watched the hidden patterns all my life."

"The I Ching," Mari said.

Anke nodded. Seemed to make up her mind. She stood, causing Rimbaud to jump down. "I have wondered if I should share this, but yes, I believe you can find value here."

Mari noticed an ivory-topped cane leaning against the divan. Anke didn't reach for it, but she did lean on a small table, then inch across the room. Understanding the extent of Anke's performance at the Polo Lounge, Mari had greater admiration for her poised entrance.

Anke approached a tall dresser, jumbled with scarves and beaded jewelry, stacked with fabric-bound books. She grabbed one and crept over to Ody, Rimbaud her constant tail.

"Ody, please check Rosenda has lunch underway. I asked her to grill a whole fish. With mint and arugula from the garden."

He nodded and slid out of the room. As soon as he was gone, Anke sat, pulled on her glasses, began to read aloud: "'His cock is beautiful. His body is leonine, fierce, hungry.'"

Mari didn't blink.

"'His atoms are composed of helium and champagne. Supercharged. Frenetic. He hears in other frequencies. Sees in other dimensions. He is the truest artist I have ever met.'"

Looking up from the page, Anke deadpanned: "It was exhausting."

Mari laughed cautiously. When Anke joined, with her shuffling chuckle, Mari let herself go. She had found her way in, and the relief they both felt was palpable. Anke read:

"'Mal pushed me in front of the others. He has pushed me before. But this is the worst. Fritz would never push me. Fritz would carry me over puddles if I would let him. Mal is sicker every day. We walk up the stairs to the house, the band, Syd, Simon, Siggi, and me. I went down on my hands, my teeth rattling in my skull, my palms striking the marble and leaving specks of blood like flakes of fresh red snow. My heart was pounding out of my chest like a freight train.'"

As Mari listened, she didn't get what was happening at first. Because Anke was recounting words from decades earlier, there was a distancing, almost performative quality. Eventually, in every project, Mari was able to coax her client past modesty or discretion, to tell her something real, which became an important moment in the book. Like any real intimacy, the revelation felt shared, and slightly charged. This was more complicated. It was almost as if Anke wasn't confessing; she was leaving that indiscretion to her younger self. But here it was—evidence of animosity, conflict, violence even. It was known Mal hit Anke. Rumored Anke hit him back. But as far as Mari could tell, Anke had never commented on it publicly.

Anke read: "'She was there, too, his ugly shadow. Nancy. She is always with him now. He makes a face when I fall. The girl laughs, that horrible sound, like a seagull or some other trash bird with a caw caught deep in its beak. He did it to impress her. Or because he hoped I would lose the baby. Or because he has gone mad. The why doesn't matter if there even is one.'"

Flustered by Anke's casual revelation of a baby in conjunction with Mal, when the public had believed Anke'd had her son with Dante, and Mal's death had left another woman's baby without a father, Mari felt her fingers slip onto the wrong keys. She took down a graph of all-caps gibberish before righting herself. But she didn't stop typing, holding her focus on Anke.

"'It is empty. As was the apology Dante shamed him into—shouldn't disrespect a lady, all that horseshit, as if we are damsels in distress, and they our knights in velvet waistcoats—'"

Anke stopped before reading the denouement of the story. She glanced up at Mari, who kept her face a perfect mask. A word floated up in Mari's mind out of half-remembered police procedurals: "motive." She thought of Syd's book, which she needed to order when she got back to her room. In the legend of the band, Syd had been a bottom-feeder, but that was often where the darkest truths lurked. She had followed enough of her former clients in the tabloids to know first-hand, there was usually a seed of truth in any gossip-mag debacle, no matter how tawdry or far-fetched, or how quickly the celebrity's team managed to squash it. Anke had always been very clear that she had been pregnant by Dante, not Mal, and any rumors to the contrary at the time of Ody's birth had never caught on. It had to mean something that Anke was revealing this secret about her son's paternity now—even if she wasn't *really* revealing it.

Anke flipped ahead, then backward, read about an impromptu house show the band's first week in LA. Mal had been so stoned on Quaaludes and rum, he'd slid down an amplifier and passed out, and the band's guitar tech, Simon, had filled in. Her voice trailing off, Anke skimmed more material. Then she looked up, and the women considered each other. Mari felt like everything—the success of the book, her career—rested on this moment. But as Ezra had suggested, she couldn't let on how much she wanted it. Needed it. She slouched a little, smiled.

Mari's mind raced through scenarios. Anke had been quite candid in several moments, and yet she had chosen to deliver this bombshell buried in a journal entry, without qualifying or commenting on it at all. Mari suspected if she called it out directly, Anke would shut her down. Perhaps she could convince her to read more and get near the truth that way.

"Not to overstep, Anke, but those passages you read painted such an evocative scene—the details, the emotion, your voice. I am your writer, but no one sounds more *you* than you." Mari's voice wobbled, grew strong. Anke watched her closely. She couldn't back down. "As for your journal—I respect its personal nature. Just to have you read a few more passages—"

"I understand the value of the journal," Anke snapped.

"Do you? To have a firsthand record of such a profound moment in rock history."

Anke slammed the journal shut. *Fuck.*

"You are the groupie. Not me! Obsessing over the Ramblers. This is my story. MINE."

"I'm not here for the Ramblers, Anke. I'm here for you. No one but you."

The two women faced off. Mari sat very still. From the outside, it looked like she was doing nothing. But as a little girl, she had learned from interactions with her dad how to soothe, how to communicate to someone lost that they were perfectly safe. Anke was so good at reading people, she seemed to observe Mari's technique, but she accepted it. Nodded.

"In the time of this writing, I was—how do you say—overwrought? I think it is better not to use the words of a young girl, very far from home. It is better for you to ask questions, for me to tell you how I understand the story, because you know how to build a book the right way."

Clearly Mari had come on too strong. Thankfully it hadn't derailed the whole conversation. Better to continue building the trust between them and work back to the secret.

"Well, thank you," Mari said. "And yes, there's a way to craft the narration, so the Anke of today is offering perspective on the Anke of yesterday. But please remember, no one would judge your emotionality—as you said, you were young and in a foreign country. You were also vulnerable. Upset. Trying to make sense of painful events with what tools you had."

"It sounds like the Mari of today offers the perspective, not the Anke."

"I'm sorry I got carried away. I was thinking about the I Ching again. You saw the future, which must have been scary, but also thrilling. What power to have."

Anke nodded. But again, she didn't reveal her I Ching reading. She tucked away the journal beneath a stack of books on the table beside her—clearly she had made up her mind.

"I trust fish and vegetables are good for your lunch?" Anke asked Mari.

Mari felt her anxiety spike, pulled it together by folding her hands on her keyboard.

"Yes, that sounds lovely, thank you," she said.

"I will go and see how Rosenda and Ody get on with the preparations," Anke said.

Mari nodded pertly, although she was forlorn. She couldn't help but feel Anke was trying to escape her, even just for the length of a cigarette. She could have easily texted Ody about the meal. Mari had never had a moment of such high tension with a client. She had been unable to keep her cool and, more importantly, to get the information she needed—that they both needed—to help Anke, to help herself, to write the book that would be a triumph for them both. What if Mari couldn't ever get the info? What if she failed? She told herself, *No*. She had never before invaded a client's privacy. But. Before she could reason herself out of it, she stood and grabbed Anke's journal, stuffing it deep in her bag. She would read it tonight and find a way to return it in the morning.

Her face was still flushed, her chest pinched with anxiety, when Anke returned to the room five minutes later. Mari forced herself to look up from her computer, as natural as could be. She was relieved when Anke told her they would break for lunch. Seated at the table with Anke and Ody, as they discussed something to do with the house's gardener, Mari's most pressing concern was her table manners. And by the time they returned to Anke's suite, she had regained her poise. Here was the possibility of a mystery solved. A bestseller. The ladder she had seen—to everything. But it must be Anke's story, not the band's. She chose her first question with care.

"How did you learn of Mal's girlfriend?" Mari stopped typing, telegraphing sympathy.

"He moved her into the house," Anke said. "This was mid-June, after we have been there around two months. The band's manager tells me of Mal's new *secretary*. I was not born a fool."

"That's awful. What did you do?"

Anke stared at her for a long moment. Mari flushed, sure Anke could see through her.

"To understand Mal, I believe you have to know the whole story, back to Berlin."

"Right, of course—Mal changed a great deal in his last summer. But you said when you first met him, he was supercharged, a true artist. Were you a big fan?"

Mari pivoted, glad for the safety of any topic that made Anke share. Anke was right, too. For readers to feel Mal's betrayal and the black hole of his loss, they would first need to feel his genius and the passion between Anke and Mal. Maybe Anke would get carried away and drop details about her pregnancy. Well, no, Anke wouldn't get *carried away*, but all intel had value.

Anke covered the androgyny of '70s fashion, the crudeness of the term "groupie," and the cultural legends who had graced the band's backstage parties. But there was never a chance for Mari to dig deeper. As the light faded, Anke announced it was time for Rimbaud's walk.

Either Anke's makeup had faded, or she had pushed herself too hard—dark circles ringed her eyes; her skin was pale. When Anke was recounting the adventures of her youth, her face was so luminous, she appeared young. But now her frailty made her seem older than she was.

Mari felt jittery with nervous energy. She wanted to beg for another twenty minutes during Anke's walk—but she wouldn't be forceful again today. She had taken the journal, and she must do everything she could to make sure Anke never suspected her, of this or of any other infraction that could cause her to fall out of favor. Mari bowed and backed out, reminding Anke memories often surfaced between meetings, and she was only a text away.

As soon as Mari found herself alone, she closed the curtains, made the ridiculous move of putting a chair against the door, and pulled out the journal. Her hands were trembling, and she was almost sick with anxiety. This wasn't her. This was self-serving, like her father. He had emulated the men in Anke's life, the bad boys of the '60s, leaving behind his own hurt women. He had given himself to the high-stakes rooms at the casinos. He had failed to pay child support. And he had corrupted his daughters' values with his gambler's fever dream. He had left Mari and V with a taste for things they couldn't afford. Like Anke, they had built lives from what they could hold onto, which had required them to be silent witnesses to the bad behavior of the men in their orbits. Well, maybe all of them, the hurt girls, would finally grow up and have their say.

Mari willed herself to use it, to not be a weakling—not just for herself, but for Anke. For Vivienne. But she couldn't make herself believe in this justification of betraying Anke for Anke's own good. She simply couldn't do it. Mari didn't even want to hold the contraband item. She again hid the journal away at the bottom of her bag, hoping she hadn't ruined everything.

FOURTH:
SWAY

People think, once a ghostwriter is hired, you sit down and ask the celebrity everything. God, no. It isn't like being a journalist. You're their employee. Meanwhile, your editor expects you to serve the book, which you're working hard to do, hoping it will lead to future projects with that publisher. But mainly, you're trying to keep your job. These two goals don't always align, especially when your client has their own agenda, to which you aren't always privy. Somehow, you must be everything to everyone, and also manage to get the writing done.

On her second morning in the desert, Mari again overslept and had to forgo exercise or personal time in order to shower, dress, and skim her notes. She was mad at herself, but she had needed the rest, having stayed up until nearly two in the morning. She had paid $200 for the cheapest copy of Syd's book she could find online, feeling the free fall of spending money after having none for so long. And then she had read a Kindle version of a book about the Ramblers, written by one of their roadies. There was nothing, here at least, that hinted at the possibility that Ody was Mal's son, or that Anke and Dante had been sneaking around while Mal was still alive. Still, Mari had tried to absorb enough of the myth to be able to deconstruct it, via the questions she would put to Anke. Then she had transcribed the day's interviews, until her eyes grew gritty.

Mari managed to appear at Anke's door at eleven a.m., their scheduled meeting time. Mari knocked. But nothing. Was Anke still miffed at her for pushing too hard yesterday? No, they had ended on a good note. A fine note, at least. Feeling exposed, Mari texted Ody:

"Good morning! Did I miss a change of plans? I'm at Anke's room and getting no response. Happy to do whatever is best for her. Thank you!"

As soon as she hit send, a reply appeared. Damn, Ody was fast.

"1 p.m."

Irritation flared up, but this was the job.

"Great, thanks!" She changed "Thanks" to "Thank you," then back. Hit send.

His terse answer burned her phone screen. Mari couldn't help but go over her standoff with Anke again. It would have been better if it had gone differently, but she suspected Anke wasn't scared by conflict. Even if Mari had fucked up, she was trapped until Monday evening. And she still needed more about Mal and his death. So, there was nothing to do but do her job well. Normally, she would have felt confident by day two, but she sensed Anke pulling back, as if she felt she had revealed too much. Mari must somehow dig deeper without showing she was.

When Mari resurfaced at Anke's door at one minute past one—be punctual but never exactly on time—she found Anke waiting for her, unsmiling. As usual, Rimbaud was at her side, and Ody was seated at Anke's desk. They all looked at Mari.

"We have so little time, it is important for us to begin promptly," Anke said, not experiencing any irony that she had delayed their meeting by two hours, Mari by one minute.

"Of course," Mari said.

Mari dove in, trying to impress Anke with her insights into the early, happy days of Anke's life. With the painful sacrifice of her first love, Fritz, Anke had left Berlin to tour the world with Mal, silencing her fears of her bourgeois mediocrity, proving she was a true bohemian, an original thinker, an artist whose medium was her life.

Careful to address the creative Anke, rather than the groupie Anke, Mari danced through sensitive topics with empathy and sanguine inevitability—as was the case with Anke, all artists must leave some detritus behind. But even with Mari at her most attentive and astute, Anke was distracted and flat. While appearing unmoved to answer a question Mari had put to her about what it was like to visit America for the first time, Anke wrapped her translucent pink shawl around her and stood. "You will excuse me," she said.

Mari's stomach lurched with anxiety. She should be getting closer, not further away.

"Of course," Mari said. "Whatever you need."

Assuming Anke had gone to the bathroom or slipped outside to enjoy a smoke in peace, Mari reviewed her notes. But given their already stilted conversation, each question seemed too personal, too grasping, especially anything to do with Anke's secret pregnancy and Mal's violence toward her, which was what Mari really needed them to discuss.

Mari couldn't bear the silence. Now was the time. Hiding the journal under her arm, she stood, observed the weather: another perfect Palm Springs day. She paused by the white flowers from their first night. Acting casual, she sniffed them and saw a florist's card: "Congratulations, You Future #1 New York Times Bestselling Author! Yours Forever and a Day, Dante." Mari wondered what Dante was like, and if he had ever doubted he was Ody's father, given Anke had been married to Mal until his death. It was all here in the room with her—the real story, the truth. Who else had gotten this close? It was still a secret, so no one, obviously. Mari could not lose this opportunity. Besides, there was nothing else waiting for her beyond it.

With a fluttering in her chest as pronounced as when she listened to a voicemail from a collection agency, Mari circled back to the table where Anke had tucked away her journal. Ody did not look up. Her muscles tensed, her breath clenched, she turned her back to him, blocking his view, silently opened a space in the stack of books, into which she might slide the journal.

"Can I help you?" Ody asked.

Panic clawing up her throat, Mari exhaled loudly. She made herself face Ody.

"Anke is very private," Ody said. "You are her guest, but that doesn't give you free rein."

"No, it doesn't," Mari said, her voice shaking. "I'm sorry."

Mari extended the journal, but when he grabbed it, she didn't let go, seeking an ally.

"I didn't read it. I couldn't bring myself to betray Anke."

He snorted, clearly not impressed. She flushed, but this was too important not to try.

"Your mother's memoir will be read very closely, and I'm not sure she understands how good the public is at sniffing out a lie, or even just an avoidance of the truth."

He stared at her silently, choosing not to validate her observations about his mother. She sensed he would want to assist her if he understood how much was at stake for Anke. But she couldn't think how to enlist his help without betraying the secret—his secret, really—and as much as she wanted her bestseller, she wouldn't hurt Anke—or him—to get it. Plus, more practically, being indiscreet about Ody's paternity would probably cost her the job anyhow. She released her hand so that he now held the journal. She wanted to cry but, of course, wouldn't.

"Good choice. I was surprised when Anke invited you here, but she said you were special. Could be trusted. I hope she wasn't mistaken. Anke doesn't like to be wrong."

"No one likes to be wrong," Mari said. "And Anke wasn't."

"Because it looked to me like you were stealing—"

"Anke wasn't wrong," Mari said again, pitching her voice to sound more confident.

Ody nodded at her, putting the journal back in the stack. Mari held his gaze, aware she had to appear strong so she would seem like she knew what she was doing. If she fell apart, she would never get what she needed from Anke. Then she would fail.

Anke made her careful way back into the room, seeming perplexed to find them both standing. Ody shot Mari a dirty look, clearly not wanting to disgruntle Anke. Mari attempted to smile with her usual warmth and ease while steeling herself for Ody to rat her out.

"What are we discussing?" Anke asked.

"Your favorite flowers," Mari said. Her eyes darted to Ody's face, which was hard to read.

"Pale pink antique roses, of course," Anke said.

Ody looked away from Mari, staring at his phone with conviction.

"A classic—let's see, we were talking about your modeling career," Mari said.

Mari used the cover of resettling themselves onto the couch to calm her nerves. Just because Ody hadn't told Anke what she had done didn't mean he wouldn't. Mari was scared, not just that she had been caught, but that she had felt so out of her depth, she had overstepped in the first place. She needed to behave impeccably, so if Anke confronted her, she could claim a momentary lapse of reason, caused by exhaustion after several late nights in a row. Even more importantly, she needed to prove she truly was Anke's writer. She willed herself to stay calm.

But it didn't matter how smart Mari's questions were or how delicately she delivered them, intent on reassuring Anke and drawing her out. Anke kept losing her train of thought, and then deciding her stories weren't interesting, even though Mari reminded her on a continuous loop: "You've had a one-in-a-million, exceptional life. *Everything* is interesting."

As much as Mari needed to make progress, fast, she wasn't going to risk embarking on a sensitive topic or implying Anke wasn't doing her part. Instead, Mari opted to salvage the day, using a strategy she had devised on her most recent project, in response to her client's ADHD and the difficulty she'd had concentrating on a single subject. A certain amount of biographical housekeeping must be done—dates, details, descriptions of people and places. It could be tedious, even for those who held their past in rapturous regard, which Anke did not. Mari decided to drive forward on this front, since Anke was already short with her. Anke pushed back at times, relented at others, but she pulled further into herself and her fortress of pillows.

Ody burst from his seat. For a few beats, they both looked at Mari. Rimbaud, too. Mari realized Anke had flagged him, perhaps with a surreptitious text. Their workday was over. Mari hadn't dared to mention the journal again—she was tempted to confess, but her instinct was that Anke would not forgive her, and it was better to risk everything on Ody's silence.

"Ody will take you to review my archives, which will fill in a great deal of this biography."

Mari nodded, even though she wanted to yell: *When the fuck is that or anything of real value going to happen?! I only have one more day before I go back to LA to start writing.* She reassured herself with a reminder of how many books had been written with even less material.

Having gathered her tools, Mari bowed good night to Anke, who had opened her laptop.

"Goddamn," Anke said. She glowered into its depths.

Mari stopped short, still cautious after her earlier missteps.

"The publisher keeps emailing me, asking for answers I do not have."

"Oh, you should have told me," Mari said, too drained by her frayed nerves to avoid the hint of censure some might hear in her response.

Anke looked up, her expression haughty. Anke was never told she *should* do anything.

"All I meant is that's why I'm here. I speak book world, so I can translate and deliver what your publisher needs, especially closer to deadline."

Mari smiled as benignly as possible.

"Fine, you do it." Anke handed Mari her laptop.

"If you forward the email, I can write to our editor, introducing myself and offering my services," Mari said, trying to hand back Anke's device. "I'll cc you, of course."

"I need you to answer the email," Anke said. "Now."

"As you?"

"No, as Lucifer." Anke threw down her reading glasses, lit a cigarette. She tried to limit herself to a handful a day and never smoked inside. This did not bode well.

"Of course," Mari said. "I'd be happy to."

Sitting, she pulled Anke's computer into her lap. Anke leaned against the open slider, back slumped, as she hissed smoke into the yard. It was easy to buy Anke's air of superior indifference, but even without knowing what Anke might or might not have to reveal about Mal's death, or Ody's paternity, Mari knew she was anxious about this book. In Mari's experience, such anxiety made her clients act their worst—not that they could be called on it.

Mari skimmed the email, which contained a perky note from their editor's assistant, Stacy. She seemed young. And eager. *Uh-oh.* Anke obviously had no patience for fools. But. Having this woman on their side would help. Stacy had forwarded the sample flap copy for the hardcover edition of Anke's book. It began: "International rock groupie Anke Berben . . ."

"Well, you're not a groupie, for starters," Mari said.

"If this is how they treat their authors, I hate to see what they say about their whores."

Mari narrated as she typed: "'Dear Stacy, you will understand why I must object to the word "groupie," which will color the perceptions of every reader who acquaints themselves with my life. I have also edited the text to be more concise, and to lead with the most vital details of my existence today. Thank you for your understanding. I look forward to our collaboration.'"

"Ciao," Anke offered up.

"'Ciao, Anke,'" Mari said as she typed. "Good? Would you like to go over my edits?"

"Your edits are fine. Danke."

Mari flushed. She approached Anke to return her laptop. Anke took it from her without looking. Mari meant to get out, fast, to decompress in her room before tackling the day's transcription. But she was overpowered by the beauty of the desert sky, as gorgeous and plaintive as the perfect song played at just the right moment, and the softness of the evening air, musky sweet with sagebrush. Mari paused next to Anke, feeling the quiet wild do its work on her. She glimpsed a fleeting motion. A tiny bunny with alert ears nibbled a blade of grass.

"They always feed at twilight," Anke said. "Look, the yard is full of them."

Mari refocused her vision, making out their white tails in the succulent-ringed yard.

"Den Hasen," Anke said. "When I look at them, I hear the German. It has happened in the recent days. I am seeing the world in my native tongue once again."

"When was your last visit?" Mari said, back to her careful word choice. It wasn't her place to presume Anke's wants, even though she was here to speak—and think—for her, at least on the page. "I'm sure your book will have a German edition, and you'll be in demand there."

"Perhaps you are right. Or not. I do not think I will see Germany again."

Mari turned to Anke, curious about the ambivalence in her voice. It was a strange, prophetic thing to say, even for Anke. In the natural light, her beautiful face was an antique teacup, webbed with fine lines. Her blond hair tucked behind her ears allowed Mari to trace the vertical artifact of her face-lift scar. And yet Mari could see the little girl she'd been in her bright, clear eyes. During the day, Anke was good at hiding the cost of it all. But as with the day before, it was now written on her face, which looked skeletal. Mari shivered, wondering what really had happened to Mal, and if Anke had been involved.

"Do you miss Germany?" Mari spoke to break the silence and force herself back on task.

"Nein. When you choose the artist's life—or it chooses you—everywhere and nowhere is your home. If I am ever at peace, it is out here. Dante always said the desert is a poultice for any sickness. Of your soul, I mean. He gave me the desert. A great gift."

"Well, you gave him a son, so you both had gifts to give."

Mari and Anke openly studied each other. Finally, Anke nodded in agreement.

"Yes, you see everything, quick, quick," Anke said. "I notice this at our lunch."

Mari took a deep breath, feeling more like her former, confident self.

"I don't want to waste anyone's time."

"Thank you, Magdalena," Anke said. "There is no time to be wasted."

Anke's compliment was an unexpected but welcome resolution to a trying day. Indicating Mari should follow her back into her suite of rooms, Anke tucked her laptop away.

"Join me on my walk," Anke said. "I have kept you too much in the house."

"Yeah? Great!" Mari said. She dared a look at Ody, but he gave nothing away.

Mari knew better than to make too much of Anke's sudden show of confidence in her, or the implied intimacy of her new nickname, but she wanted to weep with relief.

They met at the front door. Mari was surprised to see Anke approach in her giant sunglasses and an unglamorous straw hat, like gardeners wore. Holding her cane in one hand, she clipped on Rimbaud's leash as they exited the estate through a hidden door in the gate.

"Rimbaud grows bored of the yard smells," Anke said. "I feel I am safe to use my cane here. No one judges or betrays my privacy."

Mari nodded and crossed her arms over her chest so she could hold her recorder toward Anke without being obvious. The early-evening air was cool and fresh. The houses in Anke's neighborhood were stately modernist gems and elaborate Spanish and Mediterranean villas with lawns as lush as the swimming pools around back. Mari allowed herself the pleasure of feeling like she belonged to this magical place, in her own way, at least for the weekend.

"Now, where were we?" Anke said.

Mari hadn't been thinking of a particular question, but she always had one ready.

"Many people have observed 1969 was a transitory time, from the peace and love of the late '60s to the darkness of the '70s," she said. "The Manson murders. Altamont. Mal's drowning. Could you feel the shift, or is this the interpretation of distance and perspective?"

Anke opened with the usual stories, Laurel Canyon, the Troubadour, and the Sunset Strip. Mari was poised to coax her to go deeper. But after Mari had proven herself inside, earning a new camaraderie, Anke apparently felt more candid. "From these pop culture artifacts, you will see a fairyland," she said. "But the summer of 1969 was difficult. Often, I thought I would return to Germany, to my first love, Fritz. Mal was mean. Unwell. It was clear an ending of one kind or another was drawing near. But I had left one man. I felt I need to try, to stay. Then I was—let us say there were other considerations. And we were married. And he was—he was Mal."

If Mari had only trusted herself and been patient, Anke would have revealed more of the story eventually. She supposed this pointed to Anke's agenda, which Mari hadn't discerned yet—a definite concern. But that was the least of her worries now, if Ody told on her.

"Mal's genius was legendary, but so was his drug use," Mari offered.

"Drugs were the symptom. He was soul-sick. Like the black death. Every day with the band was an enchantment. That was, maybe, more the real reason I stay. But I was hurting, and I had nobody I can talk to. Anyone not with the band was on the outside. And this summer, even before Nancy, Mal is already going away from me—with drugs, with Syd. So, I send for my best friend. Sigrid, she took to the life, and she came to work for the band, and for Mal, for a time."

"It must have been a relief to have an ally, someone you had history with, who cared about you, and who wasn't swayed by the band's fame, as so many were."

"No one was immune to the band. Not even me. Definitely not Siggi. She had come from East Germany. She was very green, as you say. And they were Shangri-la."

"But she was your friend, first and foremost."

"Yes, when we were young, we could live by that idea: friends first. It is a nice code. When we were older, in America, neither of us native, life had more complications. But, still, I did all I could for her. Then I had to go. I had to."

Mari considered the loaded word "complications," but she understood readers cared more about the men in Anke's life than her female friendships, especially with a mere band assistant.

"This was later, in the mid-70s," Mari said. "After you had been with Jack for five years, and you did leave him, Sigrid, and the band. You went back to Germany, to the life you had fled. Finally, you were able to quit heroin, after trying several times."

"Ja, that is the paint-by-numbers version. But not untrue. When I left, I gave up all my power in that world. I could not do anything more for Sigrid, in terms of keeping her job or her place with the band. I got her to America, and now she had to look out for herself. Maybe it was disloyal of me, but I had to make a choice, and I chose Fritz. Women betray each other for men all the time. Men offer safety. You wouldn't understand. You have a skill. A career. To live off men, you play by their rules. Sometimes it is messy, other people get hurt."

Mari felt like Anke had broken her story into shards. She could circle back to other topics, but for now, she would follow the theme of love, seek truths about Mal, the Ramblers.

"Is that how you feel—you lived off men? But you've been a model. Published a book of photographs from your travels. You make jewelry."

"It is nice of you to say, but these are children's games, not business—not even the business of art—not the stuff by which money is made, houses kept, children raised."

"So, you found partners. They loved you. You made a family with them. They were very rich—they chose to 'keep' you, if you want to call it that, as a sign of their status, power."

"Ja, a certain kind of man, when he gets money, he acquires a watch, a car, an estate, a woman. It is a necessary expense. I see your point. But I have not had a man in my life for a long time. I prefer it as such. I was lucky to get some money when Mal died. He would have been surprised to be the one in my story who helps me, but it was so."

Again, the word "motive" bubbled up. This was good stuff. Rich material that touched on Mal's death. And how it had played out in Anke's life. But Mari knew to be careful. It was one thing for Anke to be blunt about the less-than-savory aspects of her financial realities, her marriage; anyone else who trod too heavily would be resisted. Anke was, above all else, proud.

"My son, his father takes care of him, but I never ask for more. After I no longer model, I have no income of my own. My jewelry, everyone always wants for free. This book, it is my first real work in many decades. It takes its toll, always creating the illusion of wealth out of less."

If Anke wasn't wealthy, who was? The other Ramblers. But that would have been the case with or without Mal. And they were already one of the most successful bands of all time, even as early as the summer of '69. Why would they risk getting rid of him? Anke had stopped to let Rimbaud snuffle his way along a patch of grass, and she watched Mari.

Scrambling to fill the silence, Mari lost the thread of their deeper conversation about Anke's sexual currency and its rewards. "What kind of work did Sigrid do for the band?"

"Everyone had an assistant, to run the errands. Reserve the table for dinner. Talk to management. Buy and carry the drugs."

"Your friend did this for the band?"

"Yes, for the band, and then for Mal until he is done with me and so with her—and then for Jack. It was like a—how do you say—a promotion?"

"Do you still talk to her?"

"Nein. Our paths have crossed. But when they do, there is no talking."

"Was she mad at you, then, for returning to Germany?"

"Furious. But we both make choices, and we had to see them through."

"You chose Fritz," Mari said. "She chose . . ." Mari let her voice trail off, waiting for Anke to fill in the blank, but Anke shrugged in a bored way.

Her openness was gone, and they were approaching Anke's house.

Anke paused to unlock the door, remove her hat, and light a cigarette. The magic hour had lingered, and the desert light was as soft
as peach fuzz. Bathed in its smolder, Anke's white silk dress, looped
with strands of rosewood prayer beads, shimmered as if she were a
radiant shaft of light. Mari was filled with hunger. Not to be seduced,
but to make real contact, to unearth secrets, to not fail. To climb the
ladder—inside Anke, inside her life—and to never be hungry again.

Mari tried to power on her transcription, but she was restless after
her walk with Anke and couldn't focus. She found herself online,
watching clip after clip of Mal—official band videos and shaky concert footage with psychedelic patterns projected onto him, his eyes
sparking in the colored lights. When she started to feel like he was
watching her back, she opened her slider for some fresh air. The tem-
perature had dropped. She paused, but the crisp night felt good.

She crept around the house, to the pool, aware she was overstep-
ping. Mari had never snooped—until the episode with the journal.
Before now, she hadn't even been tempted. When her celebrities
hadn't invited her somewhere in their house, or hadn't shared a letter
or picture with her, it was off-limits. If caught, she would need to beg
for forgiveness, and she was unsure if she would receive it. She knew
she hadn't yet seen Anke at her full powers. But the possibility she
might already be on her way out made her desperate to use her time
here well.

Mari's nerves pulsed. All her focus was pulled to the ground before
her. She had been expecting the usual spa-like oasis, with a jacuzzi
and elaborate plantings. Instead, she found the kind of simple concrete rectangle popular in the desert in the '20s. Still, it had a dated
luxury. She tapped the surface with her toes: It was heated. Stripping
down, she escaped the chill by submerging herself. Without any un-
derwater lights, it was spooky, Mal's ghost in her head. So much had
been written about his death, she could picture him, floating in the

pool, lungs full of water, blood full of drugs. It was even sadder if Anke's journal entry meant he was Ody's father.

Mari considered what she knew of that night. The band had dined at a trendy health food spot near their rental house. Not long into the meal, Mal had made a scene—maybe tripping, maybe ruined from the constant drugs. Anke had tried to calm him, but he'd turned away from her. Mal had been taken home, where Nancy was resting. Refusing to ride with Mal, and too upset to remain at dinner, Anke had walked down Sunset Boulevard with Dante. Syd had ferried the rest of the band to practice for the next day's Hollywood Bowl show, returning for Dante. At one a.m., Nancy had awoken to discover Mal gone. Feeling uneasy, she trailed through the house until she found him, drowned. She called an ambulance, management, but he'd been dead for at least an hour. Whatever Mal had been to her, to Anke, to the band, to the public—it was all over now.

Mari pictured Mal's limp body in the dim pool. Darts of fear almost drove her back into the house. But it was so good—silky and warm, easing the knots out of her muscles. After Anke's transcendent stories, she couldn't help but want a little magic for herself. Alone with the vast desert sky, she belonged to the story, and also to the world—beyond all books.

Mari stretched out in the water, opening herself up to the therapeutic power of the desert, which Anke had praised. She wanted more of everything, but instead, she felt like there was never enough of anything. Not enough money, or security, or love. Theoretically, life should have expanded in all of these areas after her mom kicked her dad out when she was nine and V was five. He'd been so erratic and incapacitated by his gambling that their existence had stabilized without him, thanks to after-school programs, her mom's hard work, and then her stepdad, who was a good guy. But in her years with her dad, her personality had been forged in the fires of their codependency. No one explained why he had been banished, or why his absence was for her own good. And so, she spun, rootless, until she latched onto academic excellence, vaulting into college, a journalism degree that drew on her listening skills, a job at a city paper. Becoming a music critic had led to the ghostwriting, where she had stumbled into the purpose she had lacked. But still, she never wanted to listen to anyone like she wanted to listen to her dad, and sort of like Anke and heroin, she'd had to swear him off completely. She stuck to what she could control, her books, and what she was good at, getting people to confide in her, and stayed afloat. She didn't crave what her celebrities had, because they possessed talents and charisma she lacked, but Anke made her life exceptional by living it. Such simplicity stirred something in Mari. She felt full, not just of deadline purpose but of life. She knew she hadn't earned this job with her writing résumé. It gave her confidence; she had impressed Anke on a more animalistic level, the plane where Anke thrived. Mari also knew she would never be an Anke herself. But serving as her proxy was heady enough—the pleasure and glow of this life was working on Mari in ways she'd never felt before, pushing her to risk more than ever. It hit her: *I will do whatever it takes to finish this book.*

FIFTH:

FOCUS

While your client has sold a memoir, when faced with writing a book meant to reveal so much of themselves, they are often ambivalent. Unlike a regular memoirist, who craves the opportunity to be discovered, celebrities are already known. Complicating that persona is scary. They want to be someone who is candid and wry and brave, but it is more difficult to be themselves than their persona, and so the whole experience can be fraught. Today, their whim is to write a book with you. Tomorrow, if it gets too hard, that desire could change. You must not let that happen.

A s Anke draped her shawl just so, Mari was again transfixed by the sure elegance of her movements. Mari wondered, as she had with other clients, if celebrities were born with this aura, or if it came from being observed and admired. She suspected it was a little of both. She had no bitterness about the special respect given to celebrities in our culture—the truth was, they *were* different. Most people were imperfect, ugly even, in the banal moments of their day—driving, shopping, holding a fork—but it never grew old, watching someone beautiful at ease.

Mari noticed Rimbaud asleep nearby, but they were absent their other silent companion, Ody. She didn't mention it, certain Anke would evade her. Mari flipped open her laptop, feeling the pressure of all she must do, choosing an oblique approach.

"Can you remember any assistants besides Sigrid, during your summer in LA?"

"Ack, it was so long behind us," Anke said. "There was an Andy. She had come from London. The others come and go. Later, in the '70s, there was a backup singer, Izzy, who became an assistant for many years. The band is loyal. Or afraid, maybe, of new people."

"Being that famous, it must be hard to trust additions to the entourage."

Mari thought of Syd's betrayal, but she didn't dare to mention his name. Yet.

"Maybe it is about trust, maybe familiarity, maybe laziness," Anke said. "With everything always changing—the city they play, the women they bed—they crave something the same. Sometimes, to play, they even require it. They can be very superstitious."

"I interviewed Robert Plant once, and he used to iron before every show."

Anke gave Mari a haughty look. The only rock stars who mattered were *her* rock stars.

"Superstitious?" Mari said, as if it had been her first and only response.

"Dante will play with one guitar pick only. For years, the same one. That is why, I think, they keep the same tech, Simon; the same roadies, Joel and Nigel. They stay for years. Loyal or lucky. Simon is a prick, would swagger around like the sixth member of the band. Unplug Mal. Sometimes I think he make his guitar out of tune, to have Mal look bad. Mal would embarrass himself, of course, but it is hard to see him made into a fool. Simon is never reprimanded."

"I find that surprising, given what a perfectionist Jack is known to be."

"Simon never is stupid enough to do something like that to Jack.

He knew Mal is weak. We all know Mal is weak, damaged, so we try to placate him. But Simon, he targeted Mal."

"Targeted him how?" Mari asked.

"Always bring a bottle to practice because Mal cannot stop and will be falling down. Maybe sabotage his equipment. I do not know for a fact. I know Mal was a genius musician, but not when Simon was in charge of him. I was not in the band, but sometimes I think you observe more from outside. I see Simon wants to replace Mal. But he underestimates Jack's vanity. He would not have an employee take the stage beside him. I always wondered that Simon stayed after it did not go his way. But how else would he live?"

Mari bolded Anke's comments in her notes. That sure sounded like the right setup for what seemed like the most probable sequence of events that night: Mal had ingested his usual epic quantity of drugs, and if there had been any foul play, it had been a pair of hands that had helped him into the pool, held him beneath the water, and made it look like an accident. So, there had to be someone capable of doing such a thing, with the motive to do it. Although if Simon was that intimate with the band, he would have understood Jack as well as Anke had. Unless he had been blinded by his own ambition. Mari knew a thing or two about that.

"Did you ever tell Mal or Dante your suspicions about Simon?" Mari asked.

"Nein, Mal was beyond talking that summer, and then he was gone. And when I am with Dante, we are not looking backwards, only forwards—to our new love, our baby."

Anke had said "our" baby, which Mari noted before considering the rest of her words. It was a tantalizing premise—Anke might be able to shed more light on the intimate truths of the Ramblers than anyone inside the band. Mari wasn't sure she believed it, but she didn't have to in order to use it to the book's advantage. Silently, Anke leveled her steady gaze at Mari.

"They were all so young," Mari said. "It must be a shock, especially for someone like Mal, to suddenly have so many people working for you, depending on you for their livelihood."

"Ja, and Los Angeles was a strange time. Not everyone came over from England. They thought they were careful about who was close to them, but their judgment was not always good. There were hippie kids that drift around like tumbleweeds, attach themselves to the band."

"Like Syd?"

"Ja, like the driver, Syd. I hated him. He always get money from Mal to buy the drugs. He always do too many drugs, encourage Mal to do so as well. A few weeks before he died, I find Mal, asleep, choking on his sick. Syd was fired, but he kept coming around. Mal shielded him. I think it must be a relief to be near someone more fucked than you. After Mal died, Syd tried to talk to me, but I could not look at him. Dante made him go. It felt good, finally."

"I'm sorry," Mari said. "That sounds horrible and upsetting, to have someone use Mal like that. Do you remember anything else about Syd?"

"Nein, he drift about, work for a place to stay, for drugs, for a little pocket money."

"You clearly didn't trust him, but his book must have been a shock, a betrayal of the deepest kind. He was allowed to witness the band's most intimate moments, Mal's unraveling."

"Ja, the book," Anke said, her voice flat. Mari was surprised by her lack of emotion. Anke seemed like the loyal type who would have felt justified in having Syd's head on a spike.

"Did the band know about it in advance? I'm shocked their lawyers couldn't stop it."

"It is more complicated than that."

"I'm sure," Mari said. "Major stadium rock acts are like small cities—they have economies and weather patterns all their own."

"Ja, but back when Mal die, the band was more of a family still. It wasn't such a machine. I saw that start in the '70s."

Mari didn't want to talk about the '70s yet. Yes, Anke's relationship with Jack would also earn several chapters in the book, but they were teetering on the real crux of the story. And Anke was dodging her somehow—she could feel it—but she still didn't know why. If only her copy of Syd's book were here. She wondered at the chances of Anke possessing this detested item.

Anke had begun rewrapping her cashmere shawl, as if she was on the verge of standing. Mari threw herself back into the conversation before she lost her.

"Who else was close to Mal? Did he have an assistant before Sigrid?"

"They all quit. By then, the drugs had been harder, more street."

"Was Mal different on harder drugs? Was he different in the weeks before his death?"

"Mal was different. Maybe because of the drugs. Maybe because of fame. Maybe because of his own dark cloud. He was a terror. No care for anything—except music. He always loved music the most. By that summer, he crossed over already, in some primal way."

Anke had confirmed the rumors of Mal's violence. Was it possible Anke had acted in self-defense, and that's why she didn't want to come out too strongly against Syd's book?

"He became violent," Mari said.

"He is always violent. He started—"

Mari watched Anke come to be, if possible, even more beautiful. It was the ultimate shield—an exterior so pleasing it turned the observer back from digging deeper. Anke lined up her bangles, all the stones in a row.

"He'd started to be mean," Mari used Anke's word, coaxing her to continue. Her mind flipped through their conversations, as if she were skimming the book, already written. In Anke's journal entry, she had been pregnant, and she had been with Mal. Yet now she seemed to be sticking to the official record: Dante was Ody's father. Mari wasn't so sure, and this was her chance to possibly be certain. Mari repeated a phrase from Anke's reading: "'Specks of blood like flakes of fresh red snow.' That's how you described it in your journal when Mal pushed you."

"Ja," Anke said.

Mari was so close. She tuned up her senses, reading Anke's voice and body language, finding fear, even after all these years. She leaned forward, just slightly, radiating warmth.

"When he pushed you, Mal was angrier than normal—out of his mind," Mari said. "Something had set him off—he knew that . . ."

Anke surprised Mari by stepping into the silence.

"Ja, there was no more placating him. That's why—how come I—"

Mari used all her self-control not to cross further into Anke's space and possibly spook her. But Anke backed away from confession anyhow. Sat wearing her pretty face as a shield.

"You had no choice. Anke, I heard what you wrote in your journal. I already know."

"There is always a choice. The question is who you make your choice for, and why."

"Ody, who is known as Dante's son."

"When my son was born, he came early, in March of 1970—he is a Pisces, of course—I was with Dante," Anke said. "In July of 1969, I am making a choice."

Anke reached for her cigarettes. Mari felt sorry for Anke, who had not been able to hide the vulnerability or guilt in her voice. This was it, maybe—not the official record, but the truth.

"You've said how out of it Mal was by then. Something shifted in June. Maybe with the heavy drugs, it was like he had already died?" Mari wove statements in with her questions, normalizing their conversation, modeling for Anke there was no reason for shame or fear.

"Not dead—when he was dead, it is bad to say, I should not say, but it was a relief. We were safe, then. We breathe the sigh. Before, he was like the undead. Like in old movies, walking through glass, hungry, always hungry, never satiated, a big set of hungry, wet teeth."

As she did for hours every day, Mari kept her eyes on Anke while her fingers sprinted over the keys, recording her shorthand notes. She glanced down long enough to turn on the bold function, so she could easily find the place where Anke admitted she was glad Mal was dead. But that was as much excitement as she allowed herself in the room, hoping her lack of reaction would normalize Anke's confession and draw her out to admit more.

"How terrifying. What did he do when he was angry?"

Anke leaned in closer. "I don't feel good talking bad about Mal. I am no angel. I make mistakes. And I will show that. But I lived long enough to write the history in my book. I think I must be careful how I use this power."

"I couldn't agree more," Mari said. "But there is a way to be fair. Just tell the truth of what happened, and let the reader make their own assessment. Don't call Mal a drug addict. Show how drugs ruined this magic artist you had fallen in love with. Don't pretend you were an angel—no one would believe your book if you did—but be vulnerable enough to give the reader the context for your actions, to explain your choices, to absolve you."

"You believe this is possible?"

"I have seen the power of the written word again and again. Dare to confess and the reader will dare to forgive you."

Anke nodded. It was rare for her to acknowledge Mari had landed a point, but when she picked up her narrative, she did as Mari had suggested and led with Mal.

"To be alone with him, it was terrible. But to avoid him made him worse. To prove the point, he was stronger."

"None of his bandmates, or management, did anything?"

"He was the band. He had the look. He gave them their name. Do you know how much that is worth, even back then? His songs from that year were not so good. But he wrote their first two dozen hits, signed their publishing. Up until then, it all went through him. Jack hated it, but still, they were trapped. And here he was, losing his mind. It was a nightmare. Do you see?"

"I think so," Mari said, even though she knew what she understood was just one pixel in the whole complex picture. "Financially, the band was stuck with Mal."

"Ja. No one wants to push Mal, so no matter what he does, they speak softly to him, try to make it okay. They all say, when he went dark, I was the one who could reach him. As little as I could. So, there I was, the girl in the labyrinth with the Minotaur, until I felt like I could not stand another night of his raving, lunatic self-destruction. And then, his new girl. If I am no longer the girl who can reach him, what am I? I am in danger of becoming nothing."

"I'm sorry you had to go through that. And so young. That sounds impossible."

"Danke."

Mari had learned to take that breath to empathize, to sit in the pain with her clients.

"He was fucked in his mind. His soul. Everywhere. He did not take the news well."

Anke gave Mari a pointed look, then grew silent, leaving her writer to interpret what "news" she meant. Mari stared back at her, enraptured not by her beauty, but by how real she seemed. She had lived in the world in a way Mari never had—without the filter of a book, a computer, a glass of wine, a certain ironic detachment. There were faint lines around Anke's dark eyes. She looked tired. She had earned it. She had loved. Married. Birthed a son. Seen the world. Inspired how many songs? Been a player in one of the great dramas in pop culture.

Sure, Mari envied Anke, but Mari knew things, too—how legacies were made. She not only needed to help Anke, in order to help herself, but she was moved to help Anke. She had been since she'd first noticed how Anke had only told stories peopled by famous men. Mari wanted to give her more than proximity—to give her a voice, a whole self, especially in her final chapter. If there was a buried secret that would be bad for Anke, she would help with that, too.

"On the drive out to Palm Springs, you cried. Was that for Mal?"

"For Mal, for me, for us, for how young we were, for how it could have gone."

"With Mal?"

"With everything. The truth is, Dante and I were in love when he first brought me to the desert, the summer of 1969. He had fallen under the spell of Joshua Tree. We went there first. Then spent a week in a bungalow in Palm Springs. That is where Elvis, JFK, everyone went to feed their secrets. In the desert, everyone indulges. No one tells."

Mari hesitated, unsure what in these old tales had made Anke cry other than Mal's death, which, dark as it was, Anke had admitted was something of a relief. When Anke had gotten too close to her feelings, she had left the car. She had danced around Mari's questions for days. Mari had finally broken through, at least a little. How? By being steady and receptive, by not pushing too hard, by letting Anke come to her. Mari phrased her next statement carefully.

"In 1969, you were still with Mal," Mari said. "Mal was still in the Ramblers."

"That is the truth, too," Anke said. "This was August, soon after Mal died. Dante and I both needed to get away. It was a bad few months. That spring, Mal went dark. You can see it in photos. Look beneath his beauty. His eyes are tarnished. They no longer reflect the light. He had no more light within him. I think he was evil. I do. Well, he was not evil, really. He was a sweet, sensitive boy. But he have bad influences—drugs, lies, Syd—he betray me again and again."

"It was painful for you. You loved him."

"It was painful. He hurt me. He was kicking at whatever came near him. I was there. He didn't see the damage he did. Or didn't care. He was far gone. Yet we hoped to save him."

"Dante was a knight on a white horse."

"Dante was a court jester. He made me laugh. It is a remarkable thing, to laugh when you haven't in a very long time. It is better than sex."

"Yes," Mari said. The absence of laughter was a kind of rot, along with poverty, along with loneliness.

"Did Dante know you were pregnant?"

"When I wanted him to know."

"And Mal?"

Anke looked around, but there was no tea to be made, no assistant to order about.

"You can stop protecting him," Mari said.

"Maybe I am protecting myself. Maybe I am protecting—"

"If you tell me, we can write it so everyone understands. If you don't, you will always be at the mercy of stories written by Syd, by other people. It's time for *your* story to be known."

"I want for my story to be told, for this book to be written. I do."

"Wonderful, that's all you need—to choose it. And to be honest. I can do the rest. I am here to help you, Anke. What did Mal do?"

Anke winced, but she didn't look away. "He kicked me."

Staring at Mari, Anke held completely still. Mari mirrored her, willing her to continue.

"But he was stoned. He missed. I worried about the evil, but I thought I could cure it. With love. We all pour so much love into Mal, no matter what he did. A week later, he informed me one of his new girlfriends, a cow-faced girl named Nancy, was pregnant. She was sixteen. He must take care of her, their baby, so they will get married. And like Houdini, he will be gone."

Anke lit her cigarette on a scented candle and stood. She leaned on her cane with gratitude. Mari hated seeing Anke this way, like witnessing a prize fighter wince as his ribs get taped in the locker room. But this was the real truth of Anke today, even if it would never make the book. The privilege of being allowed to view it, trusted not to reveal it, was the unspoken gift and responsibility of Mari's job. Anke opened the slider into the garden. As soon as she took her first drag, Mari exhaled. *Fuck.* It was common knowledge Mal had gotten a new girlfriend, Nancy, pregnant just before his death, but it had seemed less nasty, even had a flair of the Prince Charming, when he'd announced his intention to do right by this young girl. And then it had taken on the trappings of the tragic when he died—maybe even was murdered—just days later. But only because no one knew Anke was already pregnant with Mal's child.

Mari felt her way into Anke's life at that time, uncovered a surprise.

"It must have been a relief to have Mal put his attentions elsewhere," she said.

"It was embarrassing. I admit my pride took a blow. But, ja, you are correct. It was a relief. Being left by Mal I could live with. But losing the band—it was impossible. For me, they were realer than a backstage pass, or a bond forged in bed. They were my family."

"You were relieved, but you were vulnerable. You had to do something."

"Ja. We all stay in our house in Hollywood. Nancy, too. The band was practicing for their big show—their free concert at the Hollywood Bowl. There was tension, more than that—cracks like the cleavage that ruins a diamond. But you see, there were these papers that had been signed, for the publishing, the trademark. They were businessmen as much as artists. Even Mal. So, they would press on, pretend all was well. Anke does not do pretend."

Mari didn't move, she barely breathed, her eyes locked on Anke.

"It was the eve of the Bowl show. I knew after, everything will change. It was like a love triangle—Jack, Dante, Mal—and Mal was the past. Dante was the future. I have noticed how Dante looks at me, have felt the love there. I see a path forward for our future, but to take it, I have to act. I told Mal we need to talk. Even he feared he would appear too hateful, so he agreed. Now he will try to placate me, I suppose. I invited him to my room for tea, our ritual. I would bring the same teapot with us, on tour, nestled in my lingerie in my suitcase. So, he drank it."

She leaned her back against the door frame, brooding, smoking, silent.

Mari waited. She waited some more.

"What was in the tea?" Mari kept her voice steady, not allowing any emotion to creep in, a technique she had mastered in childhood, for after her father had gone on a bender, and she'd had to talk to him like a bad dog. She was ecstatic and terrified—not just that this new revelation might make Anke's book, but also that she was somehow going to squander the connection. After all, she had been able to talk to her dad, but what had it gotten her?

"A special blend of rose hip and cinnamon I made myself," Anke finally said.

"And what else?"

"Mal took his tea with loads of milk and sugar, like a little boy."

"And what else?"

Anke sucked down the final drag of her cigarette, stubbed it out. Anke's pause grew so long, Mari's skin began to tingle. Part of her wanted to walk out of Anke's room, out the front door, and keep going. Anke hadn't confessed to anything yet, certainly not to murder, but her loaded silence said more than if she'd continued. Mari had been in plenty of uncomfortable conversations with clients, but nothing this heavy. Surely this was above and beyond what it was reasonable to expect of her, armed with her journalism degree and her self-help vocabulary.

And yet she'd had a sometimes self-destructive tenacity hardwired into her in childhood. And she was fucked if she lost this job. This was *her* path forward. Like Anke, she must act. Standing, Mari grabbed her recorder and shook two cigarettes from Anke's pack. She lit them as Anke had. As Anke moved aside for her, Mari took a shaky inhale, let her exhale follow Anke's.

"Sometimes you have to say something out loud, to know if it's true," Mari said.

They stood side by side, smoking. She felt *alive*, as if everything tasted, smelled, felt a little deeper. But Anke had apparently used her few moments alone at the door to pull herself together, and she was no longer back in her bedroom with Mal and the tea. Her voice changed, took on the casual tone of a story she had told many times before, even just in her own head.

"Mal will fall asleep, wake up the day of the show, having missed yet another practice, and be unable to play, disgraced with the band. Dante will play his solos. That is all I know."

"But there was your I Ching reading—" Mari said. "Did Mal know?"

Anke hesitated. Finally, she shook her head, as if settling an internal debate.

"No, I never tell him. How could I? Together, the coins make the hexagram K'un. Oppression. Exhaustion. First, is Tui, the joyous, lake. But then, below, is K'an. The abysmal, water. That was always the trigram for Mal. In that formation, 'the lake is above, the water below; the lake is empty, dried up.' Confucius himself sees a bad ending here: 'For him who is in disgrace and danger, the hour of death draws near. How can he still see his wife?' This man, Mal, cannot master the oppression. And he did not. After that, nothing was good for a time."

"Oh, Anke." Unsure what else to say, Mari tried to layer these two words with enough nuance to make Anke feel supported. It was even darker than she'd expected. She hesitated, trying to figure out what Anke needed. "You were upset by the reading. Did you believe it?"

"Ja und nein."

Mari doubted Anke could be led to such vulnerability again, at least not right now, but it was her last day in Palm Springs, and they didn't yet have any future meetings booked. After today, Mari was expected to be ready to write. Mari would ask questions until her time ran out.

"How often did you do readings?"

"During that summer, every day, sometimes multiple times a day," Anke said. "Everything was at stake, and I was scared by the choices I must make."

"Did you ever get that reading again?"

"Nein," Anke said. "But once is enough."

"Did you ever do a reading about what happened to Mal?"

"'The hour of death' happened to Mal."

"Yes, of course," Mari said. "What happened to you, though? How did the legend start?"

"The next year, after Mal dies, I am interviewed for a book. This was after Ody was born. I stayed clean while I was pregnant, but after, it was a free-for-all. I don't know what I said to this writer. Dante was furious. Sued him for slander. But he was only quoting my words that he had on tape. That is how the legend started, I predict it, even though the I Ching is a subtler art."

"I'm sorry that writer took advantage of you when you were un-well," Mari said. "That's why your book is so important. It's a chance for you to set the record straight, once and for all."

"Maybe I don't care about this record, or what people think."

"I don't believe that. And I know you care about your son. What happened next?"

"Syd returned from the rehearsal space, and he came for Mal. I stay in my bed, crying."

"To bring him to practice?"

"Syd didn't care about that. To drink rum and smoke hash Syd buy with Mal's money."

"There were huge quantities of both in his blood when he died—maybe deadly amounts."

"But hash was food. Rum was water. Mal takes it all day long, from breakfast to bedtime. To give him hash, or rum, was no sin."

Mari grew flustered, wondering if the "sin" was what Anke had put in his tea, but hid it.

"So, according to your recollections of that night, Syd was the last person to see Mal. But that's not what he says in his book. Did anyone try to talk to him—the police, management?"

"He disappeared, after Dante send him away."

"That's suspicious. Do you think he wrote the book to get even for being made to leave?"

"Perhaps," Anke said.

"People were always around in that house," Mari said. "What did the others say?"

"At midnight, Syd has to go back to the rehearsal space to pick up the band after practice. But they want to go to a bar, so that is Syd's alibi. Mal goes for a swim. And—"

"The bar must have been the band's alibi, too?"

"Syd says he passed out in the car, waiting for the band, and woke up back at the house."

"So either he drove blacked out, or someone took the car back to the house—and Mal."

"Syd lies for profit. Syd lies for fun. I would not pay too much mind to Syd."

Mari raced through the possibilities. She was no police detective, and Anke had not come out and confessed to a crime, but she did seem to feel guilty about her actions. And she seemed to have taken pains to *not* pin Mal's death on Syd, which would have been the safest bet, since he was dead and his book out of print. The inclusion of this story about the tea in Anke's memoir would add a new narrative to the already suspicious events surrounding the night of Mal's death. This would undoubtedly make the book a runaway hit. But Anke didn't seem motivated by a desire for a bestseller in the same way other clients had been, even though Ody had invoked this need when he'd originally declined to hire Mari. Anke seemed driven by a deeper urge. The thought gave Mari pause. She was on the verge of her first official bestseller, and it would change her life—a change she desperately needed. But at what cost to Anke? Could Mari live with building her triumph on the downfall of someone she admired so much? And what if Syd hadn't been lying and someone else had gone back to the house that night and killed Mal?

What Anke had told her was probably enough to satiate their editor, the publisher, the readers. But in case it wasn't, Mari needed to avoid scaring Anke off so she could revisit this topic. She would not push, then, only soothe. And when she was back in LA, she would read Syd's book and dig deeper. If she had understood what Anke was implying, there was more to be uncovered. Mari wouldn't again be sold a version of events that could easily be verified as untrue. And she wouldn't let Anke expose herself unless she was sure the tea was all there was to the story, no matter what substance Anke might have slipped into it. Her eyes were drawn up by Anke's gaze. Mari wanted to give her something.

"Finally, you were free," Mari said, her voice kind.

"I am free, but at what cost? What have I done? I am despondent. Dante felt the same. He and Mal had come to blows. Dante is a proud man. He tried to be cool but despised the chain that bound them. Maybe Jack did as well. Jack hides it better. Dante felt he'd willed the death of Mal. We fell together. When I inform him about the baby, we are not just two, we are three. A family."

What, exactly, had Anke done? Or Dante, for that matter? Or Jack, even, as long as she was looking for band members with motive? Mari was queasy, and she felt relieved when Anke handed her an abalone-shell ashtray. As they returned to the couch, it felt like hours had passed.

"How did Dante respond to the news?"

"Dante was over the moon. As young as we are, he always loved kids and wanted a brood. He stepped up. I traded up. Mal had been falling apart, on his way out. Dante's star was rising, along with the band's. The sudden tragedy seems to galvanize their fans. Their free show was a happening. Their records go platinum. We make it to the other side."

Mari wanted to ask about Mal's publishing deal, and what had happened to the band's profits after his death, but it seemed gauche after such emotional topics.

"You made it. But . . ."

"Mal's ghost haunted me. I see him drinking tea—my tea. In my dreams. Behind my eyes, every time I blinked them closed. My whole world is a guilty conscience."

"You struggled with heroin. You attempted suicide."

"Ja. I am ashamed, but I take everything. I suppose I went mad. My son is beautiful, perfect. But I was afraid of him. I could not get out of bed. Dante did not know how bad it was. He was a doting papa. He woke up with the baby at night, fed him with a bottle, sang to him. I stared at the wall. Shot up in the bath. Until Jack took over. As the band's front man, he was the leader now—he will lead us all. He decided Dante cannot handle me. I suppose he is correct. Jack took me over. For Dante's good, really. But for my own good, too, or so we all thought."

"So you all thought—until . . ."

"Jack tried to turn me respectable. Rock 'n' roll is pure energy, freedom, but the life of a band on the road is monotony, backstage ass-kissing. The heroin made me sloppy, which Jack could not abide. If I stayed with Dante, it would not be so baroque. He was more of a free spirit, without shame, but Jack, he was of the society folk, the celebrities. I felt my smile was so fake it would break me in two. I enlist Sigrid, who I made Jack hire after Mal fire her. She books our travel, so she buys me a secret ticket. I fled Jack, took Ody home to Berlin to live clean. Fritz—my first love—would not see me. But then we spend time together. He built me a sailboat, where we lived. We travel the world, for ten perfect years. Then he drowned. My curse, it seems."

Mari was surprised to find tears pressing against the backs of her eyelids. This was more than being spellbound by Anke's aura. She cared about telling her story, for better or worse. Mari cleared her throat, trying to compose herself, unsure for once where to go next.

"You think I am a terrible person," Anke said.

This surprised Mari more than anything Anke had said. She knew Fritz had been alone on the boat when he fell overboard, and Anke had never been suspected. Usually elegant and languid, Anke looked scribbled and hunched. Mari was glad to be able to help her. It was complicated, though. Anke didn't want to be a good person. She wanted something trickier.

"I think you're a visionary," Mari said. "Mal was about to go over the edge. You saw a path forward where no one else would. You were young, not yet in full control of your powers."

"Now. My bed is empty. I focus on my jewelry. My yoga. My dog. My son is a grown man. He is kind enough to help me, but he is also a talented guitarist and songwriter, like his papa. He has his own career, and he can release music and tour the world whenever he chooses. I have made a life for myself, on my own. I want to write that story."

"Yes, and you will," Mari said, smiling, telegraphing her acceptance of Anke's boundaries. She felt high, ecstatic. She would have to sort the details, of course. Figure out if she could push Anke further on what, if anything, she knew of the actual moment of Mal's death. And she couldn't relax, not until she had completed this weekend. But she was so close. She was going to succeed—she could feel it—and with the book she cared about more than any other.

Anke nodded. Mari had passed. She wanted to grin, hug Anke, run around the house with a victory sign held aloft. But now was the most critical moment. Her clients sometimes felt safe enough to tell her their deepest, blackest truths, and then resented her for knowing them. She couldn't let that happen with Anke because she needed these secrets for her own survival. She was exhausted. Listening hard, and filling in the gaps as she had, was like hunting with her bare hands. But she acted refreshed, as if they'd spent the day bonding at the spa. Closed her laptop.

Anke was silent. Mari surveyed the story, looking for loose ends. It came to her: Ody.

"You have always put your son first," Mari said. She knew others might disagree, point to Anke's drug use. She had seen her own father ruined by gambling, knew it was not a choice.

"I will always protect him, but I will not always be here to do so."

Mari sensed a thread. Hesitated. Pitched her voice as gentle as it would go.

"Anke?"

"It is a cancer of the blood. I will live to see the book published. But not much beyond."

"Oh, Anke." Mari knew Anke would not forgive her if she cried. So, she did not.

"And then Ody will be—does he know who his father is?"

"Odin knows Dante is his father. That is all he should ever know."

"Dante is Ody's father, then," Mari said. She would not take another father from him, especially not now. She couldn't believe she would lose Anke. They would all lose Anke.

"How will you write it, so the reader sees?"

"There are ways," Mari said. She pulled it together. She would do this for Anke. A lifetime was seventy years. A legacy was forever. Finally, she knew just what she had to do.

SIXTH:
STUDY

Yes, there are red carpets, life-changing casting calls, and, sometimes, happy endings. But those compelled to write usually have something more earnest to convey. Being a ghost means being trusted with stories of rapes, beatings, reversals of fortune—the hardships that give celebrities the fierceness to claw their way to the top, and the price they sometimes pay upon reaching it. Always take a moment to acknowledge the trauma—a professional trick and the decent thing to do. Long before there is a book in the world, there are two people sitting alone together.

When Mari reached her room, she did a little shimmy of joy and relief, and then she sank onto the bed. This book was going to be huge. It was also going to be Anke's last act, and no one knew it yet. Mari felt a physical pressure inside her. She didn't have a moment to waste. Before she could rest, or eat a Lärabar, or pee, she plugged in all of her devices.

Her phone buzzed. Ody: "Please be in the den in 10. To see the archives."

At least he said "please." Not everyone did.

Twelve minutes later, Mari stood next to the glacier of a white couch. Two modeling portfolios obscured one whole cushion. Three gray fabric-covered boxes rested on the coffee table. Each had been labeled with a confident hand: "Band," "Boat," "Jewelry." Here was her chance to touch the past she'd spent so much time occupying through Anke's words. But she knew better than to overstep, especially as she was still awaiting the fallout of her earlier fuckup.

Ody materialized, silent in his suede moccasins. On another man, she would have found his fashion choices affected, but like his parents, he could pull off the theatrical.

"I'm sure these contain some incredible treasures," she said, nodding toward the boxes.

"Anke is very private."

Mari felt embarrassed, like he was chastising her for the journal, but shook it off.

"You've never seen what's inside?"

"Do your parents tell you everything?"

She almost laughed—the thought of her dad being transparent was so ludicrous. "Say no more. How long have you worked for Anke?"

"Since I dropped out of university and started my band. At first, she was helping me. Now, I help her."

Mari hesitated. Obviously, he knew about Anke's diagnosis. But she didn't want to push.

"That sounds like a good kind of family," she said. "What's your favorite photo?"

He raised an eyebrow, maybe surprised to be asked a question not about Anke—the designated subject—or maybe trying to anticipate what Mari would do with such info. He padded over to the piano, picked out a framed black-and-white photo. A shaggy-haired, sunglassed Dante cradled a hugely pregnant, Indian-kaftaned Anke, laughing as they balanced on a motorcycle, chrome flashing like hope in the California sun. Mari looked up at Ody, and they both smiled. If he wasn't Dante's biological son, Anke seemed to be the only one who knew.

Much like Mari had coveted the perfect boho serenity of the house, she now felt a pang of longing. She had two photos of her parents together, and one blurry Polaroid of her dad holding her as a girl—family hadn't been her dad's style, and he hadn't cared to pretend. She shook off the thought and reached for a quick joke, even though she knew it was lame.

"Four out of five doctors recommend pregnant women avoid motorcycles in their third trimester," Mari said. "But what a marvelous family portrait. They look so happy."

"That they do. She wouldn't dream of getting on a chopper now. Hates that I ride one. After the accident with Fritz in the Yucatan. Well, you've seen her cane."

"Accident—we haven't gotten there yet. What year?"

"I'm bad with dates." Ody redirected them, opening a lid. "We don't have much time."

Mari smiled. "Of course. I'll get started, then."

Peering into the first box, she found labeled, dated archive envelopes. Maybe the stereotypes were right, and we never did outrun what our youth had imprinted on us. No matter how bohemian Anke had become, she was her mother's daughter, careful of her precious objects.

The top envelope read: "1976." The year she'd left Jack. Retreating to Germany, reconnecting with Fritz, and embarking on a round-the-world sailboat adventure. In a life this dramatic and picaresque, little could be skipped over. Mari stopped herself from thinking about how much hard labor she had ahead. One thing at a time—that was how books got written, how life got lived. She lifted out the envelopes. The bottom one read: "Los Angeles. Summer 1969."

She paused, nervous. Her mind pinged with self-doubts. She knew she was stalling, but she couldn't find her nerve. Too much was at stake.

"Anke doesn't want to be here?"

"She hates old photos of herself. Says it's too painful to see how much beauty she's lost. You are to use whatever you need. If you have questions I can't answer, she will do so."

It was remarkable how little Anke romanticized her past—or present, for that matter. While the rest of the world had built shrines to her style, her place in pop culture—there were a dozen Instagram accounts and Pinterest pages devoted to her modeling days—her own social media presence was minuscule and managed with the savvy of a Midwestern grandmother. As far as she could tell, Ody wasn't on social media, except for his band accounts, which he hadn't updated much since his last album had come out three years earlier. How lucky, to have the kind of rich life that didn't need to be market-researched or padded for others.

Mari went through each photo, taking a picture with her phone and making a corresponding note in a Word doc. Faded Polaroids and snapshots, they were less satisfying than the iconic images of the band. She was struck by how many other people were always around, and by how cool the clothes were—no wonder they remained style icons, fifty years on. Jack often wore a men's suit vest, with no shirt, and a gold, flower-patterned choker with dangling teardrop bangles. He looked so current and cool, it was hard to remember how provocative and louche this had been at the time. Dante could wear a silk scarf like nobody's business. Anke had a knack for simplicity—a perfect shearling coat over bare gazelle legs and thigh-high boots, a silk shift that showed her nipples. Mari doubted the photos were high-quality enough to be printed, but it would be worth the attempt—readers would devour anything new.

Mari focused on what she could use for her writing. In any photos featuring the whole band, Mal was always on the outside, often looking away, sometimes with Anke pinned to him like a trophy. Mari was unclear whether the other people would be important to the story or not. From her research, Mari recognized the band's manager—as young as them, and even more flamboyantly dressed, often carrying a briefcase, allegedly full of cash. There were six unknowns, four women and two men—one was maybe the guitar tech, Simon. The other young man, who had shoulder-length hair and was laughing and passing a joint to Mal in one picture, was probably Syd. By squinting and doing a Google search, Mari worked out that the prettiest woman was the model Jack had been married to back then. The other women were, what? Groupies. Assistants. Nannies. One had a boyish bowl cut and always wore the same jeans and silk blouse—in most photos she was covering her mouth. When caught smiling, she had a brutal overbite. Probably not a groupie. Maybe Anke's East German friend. The busty woman, forever in a bikini, was either a groupie or the most popular assistant ever. There was no way Mari could take notes on every photo, but she managed to put her eyeballs on all of them.

Anke looked so much happier after the band, on the sailboat. Of course she was thin, fit, and tan, her teeth flashing white like the inside of an eggshell. Her clothes were even more to-die-for, plucked from the markets and bazaars in the ports where they had docked.

In Mari's three days in the desert, they'd gone over Anke's entire life story, except for this final chapter of her youth, which Mari planned to request additional time with Anke for once she was writing—by phone if Anke was in Europe. Mari knew the tragedy ahead for this young family. She could hardly bear to look at the photos, especially the last one of Fritz, Anke, and Ody grinning over a picnic on the deck of their sailboat, taken a few days before Fritz drowned.

"What was Fritz like?" Mari asked.

Ody didn't look up, and Mari wondered if he had heard her.

"I don't know, really. I was only a kid. He didn't speak English, and my German was basic for the first few years. He was nice to my mom. She was happy, and I liked that."

Mari saw the pictures on the boat in a new light—when Anke was with Jack, Ody had still been in his father's orbit. Suddenly, he had been pulled away from him, the only world he had known, carried across the globe, where he had lived in isolation with two German-speaking adults who had been deeply in love and improvising their life.

"Did you like the boat?"

"Sure, I was a little boy, and boats were cool."

He gave his voice an impish enthusiasm, mimicking his younger self. Mari smiled.

"But there were no children, you didn't go to school. It must have been lonely."

Again, he paused for so long, she began to wonder if he had heard—but of course he had.

"I never saw it that way, but yeah. I wonder if adults know how lonely kids can be."

"Especially if you're one of those kids who doesn't feel like a kid, but everyone insists on treating you like one. I seriously thought I was ready for my own apartment at eleven."

He laughed, nodding his head. "When we were on the boat, we would dock somewhere for a month or two. My favorite city was Valencia. They had just had their first elections since Franco a few years earlier. But they had been conquered by everyone—the British, the French, the Moors—they were a mutt, like me. I tried to convince Mutti to let me stay there. I was ten."

"Did you ever go back?"

"Nah, we had seas to sail, ports to explore. Fritz died when I was sixteen. My mum needed me. I did make a go at uni, but it wasn't my scene. Really, it's always been her and me."

Mari nodded and smiled warmly, but something was cracking inside her. All her smug certainty. She had felt sorry for him, but he had a place where he belonged. He had a purpose. He had been needed, and he had stepped up. Mari never missed a deadline, but that wasn't the same.

"It must have been very hard on your mother when Fritz drowned," Mari said.

"She was devastated . . ." His words trailed off; his eyes snapped up. Mari heard the telltale sound of Rimbaud's nails clacking on the tiles. Anke. "But that's her story to tell, not mine. It's *all* her story to tell, really."

Mari studied Ody's face, seeking Mal, but all she could find were Anke's high cheekbones and dark eyes. And then she was looking into those very eyes as Anke stood behind him, resting her hands on his shoulders, leaning against his chair.

"What do we speak of?" she asked. "The archives have been helpful, ja?"

"Mari asked me about when we lived on the boat," Ody said.

"And you told her what?"

"I told her about Valencia."

Anke laughed. "You were a very stubborn little boy. I always love that about you."

Mari was surprised Anke didn't seem rattled to find her son and ghostwriter in such an intimate conversation. Mari realized it was because Anke trusted him. He was perhaps the only person she did. And she was right to do so. He was loyal and true. Mari felt a tremor at her own overall lack, and her approaching return to LA.

"Ody, please bring the wine Rosenda opened for us," Anke said.

He nodded and did as he was told, also appearing at ease. Returning on his silent feet, he poured the wine. After Anke and Mari toasted, Anke sipped, allowed a tiny shiver of pleasure.

"Now we play hooky," Anke said.

"I agree, when creating, it's not good to push too hard."

"Ja, Magdalena. We all can use a break. Nothing in life should be forced. Not art. Not love. Not money. You set the terms, but it must come to you."

"You've been very lucky in all three," Mari said. She was fighting to hide how much her nickname pleased her.

"I have lived. When you forge a life of the raw stuff you are given, there is no luck to it."

"Of course. Luck is chance. And what you've accomplished is a kind of alchemy—that is, if that term seems right to you—hopefully, you'll always feel comfortable correcting my words. I've been wanting to ask you, how has our collaboration been for you?"

"You are quite good at this part. Let us hope the writing can stand up as well."

"It's a process. But it always does."

"Life is a process," Anke said. "A little attitude, and these tits take me around the world."

The women laughed. Anke had an eighth-grade education, but she had been a good student, just like Mari. Only she had excelled in different subjects—the ones learned outside the classroom, which Mari had devalued because she was not fluent in them: flirtation, poise, manipulation. Mari's younger sister, V, was also a pro—it wasn't enough to read a room; you had to know how to slice through the subtext and become the heart of the moment. Their father's favorite, V had earned more of the little attention he'd given to either of them. There it was again—more proof of the power of that ineffable spark. Others fell over themselves to be near it. Mari had to work much harder to get anywhere and would be working for a long time yet.

Somehow, they had left the script behind. Mari was torn between her desire to have a real conversation with Anke, born of affection and curiosity about her graceful mastery of her life, and the danger of forgetting Anke was her client, and therefore her boss.

"How do you feel, to be revisiting your past?" Mari asked.

"It is more difficult than I expected. Also, more immediate, as if no time has passed. This is not for the book—"

Anke sipped her drink as Mari pantomimed zipping her lips.

"Even after we married others, Dante and I remained in each other's lives, because of Ody. And we have that sort of connection—twin flames. Ring or no ring—priest or no priest."

"Oh, yes, I was reading a *Rolling Stone* interview with Dante, from the '80s, and—"

"Did you know Dante keeps bees?" Anke interrupted, as if they were two gossiping girls.

"No! How quirky."

Mari took a large sip of wine, unfurled a smile. She had been right to be cautious. Anke made the confessions, not her. Any real intimacy was an illusion. She knew this. Mari had read many features on Dante that celebrated his homegrown honey, but she wouldn't say so.

Anke pushed away her wine. "If you will excuse me, it is time for my walk."

"Of course," Mari said.

This was an abrupt end to a day of the kind of closeness she had cultivated since they had arrived, but Mari knew not to ruin the mood with too much talk. Anke did not wish to be investigated. She wished to entice. And so, Mari would be enticed. Mari wanted to reward Anke for letting her inside—to prove she belonged here, to protect her. And also, yes, she wanted to safeguard her right to remain here after work on the book ended, wanting—it was embarrassing to admit, even in her head—for Anke to admire her talent, to admire her, to *like* her.

Mari gathered her supplies. Pausing inside the door, she turned back. She thought to remind Anke of her absolute discretion, but she worried to bring it up now would make Anke question her. At least the publisher had lawyers who would know how to protect them both.

Mari was poised to ask Anke what she might like to discuss during their two-hour drive back to the city, but Anke sat still, looking exhausted. Done.

"I want to thank you," Mari said. "For your courage today. It's going to be an incredible book. I'll send you a sample soon. Once we agree we've found your voice, I can dive in."

Anke gave a curt nod. Pulling herself together, she said: "Thank you, Magdalena."

Before Mari could exit, Ody reminded her of their departure time for LA. Smiling, Mari nodded and showed herself out.

Mari couldn't bring herself to pack. She didn't want to leave, and it wasn't just because she must begin the hard labor of writing. Reaching out, she tickled her fingertips over the peacock feathers. She'd been lulled by the magic tranquility of the house and Anke's company, and now she would be returned to her slapdash life with V. Sighing, Mari uploaded sound files and squeezed in some transcription, trying not to lose momentum. As Anke had alluded to something more than milk and sugar in Mal's tea, Mari ranged her mind over the possibilities. Was it the Quaaludes from his toxicology report? Pausing the audio file, Mari considered the full implication. As she had learned the hard way, her job as a ghost wasn't just to report her clients' accounts of their lives. It was to be their first reader, their earliest critic, and, when needed, to protect them from themselves. Anke hadn't intended to kill Mal, so it wasn't like she'd committed murder. Or at least not if her version of events could be trusted. But given how cool Anke normally was, her tears for Mal suggested there was more to the story than she'd revealed. Still, with what she *had* been told, Mari suspected Syd was at least as culpable as Anke, if not outright responsible. She really needed to read that book. It was extraordinary that such a high-profile mystery could have gone unsolved for five decades. Mari had better know exactly what she was revealing and have total control over how it was told. There must be more to the story, other suspects, a version of the truth that would be accepted as definitive. With her journalism background, she should be able to track down more of what had happened that night.

But Mari had gotten off track—yes, she must untie the secret if she could, but her more pressing task was to find Anke's voice, in order to speak as her throughout her book. Mari returned to her transcription. As the shadows darkened into full-blown night, Mari kept checking her phone. Ody had said they would depart for LA around seven p.m., after the day's traffic.

Unable to focus any longer, Mari scanned her Word doc. Seeking bold items to follow up on, she saw her note about Anke's Palm Springs house. At least these kinds of Google searches, which most people made out of prurient curiosity, were part of her job. Mari looked up their address. As the results loaded, she stretched, grateful for the break from her constant typing. In an attempt to win over the skittish Anke and secure the job, she had agreed to transcribe all their interviews herself, to avoid any leaks. It was a fuckload of work. But she was more sympathetic about Anke's paranoia, given the secrets she now knew Anke had to manage.

There were several puff pieces in architectural magazines with the usual stylized photos of Anke. Also, there was the home's Zillow page. *Strange.* The house had been purchased in 1968, for $75,000. Before Anke had been to America. Did Anke buy the house in a private sale? Or didn't she own the house? If not, who did? Mari Googled around without success. Her phone buzzed: "New plan. We'll stay in the desert. Your flight is at 9:30 and your Uber arrives in 30."

This was a surprise. Had she offended Anke somehow? She needed to learn where *all* the mysteries were hidden, and who was being left in the dark. Then she remembered the queasy feeling of being caught returning Anke's journal. Had he finally told Anke what she'd done? She hadn't even read it, but of course they wouldn't believe that. The thought made her sick. But Mari could still redeem herself by making her prose undeniable.

As Mari wrangled her luggage out her bedroom door, she slowed her steps and radiated a warm smile. The hallway was empty. Still, she held onto her poise, in case Anke and Ody came out to say good-bye. She wasn't surprised when they didn't; her clients were busy and often absorbed by their next task. Also, sometimes moving in and out of the intimacy of their meetings was tricky, like a one-night stand. Mari never took it personally. When she'd climbed into the hired car, and the driver had rounded first one and then a second corner, Mari exhaled.

Anke had paid for her flight and Uber, but Mari was responsible for her ride from LAX to Anke's condo, to get her car. It would run her $50, with tip, at least. Of her final $140. She couldn't deposit her check from Anke until morning; this was a close call, even for her.

SEVENTH:
DEDUCE

You try to spend as much time as you can, not only with your clients, but also with your recordings of your interviews, even when you are making use of a transcription service. It helps to listen repeatedly on your own, to hear their inflections, their pauses, the way they lean into a question—or don't. You are listening for their particular tics and resonances, for any detail you missed during the conversation, which can lead to the crucial question that will unlock them.

Mari hadn't meant to pull an all-nighter, but the spirit had moved her. She had managed to work through her sister's rowdy return from her weekend in Malibu with the producer, and through V's tipsy decision to do her trusty old Tracy Anderson workout, before she finally drifted off, as she always did, to classic episodes of *Full House*. When the condo had finally grown quiet, Mari realized her only hope of focusing enough to nail Anke's sample material was to write while Vivienne was sleeping. So, she worked until dawn, but she wasn't quite done.

Her knees creaked as she stood. She was in need of, well, a lot of things—but she settled for a strong cup of Earl Grey. While she boiled water, she stared into the empty fridge. As she closed the door, her eye caught on a postcard from Harrah's Atlantic City. Already stung, she flipped it over: "Hey Tigger, enjoy that Cali sunshine and always put your money on black. Love, Dad." Pushing down her feelings, Mari tackled the sink of gunky glasses—her sister never seemed to eat but consumed varied health drinks throughout the day. The clean citrus scent was an escape from the linear confines of her computer, which molded her ideas into neat rows. Mari had been writing the story of Anke's early romance with Mal. The specter of his death, and Anke's insinuation about a secret related to it, loomed just off the page. Now that Mari had almost completed a rough draft of the sample, she had a little breathing room to dig, hoping if she brought evidence to Anke, it would compel her to dare to say more. As Mari ran her mind over the events of that haunted summer in LA, looking for anything suspicious, she heard a gale of rough, handsome laughter. Who in this sad, dark tale had found a reason to laugh?

Dante. His name floated up, like a text message from Mari's subconscious. Where had he been on the night Mal died? At band practice, at least some of the time. Had he known what Anke put in Mal's tea, and if so, had he been involved? He and Mal had come to blows—Anke had said so herself. She and Dante had gotten together immediately after Mal's death, becoming devoted parents to a son he adored. Anke had implied that he'd harbored feelings for her before Mal's passing. The questions arose in Mari's mind: Was Anke protecting Dante, and if so, what was she hiding, and at what potential cost to herself? Every character in this drama seemed to be a plausible suspect. It all came down to the truth of that night. The book needed it. Mari needed it.

With a fresh cup of tea, Mari returned to her desk. After the forced focus of trying to wrestle her inelegant rough draft into something with style and substance, she welcomed the delicious mental slackening of Google. She wasn't sure what she was seeking—interviews with Dante, she supposed, about the night of Mal's death, Anke, their son.

The band was so beloved, every moment of its fifty-five-year-history had been catalogued on the web. Before Mari knew it, several hours had passed. She washed up on Dante's "personal" Twitter feed. The most recent post was from last week: a short video of his still gorgeous, still modeling third wife chasing a chicken at one of their weekend homes. Through a halo of smoke, he gave arch commentary. He seemed happy and at ease, and why shouldn't he be? He was at the top of the world, and he had been for half a century. Something nagged at Mari—the landscape looked familiar. She noticed the hashtag: #jt. Joshua Tree. Less than fifty miles from where Anke had stayed behind in Palm Springs. The fact that they'd both been in the desert was probably a coincidence. But somehow the revelation made the story of Anke's book feel even closer, reminded Mari it was still unfolding. She had just hit play again when Vivienne staggered out of the bedroom in a silk nightgown, her hair done up in actual rollers. Anytime Mari was tempted to feel jealous of V's beauty, she reminded herself of the constant labor it required. V leaned over Mari's shoulder, never conscious of personal space.

"Ah, Dante Ashcombe, too bad you didn't get hired to write his book," V said.

"What book?" Mari asked.

"Everyone was talking about it at the party this weekend. It's a big deal because he's the first Rambler to do one."

"Huh," Mari said, not wanting to let on how worried she was. "I made a pot of tea."

Mari clicked tweet after tweet. She found herself a week back, in mid-January, the day she'd gone to Palm Springs. The link opened to a press release from one of the biggest NYC publishers, and trumpeted Dante's memoir. Due to drop in six months, right before Anke's.

She toggled over to Amazon and found Dante grinning from his jacket cover, displayed on the title's dedicated page, along with a pub date in June. How had she not known this?

"I'd tap that," V said.

"Ugh, please," Mari said. "He's Dad's age."

"Well, at least you'll get a lot of press for Anke's book. People love a he-said, she-said."

Anke didn't seem to be aware of Dante's memoir, or the impact it would have on hers. There was no question he would have a runaway bestseller, and Anke could benefit from the massive burst of publicity. But even if Anke couldn't see it that way (of course Anke was too proud to want to see it that way), it meant she *really* had to tell the truth.

Vivienne came out of the kitchen. Shaking up her first health drink of the day—it was always green and sometimes contained vodka—she flopped down too close to Mari.

"This is juicy. What if Dante's book has, like, a different story than Anke's?"

And what if Anke's book wasn't a bestseller, through no fault of Mari's, after all Mari had promised Anke—and their publisher?

"This is my bedroom, V," Mari said, trying to scoot away from her.

"In my house," V said. "Wanna go shopping? Skip gave me a Fred Segal gift card."

"Everything okay?" Mari asked. She tried not to put too much energy into following V's romantic adventures, because it truly was enough fodder for its own reality show, but she had noticed that V often received an expensive gift or trip right before being cut loose.

"Yeah, why?" V's voice had a little-girl quality that wasn't put on. It made Mari sad.

"No reason," Mari said. "That's so generous of him. He must really like you."

"What's not to like?" V vamped, rebounding as she always did. She cued up Tracy Anderson—it seemed to level her out; maybe it was her way of feeling like she was doing everything she could to succeed, no matter how long the odds. Mari didn't like seeing their similarities, but for once it made her soften toward V. She gave her sister a sideways hug.

"Can I make a call in your bedroom?"

"Have at it," V said. She had stripped and was putting on her workout clothes.

It was seven in the morning; Ezra would be arriving at his New York office. Mari sent the link to Dante's press release, asking for his help. Then she brought a fresh cup of tea into V's room and closed the door, trying to see all the angles.

Thirty minutes later, she heard the telltale chime of an incoming email. Her agent had snaked a copy of Dante's book proposal, which he'd attached. His message read: "Call me."

As Mari dialed his office, she was skimming the attached doc with growing alarm. Given Dante's fifty-plus years as a rock hero, his three marriages to stunning, accomplished women, his five children, his homes in four countries, his chart-topping duets with every guitar god from Chuck Berry to Jack White—and given the proposal was thirty pages, including a chapter outline, a marketing plan, and a comps list of recent best-selling memoirs by other old-school rockers—an alarming percentage of the material was about Anke. More specifically, it was about that troubled summer in Los Angeles. Its sample chapter was set at the band's house, the night Mal died, lingering on the damning revelation that the only people *not* at the practice space all night had been Anke, Syd, and Nancy, who'd been laid up in bed with vicious nausea since she'd become pregnant. Dante's description of the band's LA driver wasn't any more flattering than Anke's had been, but he also stated Syd had been away from the house for several hours, ferrying the band to and from practice and running errands for them in between. His description of Mal was even grimmer than Anke's, but instead of being gone on drugs, he seemed energized with evil intent, exposing himself at dinner when their manager suggested he lay off the wine. Dante had gone into vivid detail about how Mal had screamed at Anke outside the restaurant, before telling the others to piss off—unlike them, he didn't *need* to practice—and bounding into the limo, which had run him home before returning to take them to rehearsal.

Dante, or someone in his camp, was quite clear on the dirt that needed digging, for maximum sales. Unlike Anke, who had danced around this painful season of her life for days, before she'd been coaxed to almost confess to manslaughter, Dante seemed downright chatty.

But it had been like he and Anke were describing two different men. So, who was accurate when it came to Mal's state of mind and his drug tolerance at the end of his life?

Mari needed a tiebreaker, but not another member of the band's entourage with a subjective perspective. She needed an expert who could give her an informed opinion. She thought back to her past clients. There had been a sweet former porn star who'd done a stint on a celebrity rehab show, hosted by an addiction specialist. Mari had talked to him a few times, as her client's memories of treatment had been garbled. He had seemed down to earth and fair-minded for a TV doctor. She looked up his number as her agent's assistant put her through.

"You okay, dude?" Ezra asked. "I'm sorry I didn't already know about Dante's book."

She was embarrassed to tell him the truth, but she knew it was her best hope of salvaging this high-stakes mess: "Well, Dante's proposal has more vivid details in it about Mal's death than Anke has told me—this from someone who wasn't even at the house for most of that night. I've only slept a few hours in the past three days, and I can't seem to finish Anke's sample."

"Ugh, I'm sorry. But the sample is always the trickiest part, right?"

"Yes." Mari sighed. It was one of the most exhausting aspects of her job—having to be okay with doing her best work, having it torn apart, again and again, until she finally broke through.

"Remember, Anke threatened to walk if she couldn't have you.

And you've already spent days with her. No one wants to replace you at this stage. It's expensive. Disruptive. You'll nail it. I know you will. I don't want to add to your stress, but that's the least of your worries."

"Dante's proposal?"

"Yeah, that proposal was an exclusive submission," he said. "It's not something that went out to everyone in New York, which is why I hadn't heard about it until now. I had some leverage, but it's super top secret."

"Am I right it's bad news for Anke?"

"Could be," he said. "With both books coming out in conjunction with the fiftieth anniversary of Mal's death, his version of the story is going to be considered the official record. And his book will undoubtedly bring more attention to her book, which will backfire on her if she contradicts what he writes. Controversy will drive sales, but her reputation could suffer. And if she gets caught in an outright lie, her publisher could be pressured to pull the book."

Mari felt the borders of her vision go black like in an antique photo. Her breath grew shallow. She was mortified, as if the worst had already happened. And she was scared. Mari's eyes stung with exhaustion and tears, but she wasn't going to cry on a business call, even with her agent. She pictured the flowers Dante had sent Anke, celebrating her book deal. Given this thoughtful gesture, and the son they shared, she couldn't imagine him wanting to harm Anke. Yet he seemed indifferent to the damage his book might cause her. At the same time, Anke was ambivalent about her own memoir, and she didn't seem in any hurry to be transparent, with Mari or her readers. Still, Mari wasn't about to go down that easily. Not when she was this close to breaking through, and when the alternative was—what? Mari looked around at the tacky nouveau riche room and her sister's belongings, also held in a single suitcase. There was no alternative.

Mari had been thinking about trying to push to see Anke ASAP. But she had to be bolder.

"I need to do some outside research, maybe even talk to Dante," Mari said.

"Hm," Ezra said. It was daring, especially so early in the project. "Will Anke go for it?"

"No, but if I can find out what we need for her book, she can't help but be happy."

"Outside interviews do happen all the time. But that sounds risky."

"I know."

Mari had never attempted anything so aggressive. But she had never been this close to her first international bestseller. Or to the end of her career, if she couldn't deliver this book.

Anke was so sure she had them in her thrall. Even after all she had lived, she was naive. Dante was looking out for himself and his own bestseller—and why shouldn't he be?

"Everything with Anke goes through Ody, her son. Dante's son. What if I ask him?"

"Maybe. It's not like we can have both teams sit down and agree to what's going to be in the books. Acting like it's no big deal, and you're just doing research, could be the best option."

Mari read out loud as she texted Ody, not overthinking it, putting herself in the liminal space where she always seemed to know the right words: "'Ody, am lining up a few outside interviews for A's book. Totally standard. Can you please put me in touch with Dante's assistant?'"

"You're absolutely sure about this?" Ezra asked.

"I'm sure there's something she's not telling me. And it could sink her book, our book."

"Ah, all right, dude, send it."

"He just wrote back: 'Anke is indisposed and cannot be bothered. Don't make me regret this.' He shared the contact info for Izzy. Anke mentioned her. She's one of the band assistants."

"'Indisposed'?" Ezra said. "That's not code for vodka, like last time, is it?"

Mari was surprised by the rock dropped on her heart at the thought of Anke's illness, her death. She knew she should probably tell her agent. But she respected Anke's dignity too much.

"She's really serious about her yoga."

In the celebrity world, that was explanation enough. So, Mari had her next step. After they hung up, Mari felt the vertigo of self-doubt. But she knew she could see the whole picture, at least when it came to the two books, in ways Dante and Anke couldn't. Yes, Mari had been replaced on her last book—maybe because she had failed so spectacularly, maybe as punishment. Either way, Mari had failed. She wouldn't fail again.

Before Mari could lose her nerve, she emailed Dante's proposal to Anke, without a message. Calls were verboten unless scheduled. Texts had to be planned, so as to not disturb. Emails could be (and often were) ignored—or dealt with when time and spirit allowed. Every move was tactical. Then Mari opened a second email, typed out a short, bright message, said a silent prayer, and hit send.

Vivienne flapped around, putting as much care into her toilette to go shopping at Fred Segal as she did for a fancy date. Finally, smelling like a sex flower and looking like a young Cher on a curly-hair day, V flounced out to spend. Mari had craved the silence, but now it was stifling. The next hour crawled by as Mari compulsively checked her in-box. She knew she should be focusing on Anke's sample material. But she couldn't stop thinking about what Mal had been on when he died, and how whatever Anke had given him had acted on his system. Mari reread every article about Mal's death, especially those that referenced the original autopsy and its findings: significant quantities of Quaaludes, acid, alcohol, and cannabis. Mari didn't know much about Quaaludes, but off the top of her head, it seemed like the most likely thing for Anke to have snuck into his tea. This was something the addiction specialist could hopefully clarify.

She forced herself to work on Anke's sample a bit more. Finally, when it was ten a.m. in LA, she sent the doctor a text, asking if they could speak. He surprised her by responding immediately to say he was available. His schedule was punishing, but he was type A and smelled publicity. Or maybe he wanted to help. Either way, she was glad to be able to call him.

After a warm hello, she got down to it, asking what he could tell her about Quaaludes and how they would have impacted a known drug addict, laughing at the doctor's obligatory bell-bottoms joke. She agreed to his disclaimer that he couldn't be sure without seeing psychiatric evaluations or bloodwork for the individual. Just before asking her central question, she realized she should be taping all this. Digging out her recorder, she put him on speaker.

"*Hypothetically*, is it possible this man could have metabolized a number of Quaaludes?"

"Yes, they were just very strong, highly addictive sedatives. Casual users quickly formed a tolerance. If he took Quaaludes with regularity, for even a few weeks, maybe he metabolized them in a way that would have seemed superhuman to anyone taking their first dose."

"What if he also took acid, hash, and booze at the same time?"

"Here's the thing, autopsies measure what quantities were in the person's system at the time of death, not the system's tolerance for those amounts," he concluded. "Hypothetically, all of that could have been a regular dose for a heavy user, just doing their thing, feeling groovy. Now, of course, alcohol would have exacerbated the Quaaludes, as with any sedative."

She thanked him and signed off. It felt good to amend the story, to have an alternative perspective to bring to Anke and whomever else she would interview. She would find out what had happened to Mal, most likely by his own hand in the end. No one had poured booze down his throat, right? Feeling galvanized, Mari returned to Anke's sample. Tomorrow, she would investigate. Today, she would write. Her first job, on which everything depended: don't get fired.

Finally, at seven o'clock the next morning, Mari closed her laptop. She'd been so exhausted that she'd napped through V's preparations for her date, which didn't seem to be with the record producer. Mari knew better than to ask. As the hours ticked by, Mari had stayed up, surprised to find herself feeling protective. She had figured V would be back any minute, until at three, she'd realized V wasn't coming home. The upside was that her anxiety about her sister had put her into a kind of fugue state that had deadened her worry about whether or not she was getting Anke's sample material right and had allowed her to finally finish it and send it off to Anke.

The sudden freedom blasted Mari open with joy. The three French presses of coffee in her bloodstream made her skin feel hot and prickly, and her feet seemed to float above the ground. She had decided to surprise V by stocking the fridge with all of her sister's favorites, from pressed juices to sparkling rosé. The bins of fresh flowers at the entrance to the West Hollywood Trader Joe's were all but pulsing—red, orange, purple, pink—like the high-tech visuals at a dance club. Was there anything so delicious as the feeling right after you handed in a big chunk of writing? Perhaps the glory of trawling her favorite grocery store, with $60 to spend. She was humming along to Blondie's "Heart of Glass" when her phone buzzed. Scrambling for it, she dug in her purse. She hadn't expected notes for hours, days, depending on Anke's schedule. And it was barely eight in the morning. Mari put her hands on her device, right before it stopped ringing: Unknown ID.

"Hi, Ody," she said, too wired to play upmarket young professional. "Good morning."

"Hello, Mari," he said. "Anke has read your pages."

"Fantastic," Mari said. Trying to sound like she was at her desk, ready to take notes, she sought out a quiet corner of the parking lot. "I'm impressed by her diligence."

"We wish we could say the same," he said. "Anke detests the writing. It made her sob. We took a risk on you, even when David tried to blackball you. And you led us to believe you knew what you were doing, but clearly you don't. Given everything, I felt I had no choice but to tell Anke about your indiscretion with her journal. She is disappointed, hurt, betrayed."

Everything pressed down on her at once. Mari could hardly stand. "Okay . . ." Mari took a breath to steady herself. "I'm so sorry. But— can you say more, please? I mean, it's not uncommon for the author to give the ghostwriter extensive notes on the sample material, especially the first draft. I'd be delighted to talk to Anke and redo the draft to her liking."

Mari was floundering. She had heard Anke. She had understood Anke. Hadn't she?

"I mean, she was happy with the email I sent to our editor as her."

"I'm sure she was, but an email is not a life's work."

This was a disaster. Mari quickly dropped any thought of confessing to how far her ongoing research on Anke's behalf had already progressed. "Of course, that is true—"

"We have begun looking for a new writer," he interrupted.

Mari faced a bank of shopping carts. *Fuck.* This was catastrophic. She'd never heard of a writer getting fired this quickly. What could she even say? She couldn't admit how much she needed this job, any more than she could admit that she had already chosen her outfit for their next meeting. Or that she'd bought a round-trip ticket to Las Vegas, in order to seek the truth of how Mal had died—although it was an extreme leap, even when Anke had still believed in her.

"Ody, I have to admit, I'm not surprised. Anke is so exacting, of course she wants to rework the material. Like I said, I'd love to be able to do this for her. I *can* do this for her. If I could only get some feedback . . ." Mari knew what she had sent them wasn't a polished draft—but it was an improved version of Anke's Germanic English. It expressed her mélange of Old World manners and joie de vivre, while toning down her exuberant purple prose enough for the more sophisticated readers at most airport bookstores. Just like that, it hit Mari: She had toned Anke down. This wasn't a literary work. It was Anke's life's work. She had been trying to show off, to impress Anke, and David, and everyone with her own writing skill. She had gone too far. Mari was too smart to confess to this, or to disagree with Anke at this moment. Ody hadn't responded yet, giving her some hope. She pulled it together, tried a new tack and went bright, as if they had loved the pages. "I'm sorry Anke is upset. Of course she is. This book is everything. I understand how—"

"You say you do, but your writing does not reflect such care."

"It's truly not uncommon for the first attempt to be far off," Mari said, adopting the calm authority of a lion tamer. "Finding the talent's voice is the biggest challenge. Always. That's why I stupidly overstepped with the journal. I am very sorry. Please apologize to Anke for me."

"I will apologize on your behalf."

"You can imagine—no one is like Anke, so to try to be her, it's an art."

She had returned his sortie, as if they were fencing. And then she fell silent. You can't change the mind of someone like Anke. You must lead her to the decision but let her feel like she has made it for herself. Was Mari imagining it, or did she hear the faint chime of Anke's bracelets, somewhere in the background of their call? Her dusky rose scent came back to Mari, as if she were leaning close, exerting her will. Mari's eyes watered with the shame of having hurt her. And the fear of losing that money and what it would mean for herself, and for V.

"Perhaps."

"I can fix it. I can make it perfect. If Anke wishes me to do so, of course."

"I'm sorry, but that is not Anke's wish," he said. "I am sorry, Mari. But it's done."

He hung up the phone, and that was it. Anke was gone.

Fuck. Mari's mind flashed to her nonrefundable round-trip flight to Vegas. If she was going, she needed to get to LAX soon. At least the trip was something. Beyond that was nothing—no prospects, no money, no hope. Surrendering her cart of beautiful groceries, Mari climbed into her car. She slammed the door, her shoulders heaving, tears exploding. Her fingers gripped the steering wheel so hard, her nails cut into her palms. When she was cried out, she reversed without checking her mirrors. A horn blared. She hit her brakes. The jolt of adrenaline slapped her out of her hysteria. Salvaging any of this was up to her—she had the savvy and the skills; now she must find the focus and courage.

Entering the silent condo, Mari sighed. Her bones had turned to concrete, her mind clogged with coffee grinds—the dark side of her late night kicking in when she needed energy and clarity of thought. She was so tired. She surveyed her living/writing area: Her laptop was open, waiting, always waiting for her. On the floor was the electric kettle, which she had moved to her work space around three a.m. Half a dozen orphaned mugs, draped by tea bag strings.

While brewing fresh coffee, she skimmed her sample pages. She was still a little in love with them, but she knew better. What she had written read well. *So what?*

Mari's phone rang. Her stomach churned. It could only be Ezra.

"Hey, dude," he said, the word taking on a melancholy lilt. "What happened?"

Tears leaked with a coppery taste at the back of her throat. She didn't know how honest to be. But did she really have any other cards left to play? He was her only ally.

"I fucked up," she said.

"Mari, you told me you could do this," he said. "I didn't ask to read the sample material because you're seasoned. And it always gets rewritten ad nauseam anyhow. But I can't believe this is only about the writing. Did something go down in Palm Springs?"

Mari thought about Anke's most vulnerable secret: her death sentence. Had Anke regretted telling her? An editor had recounted this happening once: a client who had felt too exposed with her first writer and wanted them off the job. Maybe. Mari couldn't tell him that.

"Yes, I can do it. I misjudged Anke, thought she wanted to sound smarter, more polished. Anke doesn't care if her lack of education pokes through. She's comfortable being an original, and rightly so. Can't you make them let me rewrite, even just once? I know how to fix it now."

"Contractually, yes," Ezra said. "But David mentioned something about a journal."

Tears fell, and it took all her will to hold her voice steady, so Ezra wouldn't know. She paced into the kitchen, poured more coffee, went back to the living room to pack.

"I'm sorry," she said. "It was so much pressure, I cracked. I didn't read it. I put it back."

"Well, it was the wrong second to crack, dude. I don't know if I can save this for you."

"You don't have to," Mari said. "I can save it. I know exactly what to do. I spent three hundred dollars on a round-trip flight to Las Vegas, which boards soon. I'll start there."

"Eat the cost of the ticket and stay in LA."

"I can't lose this book. And to write this book, I have to know how much Anke could truly reveal—or not. I have to learn the whole story of Mal's death. If I can protect Anke, she'll be sure I'm her writer. David will be sure I'm her writer."

Mari would be sure. For once, she would have taken a risk on herself, on her life, rather than hiding out at her computer, recounting the lives of others.

"I know this feels like the end of the world," Ezra said. "But it's not. Hold tight. I'll call you back as soon as I get through to David again."

"Okay, thanks," Mari said.

As Mari hung up, she grabbed her luggage to head to the airport and show everyone, especially her growing number of doubters, just how to be a ghost.

EIGHTH:
LEAP

To master the world of the celebrity, which is not your own, you must always be listening, absorbing, processing, cataloguing an influx of information while putting forth an authentic facade. If you are a true ghost, there was probably a moment when, like a spy, your safety relied upon your skills, too. Often you were the child of an addict or a narcissist who learned to read others as if they came with dossiers. Who learned things even a secret agent hasn't mastered. While a spy must negotiate an outcome favorable to her side, a ghost must please many masters—the celebrity, first and always, but also your editor, your agent, the client's agent, the public, maybe yourself—although for you, survival always trumps pleasure.

Mari handed the driver her vintage Celine weekender with a curt nod. Belonging was an act like everything else. As they drove, Mari was struck by the light traffic. Las Vegas was the only city where the morning commute was from the poker table to the breakfast buffet. She had slept the entirety of the short flight and was feeling revived. With a shaky, caffeinated hand, she freshened up her Chanel Rose Naïf lip gloss, spritzed on Fracas. A secondary perk of being one with her laptop: Mari was a fierce eBay aficionado. As soon as Anke's check cleared, she had given herself a budget makeover. It was a risk to splurge, and that was *before* she had been fired, and before she would have to give back all—or at least most of—the check from Anke. She'd thought of it as a professional investment, like her ticket to Vegas, Syd's book, and the bootleg CDs of the band's Hollywood Bowl rehearsal and performance she'd bought online. Only now, making her initiative (and expenditure) pay out wasn't dependent on her writing, but on what she could achieve in the next twenty-four hours.

As she tucked away her makeup, her phone buzzed. She had turned it on after landing in case Ody reached out. She froze, not wanting to have to lie. She couldn't quite accept she had been let go—maybe because her childhood had taught her to persevere, even in the face of rejection. Or because she could in no way afford to lose this job.

Mari read the screen. Of course it was Vivienne, who hadn't returned to the condo before she left for the airport. V had a second sense for needing things when it was inconvenient. Mari wavered, worried. No, V would have to wait.

Mari limited her focus to what she had pulled off—talking her way into an interview with Dante Ashcombe, one of the world's biggest rock stars—and used this confidence to fuel what she must accomplish yet. She would feel out what Dante believed about Mal's drug tolerance, and if he knew what Anke had given Mal on the night of his death. Even better, Dante might tell her something that absolved Anke. Either way, Mari would try to nudge him toward a desire to protect Anke, by reminding him of the power of his book to lift up or bury Anke's own memoir.

Mari was speed-reading Syd's book while listening to the bootleg recording of the band's pre–Hollywood Bowl practice. She pulled out her notebook and listed those who had been present as rehearsal kicked off: Jack, the band's bassist and drummer, and Anke's friend Sigrid. She had been Mal's assistant at the time, but apparently had a keen survival instinct—although Mal had been a no-show, she had turned up at the space to help out the others. A few minutes in, Jack had asked her to call in a delivery to nearby Almor Wine & Spirits: brandy for his voice and a pack of cigarettes—the irony of the combo lost on those present, as they all smoked.

It was noticeable Dante and his guitar tech, Simon, were absent, as was Anke, although she was Mal's wife, and with his tenuous status in the band, maybe she felt practice was off-limits for her. The driver, Syd, had claimed to be running errands for the band that night. He had never come into the studio, so he could have been anywhere at the time of Mal's death. If Mal had died because of an accidental overdose, Mari suspected Syd was more to blame than Anke. But if something nefarious had gone down, Simon had a hell of a lot to gain, believing he would step into Mal's place in one of the greatest rock bands ever. Not bad for a motive.

Mari aimed to be as prepared as possible; so much of what it took to do her job well was instinct and reading the room. But dropping into a fraught moment in the band's history with more question marks than insight was making her tense. She couldn't afford to boff this meeting.

Mari considered the one area where she could be sure to connect with Dante: music, and more specifically, his music. She opened her phone and switched to a Spotify mix she had made of songs penned and sung by Dante—only a handful in the Ramblers' multi-decade career. He was celebrated as a guitar god, and neither Mal nor Jack had wanted to share the spotlight with him any more than necessary. Sliding on her earbuds, she gave herself over to Dante's sly bluesy sound. Mari had never noticed the distinction between Dante's songwriting and the rest of the band's music, but she found she preferred it—his songs were weirder, darker, rawer. He only seemed to sing when he had something to say. Avoiding the bombast of the band's stadium anthems, his songs drew you in, with the hushed intimacy of pillow talk, or the scuffed candor of two best mates sharing a smoke at dawn.

Against the blue desert sky, the casinos were flat white and gray stucco—their exteriors as dull as old nickels. Filled with a desire for a cup of hot tea in a quiet room she didn't have to do anything to earn, she sized herself up in the car window. Her face was hidden by enormous '60s Christian Dior sunnies. When you couldn't see the exhausted smudges under her eyes, she looked put together and poised. Hopefully she wasn't the only one who would think so.

Sinking back into the plush leather, she enjoyed the luxury SUV that Dante's team had sent for her. No generic Uber ride for her today. Her driver glided to a stop at the back entrance of the Wynn— more specifically, the Tower, where celebrities and VIPs checked in anonymously. She knew the driver was only doing what he would have done for his boss, but this little bit of make-believe helped her to glide into the hotel as if she belonged.

At the appointed hour, a curvy middle-aged assistant, with a bleached-blond buzz cut and electric-teal eyeliner, appeared in the hotel lounge where Mari was preparing her notes. Next to the woman's effortlessly cool ensemble of fitted tuxedo jacket, leather ankle-length trousers, and high-top Vivienne Westwood sneakers, Mari felt dowdy in her trusty old J.Crew blazer. At least her Anke makeover had imbued her with a little more rock 'n' roll edge, in the form of wooden prayer beads and a sheaf of vintage gold bracelets.

The older woman led them onto the private elevator for the Tower.

"I trust your flight was all right?" she said, her words touched with a British accent.

"Yes, fine, thanks," Mari said. It had been a budget middle seat.

"Would you like a cup of tea? We can ring for room service."

"That would be lovely, thanks."

"English breakfast? Green? Chamomile?"

"Earl Grey, please, almond milk on the side."

"Tops," the woman said, using her plastic room key to make the

car ascend. "Oh, I'm Izzy. I assist the band's day-to-day manager, who'll be sitting in on your meeting with Dante."

"Mari," she said, extending her hand. "Thanks for coming down to meet me."

Izzy nodded with a faint smile but stayed silent. Anke had been right about the band maintaining as many original players as they could. Mari considered mentioning Anke to see how Izzy responded, but there were too many potential land mines, and she didn't want to detonate any before she'd even met Dante. In her experience, it was better to know more than you said. Mari checked her appearance in the mirrored interior, while acting like she wasn't.

Stepping off the elevator, into the suite's lounge where the interview would take place, felt like walking the plank. There—springing from his seat with the propulsive energy of a quarter dropped into a jukebox, setting everything in motion—was Dante. He resembled a pirate king, his black hair rakish, kohl eyeliner shadowing his eyes. An Egyptian blue silk scarf circled his forehead, and leather and gold jewelry jangled at his neck and wrists.

"So, you're the ghost," he said.

"Guilty as charged. Now, are you the joker or the thief?"

With a lively, barking laugh, he pulled her close. His heavy paw warm on the small of her back, he kissed her on both cheeks. He enveloped her with his scent of wool, anise, and amber, topped with a rough sweetness that evoked old-fashioned tobacco shops, not the gross staleness of overflowing ashtrays. But her own scent was more captivating, at least for him. He held his face just above the soft curve of her neck, his hot breath tickling her skin.

"Fracas," he said. "I see you've been enchanted by Anke, along with the rest of us."

"You might say that," Mari said, willing herself to hold still, maintaining this intimate moment with this magnetic man, trying not to shake with nerves. "Or I'm a magpie."

"*Magpie comes a-calling, drops a marble from the sky,*" he sang, honeyed gravel voice.

Mari was embarrassed by her blush and hoped he would find it charming.

"Is that the old Donovan folkie about a magpie?" she asked, over-proud of herself.

"Neko Case. I haven't got both feet in the grave yet. So, you're a magpie, then, stealing from others to build your pretty nest."

"One should never steal, but I borrow, yes."

Dante laughed, at ease, as if he took as much pleasure in meetings as guitar solos, although it was unlikely. Maybe he liked life, and his had been exceptional, so why not?

Having maneuvered through the first fraught moments, Mari felt more confident. But they weren't alone. Next to where Dante had been seated was a handsome older man with thinning hair and a goatee that were both a rich brown, suggesting they had been dyed. He reclined casually, one arm stretched out on the couch back, clearly comfortable in his spot, and with Dante more generally. Before him on the coffee table was a velvet-lined case containing a vintage Gibson 335 guitar, its sunburst finish polished to a high sheen.

Behind this man was a woman who looked to be about his age, with dark blunt-cut bangs, boxy statement glasses, and remarkably dewy skin. She nodded to Izzy, who seemed to understand the command and left the room. As she glided over to Mari, her broad smile revealed white, straight teeth. Extending her hand, she pulled Mari in to kiss both cheeks.

"Mari, you have been sent by our old friend Anke," the woman said. "We are very glad to have you. I am Sigrid."

"Mari, the ghostwriter, meet Sigrid, the right hand," Dante crowed.

Sigrid laughed girlishly, although, presumably, they had played their parts in this same introduction many times. It was hard to believe, but here was Anke's former best friend, who had clung to the band's inner circle for five decades. Even with their tendency toward allegiance, she must be the best employee ever, or have the survival instincts of a fox.

Turning to the man on the couch, Sigrid clapped her hands. He radiated irritation but fell into line. Standing, he lifted the case, as if it were an extension of his body. "As you like, your majesty," he said. "But I need more time with Dante if I'm to have him ready for this tour."

"You will have whatever you need, Simon." Sigrid smiled through his aggression. "Dante will arrive at practice half an hour before the others, in order to give this time to you."

When Simon grinned at Mari, she smiled back, but only faintly. He had lived up to Anke's description as a cocky wannabe. Mari couldn't get drawn into any internal feuds when she had so little time and so much at stake. Maybe there was nothing exceptional about Sigrid, then, if they had retained so many of their original employees for all these decades. Apparently Anke was the exception because she had left. Having been fired after only a week on the job, Mari was beginning to long for this kinder, more loyal way of doing business.

"Izzy is ordering your tea," Sigrid said. "You had an early flight. You must be tired."

"Oh, but I'm too intrigued," Mari said.

Dante's laughter infected the room. She had expected this reaction, but his hound dog laugh was already familiar enough to relax her. At least she seemed to know how to handle him.

Sigrid gestured for Mari to take the seat Simon had vacated. As Dante was joining her on the couch, a commotion erupted at the door, which Izzy had opened for room service. Simon was standing off against a hotel employee, who was pushing an unwieldy cart. His posture said he was the rock star and fuck anyone who got in his way. The employee ducked her head and backed up so Simon could blaze out into the hallway.

Izzy beckoned in the server, then delivered Mari's teapot and cup and prepared to serve.

"Thank you, but I'll pour," Mari said. "I like it strong."

"I'll bet you do," Dante said.

"It's a matter of taste," Mari riffed, matching Dante's tone, even as her cheeks betrayed her with an encore flush—she knew how to play, but she would never be cool like Anke.

Still, all of Mari's nerves had evaporated. Dante was far more famous than Anke, his time more precious, and her errand more urgent. But he was easy. Mari had been playing this game with her father since she was a girl—be clever and be allowed to stay.

Dante nodded to Izzy. "Fetch me a drink, sweetheart," he said.

Mari winced internally but didn't let on—such retro attitudes could be deadly on the page. It would be wise for him to tone them down when he wrote his own memoir.

Immune after so many years of service, or a gifted actress, Izzy bowed and turned to the bar. Used to dominating enormous arenas, Dante could sure hold court, even sipping a beverage. Even at the age of—could he be?—seventy-four. He wasn't handsome so much as electric. And so comfortable in his skin, he put others at ease. Mari found she was having fun.

"First of all, thank you," Mari said. "You were very generous to invite me to your hotel, and to send a driver for me, since I'm on an errand for Anke."

That was a bit of a stretch, of course, but she trusted Ody had told Anke as much as was prudent. Dante nodded like her gracious benefactor. "I'm happy to help Anke in any way I can."

Sipping his drink, he let her lead.

"She's lucky to have such a generous friend," Mari said, careful to sidestep the word "old." "As you know, Anke is private. She has been lovely to work with—so evocative, funny, and wise—and yet she's very hard on herself. To do this book for her, and to do it well,

I have the sense we need an outside perspective. So, I've prepared a few questions for you. But I would appreciate if we could keep this meeting between us, until I can help Anke see its value."

This was a tricky move, given how much affection and loyalty Dante still had for Anke—Mari was beginning to wonder that he'd okayed his book proposal, which hadn't been negative, exactly, but had definitely leaned toward the salacious. Mari was counting on how much people—even famous people—loved to be on the inside, to possess intel others did not.

Dante nodded, as if in agreement, and she exhaled.

"I appreciate it, since you know her better than almost anyone else."

"Almost anyone—" he said, unable to resist the bait.

Mari paused. She was there under the guise of interviewing him about Anke, but she had to shift the conversation's direction.

"As research, I've been reading Syd's book."

"That garbage."

Dante held his glass out to Sigrid, who fetched him a smaller refill.

"You can't begin to imagine the muckraking and drivel we attracted at the pinnacle of our careers," he continued. "It was a blight. That's why I agreed to speak with you. And Syd, well, he was the worst, because he pretended to be our friend."

"He does call you a Gibson man. When you're all Fender, of course, except the ES."

"He says a lot worse than that, if I remember correctly," Dante said, waving his glass, sloshing booze on the floor. "You cannot believe most of what you read. Especially about us."

"I agree—it's just, I also know he was very close to Mal."

"Close enough to pick his pocket," Dante said.

Or maybe even to drown him, Mari thought.

"Touché. But there are some remarkable quotations in the book from Mal himself—"

Mari's purse gaped open, where she had set it down. Although her phone was on silent, it had begun flashing, amid her makeup, loose barrettes, and pens. After a moment of stillness, it rang again. She had misread Vivienne—she was so erratic it was easy to do—and she was apparently more desperate than Mari had suspected, even though she had just seen her.

"You appear to be receiving a distress signal." Dante laughed, but with an edge. As benevolent as he was, he was used to being the most important everything in all rooms.

As Mari powered down her phone, she glanced up. Sigrid had chosen a chair a few feet from them, but she was studying Mari. Her face was hard to read. Mari felt a prickle of unease but tried to talk herself down. Sigrid had been perfectly lovely to her, and so what if she was the band's loyal guard dog? Mari was surprised she'd gained access at all, and with no NDA—of course they were keeping an eye on her, making sure she could be trusted.

"*There's no one in the place 'cept you and me,*" Mari said, her voice a singsong.

"Sinatra, nice."

Like a stage actress, Mari returned to her mark.

"When Syd and Mal are smoking hash and talking girls, Mal says the most remarkable thing: 'Anke is a golden lovely, as if the character of Lolita had come of age under the pen of Anaïs Nin.' I mean, I get how awful Mal was to Anke, but that sounds just like her, doesn't it?"

"Mal never read a book," Dante said. "Certainly not two, in order to compare them."

"As I'm sure you recall, Dante, Jack often said something similar about Anke," Sigrid stepped in, her tone flat.

"So, for once Mal was copying Jack, instead of the other way round."

"Dante," Sigrid said.

"How interesting," Mari said. She was trying to clock the relationship between Dante and Jack and Sigrid, and what had happened there, but her real quarry was anything to do with Anke or Mal. "Was Mal a magpie, then? Was he in the habit of stealing?"

"Just women, drugs, riffs, publishing credit, money, the best seat in the jet by the bar."

"I can't say I'm surprised," Mari said, clocking the implication that Mal had been crooked in business, but not wanting to seem overly curious about his role in the band. "That's always been his reputation. And he took up with some bad characters—I mean, Syd was a real loser, right? From what I understand, he's lucky he didn't get charged in Mal's death."

Dante gave her a blank look. Sigrid remained silent, surveying the situation. Mari waited to speak, knowing she could outlast them both.

"I am surprised Anke would mention Syd in her book," Sigrid said. "She hated him so much. Remember, Dante, she had management fire him? But he kept coming around because he could get money from Mal. Until Mal is dead, and then she has you make him leave forever."

"Of course, you're right, he will only have a brief mention in Anke's book," Mari said. "But we're trying to paint a portrait of that time— how drugged out Mal was, how much his mind had disintegrated. How Syd and other hangers-on contributed."

"Dante is very busy," Sigrid said.

"Absolutely, and I so appreciate this time. Congratulations on your upcoming book, Dante—it's a wonderful way to crown your legacy. People in publishing have been wondering for years if you'd grace us with a memoir. Now you can tell your side of the story."

"Thank you. But just to be crystal clear—my side *is* the story."

"That's why I'm here, for the story."

"I find it hard to believe Anke feels the same about what constitutes *the* story."

"You're right—she doesn't."

"And yet here you are, taking time away from her book, just to speak with me—you know she was the one who left me. Almost fifty years ago, right, luv?"

"'The trick is to allow Dante to think he has all the cards, like a little boy playing solitaire who lets himself win'—*that's* what Anke said when we were discussing your relationship. But I happen to believe you see and know more, perhaps, than you let on."

"Anke, my love." He laughed with obvious and genuine affection—no offense taken.

Mari eyed Dante's drink with great longing as she sipped her tea.

"Now that's done and dusted, let's get down to it," he said.

Their banter was a dance, as if choreographed. But Mari soon understood they could talk and flirt like this for hours—days even—and yet she would never learn anything real. Her attempts to bring up band employees from fifty years ago had been, rightly, called out as a waste of time. If she was going to get what she came for, she was going to have try something drastic.

"Actually, I'm sorry," Mari said.

Dante looked up, surprised by the shift in her tone.

"You've been so welcoming, and your time is so valuable, I have to come clean. After we set our meeting, Anke fired me. I'm sure I can fix it. Even so, it's not about the job. I want to write her bestseller, of course. But. I'm worried about Anke. She—"

Mari was on the verge of telling them what Anke had implied, but she stopped short. She had already shared more than Anke would have been comfortable with—she was sure of that.

"Anke inspires great loyalty, does she not?" Sigrid said.

"She does," Dante said. "As do you, Siggi."

His voice had the tone of a father settling a spat between his children. Mari wondered if she and V would have been closer if they'd had a dad like that, shook off the thought, focused.

"Clearly you care about Anke a great deal, if you have come to Las

Vegas to help her, even without her blessing," Dante said. "Please, go ahead."

Mari was relieved. For about twenty minutes. Then her worry increased. She was trying to draw them out on Mal's drug use, and his death, while not implicating Anke. But without any leading questions, all she'd gotten from Dante were tall tales of the band's glory days, and his well-known dislike for Mal. She figured she had thirty minutes before they whisked Dante off to his next duty. She leaned back into the ergonomic furniture, teacup in hand, wondering if she should ask about band practice that last night in LA or dare another question about Mal.

Dante lit a cigarette. Before he had extinguished the match, Sigrid had the big brass ashtray emptied and at the ready. As she set it down, her eyes held his for a long moment. He nodded a quick gesture of assent. Something was happening beneath their conversation.

"I don't know why, but I trust you," he said. He sat up, leaning toward Mari.

"He trusts no one new," Sigrid piped in.

"Trust seems like an ideal place to start," Mari said. "But I thought we were talking about Anke, not about her ghost."

"What we are talking about is you doing the writing of Dante's book," Sigrid said.

"But I'm not—I wasn't even—I'm here *for* Anke's book, or at least for Anke." She turned to Dante. "And you're Dante Ashcombe. You could have any writer in the world."

"True," Sigrid said. "But we considered several writers, and they have left much to be desired. We just lost the last one, Axel. We have only six weeks until deadline, and here you are, and it could not be better. Now that Anke has chosen to fire you, you are free to write the book of Dante."

"But—I don't think it works like that. Didn't your editor give you a list of writers?"

"I'd say you need to spiff up your sales pitch," Dante said. "We're offering you a gig—quite a good one."

Mari was as flustered as she could remember being. At the same time, she wanted to laugh at her own shortsightedness. Of course, if Dante needed a writer, he would try to hire her. Even when celebrities were given a variety of sanctioned options, they loved to ask for the one thing that wasn't on offer, and more often than not, the powers that be were bent to their will.

"Dante does not take 'No' for his answer," Sigrid talked as she typed into her phone. "We will fix the details later. But you must start immediately. I am sure you can imagine Dante is *busy*. He will leave in a few days for the band's world tour—eighteen months circling the globe. It will be enough of a challenge to work around their rehearsal schedule. The bulk of his contribution to the book must be done before he departs Sunday night. We have taken your agent's contact information from your website, and I am emailing him with our offer. It is only for you to accept. And for you to know, we are grateful to have you on our team."

Dante reclined, with his long, leather-clad legs crossed at the ankle. He, too, seemed to understand the ebb and flow of selling and being bought. He flashed a sleepy, mischievous grin.

Sigrid stared into her phone. "Your agent has received our offer."

Mari reached for her bag, opened her phone. Ezra had already emailed her. The subject line read "What the F?!?!" But he would have to forgive her *now*, right? The money was more than twice her fee for Anke's book. She would get an "as told to" credit, not just the thank-you on Anke's acknowledgments page. Clearly this was a big deal.

It was as if the three squares of the cosmic slot machine had clicked into place: the favorable circumstances of this entire day, from the luxury transportation, to the cool perfection of this room; plus, the money, which would not just dig her out of her financial hole but actually allow her to breathe for the first time in years, maybe even help V; plus, the intense charm of the man sitting across from her, and the sure thing of his guaranteed *NYT* bestseller. Jackpot.

But. Honestly, her heart was still with Anke's project and the chance to give her a voice for the first time in her life, the chance to redeem herself with Anke and Ody.

Mari took a deep breath. "Can I walk around the block and think about it?"

The room fell completely silent.

And then Dante laughed his wonderful braying laugh.

"You think about it, sweetheart," he said. "Anke casts quite a spell. I oughta know."

There was no hint of sarcasm in his voice, which made Mari like him even more.

"Siggi, get Mari a room so she can have some privacy. We can spare an hour, can't we?"

Mari was so exhausted, she almost told them the truth: She had stashed her bag at the front desk, even though she couldn't afford the Wynn and planned to find a cheap room online.

"Ja, that will work," Sigrid said. "Izzy will book your room. Come back up in an hour."

"Thank you," Mari said. She felt sheepish as she stood. At the last minute, she recalled the right thing to do, bending to air-kiss Dante, and then Sigrid.

When Mari shut the door of her suite behind her, she lingered with her back against the smooth surface. She hadn't had a room of her own in nearly eight weeks. It felt so fucking good. Then, remembering herself, she threw her bag onto the bed and unzipped it, too frenzied to be neat. She ran into the bathroom to brush her teeth, then out to charge her devices, then back to the mirror to touch up her makeup, then out to her phone to check for a message from V. Nope.

Mari knew this was the chance of a lifetime, but she couldn't shake the feeling that she had let Anke down. She had been all-in since their weekend in Palm Springs. The thought of not getting to complete that book unleashed a melancholy far beyond professional disappointment. Plus, she was already fraying from lack of sleep. This was a new 75,000-word manuscript, due in just six weeks. Still, getting some real time (alone) with Dante, and Simon, would give her access to new truths about Mal's death, maybe allow her to reveal what had happened to him. She was sure that would help to absolve Anke. And it would be the kind of professional coup for Mari that would mean she would never be at the mercy of a vodka divorcée again. It could even be the career boost she hadn't allowed herself to dream of before—where her books mattered to others as much as they mattered to her, where all the sacrifices finally led somewhere good. Even if Anke was done with her, Mari would get to prove her worth. She would have her first bestseller. She needed to be brave. It would be easier to do so now that Dante had put his trust in her, which was like a gold crown on her head.

Not that it was without risk. It was a high-profile memoir that would be scrutinized by millions of die-hard fans. Dante had little time for her. But if he downloaded the pertinent intel to her and then got out of her way, that could make her task easier. As much as she needed her celebrities for their stories, their feelings, and their voice, after that, she preferred to work alone.

Plus, she wanted to prove she could do it—Dante's book, the future bestsellers it would unlock. To show her clients—and her editors, who she would hopefully work with for years to come—what she knew about herself, deep down, even if she had yet to create the external proof.

She had a rule against bothering Ezra unless she was up for a new project or absolutely needed advice. She rarely phoned him first and had only done so a few times, like when the vodka divorcée had fully melted down. On top of that, she would have to admit she had gone to Vegas against his orders. But he probably knew that. She gathered her nerve and called.

His assistant put her through right away. "Mari?" her agent asked.

"You only call me Mari when you're mad. Can I apologize later? Because I really need your wisdom right now. I've been asked to write a book for Dante Fucking Ashcombe!"

"I know, I'm impressed. What did you say to him? You weren't even up for that gig."

"I have no idea."

"I'm also more than a little worried. You went rogue. And this is a lot."

"I know. I *am* sorry. I'm worried, too. What if I can't do it?"

"I can get you out of it. But you'd never work in publishing again."

It felt good to laugh. To not be *on*. To just be.

"I jest, but it is a legitimate question. Things did not go well with Anke. I don't have to tell you how much higher-profile this book is. I talked to the agent who reps Axel—the writer Dante fired. Apparently he was really losing it—drinking too much, missing deadlines—and now no one has heard from him in almost a week. I mean, are you up for that? You do have a choice."

Mari's call-waiting beeped. Her heart leapt: Anke had changed her mind. She could write the book she really cared about, and she wouldn't have to guess how much she could handle. But it was Vivienne. Without even talking to her, Mari knew. They had lost the condo. V was proud, just like Anke, and if she could have dodged telling Mari what was going on, she would have. Mari didn't actually have a choice about this job. Better to own it, then. As if this were just another workday, Mari began making herself a cup of coffee with the little in-room setup.

"I can do it," Mari said.

"Are you sure, dude?"

"I'm sorry about Anke. I know you pushed for me, but she never gave me a chance. Who doesn't let their ghost do even one rewrite? I mean, she has to be able to give her writer notes."

"True," he said. "But writing for Dante will be pressure like you've never felt. And you should be getting transcripts, manuscript pages, from the last writer. But I wouldn't count on it."

"They have to help me get a draft done, right? They only have six weeks. I work fast."

"You are a workhorse," Ezra said. "Yeah, okay. It's really fucking hard to break through to the next level. The fact that Dante felt so strongly about hiring you, that's a testament to you. I think with an opportunity this big, no matter the risks, you just gotta seize it and do your best."

"Yeah, I want to. I think I can do it."

"You can, dude. I want you to call me every day. I'm going to talk to Dante's editor, see if I can get anymore inside intel about Axel and what happened. You just do your job."

"I was thinking, maybe Dante will tell me something that will help Anke for her book."

"I know you liked her. But don't get duped again. Seriously, Mari, you deserve better than that. Besides, right now, your first and only loyalty is to your new client, Dante Ashcombe."

She tried to feel his confidence. She had this way of playing chicken with the universe, daring herself into high-wire situations, then forcing herself to pull them off. And yet again.

Mari felt the casino lights buzzing in her highly caffeinated bloodstream. She closed her eyes in the elevator on her way back to Dante's suite. Put on a layer of lip gloss as armor.

When the doors swung open, she channeled Anke and made her own grand entrance. Dante and Sigrid were sitting together on the couch, staring into an open laptop.

"I'd be honored to collaborate with you, Dante," Mari said.

"A bottle of Dom for me and all my friends," Dante said, clapping his hands.

Izzy laughed and turned to the bar. The mini-fridge was, of course, stocked with Dom. The room filled with the particular effervescence of a champagne buzz.

"Now, where do we start?" Dante asked.

"In the middle, of course," Mari said. "That's where the story really begins."

NINTH:
PIVOT

It is flattering to have a celebrity take an interest in you, but you have to be careful. Often, they aren't used to the sustained effort a book requires. They will nudge you off topic on purpose, playing hooky from the hard work at hand. They can read the molecules in the air and will know if you aren't with them. But even as you indulge them in their asides, you can't lose focus. Be charmed but find a way to make a U-turn, never losing sight of the book, the book, the book.

S howtime. Dante sipped Dom. Mari countered her champagne buzz with a cup of tea.

"I have to finalize the collaboration paperwork," Sigrid said.

"Speaking of," Mari dared, "I talked with my agent, and he said the first writer, Axel, had transcripts and early drafts I might get access to—it could save us valuable time."

"I blathered on to the poor fool for long enough," Dante said. "I should hope it will help."

Sigrid didn't look up from her phone. "The *poor fool* is not answering emails or calls. We shall see what we can do. For now, assume you will start from scratch."

Mari's stomach twisted, the deadly combo of nerves and caffeine.

"Got it," she said. Then she dared to feel a bit superior—even when things had gotten gnarly with the vodka divorcée's team, she had always been on point. The guy must be a mess. She could do this.

"I will return in a flash," Sigrid said from the doorway.

"Sure, sure," Dante said. Waving Sigrid away, engaged with Mari.

"To begin, I was thinking, songs are like time capsules," Mari said. "I'd imagine that's even truer for the songwriter. Let's go back and talk about your early tracks. I made a playlist."

"Well, since Jack writes the lyrics and such, the songs are more about where he's at."

"No, I mean the real songs, *your* songs. They're not like the band's singles that are churned out for the label. They're all the more potent for being fewer and farther between."

"Is that right?" Dante said. But she could tell by his tone, he wanted to agree.

"I think so, don't you? Before I was a ghostwriter, I wrote about music."

She was careful to avoid the word "critic," which artists hated.

"Well, if you ever ask me in front of Jack, he's the real songwriter in the band, but I'm not gonna argue with you. It's not bragging if it's in my own book, is it?"

Dante synced her phone to the room's sound system, and his sagebrush voice serenaded them. Mari had arranged the songs chronologically. With Dante's book to be written, she needed to know the whole story now. She was soon swept up in his rollicking tales of mid-'60s London: LSD- and brandy-fueled nights out with the Beatles, Marc Bolan, and the decade's top dandies and beauties. There was a strong propulsive energy to such interviews, especially when the celebrity was as salty and likeable as Dante. She finally asked for a break to pee.

They agreed to take ten so Dante could do a quick phoner he'd missed earlier in the day—the journalist was calling from London, and the time zone wrangling had been intense. After using the bathroom,

Mari ducked onto the balcony and admired the cinematic views of the Strip. Tempted to take a selfie, just to prove she'd been somewhere other than her desk, she glanced back inside. Sigrid and Dante were faced away from her, Dante on a landline and Sigrid leaning in, as if she was feeding Dante answers for the journalist.

Mari unlocked her phone (three missed calls from V), snapped a few selfies, backed by the monorail and palm trees. She cropped the least bloated-looking shot, then paused. Anke hadn't thought to follow her on social media, as some clients did. And she had to accept it—Anke had already moved on. But she had better not accidentally betray Dante's privacy.

And yet the urge to exist beyond her work was too strong to resist. As long as Mari didn't let on which hotel she was at, or who she was with, it was probably okay. She filmed a quick story of herself, with a panorama shot that stopped just before Dante's suite. It would be deleted by day's end. But for a brief moment, she would be out there, in the world, with her friends, most people her age, and the celebrities—not just inside the words of her clients' books.

Mari's phone buzzed. Vivienne was requesting a FaceTime. If she picked up, V would know where she was. If she didn't, V would hound her until she did. And what if she was in real trouble? Mari called her right back.

"What, V? I'm working."

"You're always working."

"Where's the producer?"

"He and his wife are getting undivorced. For the kids."

"Lucky kids. I'm sorry, but I have to go. I'm in a meeting. The way you were abusing my phone, I thought you were dinner for sharks."

"Yeah, cute, that pretty much sums up my life. I called to tell you that the bag you left at the condo is in a storage locker at the bus stop."

"For real? I thought that was just a plot device in *Desperately Seeking Susan*."

Neither of them laughed. Mari saw Dante finish his call and turn to Sigrid.

"I'm hanging up. I'll call you later."

Vivienne started to cry. Not the theatrical tears she could whip up effortlessly, but the big sucking sobs that made her look ugly, which was a luxury she didn't have.

Her words were garbled, but Mari had known V her whole life, so she understood them anyway: "LA is over. LA is dead to me. I have to go to Vegas. That's the only—it should work."

Mari was struggling herself, so taking on V seemed insane. Still, Mari knew how tenuous her existence felt, most days, and she had her writing, her agent, her role as a ghost. Vivienne had her looks, her charm, and her frequent-flier miles. Guilt flared up like a bug bite.

"I'm in Vegas for a new job. Will Mr. Sin City let you stay with him?"

"Eventually, but I can't ask right away. Or go to him, looking like this."

Her eyes were drawn up by the power of Sigrid's gaze, beaming into her. Dante was strumming a guitar and didn't appear bothered in the least, but Sigrid seemed to hold everything together, and she would be an important ally if Mari could stay on her good side. Smiling, Mari waved. You never held up a one-minute symbol to a client. You just didn't.

"V, I have to go. I'm at the Wynn, but not under my name. Text me your flight info."

Vivienne was speaking—maybe thanking her, probably asking for another favor, but Mari was disconnecting. She reentered the suite.

Sigrid was saying, "You have heard my reservations—she does not have the experience of the others. That last writer had written four bestsellers, and even so, with all the pressure, he became a drunk and a deadbeat. And why does she come here and bother you with the problems of Anke? But if she is who you want, even with all that, you know I support your decision."

Sigrid and Dante turned. Mari was used to having her work, and herself, evaluated. Still, Mari had gotten the message, whether she was meant to hear it or not; she had to hold it together. She had to succeed where the last writer had not. Mari knew she was lucky to be here at all. If it had been a stretch for her to be Anke's ghost, just look at her now.

Dante was a raconteur, for sure. But his stories were all from the canon of legends that already surrounded the band. There was the time he staggered into George Harrison's limousine. The driver had been too polite to tell him of his mistake, which he had drunkenly realized when he arrived at a country manor that was not his own and found Pattie Boyd waiting for him, instead of the model he had been married to that year. And the airport bust at LAX, when they had found a roach in his pocket, for which he had barely dodged a drug charge, and which had inspired the band to buy their first private jet. Yes, his delivery was animated and studded with clever quips and British street slang. It played nicely off his way of speaking, which was eloquent and articulate, especially given the edgy reputation he'd cultivated. These classic stories were a strong foundation for the book. But for a tell-all memoir, she had to go deeper.

Mari found herself stealing glances at Sigrid, who sat nearby, tapping on a laptop. She wore knee-high black patent leather boots and a black miniskirt and matching drapey vest, over a white-and-black geometric-print blouse with a tie at its neckline. She had the figure to pull it off, and the mod outfit made her look outside of time, especially with her dark, blunt-cut bangs and cat-eye makeup. Anke also wore retro clothes, but her Lady of the Canyon vibe had come full circle, whereas Sigrid was a mixed-decade enigma.

The tambourine stomp of the last song was replaced by a wily blues lick. It had long been understood that Dante had written this ballad for Anke during the brief, sweet months they had been a family. Mari watched Dante close his eyes. A hungry smile on his face, he reached for his guitar, always nearby, and began playing along. It was fantastic, enjoying a private concert by an undisputed guitar god. He was so immersed, Mari was a little afraid to pull him out of his reverie, but she needed to capitalize on his wide-open vulnerability.

"What are you picturing?" she asked.

"Nothing you should hear me say out loud, or my wife should read."

"Fair enough," Mari said with a laugh. "A safe question. Where did you write this song?"

"The piano—" Sigrid said.

"That's right, I never could write on a guitar. It's like I know it too well, innit? My fingers get ahead of my brain—not that it's hard to do so."

He laughed, winked at Mari. She laughed, too.

"Where was this piano? The band had a rehearsal space in LA, right?"

"We always have a rehearsal space," Dante said.

"The tree—" Sigrid said.

"Oh, righto, the house we rented that summer, it was nice enough, but it was small for the band, the girls, Simon, the assistants—Siggi was there, weren't you, luv?"

Mari gave Dante his laugh, then fell silent so he would continue.

"It seemed like every corner, someone was sleeping or shagging or smoking a spliff. But we needed a piano. We always had one at the ready, whenever we landed for more than a few days. And so, we rented one and had it unloaded under this grove of palm trees by the pool. The delivery man thought we were mad. But it worked like a charm. Inspiration never strikes except for in the middle of the night, so it kept us from driving anyone batty with our noodling."

"Did a lot of—noodling happen in the middle of the night?"

Dante looked to Sigrid. His memory was concerning. Mari made a mental note to see if there were any old bios of Dante, as there had been of the whole band—even if they were trashy, they would have been written closer to the day's events, so she could trust the dates and details.

The silence in the room stretched, like a bent note that begins to go out of tune. But Mari didn't say anything to ease the tension. She wanted to understand whatever was happening between Dante and Sigrid so she could try to get a better sense of Sigrid's influence.

"Sometimes—" Sigrid said.

As Sigrid poured Dante water, Mari caught the flash of jewelry at her neck, which had been obscured by her blouse's tie. A series of small gold flowers ringed her well-tended skin. The pattern was familiar to Mari, but she couldn't pull up the memory.

"Sometimes," Dante chimed in. "It's not like we were really sleeping. A lot of everything happened in the middle of the night."

"Everything, like swimming?"

Mari had been expecting a furtive glance between Dante and Sigrid, but the allusion to Mal's death propelled each into their own little world. Dante brooded into his drink. Sigrid watched Mari, as if *she* were the one who might give something away. Mari couldn't let them know she had read Dante's proposal until they gave her a copy, but since they had led with Mal's death in its pages, Mari felt certain they would want to include it in Dante's book.

"Mal was a grand swimmer," Dante said, his voice wistful, even speaking of his former nemesis. "He'd do laps for hours. Like he was in a trance. Nowadays, my youngest, all his friends have 'stuff,' that's what the parents call it—ADHD, processing disorders—there's prescription pills, talk therapy, art therapy, equine therapy. Mal had drugs. Girls. Music. And the water. Not that they were sure to calm him down—nothing was ever sure with him."

"Ja, Mal, he did not make anything easy, not for himself, not for anyone," Sigrid said.

She wasn't talking to Mari, but to Dante.

"If he was such a strong swimmer, it must have been a shock when he drowned," Mari said. She could feel Mal, the man who had died, not the legend who lived on, in the room with these people who had known him so well.

"No one could swim with the drugs in his system," Sigrid said. "Not even Mal."

"Anke mentioned Syd buying hash for Mal that night," Mari said.

"I do not talk about hash," Sigrid said.

"Everyone knew Anke was taking Quaaludes for her nerves that summer, and no wonder with how Mal was bashing her about. So, he ended up with Quaaludes in his system on the night he died. And what of it? He surely begged them off her. Or stole them. He must have palmed a thousand joints from me over the years. None of us was there. We can never know for sure."

This was a lot to process, and Mari was trying not to influence what they said about that night. Anke had implied she had doctored Mal's tea, presumably with the Quaaludes. Even though Dante and Simon had come in late, everyone had been at practice, as the rehearsal recording had attested. So, if Anke had drugged Mal, how could anyone else have known? Anke could have told Dante later. Even in the throes of starting a post-Mal romance and a family, she had clearly had a guilty conscience. What Mari would have given to talk to Syd—after everything, his book had been a huge letdown, all dated, groovy lingo and empty innuendo, surely less of the story than he had known. Simon was the next best bet.

Mari glanced up to find Sigrid staring at her. Even though she gave Mari a broad smile, showcasing her perfect white teeth, Mari felt a sandpaper prickle down the back of her neck. She knew the term "herding cats" from her time as a music journalist—a day-to-day manager had to have the inner steel to manage the unmanageable, no matter how accommodating she seemed.

"Why wasn't Mal at practice, with the Hollywood Bowl show the next day?"

The question hung in the air. Sigrid shrugged. Dante would not be able to remember a detail so small, and she had decided not to help Mari by answering.

"I heard Anke predicted Mal's death with her I Ching—"

"I know we all love Anke, but remember, we are writing Dante's book now," Sigrid said.

Mari nodded, looked down at her computer screen to buy herself time as she weighed possible angles. "Dante, do you believe in the I Ching?"

He squinted at her, considering her question. "Don't know. Never thought about it. We believed everything back then. It was the style. I *can* tell you this. I believe in Anke."

"Which is why you wrote her that beautiful love song at the house in LA that summer," Mari said, pivoting. "The Hollywood Bowl show was the day after Mal died, and then you all flew back to London for his funeral. Am I correct?"

"Well, look at you, Sherlock Holmes," he said. He pointed toward the speaker in the corner as he sang the song's final verse.

"You wrote the song at the LA house, so Mal was still alive. But Anke said your romance started with you comforting each other after Mal's death—"

"What a peach, trying to protect me," he said. "No one could blame her. Mal debased her with his fists, flaunted his other women, broke into shards if ever confronted. But I was his mate, and I was the fox in the henhouse. See, I'd always been half mad for her, all the way back to Berlin. But nothing ever happened until that summer. It was like a magnet between us. It's my belief children have a strong will to be born. Maybe that was our son, moving us into position."

It was no surprise Dante thought he was Ody's father; that was what Anke had always led everyone to believe, and what she seemed determined to put forth in her book. But she had been very clear they hadn't slept together before Mal's death. Why would Dante lie about this? Or Anke? It was a small detail, compared to everything else, but still.

"How long had it been going on, before the baby?"

"There are some things a man remembers. The first time he goes to bed with Anke Berben is one of them—it was soon after we landed in Los Angeles. After it happened once, there was no going back. A bit like Lady H, you know?"

"Who?"

"Heroin," Sigrid mouthed, like it was a bad word.

Mari kept herself from laughing. With all the muck they had to manage, heroin was the least taboo topic she could imagine. She nodded. She was itching to ask Dante if he had ever wondered if Ody might be Mal's son, but it seemed like an intimate question for their first session. And Dante didn't need any dirt to make his book a best-seller; this point was underlined as Mari let the conversation drift away from Mal, prompting Dante to tell her vivid stories of all the albums, concerts, and honeymoons on private beaches in the Seychelles *after* Mal's death.

The five-plus hours passed in a flash, as time flew when forces aligned, and real inspiration arrived. It happened alone with the page sometimes, too. It was something to experience—like that old Renaissance idea of the muse as an external force, not an internal inspiration of the mind. And so, on some days, it felt like a possession had occurred, and when the spirit passed away, Mari was exhausted and blurred around the edges. As if she didn't quite fit inside herself anymore, or she had multiple personalities. So it was, the secret life of a ghost.

As Mari packed up her computer and recorder, she observed the others. Izzy had come in to confirm the number of people for Dante's dinner reservation. She leaned over the back of the couch where Sigrid was reviewing Dante's schedule with him on her iPad.

"Excuse me," Mari said. "Since Dante's time is so valuable, I thought I could maybe interview Simon to get some details for the gearheads out there."

Sigrid and Dante exchanged a look.

"He'll convince you it's his book you're writing, not mine," Dante said. "But why not?"

"I will schedule for you," Sigrid said. "Tomorrow. Two hours before you meet Dante."

Mari had worried mentioning Simon would make them suspicious, but if he had played a role in Mal's death, no one seemed aware of it. The mood was relaxed and fun, like everyone was just where they wanted to be. Mari found she wanted to be there, too. She had experienced this as a journalist, when she had to leave the cosseted bubble surrounding a rock star she had interviewed and go back to her overdrawn life. The sensation was even stronger now because she was on the team. She felt fickle, but she wished this weekend could go on and on. She had been enamored of Anke and her elegant home, but this was something only the rarest few enjoyed—money, luxury, insulated grace, and the pleasure of living there in perfect ease.

Not that Dante didn't work for it. He was off to dinner with his second eldest daughter, a fashion designer, with whom he was opening a boutique hotel. Then a late rehearsal. Mari was grateful to be headed for a fancy room service meal in bed, even if she'd be going over notes.

Mari slumped against the elevator wall, feeling the best kind of tired, the kind that has been well earned. Thinking of Dante on his way to dinner with his daughter, she tried to imagine a nice, normal rendezvous with her dad someday, somewhere. They would share a meal, catch up. It seemed far-fetched, maybe even dangerous. She pushed the thought of him away.

Before facing the international meat market of the hotel's exclusive section, Mari smeared on fresh lip gloss as an antidote to her J.Crew blazer. She couldn't resist the wish for a celebrity sighting, even though she was supposed to be immune to such fandom. Who would she gossip to anyhow—Dante? Izzy, maybe. As she disembarked, a familiar lean, pale figure turned down the hall. Instinctively, she retreated into the elevator. She was sure it was Ody. But then again, she was at the Wynn—most of the hotel's guests could have stepped out of a rock video.

Her nerves jangled, but she was being paranoid—he hadn't noticed her. To assume he had was elevating her own importance in the story, which she should never do.

TENTH:
INFILTRATE

Part of inhabiting the private domains of celebrities is an inherent ability to belong behind the velvet rope. It is important to honor the unspoken rules of privacy and decorum, and also to appear at ease doing so. It's exhausting for celebrities to have to always be on, to be reminded of the pressures that rest on their shoulders, and having anyone around them display the slightest case of nerves or fandom can rattle them. Act like you belong, and eventually, you will.

It had been twenty minutes since V had burst into Mari's hushed lair, and she was on her second mini-bottle of tequila. In that way of siblings, Vivienne was as predictable to Mari as Mari was to herself. Mari stared into her doc with ninja-like intensity, but she hadn't written a single word.

The neon sizzle of the Strip teasing the corners of her vision, Mari plugged her headphones into her computer, to give the illusion of focus. A text message dinged. She toggled over onto her desktop, nervous it might be from Anke. But she should have known, Vivienne:

"I don't want to go out ALONE."

Mari looked up. On cue, V dragged her fingers down her cheeks, mimicking the crying-face emoji, before being sucked back into her phone. Mari slammed her computer shut.

"I'm not going to some boom-chicka-boom nightclub and paying thirty dollars for a watermelon martini while some *Bachelor* castoff dry humps me from behind," Mari said.

"But I have drink tickets!"

"Yeah, well, you came out of the womb with drink tickets."

Even more maddening, V hadn't looked up, so Mari was fighting with the crown of her head. As usual, V's hair looked as if she had just stepped out of a salon. Mari already looked like she had just been dropped out of a plane, and she was on day one of a six-week book deadline.

"Ooh, you can't say no if it's research," V said.

Mari's computer chimed. The text was a screenshot of an ad for an event:

"Mal Walker Birthday Tribute Show!!"

"Fine," Mari said. She wasn't about to let V know this was exactly what she needed.

Of course V's ever-present phone had vanished the moment it was time to order a Lyft. Mari didn't care about paying—it was a write-off anyhow—but she had been talking herself into being more generous with V, and her current level of irritation was making her feel uncharitable and cranky. At the club, Mari eyed the twenty-person queue, wondering at her chances if she pretended her name had accidentally been left off the list at the door—an old trick from her music-journalist days. But V was already moving to the front of the line. This left Mari trapped between their Lyft and—Austin Powers. Well, not *the* Austin Powers, obviously. The thick, black-framed glasses and buckteeth seemed to belong to the man, who had completed his costume with a cheap white ruffly collar over a gaudy purple turtleneck.

"Yeah, baby, yeah," he said. "Five dollars for a photo."

"Sorry, but I never have cash," Mari said. "Wouldn't you have better luck over by the casinos, where there are more tourists?" Feeling the bottomless pit of his addiction and the sharp claws of his need, she moved her gaze up and down the street, unable to maintain eye contact. The club was the only obvious life in a grim neighborhood of dark, derelict warehouses.

"Um, yeah, see, baby, I'm over here meeting some associates, and I just need to—"

The words were different, but the inflection was familiar—she had heard her dad make a million excuses in just this tone. Such was the wreckage that would have consumed Mal if he hadn't died. Such was the inevitable destination of those who couldn't fight back from the edge.

V turned, clocked what was happening. Grabbing Mari's wrist, V flounced back to the doorman, a tattooed linebacker type wearing a tight-fitting black T-shirt, even though the desert air was cool. V put her hand on his arm, not sexually but intimately. Mari thought of Anke, and Dante, and her father (on his good days, if he still had them), and how they could make you feel like you were the only other person alive. V was talking quietly, causing the man to lean in. Mari gleaned V had been here with the club's owner, and it gave her clout.

"Thanks, Dario," V said. He swung open the door.

How did she know everyone's name? Mari was more in awe of her sister than she liked to admit; it made her even more scared for V, as her powers seemed in danger of fading.

"Thanks," Mari said. The man didn't look up from his phone. *Yep.*

They pushed inside. Mari's lungs felt constricted, like they were trying to get air in a hot sauna. She stayed close to V, even though it irritated her to rely on anyone, especially her sister.

The venue held about three hundred people, to achieve maximum exclusivity. Judging by the well-heeled, white-wine-drinking crowd, the ticket price had been high enough to dissuade most younger fans of Mal or the band. Mari craned her neck, looking for Dante in the VIP area.

Somehow, without ever lining up for the bar, they were each handed a glass of white wine. Mari smiled with gratitude. As they drew near the stage, Mari sipped her chardonnay. Looking up, she recognized a celebrated psych rock band, sludging its way through one of Mal's later sitar-laced drones. She was startled to recognize Ody onstage. With a guitar in his hand, he was transformed. Head bowed, lean body taut, he radiated a youthful, animal grace. Mari could see both of his parents in him—all three of his parents, really—and she was struck by envy. Then it hit her—she knew more about his family tree than he did, and she felt the intimate gift of Anke's secrets and the shame of her firing all over again. The thought of facing him made her queasy with nerves, but she also felt sure they had genuinely connected in Palm Springs, and she couldn't miss the chance to see what he would say about, well, everything.

V was never satisfied until she was in the best, most exclusive place. The doorman outside the greenroom remembered V, and accepted a kiss on each cheek as she swanned inside. Mari searched for members of the Ramblers' entourage, but she didn't spot a single familiar face. A few minutes later, the psych rock band rolled into the room in a wash of sweat.

Mari nursed her wine, poised for when Ody noticed her. He emerged from beneath a hand towel, mopping his tangled dark curls. He didn't smile, but he nodded in acknowledgment. Her heart bucked in her chest. V slid over, as languid as smoke. The instant a man paid attention to anyone but her, V materialized. Holding a bottle, she topped off Mari's glass.

"You know Dante's son Ody?" V asked. "Why didn't you have him get us in? He's cute."

"Don't," Mari said.

Realizing Ody wasn't coming over, V flitted off.

Thirty minutes later, Ody slouched across to Mari, who tried to channel Anke's poise.

"Good set," Mari said. "Is Dante cool with you playing tonight?"

"Grudgingly. Neither he nor Jack would deign to be in a room where Mal's name is mentioned—unless they're top of the marquee. I'm meeting Dante at practice in an hour. He's hired me for tour, as his backup guitarist and tech. There's a few songs he wants to go over."

His phone buzzed in his hand.

"Anke," he said, indicating his screen. "She's on the fence about the new writer."

If Mari had a normal survival instinct, she would have been glad for the easy excuse to leave Anke and her book far behind and focus on the real prize—Dante's memoir. But their doubt in her made her want to win them over, even if it would be a meaningless victory now.

"What's your wise counsel?"

"Do nothing until I'm back on Monday," Ody said, typing as he spoke.

Mari tried to catch sight of Ody's text, but he had been conditioned to be cautious when it came to his parents. Looking up, Mari counted four young women giving her dagger eyes. She was used to being envied by strangers for the company they saw her keep. She looked at Ody. Handsome. Musical. To the rock 'n' roll manor born. Presumably rich. Yet he couldn't see beyond the seventy-one-year-old vixen who kept him on call. He wasn't free to revel in the full scrappy mess of life, any more than she was. *Sucks to be us*, she thought. *Nope. Does not suck to be him.*

One of Ody's admirers had decided that, even with her recent, Anke-inspired makeover, Mari was no real competition. She glided over.

"I'm about ready, luv," Ody said. "Maybe freshen up, and I'll meet you by the door?"

When would Mari see Ody again? Plus, she still felt the cord of their earlier talk.

"So, you told Anke you saw me with her journal?"

"I had to, didn't I? I've watched people try to take advantage of her my whole life. She deserved to know. She really liked you, but after that, and reading your pages, she freaked."

"I get it. *I'm* sorry—it was fucked-up, a momentary lapse of judgment. I couldn't even read it. I just wanted to kill it for her. I am actually good at this. That's why I was so upset Anke wouldn't let me rewrite. I could have nailed it for her. I was so close to getting it right."

"I know. That's why I asked Dante to meet you. He texted when they got your email."

"Oh, wow, thank you. I had no idea."

"You're welcome. I had no clue he would hire you—can you handle it?"

His voice wasn't teasing; it was kind. Mari sensed he was looking out for her, in a way.

"Yes? I came here to do research, at my own expense, even after Anke fired me, because I was worried for her. But what was I supposed to do when Dante wanted to work with me?"

"Is it really as bad as all that for Anke?" He leaned in close. She could smell cigarettes and bay-rum-and-lime cologne. She studied him, wanting to trust him, unsure if it was wise. But if there was one person who really cared about Anke's success and happiness, it was him.

"She didn't come right out and say it, but she blames herself for Mal's death. She implied she drugged him, at the least. You have no idea the scrutiny she's going to be under when her book drops, just a few weeks after your dad's. His proposal is full of stories about her and Mal. If her version differs, the public opinion will go with Dante. He's the bigger, more beloved star."

"No," Ody said.

"No? I don't like it any more than you do, but that's how publishing works. How pop culture works. Why do you think I came to talk to Dante? Not that I've brought it up yet."

"No, my dad and mum get along. They don't see each other much these days, but he's very loyal. He would never do anything to hurt her or make her look bad."

"Well, then, who wrote the proposal? I read it with my own eyes."

"I haven't the foggiest, but I know my dad. You're juggling a lot of fruit, luv. Are you sure you can keep it all in the air?"

"I learned to juggle before I could write. I'm ready for the big top."

He laughed. The fact that he didn't scoff at her bad, awkward jokes made her like him.

"Good," he said. "I'll take care of Anke. She's just—she's anxious about this book."

"Understandably," Mari said. "It's her first and only chance to tell her side of things."

"And—she told you about her diagnosis. I think she regrets it. That was part of why she had to let you go. She hated that you might think she was weak. She won't tell the other writer."

"Of course. Through everything, she's maintained her dignity. She feels it's all she has."

"You get it. I knew you did. Not to mention—Anke is very head-strong."

"You think?"

They laughed.

"Be careful, please. I don't doubt your skills, but you've never been in a circus like this."

She nodded, and they shared a smile. Swooping down, he kissed her on both cheeks, surrounding her in his citrusy, androgynous scent. She was well aware the kiss was a cultural habit. But still, she blushed. And still, she hoped he might turn out to be an ally.

Back at the hotel, Mari tried not to worry about V. It *was* Las Vegas. And Mari had so much work. She comforted herself with her swanky room, the pot of tea and fruit plate she would order, maybe even the mini chocolate torte. When writing, she was bad at saying no to herself. It was all a justifiable expense—writers needed caffeine like rock stars needed applause.

The exhaustion was brutal but worth it. There was a real life for her on the other side of all this labor and risk—one where she could decline D-list assignments; where an eight-hour day was sufficient; where she had a little extra money for V; where someone was waiting for her beyond her computer with a glass of wine, dinner, conversation not about work. There had to be.

Mari opened her door. It was like stepping into a club—pot smoke haze; Tricky's throaty, coaxing vocals: *You stare, you stare and look confused / Your fruit is slightly bruised.*

On the bed, Vivienne inhaled a joint. Looking ready to eat V up, a young man with neat dreadlocks passed her a bottle. Fatigue throbbed behind Mari's eyes like a strobe light. She wanted to cry. If she ever needed to put on a show, it was for V. She had Mari's same supersonic powers of observation but had turned her talents to the dark arts of manipulation and survival.

Mari took the bottle from V, pouring liquid fire into her mouth, shimmying to the music. She drank more, craving its muffle—the opposite of being *on*.

"Who's this, then?" the handsome Black man asked, with a British accent far posher than Dante's. He nodded to Mari and pulled Vivienne close as V introduced her sister to Liam.

"We share the same DNA, including the back-alley blood of our Daddy dearest," Vivienne continued. "He's banned from Atlantic City—I mean like the whole state."

"She means like the whole *city*," Mari said. "And yet he lives there. He loves that story."

"Mind your p's and q's. She's a writer. She'll rewrite your dialogue with her red pen."

"Your pop is a gambler, then?" Liam asked.

"Affirmative," Vivienne said. "And a mystic. He used his powers of divination to predict winners. He read Jack Kerouac once did it in New Orleans."

"How did that work out for him?" Liam asked.

"He lost it all," V said. "Hundreds of thousands of dollars. Cars. Houses. Women. Two daughters. A kidney. We'd need some coke to get into that one. So, from the perspective of a gambler, it worked out terrible. But losing everything, that's the start of every mystic's journey, so I've been thinking, maybe he was onto something after all. Not that I'll ever tell him that."

Mari laughed. She shouldn't forget, V was their father's daughter, with the same dexterous, fascinating mind, as well as his talent for trailing chaos and frustration behind him. Maybe she would ask V for his number. Or maybe not. They'd never really reconcile. She should focus on V, getting a little hot food into her. Liam smiled and sleepily inhaled the joint.

"Sure, there was the obvious fallout—no money, no safety net. Plus, his philosophical approach to life. Like the time I got arrested in New York City for solicitation—a silly misunderstanding. I was asking the gentleman for what we entrepreneurs might term a bridge loan. I called Dad, and he told me, 'You need to interpret the hidden message from your subconscious. Then you'll be free.' I think that was him being too broke to get me out."

"Who paid your bail?" Mari asked. She couldn't resist going there, lulled into the feeling of belonging to her own life, not inhabiting the emotional viscera of others' lives for once.

"Eight hours later."

"Because I had to take a bus from Boston."

"That's my sister, she's taking the bus, but she'll get there eventually."

That's Mari, bailing everyone out, never being bailed. That's Mari, watching from the shadows, never starring in the show. That's Mari, writing as others, never telling her own tale.

Seeing herself through her sister's eyes hurt, but she acted with everything she had.

"Speaking of getting there eventually," Mari said, "I'm on deadline. Break's over."

Mari reached behind Liam, grabbed her computer, and powered it up. Vivienne clamored out of Liam's eager lap, hesitated. Oh, how Mari loved to cause even this brief wobble in her sister's glam life—maybe they were both pretending, but what mattered was pulling it off.

"Let us finish our drinks—we're going to an after-hours that doesn't kick off until two."

Mari flashed her a peace sign—the passive-aggressive version of the middle finger.

"I'll be home in a few hours," V said, bottle in hand. "Thanks for the place to crash."

Mari let her bowed head be her answer. She was furious at herself for slipping up like that, and she knew nothing would soothe her like work. Popping on her headphones, she let in the raw-wool scratch of Dante's voice: "First time I saw Anke, just the sight of her was like honey. You know, the distillation of all those flowers into a sweet living drop of perfection.

"Truth was, I never thought much of Mal. He was Jack's boy from the word go. Looked the part of some Romantic poetry twit. But once he had Anke, that got my attention. Used to gnaw at me, watching them together, how addled he was, how poorly he treated her."

Watching from the shadows.

"I knew I wasn't the best-looking lad in the band. I wasn't telling anyone how things would be done, either—I'm no leader. But I had one thing that counted: I made her laugh."

Writing as others.

Mari rewound the audio, hit pause in disgust. Who was she fooling, other than V? Mari thought of how effortless V appeared—how she *made* things happen. Then Ody's revelation that he was meeting the band at a late-night rehearsal. She picked up her cell phone.

As Izzy led her into the practice space, Mari felt like she was falling back in time, into the heart of the cultural revolution that millions of people still wanted to touch. What grabbed her first was the music, a country rock ballad from the early '70s. It sounded fresh and intense, like it had just been written. The song was so fucking magical, and sexy, and alive—just being there, she was all of those things she had felt in the music; it didn't matter how or why.

Dante finessed his solo. The way his back arched with the energy of his playing, as much as the sound of the bent notes, was as familiar to her as an adoring John, naked and wrapped around a beatific Yoko, or a scruffy Kurt hiding behind bug-eyed white sunglasses. These were the artists who had created the emotional tone of our collective lives.

Jack was small, but he took up a lot of space, like a hummingbird surrounded by an aura of its own speed and motion. His hair was spiky, his skin clean-shaven, every detail curated to look as young and vibrant as possible—and it worked. He was a live wire of virility, and it was very attractive. Still, he lacked something Mal had oozed in the endless loops of video Mari had absorbed. Mal glanced through life like he didn't care, which was sexy as hell. Jack clearly did. That's why she was here—to see the major players up close, in their element, and to try to figure out if any of them had helped Mal drown. Even though Dante's book didn't need the story of that night in the same way Anke's had, Mari couldn't let the mystery go now—she was too invested in solving it, not only for Anke, but also because of what it would prove about herself. If nothing else, tonight's band practice would be a vivid scene for Dante's book. He probably would have invited her himself if his team wasn't on edge after the last writer went off the rails. Mari didn't have that luxury. She always found a way to hit her deadlines.

When Jack's gaze locked onto hers, from where he sang at the center mic, Mari smiled. His nostrils flared. He tore into the next verse, smacking a tambourine against his narrow hip, clad in a red tracksuit bottom. The less threatened Jack was by Dante's book, the more likely he was to help the process, or at least not hinder it. Mari slowed her pace but kept moving forward.

"Hold up, hold up," Jack said into the mic, mid-verse. "Let's take five. Sorry. I lost my concentration there." The band shambled to a confused halt.

Oh, fuck.

"Who's this, then?" Jack asked. "The masseuse?" Jack's tone was condescending, but he flashed a million-watt smile, as if she wouldn't notice the subtext. "I'm sorry, darling, you're an hour early, aren't you? You'll have to wait back at the hotel until we're done."

Izzy stopped dead. Mari strode right to the de facto stage. She had been throwing herself into the fire of her father's narcissism since before she was old enough to know the word. She could handle a rock star, even *the* rock star. Out of the corner of her eye, she saw Dante and Ody watching her, but she went straight to Jack, made herself smaller, so he was almost her height.

"With my sad-banana posture?" she said. "I couldn't be a masseuse. I'm Dante's guest."

Flashing her own million-watt smile, her shake extra firm, she telegraphed her insider status to Jack. No one who didn't belong would behave that boldly. His smile transformed into something shaggier, more boyish. Satisfied she had won the moment without having to identify herself, she turned to Dante. They kissed on both cheeks. Ody nodded at her.

"Sounds incredible," she said. "Adding the slide guitar really makes the heartache sing. Please, don't let me stop you. I'm sorry to have interrupted."

"Thanks for the feedback, pet," Jack said. "I don't know how we made it without you."

The room erupted in laughter at her expense, and Mari stood and took it. Satisfied he was still top dog, Jack released a hiss of tambourine, returned to his mark. Mari kept her eyes down, giving him the victory. Now she could observe him, and he wouldn't give her another thought. On an island of expensive-looking Moroccan rugs were two couches filled with (mostly young) women—it was hard to tell which were the assistants, which the band members' third wives. So, she acknowledged each in kind, and then air-kissed Sigrid, taking the empty seat next to Izzy.

As the band members circled up, she watched Ody, wondering why he kept helping her—this time, to gain admission to practice. Was it possible he had felt the same connection she had sensed in Palm Springs? At least he seemed to trust her to help his parents. He slouched against his guitar cabinet, an acoustic Gibson across his chest. She got that he was going out on the band's tour, which Sigrid had said would last for more than a year. It was hard to believe Anke could spare him, especially if she was sick. Mari sensed some deeper motive, other than a mother's desire for her son to earn his keep and spend time with his father. From the side of the ad hoc stage, Simon slouched over a guitar he was tuning as if he was playing a solo. As brash and annoying as he was, she couldn't fathom why the band had kept him around, no matter how loyal they were to insiders. *Unless.* Maybe he had been rewarded for taking care of a problem.

A man in pristine basketball high-tops, skinny jeans, and a giant oversized hoodie squatted down, blocking her view. Mari snapped back to the job at hand.

"Hi, miss," he said. "Sorry, if you want to hang out during rehearsal, I'll have to hold your phone. I can charge it for you. And if you wouldn't mind signing this."

With a practiced gesture, he pushed forward a stack of stapled papers, flipped open to the last page. As it hit her lap, he extended a pen. "Standard NDA," he said.

She couldn't help but be impressed with their efficiency as she nodded, reaching for her phone, while signing. She would let the publisher's lawyers work out whether the NDA was trumped by her contract with Dante, which gave her access to his inner world, for the good of his book, for the duration of the time it took her to write it.

NDA dude scuttered off with her phone. Dante was standing next to Ody, his guitar angled away from him with practiced nonchalance, his arm slung over Ody's shoulders. Ody was Dante's son in all the ways that mattered. Dante had even confessed to betraying his bandmate in order to secure the fact of his paternity. So, who was lying about when they'd started their affair, and why? And did it matter if everyone was unified in their truth about Ody's lineage?

Ody must have felt the weight of Mari's gaze. He looked up, winked at her. She had no idea what that—or anything—meant. Mari had to be careful not to let her personal feelings cloud her judgment. Even so, there was something so nice and normal about seeing Dante and Ody together. Who was Mari to fuck that up? She'd better be sure of what she was doing, and why, before she made any moves that might change the story. Very sure.

It was two a.m. when the band hit the lobby and scattered like champagne corks—the other members off to their hotels with their wives; Ody to his sleek BMW motorcycle, before Mari could say thank you or goodbye; and Dante to his own black Mercedes Sprinter amid the purring fleet.

Dante seemed to be talking to his wife on the phone. Mari gave him space while standing near the open door, at the ready. For once, Sigrid wasn't glued to Dante's side. After the other cars pulled away, one other van was left idling. She realized she hadn't noticed Jack emerge.

Mari leaned toward Izzy, seated in front of Dante, working her phone. He had wrapped up his call and was meditatively reshaping a joint.

"Should I call an Uber?" Mari asked.

"Nah, I mean, I don't see why we can't run you back to the hotel. It'll give you a few minutes with Dante. I'll clear it with Sigrid when she's here."

"Thanks," Mari said. "I'll just pop into the bathroom."

"Ah, yeah, but hurry. Dante has an event."

"That Sigrid scheduled for me," Dante said. He was laughing, but the fact that he'd mentioned it suggested he didn't like to be kept waiting. Of course he didn't.

An awkward silence fell. Mari nodded and rushed into the lobby. She was brought up short by Jack and Sigrid huddled inside the door.

"Well, if our first date is in Los Angeles, maybe her ticket should be to—"

"Berlin?" Sigrid said. They both laughed, then noticed Mari.

There was something guilty in the way they sprang apart. If they had been anyone else, she would have thought one word: "affair."

"Ja?" Sigrid said, her bearing nonchalant, her voice genial as ever.

"I don't want to be any trouble, but is there a bathroom I could use?"

"There is a bathroom at the hotel," Sigrid said.

Without a farewell to Jack, Sigrid herded Mari out into the car, filling Mari with relief.

Dante had slid into the back row, with Sigrid next to him. Mari sat down beside Izzy. She was still getting used to the unsettling directness of Dante's gaze, which was pointed straight at her. During their hours together, he'd picked up his ringing phone a few times—because it was his wife or one of his kids. Other than that, he didn't have much use for the screen, making him remarkably present, even if he was cloaked in a pungent funk of marijuana smoke. Mari would have accepted a toke, if invited, but Dante kept his joint to himself.

"Is Jack upset you're publishing a memoir?" Mari asked.

"Dunno, never asked him. Even though we lurch out of our castles every couple of years to go on tour, I think the last real conversation we had was in 1971."

"The year he and Anke got together."

"The year he stole her from me," Dante said. "Time is a river, and the tiniest violins play the sweetest melodies and all that, and of course I love my wife, been with her thirty-five years now, if you can believe it. Clearly she's the only woman mad enough to stand me for the long haul. Oh, pardon me, and Siggi, of course—"

He nodded in the direction of his girl Friday, who answered with a smile.

"Your loyalty has surpassed any woman I've known," Dante said, puffing his joint. "Plus, you're the only day-to-day manager I know of who can make a proper margarita."

"It has been the ride of a lifetime," Sigrid deflected.

Mari surveyed Sigrid, who watched Dante as if he were a child prone to wandering off. When Anke had left the band's orbit, Sigrid had been an assistant. To graduate to a manager, even on the day-to-day level, which didn't require industry contacts and business acumen like the band's broader management, she must have made herself indispensable. Mari was intrigued.

Dante seemed more subdued than usual. Maybe it was all the talk about Anke, or maybe he was susceptible to the late hour and the marijuana, just like mere mortals.

"You've never forgiven Jack," Mari said, sliding out her mini-recorder.

A burst of rainbow neon lit up Dante's face as they reached the Strip and passed one of the endless casinos. She was always running out of time.

"Maybe not, but also, maybe he was what Anke needed," Dante said.

Mari processed this, clocked what she assumed was his allusion to Anke's heroin habit, which Jack had helped her to curb, if not kick completely. Even though Anke had clearly loved Dante, she had loved Mal before him, and she had nearly self-destructed after his death.

"Although from what everyone says, Mal was very unkind to Anke, she loved him," Mari said. Watching Dante wince, she pushed on anyhow, or maybe because of it. "She did. He made his mark on her. Did you worry about her after he died?"

"Anke may come off like an Italian greyhound, but she's a sheep dog—wants everyone to be all right—and she felt bad about what happened to Mal. Took too much responsibility, which I told her time and again."

Mari bolded her notes, in order to go back to them, as his words were warmer than what Dante—or someone—had written in Dante's proposal. He was a great talker. Sentences rolled out of him with a wild variety and brash color that would read well. But there was something detached, Zen even, about how he'd recounted such painful events. Maybe because of the many years that had passed. Maybe he was flattened out from decades of heavy drugs. Or maybe, just maybe, he was distanced from the story because it was made-up, with no real emotional stakes.

Lifting her head, Mari reconnected with what Dante was saying:

"Mal was dark, a nutter, a one-man A-bomb waiting to detonate. But she felt guilty. After Ody was born, it got heavy. She went very far away from me, from this world, even."

"Dante, do not protect her," Sigrid said. "Anke has made her own choices."

Once again, Mari felt how little she understood Sigrid and Dante's relationship, and wondered if they shared the same goals for his book.

"Anke was a good girl," Dante said.

Sigrid didn't respond. Instead, she returned to work on her phone—or pretended to.

"Anke went deep into her own darkness. The strong hand she reached for on the other side wasn't mine, to my great disappointment. But that's her story. And it was a lifetime ago. I have always wished her well. She's one hell of a woman. And a bang-up mother."

Now Mari was sure they were both alluding to Anke's drug use, which had been very bad until she'd landed with Jack and had, publicly, gotten her act together. To speak about it felt like a betrayal of Anke, especially when any conversation they had now could be expected to end up in Dante's book. They were idling at the back entrance to the Wynn. Before Mari could come up with her next question, Dante leaned in to kiss her cheeks.

"My better half awaits," he said. "Until tomorrow, Little Marie."

With surprising agility, given his age and blood alcohol level, he slid from his seat. Dante blew the ladies a kiss, sauntered off, singing Chuck Berry's "Little Marie," to his waiting wife.

Sigrid and Izzy said quick, business-like goodnights. Mari matched their tone and body language, staring into her phone. She had a missed call from Ezra, but it was too late to call back. She didn't know how much Sigrid micromanaged Izzy, so she kept her text neutral:

"Hi Izzy, fancy a nightcap in the lobby bar? My treat x Mari."

Deciding to be optimistic, Mari found a table in the darkest corner. The waitress approached. Mari wanted a drink, felt like she should wait, but then couldn't.

"I'll have a glass of red. Pinot if you have it."

"You got it, doll," the woman said.

Izzy approached the table. Mari nodded for the waitress to take her order.

"I didn't know what you'd want," Mari said. "I would have guessed a gin martini, but—"

"Fuck me, long day," Izzy said, sitting. "A martini might just do it. Gin is grand, thanks."

"I know you're probably immune by now, but *wow*, it was cool to see the band practice."

"They are a force indeed," Izzy said. "Still gives me a thrill, I must admit."

Their drinks arrived, and Mari clinked her wineglass against Izzy's cocktail before taking a sip. Izzy was reaching for her purse, but Mari had her card at the ready.

"Thanks, pet," Izzy said. "But the band still gives their staff an expense account. They're old-school. Just ask me a question for Dante's book, and it'll be a write-off."

"Cheers," Mari said. "Were Dante and Jack ever friends, like back when Mal was alive?"

"Well, they definitely weren't friends with Mal, and I think Jack hated him most of all."

Mari weighed her response, surprised Izzy had been so bold. But everyone knew Jack was in conflict with Mal at the end. Still, was Izzy alluding to something deeper than a simple tussle for control of the band? Izzy seemed direct, so Mari decided to see how far she could get.

"What do you mean Jack hated Mal—like he was jealous of him?"

"That was before my time," she said. "Anyhow, Jack's name had better not darken the pages of Dante's memoir."

"You're suggesting I write an entire book that doesn't mention Dante's bandmate?"

"Tell me that's the craziest suggestion you've ever heard. Now, please excuse me."

Mari laughed as Izzy pried off her narrow, spike-heeled shoes. "Another reason I have a job where ninety percent of my time is spent in yoga clothes."

"Sounds lovely," Izzy said. "Thing is, I'm a singer. I couldn't travel when I was pregnant with my daughter. So, the band switched me to office work, and now they rely on me. But I can't ever let them stop picturing me under that spotlight—I'll get back out there, you watch."

Izzy seemed inclined to candor, but Mari had found direct questions could end that fast.

"The band seems very loyal," Mari said. "It's refreshing."

"Here's the thing. Loyalty goes both ways, and I don't fancy you hanging our dirty knickers out for everyone to see."

"Dante hired me. Besides, that's not how memoirs work."

The two women sized each other up, wavering between potential friendship and professional caution.

"What are you here for, then?" Izzy said.

"I'm after the truth," Mari said. "But the truth doesn't necessarily belong in the book, at least not all of it. There are many ways to tell a story."

"I get that. Just, tread gently. I don't wanna see Dante, or anyone, get hurt. Except for maybe Simon. He can rot."

"I noticed his charm," Mari said. "Got the impression he thought he was the next Mal."

"He's stroppy all right. I'm sure he thinks a lot of things. There the band goes with that old-fashioned loyalty again. We're family. Overall, I'm grateful. It's a lot worse out there as a female performer, flying solo in a universe of perverts."

They laughed. Mari liked Izzy's dark wit and was impressed by how deftly she filled her professional role, while keeping sight of her own opinions and goals. She hesitated, not wanting to blow their burgeoning bond, but also short on potential allies and time. Often, for the length of projects, her clients' assistants were tasked with helping her out a bit.

"Oh, hey, this may be beyond your job duties. If so, please, tell me to back off, 'cause you certainly don't owe me any favors." Mari made a face and was relieved when Izzy laughed. "But could you please look this up for me?"

Mari had scribbled her questions on one of her business cards. Izzy glanced down.

"For Dante's book?" she asked.

"Yes," Mari said. Then, realizing the info she was after might not all end up in Dante's book, she added, "It will help Dante."

"You got it, toots," Izzy said. "I would love four more of these, but I've got work."

After Izzy had air-kissed her good night and gone to her room, Mari lingered over her last sip of wine. She didn't have any time to waste, but she was afraid if she rushed herself she might miss something important, blow up this insane opportunity she had created. Mari knew how to do her job, but she wasn't sure how anything else was supposed to go anymore. By coming to Vegas, she had stepped outside her normal role as ghostwriter. She was in the story now.

ELEVENTH:
INTUIT

You can sometimes earn a client's buy-in by suggesting a line of questioning was their idea, and without them realizing it, they are now invested in telling you this very tale. It feels wonderful when a query unfurls a juicy confession or intimate anecdote. But it's okay if the storytelling is mostly workmanlike. It's remarkable how little time it takes to share a whole life— maybe thirty or forty hours. Of course, some books are written with even less collaboration. You can fill in background with research, outside interviews, and your own intuition. As long as you have learned to think—and speak—as your celebrity, you will know how to weave the info into their own story.

The night passed in a haze of caffeine and writing. As the sun rose over the burnt-out Strip, Mari brewed coffee to kick-start her morning. To kick-start her face, she completed a mini-version of her new Anke-inspired beauty routine with organic serums she'd found on markdown.

Mari was startled by a burst of noise, but it was only Vivienne stumbling back from her after-hours. Mari looked at her computer's clock. It was 8:10 on Saturday morning. She opened her mouth, but she had worked all night, except for a quick nap. Everyone had their vices.

"You're welcome to use my room today," Mari said, grabbing her bag. "I have an interview, and a long meeting with Dante, so I'll be gone until tonight."

"Thank you a thousand million trillion times," Vivienne said, flopping down on the bed. "Are you happy now?! Besides, you should be thanking me."

Mari was halfway to the door. She willed herself to keep going. But she could never resist. "What?" Mari asked. She hoped, whatever V had done, Mari wouldn't have to pay.

"You'll never guess who was at the after-hours," V said. "Sir Dante Ashcombe."

Of course she couldn't have one thing of her own. V had probably fucked him in the toilet, causing him to divorce and shelve his memoir, because the optics would be all wrong.

"Just tell me," Mari said. "Or I'll get it out of Dante."

"Well, you'd have to be a pretty fucking good interrogator since he had no idea who I was. Or that I was eavesdropping while drinking champagne with his lovely wife, Fiona."

"I didn't request your help with Dante," Mari said.

"It's not Dante you should watch," Vivienne said. She pulled off her false eyelashes. Under her makeup was the last remnant of a black eye.

"Oh, V, your eye," Mari said, immediately regretting her tone. Like her, V was proud.

V ignored her, continued undressing. The empty feeling of being ignored reminded Mari of Dad, and she hated it. She had been trained to only push so far, so she kept silent and still.

"It's Sigrid who pulls the strings," Vivienne said.

"Day-to-day managers keep the trains running on time, so that's normal," Mari said.

"Maybe usually, but she and Fiona had the most covert fight I've ever seen—you know, all smiles and air-kisses on the surface, but fire and brimstone beneath. Just because Fiona suggested Dante was working too hard and should be resting before tour."

It was possible V had some power for good within her after all.

"Maybe you misunderstood," Mari said. "Sigrid seems quite devoted to Dante."

"Or to what Dante can earn for them," Vivienne said. "She was obsessed with his book. Coaching him on what he should say to you, about stuff that happened fifty years ago—I mean, please, the guy's a sweetie, but he's burned holes in his memory with all the reefer. And it was two in the morning. Fiona said Sigrid and the band have him booked twelve, fourteen hours a day. But the more you earn, the more you need. It's the kind of quality problem I'd like to have."

Vivienne gave Mari a pointed look. "Thank you," Mari said, meaning it.

One refreshing anomaly about Vivienne was that she was indifferent to celebrities. She'd had enough weird flings with too many of them—usually the ones with drug problems—to hold them in high regard. She would enjoy the perks of their money and their fame, but she never lost her head around them. Although she had downplayed it, Vivienne had gotten close to Dante out of loyalty to Mari, unlike anyone else, who would have been agog just to land themselves at his table. It was a kind gesture. V wasn't really a monster. Just scratched up inside with the same wounds as Mari, camouflaged in a flashier, more self-destructive package.

Mari vowed to make time. She had to survive this day, this deadline. Then it would all be okay. Maybe they could even go away together. It was hard to picture, but for once, Mari tried.

Mari was feeling exhausted and overcaffeinated, and she knew Simon's sharp edges would further snarl her nerves. But she was also eager to see what she could get out of him. Her conversations so far, and Syd's book, had eliminated him as a potential suspect. They had also supported Anke's assessment that Simon had seen himself as a bandmember who should have replaced Mal. He wasn't the only one in the inner circle with a motive, but he would have seen the biggest improvement in his circumstances after Mal's death—if things had gone his way.

It was no surprise Simon was fifteen minutes late. Normally, she would have been polite, as Simon worked closely with Dante and had made time for her during a busy day of tour prep. But he soon made it clear a different approach would be necessary to get anywhere.

"You're the last person I would expect Dante to hire as his ghost-writer," Simon sneered.

"Why, because I'm a chick, and we don't know anything about gear?"

"You said it, not me." But he let a snort of laughter escape, which felt like a victory.

"Well, I do know Sir Dante Ashcombe is a Fender man, except for his '59 Gibson 335, which he plays on songs that call for more of a bluesy, vintage B. B. King sound. And that while most rock guitarists favor a Marshall full stack, especially for stadium shows, Dante prefers a Fender Vibrolux, as he has for decades."

"Listen to all the pretty words she knows," Simon said.

"She even knows what they all mean," Mari said. "Now let me buy you a beer."

He didn't pretend to protest, although it was just after nine in the morning. He wasn't exactly pleasant, but he did give up his perch on the table's edge and move into a chair.

After the waitress had dropped their beers, and Mari had made it clear she would be paying, Simon was as relaxed as she had seen him. It was remarkable, really, that the band and their entourage had put up with his attitude for so many years. It was usually a must for the support staff of stars to be unfailingly pleasant, or at least mellow, since their way of life necessitated lots of time together in close quarters. Mari was even more curious about this guy.

He wasn't the least bothered when, after a few easy questions about how he had come to work for Dante, and his duties in the studio and on the road, she nudged him toward Mal.

"You must be the most veteran employee—well, except for Sigrid."

"I was there the night Anke met Mal, and she didn't come on the scene until after."

"Wow, you've seen it all," Mari said. "In fact, you're one of the few people who was around on the night Mal met his tragic end—"

Before she could ask about Syd, to suggest she wasn't suspicious of Simon, he cut her off. "Tragic?" he said. "I may be an asshole, but that guy makes me look like Mother Teresa."

"Yes, I've heard he was violent, untrustworthy, abusive," Mari said. "But he was also very young. Were you surprised when he died?"

"And here I thought you wanted me to tell you about Dante's gear, how we achieve his trademark sound," he said. "These questions are above my pay grade."

"In my experience, most of a band's entourage thinks they're at the same pay grade as the members themselves, but perhaps you're the one exception—"

She paused for ironic effect, and he smirked at her, drained his beer, waved for another.

"You were at practice that night, helping Dante?"

"That I was. It was a big show for 'em, and they wanted to sound sharp."

"Even without Mal, the founding member and leader of the band?"

"Mal had vision in the early days, I'll give him that. But by that summer, he was a drag on everything—the live sound, the overall morale. What they needed was a reliable rhythm guitarist to take his place, allow Dante to step forward, where he belonged, and shine."

"Who did you have in mind?"

"The band could have had anyone in the world at that moment, but Clapton, Bolan, they would have just been more flash. Jack and Dante had that in spades. A working guitar player to hold down the back end of the songs, be a bridge with the rhythm section."

Mari was starting to feel bad for Simon—he'd had a whole plan. She wondered that he had been able to remain so close to the band after such a vicious letdown. Or maybe it underlined how remarkable it was Anke had left. After only one day with the band, Mari wanted to stay.

"You and Dante arrived at practice late that night," Mari said. "Were you together between dinner and turning up at the rehearsal space?"

"That's my job, to be with Dante."

"Why were you late, then?"

"Syd was supposed to pick us up, but he had taken the band's car to score drugs for Mal," Simon said. "So, we waited at our usual bar till he turned up."

"Did anyone ever question Syd about Mal's death?" Mari asked. "I heard he was fired."

"Fired? He overdosed the day after Mal died. I found him in the loo. Resuscitated him. By the time he got out of hospital, we'd gone back to the UK for Mal's funeral."

"Did you read his book?"

"'Course, wanted to see if he made me look bad. Wouldn't you?"

"And?"

"We all looked bad. But—" Simon shrugged. Syd had not made any friends in his lifetime, except maybe Mal.

"Bad, like murderers bad?"

"Cheeky," he said, laughing. "You should read it yourself."

"I have," Mari said. "Why didn't you get dropped off at ten with the rest of the band?"

Simon drained his beer. Crossed his arms against the idea of having a third, gave in. "You are going to talk to Dante for his own book, are you not?"

"We're meeting all day."

"Ask him, then," he said. "I can talk downtuning. Beyond that, it's not my tale to tell."

Mari sighed as she turned to the gear talk that would have to be worked into Dante's book as elegantly as possible. The only juicy detail was his aside expressing displeasure about being supplanted by Ody as Dante's guitar tech. A lot of trouble had been taken to shoehorn Ody into this tour. Mari again wondered if it was just so Dante could spend time with his son.

Then, as Simon was talking about amp wattage and, yes, about Dante's unique approach to downtuning, Mari had a flash of insight. As Simon had noted, he was one of the few inner circle people left who'd known Anke all this time. She tried a new tack.

"You were there the night Mal and Anke met," she said. "Were they an obvious match?"

"She and Dante were the first to start talking," Simon said. "But Mal caught sight of that and wanted in on the action. He could be very greedy."

"Well, I suppose it all worked out for the best," Mari said.

"Not for Mal, the poor bastard," he said.

"I'm surprised you have sympathy for him."

"Didn't like him, but I'd have been content if he'd left the band to people who had half a brain cell to play with. I thought Anke's plan was grand—just have him fall asleep was all."

"Wait, you knew?"

He picked up his new beer bottle, put it to his lips.

"That definitely wasn't in Syd's book."

"Syd might have been the only one who didn't know—and Mal, of course. In a real band, one built to last like the Ramblers, there are no secrets. You can try, but everybody'll find out."

Of course Simon would think that because he wanted so badly to believe he was on the inside. But Mari had only been around the band's inner circle for a week now, and she already knew a secret that had been kept from most of the players, if not all.

"Did people blame Anke?"

"Not any more than they blamed themselves."

"How so?"

"All I can say is, if I'd known which way Mal would go, I would've warned Anke off," he said. "I guess she did all right in the long run, but I wouldn't want my daughter to wind up with any of the lot of them. Well, not Dante, he's different—he and Fiona have a good life."

"It does seem like women were a bit"—Mari considered her next word—"disposable."

"You said it, not me, but yep. And you shoulda seen Anke. She was a stunner. I don't know how to put it, except she glowed. She and I always got along well. We're both direct, if you know what I mean. She was fierce. But still, Mal wasn't satisfied. He went off and got that other poor girl in the family way. If Mal had lived, Anke would have been out."

Except she was secretly having an affair with Dante, or about to launch one—a wise tactical move, although it did seem born of genuine passion. So Anke was fine. And since Simon had stayed with the band, even when he hadn't been upgraded to rhythm guitarist, he had been fine, too. Who else had been poised for a downgrade or promotion?

"Since Anke got Mal to hire Sigrid, she would have been out, too," Mari said. "That's crazy, given how important she's become to the band."

"Anke brought Sigrid over from East Germany. You didn't hear it from me, but—"

Mari's breath caught as she waited for Simon to spill.

"—the overbite she had on her. Could have cut timber with those teeth. But she got herself made over. And got herself promoted. Made herself useful in the end, and still, to this day."

Mari felt for Sigrid. She could relate. She doubled down—something crucial was here.

"You said Anke would have been out, but Dante was in love with Anke," Mari said.

"That may be, but Dante fell in love every other week back then," he said. "He would have moved on. It wasn't until he became a dad that something in him changed."

"You don't think their relationship would have lasted, if not for Ody's birth?"

"It didn't anyhow, did it? Anke got lucky where she landed. Sigrid saw to that. A lady-in-waiting is only as powerful as her lady."

Mari nodded, trying not to let on how excited she was, formulating her next question. The hair on her arms stood up, and Simon got to his feet, still sipping his beer, as Sigrid materialized.

"Enough, Simon," Sigrid said. "If you drink like this, we will have to question the wisdom of having you out with us for this tour. For your health."

There was no edge in Sigrid's voice, but she was serious. She handed him a to-go coffee cup. "The driver will take you to the rehearsal space to pick up items for Dante."

"Ta," he said, downing an obliging sip. He nodded and, with a salute to Mari, hurried off.

Mari hoped Sigrid noticed she had ordered only one beer—and it was mostly full—unlike Simon's three beers. But having supplied him with booze seemed to be enough of a sin.

"Sigrid, I'm so sorry," she said. "I didn't mean to get Simon in trouble."

"No one is in trouble," Sigrid said. "But he must pace himself. The days are long, and not everyone has the constitution of Dante," she said. "No one has the constitution of Dante."

"Too true," Mari said.

The two women paused for an awkward beat. Mari was all but certain Sigrid had been eavesdropping, but she couldn't see an obvious hiding place. And Sigrid had given her blessing for the meeting, had seemed pleased at Mari's suggestion it would take work off Dante's shoulders. Sigrid stood there, innocent as could be, extending a holder of to-go coffees to Mari.

"I am on a coffee run," Sigrid said. "I am aware you prefer tea. But would you like one?"

"Yes, thank you," Mari said, gently pulling out a cup. "So, I'll see you—"

"You will see us at eleven, as we have agreed," Sigrid said. "Ciao."

Mari tilted her face for the air-kisses, sitting only when Sigrid had walked away. Simon had suggested Sigrid had more influence when she had first arrived than would have seemed likely. But it was obvious he had a personal agenda on just about every front. What was more surprising was the possibility he had known about the Quaaludes. That everyone had known.

There was some significance there, some key to the inner circle; Mari just had to see it. Until she could, her best hope was to keep asking Dante questions, she supposed. Because from what the celebrity doctor and everyone else, except Anke, had told her, the Quaaludes had been only a blip in the grand toxicology report of Mal's life. Everyone in the band's circle had been routine users. And they had all been sick of Mal's bullshit. Even if Anke had drugged him, it wasn't a secret, and no one seemed to think it had caused his death. Not even Syd, whom no one believed anyhow, and who had caused his own premature death. Mari needed greater access.

Then it came to her: *Izzy.* She seemed inclined to help. Mari knew from experience, assistants were often the most powerful people to befriend—they could smooth over gaffes, offer access and intel, if so inclined. Make phone messages and emails disappear, if crossed.

Izzy hesitated on the threshold of Dante's suite, surveying Mari.

"Izzy, I'm sorry I'm late," Mari said. "Are they waiting on me? Ugh, I'm so embarrassed. I was typing up notes for today, and I lost track of time. I swear I wasn't playing the slots."

Izzy gave Mari a quizzical look. She had witnessed *everything* during her tenure with the band, and Mari suspected she could see right through her. But would she help her anyway?

"Morning," she said. "Your meeting isn't until eleven. You're quite early, actually."

Mari held up her phone, as if checking the time. "No? Yes! Now I *am* embarrassed."

They both stood on the threshold of the suite. Mari was an insider because she worked for Dante. But one drink together was only that, and she respected Izzy's caution. Opting for the nuclear option, Mari said a silent eulogy for her untouched matcha latte, handing it to Izzy.

"Have you had the Japanese tea latte from the Urth Caffé downstairs?" Mari asked. "It's like a seven-day juice cleanse with a caffeine buzz. I grabbed you one."

"Thanks?" Izzy said, trying to catch all the ping-pong balls of conversation Mari was serving up. But she pulled Mari into the suite, lowering her voice.

"I have my own office," she said. "Correction, Dante and Sigrid both have suites, which means I have the lone room down here. You can hang there until eleven."

"You're an angel," Mari said. "Of course. Can't work in these circles and not have the personality of the Dalai Lama dancing backup for Beyoncé. I knew I liked you." Izzy's back stiffened. "But I've been wrong about the Dalai Lama before."

A ripple of laughter passed along the back of Izzy's Alexander

McQueen sweaterdress, where it was bisected by a bold silver zipper. Mari fell silent. She was always on her best behavior in her clients' private spaces. Except for Anke's journal. And she had paid for that.

"This is primo," Izzy said, sipping her latte as she closed the door to her office.

Izzy's phone, resting on the coffee table, buzzed. She snatched it up. Close as the two were sitting, Mari could hear the call.

"Come to Dante's room," Sigrid said. "We need you before he starts with the writer. And watch her. I don't believe she has worked with a star of his caliber. And you saw what happened with Axel. When he went AWOL, I have to clean out his room—empty bottles up to your elbows. But no documents or notes. We don't need another drunk and disorderly on our hands."

"Righto," Izzy said, offering Mari an apologetic grimace. "On my way."

Izzy zipped to the door. Mari had never witnessed anyone throwing hairbrushes or f-bombs at their assistants, but of course she had heard the legends. And Sigrid had an imposing strength behind her pleasantries and accommodating smile.

Grabbing a stack of printouts, Izzy left. Her laptop was open, and Mari couldn't help but notice the screen was full of news items about Mal's death. Was Sigrid boning up Dante on his story? That was the impression Vivienne had gotten last night.

The coffee table—set up with a laptop, calendar, and stacks of paperwork, as well as a water bottle and Weleda hand cream—was clearly Izzy's improvised office. The doorknob turned. To deflect any suspicion of snooping, she stood quickly, purposefully tipping Izzy's cup, splashing liquid across her computer. As Izzy entered, her gaze jumped to her ruined keyboard, which dripped green liquid from where Mari held it aloft, as if she'd just rescued it.

"Bollocks," Izzy said. "What happened?"

"I'm so sorry. I was digging in my bag for my mini-recorder, so I'd be ready. I must have tipped over your drink. I'll pay to fix your computer, of course."

Izzy started to laugh. Mari was jittery with nerves and caffeine, but relief crept in.

"Seriously, pet, your face. Don't worry about a thing. It's all on the cloud. I'll pilfer a laptop from the production office. I'm the only one who knows how to turn them on. They still message London via fax. I have to sleep with the travel fax by my bed—" Izzy stopped short. "That's not, you wouldn't—none of that is for the book."

"I'm sure Dante's fans would be titillated by his fax habits, but we're already overlong. I'm desperate to keep us on topic." Mari glanced casually down at Izzy's open computer. "Oh, great, you were pulling articles on Mal for Dante. He wants to talk about Mal today. Could you please print me a copy of those stories—you know, in case Dante's recall is a little—*foggy*?"

"Ace, he told you about his memory thing, then—that's a relief," Izzy said. "I'm never sure how to handle it if he doesn't."

Mari suspected there was more to Dante's "memory thing" than anyone was letting on, but at least she now had a truer idea of the landscape. And maybe it was because he had just gone over them with the first writer, or because Mari knew how to draw him out, but Dante was proving to be full of hilarious and heartfelt stories from all eras of the band's reign. Feeling less worried about whether she could get what she needed from him to fill out his book, Mari decided she could safely turn the conversation back to Mal's death, as the clock ticked down. But although Mari had implied otherwise to Izzy, she'd gotten no promise from Dante to talk about Mal. Izzy had just ushered Mari into Dante's suite and returned to her own office. After their usual warm hellos, Mari studied her notes for an entry point. Dante started fidgeting with his Zippo.

"Have I told you about my honey, luv?" Dante asked.

Not the goddamn bees again, Mari thought, smiling and nodding. "Yes, let's start there."

"Golden," he said.

"Which brings to mind your wonderful lyric *Love like golden honey from your hive*," Mari improvised the best pivot she could. "Now, with Jack and Mal writing for the band, it must have been hard to get your songs included on the albums. How did you handle your frustration?"

"Dante has never been the least bit insecure about his role in the band," Sigrid said.

"Even with Mal clinging to a leadership role he was too far gone to handle?"

"You want to talk frustration with Mal," Dante said. "That was all Jack."

"You didn't get worked up when Mal was burning the house down around you?"

"Getting worked up ain't my scene, pet. When did that happen? I remember, of course, but if you could just give me a wee jog. We were in—"

"Yes, you remember, Dante, we were in LA during Mal's final summer," Sigrid said. "Mal had gotten it into his head he should have a séance."

"That's right, he was lighting—"

"—candles," Sigrid picked up the thread.

"Candles, that's what I said, and his kaftan went up, like a string of firecrackers. But a lot of fires were happening back then—literal and metaphorical. *Come on, baby, light my fire*, an' all that? We weren't the knights of the realm we've since matured into, were we?"

"Yes, good point, you were babes in the woods—barely twenty-four. And full of *fire*. I know toward the end Mal had to be coddled. But you mentioned you came to blows on occasion. The first time you punched Mal, you must have been frustrated. Angry. Over the edge."

"Fucking pathetic worm hit Anke in her lovely face. I couldn't not."

"Although it must be admitted, Anke could be provocative," Sigrid said.

"I'm surprised to hear you say that," Mari said. "I think of Anke as so elegant and cool—like a goddess, almost. Above the petty fray of us mere mortals."

"I like that, I like that," Dante said. "Write it just like that in the book."

Dante had slid toward Mari and was gesturing with his cigarette. He was so present in his body, the weight of his attention was magnetic, heady. It made Mari realize how distracted most people were, only giving half their focus—like her, for example, always scheming beneath the words she spoke, trying to shape the narrative to her favor. Anke was like Dante. Immediate. You either had her, or you didn't. Together, they must have been combustible.

"I'm just making sure I have that down in my notes," Mari said. She was typing her own observations now, while throwing out asides to buy her time.

"Coolio," Dante said.

Mari became aware of the weight of a stare and looked to Dante. He was stretching his gnarled fingers across imaginary keys on the coffee table as he hummed "Light My Fire." It was Sigrid. When Mari caught her eye, she smiled, but she'd been watching Mari closely.

"What was Mal like as a bandmate?" Mari quickly asked, to break the tension she felt.

"There are several adequate Ramblers biographies I could point you to."

Sigrid smiled warmly, as if she wasn't trying to brush off Mari's inquiry. "If we were in London, I would give you copies. But we are a band on the run these days."

"Yes, but what did you think of Mal as a bandmate, Dante?" Mari kept on.

"We used to call him Mad Mal, didn't we? Toward the end, I mean. It was sad, really. He went away for treatment twice that year, and he only lived to see midsummer."

"Treatment?"

"Nervous exhaustion. That's what management called it to the press. I guess it was the drugs, but he was always a few notes short of an octave if you ask me. Jack was the one who wanted him in the band, not I. Well, at least until he didn't anymore. And there was the matter of the publishing and that whole ball and chain. I stayed out of it."

"Out of what?"

"Everything, if I could help it."

"Did anyone ever think to tell Mal no?"

"'No' wasn't in our vocabulary, luv. We were the poster boys for a Dionysian revolution, not three square meals and a pint on payday. That was the whole point of all we stood for—you must say yes to everything."

"Did anyone consider the possible fallout when Mal moved in his new girlfriend?"

Dante exchanged a long stare with Sigrid, but Mari couldn't read it.

"We didn't think it through," he said. "Things just happened. It was a long time ago."

Mari was no expert on memory loss, but she was beginning to be sure at least some of Dante's issues were a way to avoid answering questions that got too close—but to what?

"You had practice the night Mal died," Mari pressed on. "Yet he wasn't there. Why?"

This time when Dante looked to Sigrid, it seemed clear he wasn't dissembling—he was floundering, seeking answers.

"You recall how Mal was crazy at dinner," Sigrid said. "He made such a scene at the restaurant, the driver took him back to the house. You and Simon went by to check on him. He didn't like you smothering him, and he cut your guitar strings, as if this was the height of wit. You wanted to hit him. Anke, she got between you two. She said she would take care of him. She sent you away. The rest of the story you heard later. About the Mandrax she gave him."

"Mandrax?" Mari asked. So, this was the story Simon had said wasn't his to tell.

"That's what we called them in the UK," Dante said. "Everyone did them, especially Anke, that summer. Quaaludes. Liquid Sunshine was my nickname. I still maintain Mal stole most of his drugs, but if she did drug him, I'm not surprised. Anke was not to be messed with, and he was a nightmare by then. Violent. Ugly. Maybe she just wanted some peace and quiet."

"You were at practice," Mari said. "How can you know what happened at the house?"

"He knows because Simon knows, and if he knows, everyone knows," Sigrid said.

"It's not important," Mari said, wanting to protest that *not* everyone knew, but trying to avoid a confrontation. "I just meant who knows what happened, except those who were there?"

"This is the kind of night you do not forget, ever," Sigrid said. "Dante, we talked about this when we wrote your proposal. Do not give the power to Anke. Do not protect her. When did she ever think of you? *You* tell the writer the whole story for *your* book. Start with the Mandrax."

He nodded, and as Mari considered the "we" who had written his proposal, she again wondered about their relationship—she had seen managers who wielded total control. It had surprised her until she'd witnessed how insecure some celebrities could be. Sigrid's influence looked friendly but seemed ironclad, even if it was supposed to be for Dante's good. If Dante was as liberated as he claimed, what role did Sigrid play in creating or putting boundaries on that freedom? Whatever the truth was, he was adept at appearing as if life itself did his bidding.

Again, he nodded at Sigrid, but he held off on speaking.

"She served him four, in his tea—" Sigrid prompted him.

Dante gave Sigrid a long look that seemed full of reluctance. Lit another smoke.

"Four Quaaludes was a king's ransom," he said. "But not for Mal. He was a hoover for drugs, girls. Sucked them all up, then came back for seconds. No care for anything. Or anyone.

"Drugs weren't what was wrong with Mal," he continued. "If anything, they set him straight. Once, back in London, we got some acid. I took one hit and lay in bed tickling myself with a feather. For eight hours. I had the consciousness of a sticky toffee pudding. Mal took three hits. He was fine. Went out to see the Yardbirds. He even sat in on sitar. Came home, wrote a song. A good one. You know how some fellas have a wooden leg? Can drink the bar and still be standing? Mal was like that with drugs. He metabolized them like nothing, like fuel."

"Sure, there are the legends—Keith Moon. Iggy Pop. But is there any chance your recollection might be a little, shall we say, impaired, by your own altered state?"

"Could have been that night, or any Tuesday in May. He was the same, always. Pot. Hash. Mandrax. Acid. Dope. It was yet another reason he was no fun. Wins over all the girls. Does all the drugs. Gets into fights with his shadow. What's to like about that in a bandmate?"

This was as the celebrity doctor had suggested—Mal had probably been "sober" when he left Anke's room. Making a quick, bolded note to go back to Anke's description of that night, Mari returned her focus to Dante. His memory had switched on, and he was rolling.

"Yeah, Anke was at the house, but Mal stayed behind with his latest conquest. She was a sixteen-year-old model. Gorgeous girl, I don't mind saying. But just a child. She phoned a little after I got to practice, said Mal was too shattered to come meet us, which, mind you, there was no such thing for him. I figured she wanted him all to herself, and it was easier, given the state of him that summer. The second call came in later. Mal had drowned in the pool. No one was surprised. Or devastated, truth be told. He had been our mate once, sure. But for the last little while, he'd been a drug-addled, fame-hungry monster. Anyone who could look into Anke's beautiful face and mar it with his fist. He got what was coming to him."

"Yes, but you were sad," Sigrid said. "We all were sad when Mal was no longer with us."

"I'm sorry for your loss." Even though it had happened fifty years ago, Mari paused a respectful beat. "Was Anke usually at band practice?" she continued.

"Not always. But during our time in LA, it was different," Dante said. "One long midsummer's night dream."

"Was she there, that night, even for part of practice?"

"You know how Dante's memory is," Sigrid said.

"Yes, thank you, Sigrid," Mari said with a fake smile.

"What was the mood before Mal died, I mean, at least in your mind, Dante?" Mari said.

Dante gazed off into the distance, as if watching an old home movie.

"In that moment, summer of '69, I'd pulled the sword from the stone. Anke and I had been sneaking around for more than a month, which, in retrospect, was when he met"—turning to Sigrid—"what was her name?"

"Nancy," Sigrid said.

"That's right. We knew it would come to a head. I was afraid Mal might kill Anke if she tried to leave him. I once saw him smash a guitar he didn't like the tone of, into bits. It was a beaut, but it was like, if he wasn't going to play it, he didn't want anyone else to, either. But when Anke became pregnant, we knew we would have to tell him."

Mari made a herculean effort to appear calm. Had Dante killed Mal to be with Anke? No, that was crazy. It was 1969—they'd traded girls back and forth like sharing a joint. But he had loved Anke with an incredible passion. And Dante had feared Mal might hurt Anke. Had he killed Mal to protect her? Holding him under the pool water, after Mal had left Anke's room, those four Quaaludes in his system? Maybe he had implicated Anke in his proposal to avoid the revelation of his own role in Mal's death, and Mari hadn't wanted to see it. Had Mari allowed her romanticism to blind her? But why commit murder for Anke and then implicate her?

Mari had allowed a lull in the conversation. Dante and Sigrid were both staring at her.

"Did you have any fear, possibly, the father of Anke's baby had just died? I mean, if—"

"Not to be crude, but the only thing Mal could get up by that point was a bar tab."

"But Nancy became pregnant that summer."

"I'd say that's between Nancy and the vicar, innit? Not that she'll ever dare to write her memoir, I'd imagine. Jack had the band's lawyers pay her off years ago."

Now that was an intriguing footnote, but before Mari could ask more, Sigrid stepped in.

"I can understand Mal must make some appearance in Dante's memoir, in stories of the band's early years, but I cannot see how this is relevant," Sigrid said.

"Of course. We've been capturing some inspired material today, especially about the '70s and '80s. Once we do our final interview tomorrow, I'll have enough for a sample, to get the voice down. Speaking of, if you could please send me—or my agent—the first writer's files."

"As you can imagine, we have much to prepare for the tour," Sigrid deflected.

"Exactly, I don't want to waste any more time after what happened with the other writer."

"Axel was a foolish man," Sigrid said. "He kept his focus all over the place. This is the book of Dante, not Mal. You will not make the same mistake. We have talked enough on Mal."

"Thank you for the direction," Mari said, keeping her voice bright and her recorder running. People often said something candid after she closed her computer for the day.

"The nice thing about books is you can go beyond the sound bite and dig into all the complicated ways we feel about the people we love."

"No sound bites here," Dante laughed. "Not really my cup of bourbon."

"Which is why you're a natural author," Mari said. She knew she was pandering, but she was too preoccupied to be authentic. She thought of her conversation with Ody and his certainty that his father would never harm Anke. If Dante wouldn't hurt Mal, either, had anyone?

TWELFTH:
LEVERAGE

Even if they lack the formal education to write a book themselves, most celebrities are inspired storytellers and quick with a clever turn of phrase— maybe from keeping company with culture's crème de la crème and journalists seeking sound bites. It's wonderful when they hit their stride, and you can let them run, almost seeing the book pages pile up. Sometimes that's the key to being a good ghost, intuiting when not to talk, or when to talk just enough. Listening is also the most fun, especially when you are made to feel like you are there as their confidante, their friend.

For maximum flake and puff, it's all about the cut of your butter. I keep a pound of fresh-churned French gold in the freezer around the clock. In case I have need of a toot."

Mari was taking notes, propped up on a pile of pillows on her bed. Dante's gruff, salty voice ricocheted around inside Mari's headphones, as if he were whispering his juiciest secrets. Mari had found it difficult to believe Dante's skill as a baker was anything more than a publicity stunt—until he talked about heroin. It was easy to look back now and label Mal the mad one, the one set to self-destruct, but Dante had been wild, too. Luckily for him, he had also been indispensable and never allowed to get too lost. Finally, in his late thirties, he had met his current wife and seen a window into a domestic bliss he had previously lacked the patience or imagination to want. Having finally kicked junk, he had found no better antidote for staving off the midnight scratch of his dark hunger than an intricate recipe that required total precision and focus. And no better feeling than the delight on his kids' faces upon seeing his piles of scones.

"Being Papa, it's the best," he said. "Playing for a sold-out arena, sure, you feel special. But your son runs up and hugs you, straight through the heart, all the clichés apply, there's no distancing of logic or ego. It just is. Pure love. Love. That's all you need. John had it right."

"You were the first member of the band to become a father?" she asked.

"Nah, Mal was a rabbit. Had three kiddos when he met Anke."

"Was that a problem?" Mari asked. "I read the Beatles had to hide their girlfriends because management didn't want to upset their fans. A baby would flatten the fantasy."

"We weren't the Beatles, were we? Girls wanted to shag us, but I don't think they had the whole castle-and-a-pony fantasy with us. Sure, there were things management wanted to keep out of the paper, especially when it came to Mal, but I don't know if it was really for the fans. It feels weird talking about myself like some kind of fairy-tale Prince Charming."

"Well, you must know you're an international sex symbol."

"Is that so?" he said, going there, as she had hoped. Flirtation could be a valuable tool.

As Mari listened to the interview, she could almost hear the sizzle. He had eased toward her, in that way men do—the confident ones—sizing up their chances of getting laid. Of course, in their dynamic, sex was theoretical. She might flirt, but she would never cross the line. There was too much at stake, and more power—always—in withholding. Being willing to put sex on the table, without acting on it, showed she wasn't a prude. She could hang. But she wasn't any risk to him or his family. It was safe for him to open up. It was a delicate balance to achieve.

Bored with their flirtation, Sigrid had excused herself to make a call to London. Mari wasted no time, knowing she might never be alone with Dante again.

"What kinds of things did management try to keep out of the paper?"

"Well, if I told you, that would defeat the whole point, now, wouldn't it?"

"I'd say anything that happened fifty years ago is fair game. Wouldn't you?"

"Believe me, babe, there's no expiration date on secrets," he said.

Anke had also referenced the danger of old secrets, back when Mari had been naive about the hidden truths they were discussing. Dante, too, seemed aware of the dance between being authentic and revealing too much, which Mari was struggling to master. Their wisdom was earned, she supposed. Anke and Dante had begun on the down-low, and both had remained discreet about their shared history for decades—until they had each sold a memoir.

"Sigrid was Anke's best friend—did she help you two keep secrets?" Mari asked.

"Sigrid has been a fixer so long, she's seen and heard it all, going back to original sin."

"Was that one of her jobs, as a fixer, killing unfavorable news stories?"

"Who'd want to write an unfavorable news story about me?" he teased.

"Sigrid must have done something right, to rise up from assistant to manager."

"It's a rare thing, finding someone in the music business you can trust. Sigrid proved her loyalty to us long ago, and she continues to prove it every day. That's all I'm gonna say."

Mari knew all managers were fixers, but his casual reference to Sigrid's subterranean role intrigued her. Dante had only been caught

with drugs once, even though he'd been a known enthusiast for decades, and the band was constantly traveling. Had Sigrid "fixed" that
for him?

"But you're famous for being a one-woman man, and you've been
off junk for more than thirty years," Mari said on the recording.
"What can she possibly need to fix for you?"

"The thing about a band is, the welfare of any individual member
is the same as the welfare of the whole—you get my drift?"

He had said he wasn't going to talk about it, but he was letting
her into the band's inner circle. Why? Because he resented Jack, and
there was dirt he wouldn't mind spilling.

"Jack has eight children with six women. That must have required
some fixing."

"You're good, Little Marie," he said. "I'll give you that. But it's not
for my book."

Just then, Sigrid had returned. "What is not for Dante's book?"

"Jack's Johnny Appleseed approach to his family tree," Dante said.

"It most certainly is not," Sigrid said.

Dante had disappeared behind his bumbling Rasta-man vibe, nodding to Izzy for a beer, playing air guitar in his lap. Having seen how
Dante had been prepped for their earlier meetings, and how unforth-
coming he was with specific memories, Mari again wondered if he could
recall much. Or if he had found the perfect ruse to avoid off-limits info.

"Times have changed so much, with America's posh pot shops,"
Mari said. "Housewives microdosing, as their mother's little helper. I
think it will be important to remind readers how different it was. Back
then, there was the risk of incarceration. But Mal was quite brazen."

"I'm not sure I see the point of this line of inquiry," Sigrid said. "I
do not wish to insert myself, but we have so little time."

She looked up into dark eyes, darker than she had ever seen before.
But they were familiar. Something was wrong. They belonged to a

man, and he was on top of her, pressing into her, and they were in the dark water, and his body was holding her down so she couldn't get free. Mal.

Jerking awake, Mari knew she was late. For something, somewhere. In fits and starts, her room came into focus: the weak circle of light from her bedside lamp. She had been spending so much time with Mal and his waterlogged specter that he had entered her dreams. She pushed herself up against the pillows, closed her laptop, which had waited for her while she slept.

Mari shivered, feeling Mal recede. She was blue in a vague out-of-time way, like waking up from an after-school nap to the smell of roasting chicken at her mom's house. Even as a kid, she'd been filled with a kind of pre-nostalgia, a sense that she'd be forever searching for the return to a belonging she had never quite felt.

Blurry with exhaustion, Mari staggered through her room, zipping her boots as she walked. Shutting the door behind her, she went downstairs in search of the strongest coffee she could find. Maybe with a shot of cognac. Her Mal dream had spooked her, made her feel like she was failing him, and she certainly didn't need another master.

As she waited for the hotel elevator, she felt like a giant clock hung over her head, ticking down the minutes. She didn't have much longer in close proximity to this story's major players. Running her mind back over the interview with Dante she had just listened to and her conversation with Izzy, it struck her that both of them, although indirectly, had pointed to Jack.

Was Mal afraid of Jack? Was Dante still afraid of Jack now? It sure seemed like it. At the very least, Dante preferred to fly under Jack's radar as much as possible. Jack was a perfectionist who insisted on the smallest details going his way. Not to mention he had stolen Dante's woman. But when coupled with Izzy's allusion to Jack, Mari wondered if there was more to the story than that. It came to her—the

CDs of band rehearsal for their Hollywood Bowl show. Dante had been furious at Jack for disappearing for an hour. Had he left practice?

Jack had gained something from Mal's passing—he had become the new band leader. He had decreased the number of people with whom he would have to share future publishing profits. And while Dante had gotten there first, he had won the hand of Anke, who was the crown jewel in the band's value system in those years. Yes, Mari was interested in having a solo conversation with Jack. Before she could figure out how, her phone buzzed with a call: Unknown ID. Not expecting anyone, she figured it was the celebrity rehab doctor, wanting to approve his quotes.

"Hello again," she said.

"Hello again," Anke said, her tone frightening, or maybe it was the German accent.

"Anke, I'm sorry, I thought you were someone else."

"But who else could I be?"

With dread, Mari saw the elevator car was approaching her floor. While of course she had a right to be anywhere, she felt nervous, like Anke would know where she was and why. She speed-walked the hall toward the emergency exit and the twelve flights of stairs to the lobby.

"The one and only Anke, of course," Mari said. "I just didn't expect to hear from you."

"I have to tell you, Magdalena, I begin to question the wisdom of this book."

Fuck. Was she not just doubting Mari, but the entire project? Writing a memoir was a vulnerable process—having it written for you must be worse because you had only peripheral control. Mari should have been thinking about more than just her own role, her own glory.

"I hear you, and I know how grueling the experience can be. Excavating the past. Forcing yourself to get down what happened, how you felt. I imagine you are in the process of hiring another writer who will lighten your load. Is there anything I can help you with, until then?"

"Perhaps. I do not know how much you or anyone can do. My heart is not in it."

It was bad enough that she had been fired. What if she somehow made Anke shelve the project altogether? She knew how quickly stories traveled around the publishing world—that would likely give her a reputation for chaos. She didn't have time for this, now that Dante had hired her, but she couldn't seem to give up on Anke's book, even if Anke had already done so.

"I don't mean to overstep, or make myself sound bad at my job, but you are not my only client who hated the first draft I sent them. Usually it takes several tries, at least, to get it right."

"Okay. But you do not steal from your other clients, or you would have failed long ago."

"Anke, I'm sorry. I wanted it so badly, I lost my mind. But I didn't read your journal. I couldn't."

"What is it that you want so badly? To give my secrets to the hungry world?"

"To *protect* you from the hungry world."

"You could have said. As you might guess, I am not unfamiliar with losing one's mind."

Mari dared a laugh. Anke joined her, which gave Mari courage.

"I will text Ody for some dates and times?" A statement, softened with a question mark. "We will sit down together and talk about all the possibilities of your book—the promise."

There was a long pause on the line. Anke sighed. "Tomorrow afternoon, then. The new writer is supposed to start later in the week."

Mari felt triumphant until she thought it through. Tomorrow was her last interview with Dante, and even if she flew out right after their meeting, the afternoon was impossible.

"I feel I have already wasted too much of your time," Mari said. "I could use another day to prepare. So as not to do so again. I'll transcribe the rest of my interviews—as a gift to you."

"Hm."

"I could text you some homework in the morning, questions I was eager to ask you more about during our weekend together. Write as much, or as little, as you feel moved to. Send your answers, I read them, and I reread them. We meet on Monday afternoon, both of us with an even deeper understanding of the story as spoken—and written—in your own distinctive voice."

"I always hated homework, never did it. But for *my* book, that would be different. I am interested to see your transcripts. And these questions. Maybe they will help me find a way in."

Not a moment too soon, as Mari had reached the casino level of her hotel. As soon as she opened the stairwell door, the cacophony of the slot machines would explode around her.

"Where should I text the questions?"

Anke paused. Mari feared she would tell her to text Ody. But Anke read off the numbers in her deep, languorous voice. Mari barely managed to open her laptop and type them into her doc.

Mari stood by the elevator bank with her triple cappuccino in a to-go cup. She couldn't bring herself to go up to her room. It was eleven o'clock on Saturday evening, and she felt restless. Her drink with Izzy the previous night had been such a rare break of normality. Now it was harder to put her blinders on and squeeze the necessary discipline out of herself. She found the quietest bar in her hotel and ordered a Pinot. As she alternated coffee and wine—the ghostwriter's deadline speedball—she wondered if Anke would ask her to return to her job, which she wasn't sure she could accept. But she didn't have time to think about that until it happened.

While she was near the Ramblers, her real focus was them. And her new suspicion: Had Jack gotten rid of Mal, to secure his role as the band's leader, and to win Anke for his own? Mari had to do something to try to find out, but what? The band was rehearsing, but she couldn't turn up a second night in a row and ask to speak to Jack. It was late enough that she would be annoying if she reached out to anyone in the band's entourage. But it was rock 'n' roll, and this was Vegas. She figured the person it mattered least if she pissed off was Izzy. A text was the more polite option but risked being ignored. She was hoping their burgeoning friendship wasn't all in her mind. She dialed and let it ring until Izzy answered. "Mari, everything all right?"

"Yes, I was just thinking, Sigrid hasn't had a chance to give me the first writer's notes yet. But they would be so valuable. If it's not too much trouble. Our deadline is in six weeks."

"I'm not sure she's been able to pull them together as of yet—there was nothing in his hotel room, so she emailed his agent. It's eleven o'clock at night. Don't you ever sleep?"

"Yeah, after our deadline in six weeks. What about you? You're a machine. I was sure you'd be working. I figured Dante is out, right? Sigrid is probably with him? If Sigrid does have the files, I'd be happy to go through them on my own, so as not to be in anyone's way."

"I have a few things to finish up," Izzy said. "I can stay a little longer. Let me ask her."

"Great, thank you," Mari said. "I can come up, then?"

With the ambient noise in the bar, Mari couldn't be positive, but she thought she heard a text come into Izzy's phone. There was a brief pause, as if she was reading it.

"Give me thirty, please?" Izzy said. "Sigrid is texting me with her instructions."

"Of course," Mari said. "I appreciate it."

"Righto," Izzy said. "I guess I'd better order some tea. I'll see if they have a samovar."

Mari was feeling triumphant when she knocked on the suite. And then Sigrid opened the door.

"Come in," she said.

Of course, even if Izzy did like Mari, she wasn't looking to get fired. And the elder woman had wanted to chaperone. Sigrid stepped back and allowed Mari to settle on the couch. Still wearing her jacket and holding her Chanel tote, Sigrid had clearly just come in. As she sat across from Mari, she slid off her jacket and scarf. When the gauzy black fabric was removed, it revealed her gold flowered choker, dripping with small coins that shimmied with her motion.

Izzy stepped toward Sigrid, papers in hand. "Sigrid, we got some faxes from the London office about the band's Brazil dates. The contracts seemed urgent. Since they're about to get in for the day, I thought you might want to go over them before they call."

Sigrid hesitated, looking annoyed. Mari also wasn't sure what was happening.

"Izzy, please order tea and anything else Mari desires. I will take a Diet Coke."

"With a side of lime," Izzy completed her thought.

"Excuse me," Sigrid said to Mari as she stood, flashing her toothy smile.

As soon as she exited the room, Izzy sat close to Mari, who listened for the faint click of Sigrid's door. But Sigrid seemed to have left it open. Izzy slipped Mari the card containing her "research" question, which had been worded to reveal as little as possible: "Can you please write down the full names of Dante, Sigrid, Dante's wife, and all of his children, so I'll have them for the book? Plus, their ages and the country of their nationality/passport?"

> David "Dante" Ashcombe (age 74, passport British)
>
> Fiona Ashcombe (wife, age 53, passport American)
>
> Odin "Ody" Ashcombe (son, age 49, passport American)
>
> Ruby Ashcombe (daughter, age 39, passport British)
>
> Opal Ashcombe (daughter, age 37, passport British)
>
> Serenity Ashcombe (daughter, age 17, passport American)

Basel Ashcombe (son, age 9, passport American)
Sigrid Wagner (age 70, passport German)

Mari nodded her thanks. Her eye lingered on Sigrid's name. Even after fifty-plus years with the band, who all lived in Britain or the States, she still had her German citizenship. Mari wondered if this was by choice.

As if realizing they had been quiet too long and might arouse suspicion, Izzy leapt up and crossed the lounge to dial the hotel phone.

"So, the usual, then?" Izzy said, her voice loud. "Pot of Earl Grey, side of almond milk?"

"Yes, thanks so much," Mari said. She opened her computer.

Just as Izzy was hanging up, Sigrid bellowed from her room, "Izzy, come help me with this box."

"On it," Izzy called back.

Mari wondered about Sigrid's citizenship status. It seemed strange, since she hadn't lived in Germany in decades, and Mari knew from a French writer friend that it was expensive to keep renewing a US work visa. Of course the band would pay that expense, but couldn't they just get Sigrid citizenship?

Izzy and Sigrid entered as one. Between them was the big file box she'd had Izzy carry out with her. Mari's heart sank. At least there were notes, and maybe drafts. But the first writer really had been a mess, if he was so disorganized it required two sets of hands to move them.

"Thank you for agreeing to meet so late—I'm a perfectionist, so I can't help but keep working." Mari gave Sigrid a peacekeeping smile, which Sigrid returned. "Not everyone gets it."

"I understand," Sigrid said. "People think rock 'n' roll is the pleasure dome. But Dante, he does twelve-hour days when he is on. After tonight's practice, he and his wife will entertain business clients. In this band, we all work hard."

"May I?" Mari asked, indicating the box. "And my recorder is on, just so you know—"

Sigrid nodded in assent. Mari found dozens of files organized by date. *Jackpot.*

"I am in the process of going through Dante's private photos to determine those appropriate for you to see," Sigrid said. "In the meantime, here are his publicity photos."

"Oh, thank you," Mari said. "But I'm not sure—I thought I made it clear to Izzy that what I need access to is the interview notes and drafts from the first writer. So I don't end up wasting Dante's time by asking him too many duplicate questions. Our deadline is so tight."

"That would be a nice plan, we are agreed," Sigrid said. "But the other writer has gone. And so has his laptop. He gave us nothing before he disappeared."

"Not to speak badly of a peer, but that's crazy unprofessional. I've never heard of anything like that in my years as a ghost. And his agent can't help us track down the files?"

"It seems no one can help. We have been more than generous. We have kept his room at the Wynn, in case he comes back from his bender. We are concerned for his safety, of course."

Izzy ushered in their room service. She placed Mari's tea on the coffee table. Zero eye contact. Mari smiled to herself, feeling like she was getting the hang of this room, this world, hopefully in time to learn everything she needed for Dante, and maybe even Anke.

"Thank you, Izzy," Sigrid said. "I am sure you are eager to return to your work."

Sigrid opened the top file and fanned out black-and-white glossies. Mari felt a pang of nostalgia for the days when record labels sent out such promo materials, with physical CDs, to music critics like her younger self.

"I am certain Dante's fans will be interested to learn more about his time recording in Trinidad with his side project that has sold millions of albums."

"Of course," Mari faked. Exhaustion set in as she examined the staged photos, which she would have to pretend to examine for at least an hour, to show her appreciation of Sigrid's effort.

"In this particular photograph, Dante is holding his most beloved guitar, the Duchess. He has played it since 1965. And, since you have a crush on Mal, you can flip back to see the earliest photos of the band with him in the original lineup. Very rare treasures of their archive."

"Interesting," Mari said. She felt like Sigrid was fucking with her, but she couldn't not seem interested, so she took both stacks of photos— the Trinidadian side project and the original lineup. She could sense Dante and his team losing patience with her frequent mentions of Mal, and she could understand why, especially if they truly weren't hiding anything. Mari looked at the newer pictures first, trying to appear diligent, then flipped through the older ones, slowly. She was looking for anything that telegraphed tension between Jack and Mal, or even Dante and Mal. But as sexy and compelling as the images were, they came off as self-conscious and staged. She knew better than to read too much into them. This was all turning out to be a colossal waste of time she didn't have. And then she stumbled upon a band shot from 1969, in which Jack was wearing a gold choker with dangling coins that looked familiar. Slowly, she pulled out the photo and glanced up at Sigrid, whose eyes were on her phone. Of course the gold coins were familiar: Sigrid was wearing *Jack's necklace* right now.

She still wasn't sure what Sigrid was hiding, other than all the band's secrets, but she had to get what she could out of her, without arousing suspicion, while they were together in Vegas. Among the most valuable assets Sigrid controlled was Mari's only access point to Jack.

"It's interesting that you and Jack are so close, when you work for both him and Dante, and they can't stand each other. Such good friends, in fact, that Jack gave you a gold necklace he once wore quite a lot—I would assume as a token of appreciation."

Sigrid's hand flew up, fingering a coin out of habit. She stalled, assessing the band photo.

"If you are such bosom buddies with Jack, you must know many intimate details from his life," Mari continued. "Like where he was at the time Mal died."

Sigrid's nostrils flared. So, she had been shaken by Mari's reference to the necklace or to Mal's death. She patted down her jacket, as if looking for the cigarettes she no longer smoked.

"You know you are the second writer for Dante's book, and we have a possible third in the wings," Sigrid said. "I humor you now because I want to make sure you are very clear—Jack had nothing to do with Mal's death. Nor did Dante. But I grow weary of you. Jack was at practice. Dante was at practice. Everyone was at practice except for Mal. Nancy. And Anke."

"So, you wouldn't mind if I asked Jack a few questions about practice, the set list, the band's mood going into their big show, since Dante's memory is a bit—well, *you know*—"

"Why don't you ask Anke since she was at the house? Oh, that's right, she fired you."

"I did ask her, of course. She's protective of her old friends. It would be such a shame to reopen any cold cases related to the band—their role in Mal's death, their tax filings, or—"

"I do not know what game you are playing," Sigrid said. "But I could make Dante's book go away so fast. And with publishers knowing you had alienated such an important client, such an A-list celebrity, not like some meager little groupie turned jewelry maker. You would be persona non grata in the New York publishing world. You might never work again, in fact."

"And having come to respect and admire Dante as much as I do, I would *have to* speak with him before I left Las Vegas," Mari said.

"To ensure he was aware of the true loyalties of those who work most intimately with him—he calls you 'the fixer,' but I'm not sure he understands how much this is true when it comes to your relationship with Jack."

Sigrid flinched, as if surprised Mari had earned such candidness from Dante.

"Well, since you do appear to be doing such excellent work on Dante's behalf, and we both share the desire of protecting his best interests, perhaps we should return to our research."

Mari was wired with adrenaline. Sigrid was so pleasant, so obviously devoted to the band, Mari feared she had overstepped. But she had found Sigrid's Achilles' heel—she wasn't as sure of her own power, or place within the band's hierarchy, as she projected. Mari pulled out her phone and snapped a few pics of the image with Jack in the necklace Sigrid was now wearing—she wasn't sure what it said that Jack had given it to Sigrid, but it meant they were close, potentially in a way that would have infuriated Dante if he knew everything.

"There was just one more thing. It's tiny, so very minuscule."

"What is this tiny, very minuscule thing?"

"It would be so helpful to have even ten minutes of Jack's time," Mari said. "I'm sure, if you presented it to him in this light, Jack would see it's in *his* best interest to have certain events described in Dante's book in the way that's most favorable to him."

"Jack could not be bothered to worry about such—"

"Jack seems quite bothered by the smallest things Dante does. I think it's this tension that keeps the music so vital, but that's my private observation. Not for the book."

"I will see what I can do," Sigrid said. "Is that all?"

Izzy leaned on the doorway. "Need anything from me, then? Photocopies? Water?"

"We are finished for the night," Sigrid said.

Mari projected calm confidence as they confirmed her meeting with Dante the next afternoon. But once in her room, she fell onto her bed, her muscles shaking. It was all catching up with her, risking a showdown with Sigrid, making herself vulnerable with Anke—not to mention the caffeine she had been mainlining for days now. She opened a tequila, drank half. Ody had been right—she was juggling a lot of fruit—and in moments when exhaustion addled her, she felt sure she was about to drop everything and let everyone down, most of all herself.

THIRTEENTH:
DISCOVER

Being a ghost means becoming indispensable by figuring out what is needed, by your client, by the story, by the reader. Memoirs are meant to be tell-alls, but of course some only give the illusion of transparency. As a ghost, you must possess a second sense for what a story requires and what readers will and won't believe or tolerate. Sometimes the truth is just too much, and sometimes it's not enough. You are a conduit for the story, but you don't control it, any more than you do your client. When handled with craft, though, even flawed tales can provide valuable takeaways and add up to more than their individual parts.

Mari had come a long way since her job interview with Anke at the Polo Lounge, a week earlier. On this Sunday morning, she assumed the Anke role, striding through the dining room at Bouchon, Thomas Keller's Las Vegas outpost, behind the maître d'hôtel. As she entered the private dining room and pulled out a chair, Jack appraised her. "Hello, Miss Masseuse."

"Hello," she said. "I'm actually a ghostwriter, but you know that."

Mari gave Jack her most winning smile, turned to the maître d'.

"I'll have a glass of champagne, please," she said. "Would you like one, Jack?"

"So, I have Sigrid to thank for this tête-à-tête, then?" Jack asked, ignoring her question.

The maître d' hovered, unsure if he'd been dismissed.

"To be fair, I didn't give her much choice."

"I'm impressed. Please bring me a champagne." Jack nodded to the man, and he left.

"I'm sure you'll hear all about it, along with the update she was meant to give you today on whatever she's fixing for you," Mari said.

"You make it sound like something out of le Carré, but she's the band's day-to-day manager. Yes, she may keep a closer eye on Dante, so he doesn't dodder off in his book, which I have no idea why he's writing, given his memory. But we're in constant contact, about travel plans, costumes, staffing issues, dinner reservations—don't faint from the intrigue of it all."

Their two chilled flutes arrived. Mari lifted hers, clinking it against Jack's glass.

"Cheers," he said dryly. He took a robust sip.

Mari waited to say more until the waiter had taken their order and gone.

Jack was the picture of relaxed ease as he held his drink. Like Dante, he had been at the top of the heap for so long, little could rattle him. "So, you have come to interview me, then?"

"Something like that."

"Lucky me," he deadpanned. "Well?"

"I'm not trying to annoy you," Mari said. "It's for your own good. You may have known about them, but I was surprised to find several bootlegs of your Hollywood Bowl show."

Jack looked irritated, and Mari hurried it along.

"Anyhow, I thought it would be helpful for my research to hear them. When I'm ghosting, I like to *immerse* myself in the world of the book."

"How fascinating."

"When I got the Japanese version, it came with a bonus album, of the previous night's rehearsal. I guess there was a recording made off the soundboard."

The waiter reappeared with their entrées, and fresh champagne. When you were rich and famous, people gave you all the nicest stuff. It was up to you to exercise self-control. Mari sipped her water, determined not to outpace Jack.

"There have been many leaks over the years," Jack said. "That's why we keep any loyal staff we can find, such as Simon, Izzy, and Sigrid."

"Yes, Sigrid is very devoted to you, isn't she?"

"Just remember, Marianne Hawthorn, I could have you removed from this dining room at any moment, from your hotel—the Wynn, I believe?—should I choose."

If he knew all that, then Sigrid *was* feeding him intel, and there was something to be uncovered. Her risks were merited, even if they hadn't paid off yet.

"I never forget how tenuous my position is," Mari said. "I'm always in the room at someone else's whim. A perilous way to live, but also not without its advantages."

He looked at her with a seriousness he hadn't shown before, perhaps startled by this confession. She allowed herself a mouthful of champagne, even though he had not touched his.

"So, back to this long-lost recording," she said. "The practice kicks off at ten—you come in with Sigrid, your then manager, and the band, except for Mal, of course. And Dante. At first, it's like playing hooky. You do 'A Change Is Gonna Come.' Always been one of my favorites. You play around with a new song, 'The Strip.' At eleven, Dante comes in. Someone speaks into the mic like it's a war documentary: 'Oh-twenty-three-hundred hours, all quiet on the western front.' Dante tunes up. The weed guy stops by. The band prepares to run through the Hollywood Bowl set list, from 'Portrait of the Artist' to 'On the

Lash'—but you're not there. Dante pitches a fit. Even though he was an hour late."

"Typical," Jack said.

"Your wife comes in, looking for you. The band does a riff on 'All Along the Watchtower.' At midnight, you're back at your mic. This time, it's on the recording, because Dante is sure to tell you how late it is, what he thinks of your tardiness. Anger does seem to be a kind of fuel for the band, as you tear through the whole set in ninety minutes. Pure fire."

Jack reached for his champagne before responding. "Please don't tell me that we're going to go through every night in such detail."

"The time I'm interested in is between eleven p.m. and midnight. That's when the coroner estimates Mal died. Of course, back then, the science of forensics was not what it is today. But they can say with a fair degree of certainty. Plus, Nancy told the police she got up at one a.m. to use the bathroom, and that's when she made the discovery—"

"I was at practice, with my ex-wife, only she was my wife-wife then."

"She comes in without you, on the tape, and she's pissed. Something about you forgetting to send a limo. She had to take a taxi to rehearsal. You try to put her in the limo to go back to the hotel, but Syd's taken off with it. You yell for Sigrid to call your wife a cab, but—"

"Fine, then. My wife should never have come to LA that summer. I'd warned her. Sigrid even *mistakenly* booked her flight to Berlin instead of LA, but she was stubborn. Truth is, we were out at a club the night before, and I'd met this—cigarette girl?"

Mari nodded, her mind caught on the "mistaken" ticket, but she didn't want to lose focus.

"Anyhow, I had her come round the studio. She waited for me in the loo in case I needed to relax between takes. When Dante was a no-show, I nipped in. I can't see how my bathroom shag merits mention in the books of either Dante or Anke. Well, at least *that* bathroom shag. Anke can say what she likes. She didn't take any money from me. She's a free woman."

"It's just interesting because you were the one who had the most to benefit from Mal's death. You shared the most cowriting credits with him, so when he died—"

Jack's posture relaxed. He lifted his napkin from his lap, dabbed his lips.

"You must be aware of Mal and Nancy's son, Byron," Jack said.

Mari nodded stiffly. She did not like the relish in his voice.

"What about Brenda O'Shaughnessy, in Ireland? She's got a daughter who bears a startling resemblance to Mal. Plus, there's three children who were known to him before he married Anke. Altogether, there's five, all over the world. Of course, the bulk of his estate went to his widow, Anke, I believe. None of it had anything to do with me—I wasn't privy to the details, but I'd imagine when Anke goes, his kids will turn up, if they haven't already. These kinds of high-profile estates are always in and out of the courts."

"Oh," Mari said.

She didn't like being wrong. She studied Jack, weighing whether he would retaliate for her vulgar questions, and wondering how to smooth things over.

"So, you're the girl who's been entrusted with writing Dante's book? Have you written anything I've read?"

"Do you watch any *Real Housewives*?"

He laughed. "No, somehow I haven't had the time. Touring the world. Getting knighted."

"You'd be surprised. People *love* the Housewives."

"You must have done something right. Or Sigrid would never have let you get this far."

"I can be way more charming than this."

"Not a commodity in Sigrid's world, although she can turn it on," he said. "She may be the only one left who's immune. Makes her incredibly trustworthy and a great fixer. Is there anything else?" He checked his phone, looking as cool as the cucumber in a Pimm's cup.

Mari pulsed with anxiety. Jack was describing a much savvier, more conniving Sigrid than how the manager presented herself. Had Mari allowed herself to be tricked when she gave herself credit as the one who could read any person in the room? She willed her attention back.

"You tell me, Jack—"

He ran his fingers through his hair in a practiced, rakish way. "There are many lies on the internet. Now that you've punctured my privacy, have Sigrid put you in touch with me if you're ever in doubt. I'll *never* write a book, by the way. Can't see why anyone would. But Dante needs the attention. Anke, probably the money, a small place in history."

"What kind of mistruths?" Mari asked.

Jack had eight children by six different women, and those were just the acknowledged ones. He had been the lover of several of his generation's sexiest male rock stars. He had been avoiding full taxation for decades. What could he care about correcting in print?

"I'm five-seven. The internet often says five-four. But that's wrong. Measure me."

"That won't be necessary. I'm getting five-eight from here."

"You *are* good," he said. "Now, there are six places I needed to be thirty minutes ago."

"Of course," Mari said, accepting air-kisses. "Thank you for your time."

"Oh, and Marianne," he said, turning back. "Sigrid has been with the band so long, it's like a marriage. Don't try to dissect it. You'll never get all the nuance."

"A convenient way to describe someone who does your dirty work for you."

"If I thought of it as *dirty work*, I'd never have made it. Sigrid prevents the unpleasant and inconvenient from intruding on me so I can be creative. I don't ask how she does it."

He blew Mari a kiss on his way out, and she found she believed him.

Mari reached for Jack's untouched champagne flute and downed it in one go. When the waiter returned, she was sipping her own second glass.

"Is there anything else you desire, mademoiselle?" he asked.

"No, thanks." She held up her glass, indicating when she finished, she would leave.

"Excellent," he said. "I'll leave this for you. No rush."

With dawning horror, Mari realized Jack had stuck her with the bill.

Nicely played, prick.

She sighed and pulled out one of her credit cards. Jack seemed to be telling the truth. She had eliminated him as a suspect and somehow gotten him to be available to her during her research and writing, which she had never expected. So, $100 well spent.

As she stepped out into the glare of the noonday Vegas sun, Mari felt woozy from the champagne and multiple nights without proper sleep. This was her last full day in Vegas, and if Jack was guilty of nothing more severe than vanity and a wandering eye, that left her no closer to learning what had happened to Mal. She had been pushing for answers from every possible direction, but she had encountered nothing but dead ends. And now she wasn't feeling well.

When Mari got back to her hotel, she was in desperate need of a nap. She'd have to hope pounding some caffeine would help. She had only a few hours to make real progress on Dante's sample material before their next—and final—meeting. Mari was heading to the Urth Caffé for a matcha latte when she got trapped between the front entrance and a blitzed bachelorette party. The bride-to-be lurched toward Mari, who reversed away from her just in time. Feeling herself back into someone, Mari turned around, already saying, "Excuse me. I'm so sorry."

She was startled to find it was Sigrid she had bumped into. And then she wasn't. "If I didn't know better, I'd say you were following me," Mari said, keeping her tone light.

Sigrid laughed and stalked away. Mari felt relief, but her time here was almost up. She had to force herself to keep pushing, while not letting on that she was. She ran after Sigrid.

"Wait, Sigrid, can I buy you a drink?" Mari said. "I wanted to thank you for your help."

As soon as they found a table and ordered, Sigrid leaned toward her. "Well, ask your questions."

Mari smiled, about to reiterate her gratefulness, then realized it was pointless.

"So, you seem very interested in what goes into Dante's book, and what doesn't."

"That is my job, to care."

"Do you care what goes into Anke's book? She seems quite ready to blame herself for the four Mandrax she thinks caused Mal's death."

"Maybe it would be good for her, to take responsibility, for once," Sigrid said. "Why is it *you* care since she is seeking your replacement? You work for Dante now, remember."

"I'd expect more loyalty for your oldest friend. She is why you're here, and me, too."

Sigrid leaned around the waitress as she served their wine, losing her masterful control.

"No, Anke left me to be thrown to the wolves. She got the papers signed. She got me a job with Jack. But then she loses herself to the drugs. She is selfish and lazy. She cares only about herself. It nearly cost me everything. If Anke goes down now, what is that to me? She has had a good life, so maybe the tab comes due. I am here today because of no one but me."

Mari nodded her head, relating more than she cared to admit. It took a specific kind of courage and tenacity to live by your wits,

to remain indispensable. With no safety net, the stakes were even higher. She studied Sigrid, seeing one of her own potential futures, wondering if it was a good one, compared to all the other possible ways to live.

"I don't believe you no longer care for Anke," Mari said. "But you're right, that's not my business. I'm here to write a bestseller for Dante. To do that, I need to get at Mal's death. We *all* know four Mandrax was nothing to Mal. I know Anke wasn't responsible for his drowning."

Mari held her breath.

Sigrid had been drinking with workmanlike efficiency and had one swallow of wine left.

"So, was Dante somehow responsible for Mal's unfortunate final swim? Is that why you're micromanaging his book?"

"Dante is old," Sigrid said. "Jack is old. No one likes to see them as such, but they are. Dante's memory is the Swiss cheese. To write the proposal to sell his book, we had to hire a private investigator to uncover the stories Dante cannot recall. Don't you think he would have found out if Dante had killed Mal? You are grasping at ghosts."

"But—"

"Your fantasy has wasted my time. We are busy. Do the job the first writer could not."

Sigrid was calm and collected once again; their conversation had clearly put her at ease.

Mari was more uneasy than ever. And less sure of what she should do next. What wasn't she seeing? Simon had sauntered into the bar without noticing them and was ordering a drink. Sigrid called out to him. With her would go Mari's access to the band. She couldn't lose that.

"You said Anke almost cost you everything, but Jack kept you on anyway. He gifted you his favorite necklace. Had you serve, for all these years, as the band's day-to-day manager."

"Not the necklace again. It is a cheap trinket. But yes, Jack is loyal. So am I."

"'Loyal' is not a word I'd use to describe Jack. But you're different. You're his fixer."

"You like to throw this word around, but you have no idea what it means," Sigrid said.

Holding his beer, pretending he hadn't heard Sigrid, Simon strolled onto the casino floor. Sigrid stood to leave. *What do I mean?* Then it came to her, Jack's "mistaken" ticket. When Jack got tired of a woman—his first wife, Anke, his current wife—Sigrid made them go away.

"I know you fix the plane tickets," Mari said.

"A common job of both the assistant and the band manager," Sigrid said, shrugging. But she didn't turn to go. Simon would get to enjoy his drink after all.

"And Jack's preferred method for disposing of women."

"Those are your words. Just because a woman is given a ticket to a city where the band is not, it does not mean she must go away. Maybe he is just asking for a little break, a little space. When she decides to leave him over this matter, that is up to her. If you want to hurt Anke by bringing up this story of Jack's plane ticket, now, so many years later, that is your choice."

"Anke's version of her breakup with Jack is good enough for me, and it's not my story to write anyhow. But I am interested in this band's longevity, and how a fixer might have been compensated for everything they fixed to ensure that longevity."

Sigrid shrugged, as if excusing any moral laxness Mari was implying.

"It is fortuitous we have met like this," Sigrid said. "There has been a change of plans."

Mari's self-assurance had been growing, but now it teetered.

"As it is Dante's last night before tour," Sigrid continued, "he has decided to have what he would call a proper send-off, at his house in

Joshua Tree. He will leave this afternoon, and so your final meeting must be truncated. You will ride with us to practice now."

Mari couldn't let herself get pushed to the outside. She needed more interviews with Dante. She needed this book to not fall apart. She needed to prove she could pull this off.

"It would be incredibly helpful for me to attend Dante's send-off tonight," Mari said.

Sigrid smiled, but her voice said no: "Don't be ridiculous."

"I need as much time as possible for his book, especially if there are no files from the first writer, which is unheard of. And. That is the cost of my silence about what you do for Jack."

"Who cares what I do for Jack?" Sigrid said. "You will have to try harder."

"The people who renew your work visa might care," Mari said. "Since you've never succeeded in becoming an American or British citizen. I wonder why . . ."

Sigrid looked startled. She hadn't counted on Mari's skill at gaining insider information. Mari knew her accusation had glanced off the top of Sigrid's secrets, and she had better be sure of what she was doing. But at least in the moment, Sigrid nodded her head, deferring to Mari.

"You will come to Dante's dinner tonight," Sigrid said. "Because it is good for his book."

"Thank you," Mari said, making her smile as pleasant as possible, since they were about to step into tight quarters with the man himself.

The aroma of marijuana and old-fashioned shave cream hit Mari when she climbed into Dante's Sprinter van. Mari had decided not to mention she would be attending his family party.

"Dante, thank you for letting me tag along," Mari said. "I won't waste a moment."

"Sure, luv, I'm all yours."

"Yesterday, we were talking about the summer of '69. What do you remember of the Hollywood Bowl show?" Having been warned off the subject of Mal, she didn't mention it had become an impromptu tribute to him in the wake of his death.

"The show was highly regarded," Sigrid jumped in. So, she would give Mari time with Dante but domineer the conversation. "The band set attendance records for the Bowl. And the critics adored it. Even Lester Bangs, who was the biggest crank."

"Is that so? Well, you know, I never had much time for critics. If they think they're so grand, why don't they learn three chords and piss off? But yeah, we played well. Without Mal, we zipped up into this tight unit. It sounded good, which felt horrible, to be honest."

Mari dared a look at Sigrid. If Dante, not she, brought up Mal, surely it was okay.

"You were glad he was gone."

"You know when you've met your soul mate, found a hundred pounds in the street, and won the Nobel Prize, but your best mate just got bit by his dog and left by his wife?"

"I'm usually the one with the dog bite," Mari said.

Dante laughed with gusto.

"Don't fret, luv, your spaceship will come in—for everything there is a season."

"Your season has lasted a long time," Mari said.

"My season has lasted a long-ass time. But I've had my share of knocks."

"There's a rumor, deep in the fan chat rooms, that your drug bust in the fall of '69 was the authorities' cover to bring you in for questioning about Mal's death," Mari said.

"All right, Woodward and Bernstein, whose book is this?" Dante asked, waving to Sigrid.

She poured him a drink from a cut glass decanter.

"I didn't mean to offend you," Mari said. "I've found it's best to beat your critics to the punch. Anticipate the worst thing they might say, any reason they might dismiss your book, and walk right into the line of fire. If you go there first, what ammunition do they have?"

"I like that—'walk right into the line of fire'—that's on the short list of titles."

Mari let herself relax, having dared to be brash and (hopefully) earned respect.

"But—" she said.

He laughed, once again at ease, sipping his drink. Having been on top for as long as he had, he wasn't scared of much. That's how it was to be king of the jungle.

"But my dear," he said, "I don't care what some rotter has to say in some chat room somewhere. As long as people still buy tickets for our concerts. And people will always buy tickets for our concerts. If the past fifty-five years are any measure, there will be an audience for this book. As far as Mal or Anke or Ody goes, I don't have to say squat about diddly."

She smiled, signaling she wasn't ruffled and Dante should continue. By now, Mari was convinced Dante hadn't read his book proposal, but how to find out without suggesting he wasn't aware of what his team had written?

"Mark my words, none of us are as relevant as a redwood in the grand scheme of things. But I'm not afraid of anything you or anyone else can ask. It was lousy of me to go behind my bandmate's back, with his girl, but the way he was treating her was worse. As soon as I found out we were pregnant, I put her on the highest, shiniest pedestal I could build. By now, you've heard me go on about Ody for hours—you know how proud I was, and am, of my firstborn son."

Their vehicle had reached their destination. The driver had been instructed to take her back to the Wynn. Mari felt so close—she wasn't sure to what, but to something crucial.

"And?" she prompted.

"And yes, the police asked about Mal's death. I told them what I'd tell anyone. I was fed up with his violence and his soul full of garbage. But I didn't kill him. Don't have it in me. Had no reason to, because by the time he died, Anke had agreed to be my old lady. He'd moved on to Nancy. And he was walking over his own grave by then anyhow. Nothing left to battle for."

Mari didn't believe Dante, but he appeared to be lying for his son. Everything he had said about Mal seemed true. Dante glanced out the window at the practice space, where Simon stood waiting for him with a guitar case in each hand. She was losing him. Just in time, it dawned on her. "Oh," Mari said, "I realized I never asked for a copy of your book proposal."

"Whatever you need," Dante said. He kissed her cheeks and glided out of the van.

Sigrid watched him stroll away. When she turned back to Mari, she wore her normal smile, but it was rigid, as if she had snapped it onto her face like a mask. A shiver raced down Mari's spine. She thought of her sister, her dad, herself, understood that surviving was the goal, but what was required to pull it off could wreck you in the end.

"I will call with our travel plans," Sigrid said.

Mari nodded. She was often frightened by the challenges of her job, but they were just social anxieties, fear of failure. Now she was scared. There was still so much she didn't know.

FOURTEENTH:
UNDERSTAND

It's not about the quantity of hours, but the quality. People repeat them-selves, anyhow, curating their lives into the top three or four stories about childhood, first love, career highs. Sometimes asking specific, provocative questions or presenting multimedia related to a moment they haven't de-scribed will evoke something fresh. More often, they circle back to their gems. You let them go through it again, for new details, but after you've heard the iconic stories twice, you must write. Gaps are inevitable. It's your knowledge of them as a person that's the key. If you understand your client on a deep level, you will present the narrative in a way that feels con-scious and complete.

Mari sat at her laptop, as usual, but she couldn't concentrate. She checked her computer clock—one p.m. on Sunday. A benign time—neither too late nor too early. Before brunch, she had emailed Anke the "homework" she had promised her, but she hadn't received any response. Now was the moment to be brave, to do whatever still could be done. She texted Anke: "Hi, I hope you're having a lovely Sunday. Could you please call me when you're free? Thanks, xo Mari."

Her phone buzzed.

"Anke, thank you for responding so quickly."

"Hallo, Magdalena, I am doing my homework. I thought it would be good for me to read, so you can hear my voice and give your feedback."

"How wonderful, but—" Mari leapt in before Anke could begin.

Every time nonwriters scratched out half a page, they wanted a trophy. Often refused to let their rare and precious words be edited. Mari was sympathetic. She could remember, when she had studied writing in college, how she had labored all weekend over a paragraph. Even now that she was a veteran, she loved words, found them precious, and could fall under their spell. But Mari knew she had to be careful. Anke had softened toward her for some reason she had yet to share, but another writer already waited in the wings. And Mari had a new job. She could tell herself she was just being kind to Anke, in feminist solidarity, but she couldn't let it go too deep.

"I was hoping you could text me pictures of your writing, so I can digest it. I will have detailed notes tomorrow. I am happy to help you, as your friend, until you hire your new writer."

"Hm," Anke said. "But that is not my process."

Mari swallowed her sigh of frustration. Anke had fired her, but in this moment, she wanted to write, and Mari was the only one who was available to listen, so Mari would help.

"I want to support your process. So, yes, you should read your pages to me. I can't wait. Could I please just ask you a few questions first?"

"What questions?"

"We have spoken a great deal about Mal and Dante and very little about the rest of the entourage, like Sigrid. Or even Jack. What can you tell me about him?"

"He is not five foot seven," Anke said.

Mari laughed. "If you don't want to get sued, maybe go along with his Wikipedia page."

"Men. Little babies. Except my son. I raised him to be strong. To not care for gossip."

"That must have been a great gift for him, given the circumstances in which he grew up," Mari said. "Did you ever want a child with Jack?"

"He was the child."

"But you loved him."

"Jack is like a comet. If fortune brings him across your path in your lifetime, you take it."

"I can't imagine comets are easy to love."

"Most people are not easy to love. I am not. I am not sure that should even be something to aspire to—I was no catch. Heroin and love cannot coexist in the same body. It was not until Jack had me for his own that he learned the truth of my condition. We struggle and fight, until we can't anymore, and I end up back in Berlin. There is a version of the story where he saved me."

Mari thought of the "mistaken" plane ticket, but she wanted Anke to feel close to her.

So, she stuck with Anke's version. "When you left Jack, you followed your heart."

"I missed Fritz. I missed the real world."

"The real world outside of rock 'n' roll?"

"The real world outside fame. I wanted to walk to the café in the morning, take my son to the park. I wanted to be free to go where my whims carried me."

"Jack is not known for being generous to his exes."

"It was a breakup after five years of living together, being together every day. It is a horrible rupture. Why should he be generous? I am not sure what you are asking."

"If you had married him in California, you would have been entitled to half of everything. In two more years, you would have been considered common-law partners."

"Jack is exceptional—I mean it. Even more so than Dante or Mal. Just full of so much light, it can dazzle you, project to the last seat in the arena. I have seen him perform for a literal million people and make each and every one feel special. But he is not so good as a husband. Why would I marry him when I already make the mistake with Mal? I have a little money after Mal die. I have a son, but Dante helps me with him. I take care of my family, take care of myself. Maybe because of this way I live my life, I am not Jack's problem, and so I am not a problem."

Of course. How had she not seen it before? Anke had been Mal's *wife*.

"How much was Mal's estate worth when he died?"

"Mal never save a penny in his life. Owe debts all over town, for clothes, for drugs, for the three other children he has. Thank God Sigrid take care of this for me."

"But you said there was a little money—"

"Not for a year. It takes the lawyers that long to untie all the knots. For that time, Dante, he provides for me and his son. He is a good man. He is fair. Then Sigrid sort out the lawyers and the estate, and there is the trademark and the publishing. Mal wrote on two albums, but he also name the band, come up with the logo, and all together, it is enough."

"I don't suppose you still have Mal's will? It was fifty years ago."

"Sigrid was the executor, not me."

Sigrid was the band's fixer, and maybe she fixed this. But when were the papers signed?

"I don't see how this is relevant," Anke continued. "I am not writing a story of marriage agreements and what famous person was at the party on what night. This is why I question the whole endeavor. This book is my legacy. I will be gone soon. It must have poetry at its soul."

"It does, and it will, Anke, because that is how you live. Please, trust me. Getting all of these facts right, even just in passing, allows the reader to trust you, to believe in your poetry."

"Ja, okay. Now I read."

Mari was rattled by Anke's reminder of her illness. Something thudded against her door. In her ear, Anke read about the boat, Fritz, and her boy—about diamonds of sun on the water.

Leaving the security lock engaged, Mari cracked the door. Pitching Vivienne's deadweight forward. Mari opened up and caught Vivienne as she fell inward. Vivienne sprang back, scratching at Mari's face. Mari caught both of her sister's hands without dropping her phone. But Anke must have registered Mari's sharp intake of breath.

"Are you okay?" Anke asked. "Where are you?"

Making a dramatic shushing gesture to Vivienne, Mari kept her hand around both of Vivienne's wrists as she led her inside. Mari leaned V up against the wall.

"Yes, I'm at my desk," Mari said. "My chair tipped back, and I had to catch myself. I'm sorry to have interrupted. Your writing is wonderful. I can tell you've found your true voice."

"Ja," Anke said, her tone flat.

"Do you feel up for writing about the accident aboard the boat?"

"I do not know—"

"We can wait and talk about it together, figure out the best way for you to handle such sensitive material. With respect. With sensitivity. I just thought, by writing, you might access deeper memories and feelings—if it's not too hard."

"The accident hurts even after so many years, but I will try. You like my new writing?"

"Very much," Mari said. "It's going to be an incredible book, Anke. I know it can be painful. I know it's a lot of work. But you will have a writer to help. It's worth it. I promise."

"Ja," Anke said, again managing to express volumes with one little syllable—the weight of her legacy truly seemed to hang in the balance of their task, and Mari felt it, intensely.

"Thank you," Mari said. She was trying to figure out how to work the conversation back to Mal's estate documents, but before she could, V released a gentle moan. She'd better sign off.

"I look forward to seeing you, and going deeper, tomorrow."

"Okay, until tomorrow."

Mari got right in her sister's face. "Fuck, V, how drunk are you? I'm working."

"I'm working, I'm working," Vivienne mimicked her. Stumbling over to the bed, she missed and landed on the floor. There was the scratchy, nauseous sound of fabric ripping as she puddled into a heap. She was wearing a snug black sheath dress with expensive-looking drapey net across the chest and hips, and the rip at one thigh spread higher.

Mari crouched down next to her sister, touched her hand. "I'll help you unzip. Sit up."

Grabbing V under the armpits, Mari piled her onto the mattress. As she tugged the zipper down, Vivienne yanked out several tags.

"Guess I'm not returning this dress," Vivienne said. "Oops."

Mari didn't want to look, but she had to know: $3,800.

"Christ, V, you didn't pay full retail, did you? How did you scrape together that much?"

"*He* bought it for me," Vivienne said. "And a Chanel purse, which is—"

Vivienne swiveled around, in search of the missing bag, nearly tumbled again.

"Of course you would lose a Chanel bag," Mari said. "God, you're so frustrating."

"Right—because you've had such a tough day," Vivienne said, pulling her phone out of her bra.

Mari realized she wasn't as drunk as she had first appeared. Whatever was happening to her system was much worse—shock, maybe, or some kind of total internal collapse.

"Boo-hoo, I have to eat room service and write words, and it's so fucking hard. Poor me. Try getting finger-banged by a sociopath in front of his friends, and the limo driver, just to show you—and them— that he can do whatever the fuck he wants, and then, when you won't agree to let him *share* you, because that wasn't your deal, he pushes you out of the limo at a stoplight, throws the Chanel purse at you. So, yeah, I lost my bag while I was trying to not get hit by a car on the Strip. I'm not even going to tell you what happened after that because you'll just—"

"Oh, V."

"Don't-you-dare-judge-me—" Vivienne said, standing and pushing across the room, her unzipped dress dragging behind. "You don't *know*."

"I'm sorry," Mari said, spinning her around, holding her in her arms, even though she smelled like cigars and sex and the sour funk of fear sweat. Mari held her, and held her, until V's nerves stopped fighting. She started to cry, heavy, shuddering sobs.

"He was so mean. Why do they have to be so mean as soon as I try to say no?"

"Men don't like to hear *no*."

"Oh, that's bullshit," Vivienne said, struggling out of Mari's embrace and wiping her tears on the edge of her expensive, ruined dress. "Those are the words of someone who spends very little time with men. Men are easy. Women are fucking scary. Do you know who set me up with this guy? His female assistant. I met her on a flight back to LA, and she purred, talking about how great he was, what a catch. She told me, when I was in Vegas, I just *had* to look them up. It was like she couldn't stand me—hated everything about me—my face, my body, the way she knew he would look at me, the way he *did* look at me. When the doorman was putting us into the limo last night, she leaned into the car, looked right at me, and said,

'Have fun,' only her voice said, 'Fucking die.' She smiled at her boss, and she shut the door."

"Do you want me to take you to the hospital? We'll get a rape kit."

"I didn't say *no*. I never say *no*. Because the one time I tried to, look what happened."

"It can still be—"

"I just want to go to bed," Vivienne said, yanking at the comforter, covering herself.

"I know you do, honey," Mari said. The word felt strange in her mouth. She hoped her sister could feel her empathy, her love. "But you've got to tell me what happened. Who is he?"

"No way. I don't ever wanna hear his name again. Fuck him. And no police!"

"We can't let him get away with it."

"This isn't one of your books where we can just write a happy ending," V said. "No."

Mari knew how stubborn her sister was. So that was it. She glanced at her laptop clock.

"V, it's 1:30 in the afternoon. We should get you some fresh air, some hot food."

"I don't want fresh air. I want to fucking die. I'm so tired, I could sleep until I was dead. Cocaine is disgusting. And then, well, let's just say I didn't go to bed last night."

"Look, I hate this, but I have to leave in a few hours, to go to Dante's house in Joshua Tree. You know what? I'll cancel and stay here with you."

"No," Vivienne said. "You can't fuck up. You're the only one making it."

Nice to be acknowledged, V, but not helpful.

"Don't worry, V, I'm not fucking up. I can do a phoner another day instead."

"No. Do not fuck up. What would happen to us then? Mom does

her best, but she's got a new family. And Dad, he's like an *Ocean's Eleven* Halloween costume. I need a drink."

"You do not need a drink. Here, I'll run a bath, and I'll order eggs Benedict, extra bacon, just the way you like."

"Believe me, I know what I need right now, and it is 80 proof."

Marie understood she had no idea what V had really been through, and she nodded. Running out to the minibar, she grabbed V a tequila. After bolting the liquid, V seemed steadier. Mari stripped V and piled her into the suds. V looked amazing in clothes, like a dream, but naked, she was too skinny, her ribs showing, dark bruises on her hips and thighs. Seeing the fingerprints on her sister's pale skin made Mari want to cry. She focused on her task, to steady her nerves. With the room service on its way, Mari sat on the tub's edge, scrubbed V's back like she might have done when they were little girls, if they'd had that kind of childhood.

"Remember how amazing it was when Dad was winning—he was so proud, even of us," V said. "He'd introduce us around as his daughters. Give us hundies. Promise us the sky."

"Yeah, until he lost, and he always lost."

"I'd like to win again someday."

"Yeah, me, too. I'll be in Joshua Tree, but you can have the room tonight. Where will you go after this?"

V slid lower into the water. Mari thought of how hard the next few weeks were going to be. And then it hit her: V had lost the condo. Where was she going to write Dante's book?

"I'll find a cheap sublet when I get back to LA, and you could stay with me," Mari said. "I have a book—possibly even two—to get written in the next few weeks, so it's gonna get primal. But there's a lot of cute boutiques on the east side—you could get a part-time job—"

"I'm not going to sell fifty-dollar hemp candles to stay-at-home moms who take turns going to each other's birthday parties and giving each other fifty-dollar hemp candles."

Mari wanted to laugh and scream: *I don't get to say no to work!*

She willed herself to be kind. "Oh, honey, I know, but it would be temporary."

"You don't understand anything. If I do that, it's like climbing into my own coffin and closing the lid. You have options. My only chance is to get lucky."

"Fine, I don't get it," Mari said. "But tell me, since you do, what's your brilliant plan?"

"Bring me my purse."

"Your plan had better not be cocaine."

"Gross, no."

Mari came back to the side of the tub with Vivienne's Gucci tote.

"Pillbox and wallet, please."

When Mari looked inside the bag, she felt a maternal pang. Vivienne had a leather-bound day planner like the kind executive assistants used to carry, and her purse was as organized as if it were her arsenal of weapons. It contained six lip glosses in shades from pastel pink to fuck-me red, her bedazzled pillbox, and a Louis Vuitton wallet. V swallowed a pill dry, in a practiced way, and lined up objects on the fat lip of the oversized tub: three chips from different Vegas casinos; a canceled Amex black card that V carried to look like she could pick up the tab sometimes; a piece of folded paper—at least her sister had a little cash.

"Is that your secret stash?" Mari asked.

V snorted and handed it to her. When Mari opened it up, it was a $2 bill. She turned it over. On the back, in their dad's florid handwriting, was a phone number. Of course Mari knew they were in contact, but this proof of their deeper connection still stung.

"You're gonna call Dad?"

"And have him ask me for a loan? No, thank you." V pulled out several electronic keys. "Guzel gave me a key card for the elevator that accesses the Tower and one for the room next door."

"Guzel?"

"I'm a Vegas regular. The hotel maids can get *anything* and know the best after-hours."

Vivienne still exuded a party girl verve, but she was focused and organized, and Mari realized she was accustomed to bad nights. Mari tried to catch up to where her sister was headed.

"I know bands usually book blocks of rooms for their entourage, so everyone stays close together—for working, partying, and keeping tabs on flight risks. It's one of the band's rooms?"

"Exactly, and everyone leaves tomorrow when the tour kicks off. But that room has been rented through the end of the month for some reason."

"So, someone's staying behind?"

"No one's been using it for a few days. It's a mess, because the 'Do Not Disturb' sign was left on the door, and the maids can't go in—I mean they go in; they just don't touch anything. Anyhow, it's total crazy hoarder alcoholic—papers everywhere, empty liquor bottles, all these stacks of books about the Ramblers. But it's quiet. I go there when I need a break from you."

"I wish I had a magic key."

"What can I say? Tip better. So, I can stay there for a few weeks, no one will notice."

"And then, after that?"

"There's a man in Chicago. He always takes me back. He's not nice. But if I don't make him mad, it can be okay for a few months, maybe longer."

Dante's book had bumped Mari's rate up from the low five figures to the low six figures. It wouldn't go far in LA. But then she thought of Anke, walking out of her fancy life. Mari's fear had kept her dreams as narrow as her focus: on survival. But actually, options abounded.

"Can you last six months?" Mari asked. "If you can give me that long, I can get us a house, maybe not in LA, but one that is ours. No more sociopaths. No more crazy deadlines."

"Six months is a long time."

"Not really, it isn't."

A half hour later, Vivienne was comatose on the bed. Mari hadn't been able to coax her to eat anything, but she had passed out from her pill. Mari was relieved on many levels. She didn't know what to do for her sister, but she felt like she had failed her by not convincing her to go to the police station for a rape kit. And if this guy in Vegas had been her first-choice destination—would her Chicago option be even worse?

Mari was sitting on the couch, trying to get back to business as usual, when the day caught up with her. She was about to leave her sister alone, after a bad drug bender and sexual assault. And sure, V had theoretically agreed to Mari's little plan. But who knew what state V would be in when she woke up? At least she had a free hotel suite as a buffer before Chicago. What V had told her about the room nagged at Mari—it sounded like her work space when she was on a tight deadline, except her liquor bottles were dirty mugs and empty almond butter jars. She needed to check it out. Mari led with caution, but when the stakes were high, she was fearless—it was the combination of these two qualities that had gotten her this far as a ghost.

As Mari was leaving her room, her phone rang: Sigrid. She darted into the hall to answer, feeling a burn along her nerve endings, as if Sigrid knew what she was about to do.

"You will fly with us on the jet. Please meet us at the hotel's private entrance at five p.m."

"I'll be there. Thanks again, Sigrid. This will be a big help for Dante's book."

"That is what we all want," Sigrid said. "To help Dante's book."

Mari sighed with relief as she hung up. Maybe she had been reading too much into her earlier conversation with Sigrid. It wasn't just her clients who became stressed out during the penning of a memoir—she had seen managers freak, too. There was so much pressure to get it just right. And for nonwriters, it was a tremendous leap of faith to put the job in a ghost's hands.

V hadn't been exaggerating: The room was a mess. Heaps of clothes on the floor. Piles of papers covering every inch of the couch. Mari lifted a stack, holding them in her lap so she could sit down. Looking at the top page, Mari saw a Word doc printout of a manuscript. Her eye caught on Dante's name. Of course, this must have been the other ghostwriter's room. Sigrid had said they'd continued to rent it for him, as a sign of good faith, in case he came back.

Mari flipped pages as fast as she could. Why had Sigrid lied and said there were no files when they had been sitting here all along? Mari thought of how closely the band's entourage worked together; if they were files Sigrid didn't want anyone to see, this was a safe place.

Next to the stack of manuscript pages was a manila envelope with a return address in Flagstaff. Mari opened it and found a note, addressed to Axel, thanking him for visiting a lonely old widow in her twilight years, and signed by Nancy, Mal's final girlfriend. Apparently, during his time at her house, Axel had somehow gotten her to send him Mal's estate paperwork.

Beneath the will was a piece of paper, torn at a diagonal. A vertical line of phrases was written in black marker: "On the Lash," "A Change Is Gonna Come," "Portrait of the Artist," clearly the set list from the band's Hollywood Bowl show, which Mari had memorized. In the far right corner was a scrawled note in a large childlike script: "Please forgive me. It is not my choice, but how can I escape my fate? For him who is in disgrace and danger, the hour of death draws near. You will both be better off in the end. Lovingly, Mal."

Yes, it was formal and pretentious for a love note—even for a suicide note. But that was so Mal. Mari laughed, giddy with her triumph.

She knew it was true because she knew Mal so well, just like she knew Anke and Dante. So well that she had kept the project no one had really thought she could handle, and also she had cracked the case no one else *ever* had. Well, except for the other writer—but where was he? Not about to churn out a bestseller like she was.

Her pride in her accomplishment was so strong, and so unexpected, it was a kind of high. It was also a moot point. Mari wasn't sure if she could write about this revelation, or even admit she had found it. Clearly the first writer had not been a fuckup. He had been very, very skilled at his job, and what had happened to him? A dank fog of fear settled in her gut.

Mari called Ezra on his cell. He picked up right away.

"Dude, why haven't you been answering my calls?"

"I'll explain everything. But I need help ASAP—you went to law school, right?"

"Yeah, what's up?" She was grateful that he would still hear her out, even now.

"Long story—but I just stumbled into the first writer's hotel room. They've been saying he didn't leave any files, but they're all here, including Mal's suicide note. And his will."

"Are you serious? What are you even telling me right now?"

"I know, dude. It's a lot, but we've got to focus. I don't have long in here."

"Hey, look at you, number one ghost! Does anyone know where you are?"

"No, so I'm not sure I can use the note. I took a picture just in case."

"Okay, okay, let me think, maybe not, but the will, that should be in the public record, no matter how the rest of the band feels about it coming back into the light now. What does it say?"

The typeset was hard to make out in places—the document was fifty years old.

"Because Anke and Mal were married when he died, Anke received everything, except for a stipend for Mal's parents."

There was no mention of Anke and Mal's unborn child, which Mari didn't bring up. There were no other beneficiaries, so as Jack had suggested, Mal's acknowledged children hadn't gotten anything when Mal died. When Anke passed away, maybe they would try for her estate. Maybe not. Ody would get whatever Anke gave him in her will, so from a financial perspective at least, his paternity would be a moot point.

"Wow, does that make Anke look like a suspect or what?"

"I don't know. The estate didn't include much—one country manor outside of London, one Rolls-Royce, a few rare instruments, a life insurance policy purchased earlier that year, and the most valuable assets: Mal's share of the band's trademark, plus publishing on twenty-two songs he had cowritten, all of which remained classics, and a few of which were essentially standards."

"Even one-fifth of the money from those had to be significant," Ezra said. "What else?"

Mari reached the final two documents—the signature pages. It hit her like a double espresso: The will had been signed August 5, 1969—two days before Mal died—with Sigrid Wagner as witness and executor. Anke had told her Sigrid had handled the estate, but Mari hadn't understood the significance. And then she thought of the bootleg recording of band practice. Jack had called out for Sigrid to fetch a cab for his furious wife, partway through rehearsal, but she had left the room without anyone noticing. So, Sigrid had an alibi, but only until midnight. Mal's body had been found at one a.m. It wasn't much time, but it was enough. Even if he had stumbled out to the pool, intent on killing himself, he might not have gone through with it. But what if he had encountered Sigrid, and she had made him take that swim?

"Anything else, dude?" Ezra said. "You're not protecting Anke, are you?"

"Of course not," Mari said. "It's all a little intense, but I've got it! I'm having dinner at Dante's house in Joshua Tree tonight. And meeting with Anke tomorrow. I'll call you after."

"Hang on—what happened to the other writer? Don't go anywhere until we know more."

"Don't worry, dude, the other writer cracked. It's Vegas. He's probably been playing poker for seventy-two hours. Or he had a vision and wandered out into the desert. I'll call you tomorrow!"

"All right, but just in case, I'm calling his agent. We came up at the same agency."

Mari had kept her voice bright for Ezra, but she was shivering. She knew the most intimate moments of this story so well it was as if she had lived them. Back at the house in Los Angeles, Anke was lying on her side, staring at the wall, crying. Mal was floating, angelic in death, his blond hair haloing him. Sigrid was standing in the water, pressing his head under. Or poisoning him with words, pushing him to do it. Deep down, Mari knew it was some version of the truth.

Hands shaking, she took photos of the will documents, making sure to get a good clear shot of the signature page and Mal's possible suicide note. It contained the exact language of Anke's I Ching prediction, which she claimed not to have told him. It said "he didn't have a choice." Both Anke and Dante had alluded to how broken Mal's mind was at the end. As frustrated as they were, they had coddled him, trying to hold him together. Anke had drugged him, not confronted him. What if Sigrid hadn't held his head under, but had filled it with black tar that made him do it? Had stood by the side of the pool so he had no exit, no escape, no help?

That might account for one mystery. But what about the first writer? If V's hotel source could be trusted, he hadn't disappeared until a few days ago. What if Sigrid had been fucking with his head, too, but had waited to get rid of him until Mari had appeared as the possible next writer? Mari felt much as she did when she was working on an early draft of a manuscript, identifying each individual thread of the story, which obviously wove together, only the question was where and why. She sat down at the desk. On top of Axel's computer was a smartphone.

She checked her own phone and saw she had half an hour before she had to meet Sigrid. This wasn't some movie where she could magically deduce the password of a person she had never met. And besides, even before she had been entrusted with the kind of pop culture secrets millions of people wanted to know, she and Ezra had never written anything sensitive down in an email or text, unless they wanted to create a paper trail of a celebrity's bad behavior for potential contract disputes. She doubted there was anything on Axel's devices to find. She had better use her time as efficiently as possible. Just in case these documents disappeared, she took shots of the manuscript pages, too. And then a few pictures of the room. She sent everything to Ezra. At the last minute, though, she didn't include the signature page of Mal's will. She didn't know what Sigrid had done, but she knew she would have to confront her.

Mari was surprised when Ezra called her a few minutes after the last photos had gone through. "Okay, you cannot let on that you know this," he said, devoid of his usual playfulness.

"Dude, at this point, I'm holding so many secrets, I'm not saying anything to anyone."

"Good. Axel is in rehab. That's why he doesn't have his phone. Obviously his agent doesn't want it getting out in the industry so he can still get work. Losing Dante's book was bad enough. He doesn't have health insurance, so Sigrid had the band take care of it as his kill fee."

"Wow, I can't believe they fucked him up that bad in a few months."

"Worse than that. He was sober for ten years before this job. His agent thinks maybe he wanted to seem cool to Dante—who wouldn't, right? But the coke is what unraveled him."

"Dante is Dionysian, but he doesn't do coke."

"Exactly. But some of the guys in the entourage do. I guess they were staying on the same floor as him. That's when Axel crossed the line and Sigrid called his agent. Somehow she knew about this clause in Axel's custody agreement for his daughter—he had to stay sober."

"Wow. She's good."

"Yeah, good at being evil."

"Depends on your perspective. She's taking care of her band, everyone else be damned. I think she felt threatened by Axel because he didn't just buy her official version of events. Better to push him out and start over with me. On such a tight deadline, she probably figured I wouldn't have time to step out of line and do any digging of my own."

"So, you're seeing her tonight, but Dante's going to be there, right?"

"Yeah, we're having dinner at his house in JT with his whole family."

"Okay, you don't know any of this. Especially not about the will or about Axel. Just get out of there without making Sigrid suspicious, and we'll sort it all out when you're safe in LA."

As Mari put on her lip gloss and Fracas—armor for the hours ahead— she practiced a smile in the mirror. It looked fake as hell, but hopefully, no one would be looking that hard. Her phone buzzed. Dante's driver was waiting for her. She was scared, but she was going to pull this off.

FIFTEENTH:
SURVIVE

There is an art to finessing a conversation into areas where people prefer not to go. There is a reward, too, as their revelations are more authentic because of their freshness, never having been shared before. This is one of the most valuable skill sets for a ghost—being able to get close enough to your clients to help them find the meaning in their lives, and then to bring it to their readers, who are seeking meaning of their own. Do this without leaving any sign of your own fingerprints on the material, and you will prevail.

The flight attendant standing before Mari was prettier than many models and wearing a fitted skirt and sheer silk blouse. She extended a tray, holding a single cobweb-thin flute.

"No, thank you," Mari said. "I'll wait until everyone boards."

"As you like." The woman smiled, retreating.

Mari pulled out her laptop and recorder so everything would appear normal to Dante and Sigrid. She couldn't take her eyes off the cabin door. She didn't know how she was going to hold it together. Quickly reading her list of remaining questions, she decided she'd assess his mood and ask him about either his father's passing the previous year or, for a lighter tack, his collaboration with Stetson on a signature hat. It seemed impossible to look Sigrid in the eye. Mari forced herself to breathe.

Sigrid glided into view as she climbed aboard the jet. As Sigrid approached, Mari watched the iron-bar rigor of her spine. Feeling her nerves prickle, she tried to forget her suspicions, as if Sigrid would be able to read them on her face. Mari used her childhood acting skills—put the other person at ease, have no feelings of your own. She plastered on a cool smile.

Sigrid sat down across from Mari, but still, Dante didn't appear. The flight attendant closed the door. Mari wouldn't give Sigrid the satisfaction of asking where he was.

"Diana," Sigrid said, turning to the flight attendant, "bring us some champagne."

In a flash, the woman was at their elbow, tray extended, with two flutes of bubbly. Mari's nerves sparked. Sigrid was flashing her usual smile. Having spent the past week immersed in a story about a secret drugging, and the past hour in the room of a writer who had been blackmailed into rehab, she felt suspicion was warranted. But when Sigrid reached for a glass, Mari couldn't see a way to refuse. She focused on keeping it together while taking a small sip.

"Thank you," Mari said to the woman. She nodded to Sigrid. Hopefully, the champagne would soothe her and help her to play along.

"Dante sends his regards," Sigrid said. "He had a last-minute band meeting. The plane will fly back and retrieve him."

Mari nodded, although this made no sense. If there was a band meeting, why wasn't Sigrid there? And why would they fly Mari on ahead by herself? Her mouth went dry.

Sigrid reached into her giant Chanel bag, and Mari's heart stuttered. But Sigrid only pulled out a stack of manila files.

"Since you have told me how you are a perfectionist, I brought you Dante's press photos you did not yet look through. I know you will want to see each and every one."

Again, it felt like Sigrid was fucking with her, but she couldn't see why. Rather than thwarting her or wasting her time, Sigrid should have wanted to help Mari succeed at her job—so Dante's book would not only be a bestseller but also well reviewed. Mari took the folders, but she didn't open them. She must keep pushing, as long as she still had access.

"Since this is our last day, I was hoping you could answer—"

"No, I am sorry, I cannot," Sigrid said. "I have important work to finish. As do you."

The flight attendant reminded them to turn off their cell phones, and then she took her seat, and Mari was alone with Sigrid. The plane rose into the air, and Mari sipped her champagne, trying to pace herself. But Mari had never been good at moderation—that's why she was such a stellar ghost, her obsessiveness, her ability to forgo her own comfort. After the day she'd had, Mari was on the edge of panic. She accepted another glass from the flight attendant. As she drank it, she pretended to look at the press photos while trying to get inside Sigrid's mind. What made people do their worst? She thought about her own transgressions of the past week. Fear.

Flipping her perspective, Mari wondered how scared Sigrid had been when Anke had almost lost her place with the band and Sigrid had nearly been sent back to East Germany. And then, once Sigrid had done the criminal, or at least the hateful, certain she had earned her safety, how it had felt to have Anke leave her behind. Or maybe this was Mari's romantic projection. She considered what V had said about the cruelty of women. How much more at ease Sigrid seemed around the band without the wives. Sigrid had done well for herself after Mal died, on her own, whether she had orchestrated his death or just Anke's incorrect flight. But it had to be the darker version of the story, or else the first writer would still be here instead of Mari, right?

As hard as Mari had been pushing for the truth, she hadn't believed she would uncover a suicide, let alone a murder and blackmail. She had no idea what to do. What did Dante know of all this, and how could it ever appear in his book? Even if she told Anke everything— her trip to Vegas, her attempt to help her sister—she doubted Anke trusted her enough to let her make use of this material in *her* book. Mari needed to tell Ezra *everything*, but there was no time now.

When Sigrid dozed off, Mari was so wound up, she accepted a third glass of champagne. Nervous as Mari was, the jet was luxurious, the service impeccable. She had said no to herself every day for years, forcing herself to sit, endlessly, at her computer. It felt so good to say yes. Hopefully, a light buzz would ease her approach to the obstacle course of dinner.

The little plane bumped down in Palm Springs, and Mari drained the last of her glass, to avoid letting the liquid spill. She had trouble putting the glass down on its base, and she could barely keep her eyes open. It felt like she'd had three bottles of champagne, not three thin flutes. She should have given herself enough time to grab that double capp before she had left the hotel. She had no idea how she would get through the long night ahead, especially with as little sleep as she'd had. The wine would be abundant, and she would have to pull it together if she was going to seem laid-back and fun—worthy of her inner circle status. Sigrid's eyes remained shut until the plane stopped. Then they popped open, and she looked straight at Mari, who was already smiling in answer to Sigrid's familiar grin. The hair on Mari's arms stood up.

Sigrid left the plane without saying a word. Apparently they were done with niceties. In a way, it was a relief when she wondered if she could even speak coherently. At least she could disappear into the chaotic frivolity of the family dinner. As she stood, her insides shifted in a strange way, like her blood was sand. But she forced herself to act normal. She was glad Sigrid didn't see her smash against the leather seats as she tried to walk down the aisle. Just before the door was a basket of drinks and snacks, and she grabbed a Coke for its jolt of caffeine.

A black Escalade waited on the runway. Sigrid was seated in the back. Deep within Mari, a voice told her to run back onto the plane and insist they return her to Vegas. Or to take a taxi to Anke's house in Palm Springs. But as usual, she silenced her inner protector and did the scary thing to maintain the status quo. Now she had even more at stake—she had made a promise to Vivienne, and she felt responsible for the other writer, not to mention Dante and Anke.

The romance of the wild landscape was revealed in swaths by the sweep of the car's headlights. As they made the right turn onto Highway 62, she and Sigrid locked in cold silence, Mari's thoughts fuzzed into static. The car raced up the long gliding hill to the first town of the high desert, Morongo Valley. They careened up the second hill, to Yucca Valley, where the windswept magic gave way to the generic everywhere of strip malls and fast-food spots.

Mari felt like her neck was a pile of loose rocks as they bounced down a long dirt driveway, no lights visible anywhere. Sigrid remained still. It was a relief when they pulled up to the well-lit house. Mari could ask to turn a spare bedroom into a temporary office, close the door against Sigrid's prying eyes, and sneak a nap before Dante arrived. She felt so tired, her eyes drifted closed. This was unlike her, and it was very bad.

Stumbling out of the van, she was slapped awake by the cold, fresh air. The vast structure was made of white stuccoed adobe that glowed against the dark hills. Mari put on her game face to meet the family, but the hot kitchen was silent.

"The bathroom . . . please?" Mari slurred.

These were the first words she had spoken in an hour, and her throat was silty and parched. Sigrid pointed to a wooden door that was ajar. Mari did her best to walk like a sober person, Sigrid's gaze boring into her back. Mari caught sight of framed photos, which she was sure were incredible cultural artifacts, but she couldn't trust herself to turn her head and look.

It was a relief to be alone. When she was done, she fixed her clothes, shut the lid, and sat down. The gears of her brain were jammed, and she couldn't make her thoughts move. Struggling with her bag's zipper, she found her phone. She had to get out of here. She had come because she believed Dante and his family would be here, and Sigrid continued to think she had Mari fooled. This situation was clearly way more dangerous than making a social gaffe or losing a client. She hadn't been sure what she would do, now that she was so close to the truth of what had happened to Mal. But she could feel Sigrid in the process of forcing her to decide, *now*.

Vivienne was not trustworthy or dependable, especially today. Anke was still evading her, while dangling the prize of her book. Ezra would tell her to flee. Izzy was the only friend Mari had made in a long time. She tried FaceTiming Izzy, but she had no signal. She recorded a short audio text. Before she could talk herself down, she hit send, desperate for an ally, or at least a witness. The bar crawled across her screen, inching toward completion, then got stuck.

Mari slapped her cheeks, ran cold water over her wrists. She could barely keep her eyes open. Hopefully, Dante would arrive soon. But the silence in the house felt spooky and resonant, and she couldn't picture dinner. She opened the old-fashioned casement window. Teetering for balance, she stuck her phone into the night sky. Reaching with her other hand, she hit retry on her text to Izzy and nearly fell over. Her phone caught a bar of service, and after what felt like three days, her message went through. The knots in Mari's stomach loosened.

After several goes at the latch, she managed to open the door. As she did so, an incoming text chimed nearby.

Sigrid stood on the other side, waiting for her.

"Oh, maybe she forgot to tell you. Izzy has a new phone. A new number."

Sigrid held out an iPhone so Mari could see its home screen, featuring a picture of a younger Izzy, singing backup with the band. There was a text notification, from Mari.

"What did you do to Izzy? She's my friend."

"Izzy is smart. She is a survivor. She has told me about your Hercule Poirot game and how you asked her many questions. She will go far. Dante will produce her solo debut for her."

"Ody won't let you hurt me. He'll be here for dinner soon."

"He was called to Palm Springs at the last moment. Anke needed him right away. She never could wait for anything. She always take, take, take."

"You're lying," Mari said. She leaned against the wall, willing herself not to sit. But she could imagine Anke inventing an errand for Ody, too proud to admit her own human need.

"It is for the best. When the secrets show their bones, Ody will get hurt. Lose a father who is dear to him. I have always known, but now you have given me the need to use this intel."

Too late, Mari caught up with what was happening. Whether it was drinking on an empty stomach, being at altitude, running on coffee fumes for days, or something Sigrid had put in her drink, she had let herself fall into a terrible state. And Sigrid was confronting her. Realizing she was way past making a good impression, she opened the Coke and chugged it, forced her shattered molecules back together as much as she could.

"But why would you hurt Dante like that?"

"Yes, it hurts father as much as it hurts son. But it also hurts Anke."

The sugar hit Mari's empty stomach and, psychosomatic or not, she felt a little better.

"You're afraid Anke is going to expose you in her book."

Sigrid gave her a long look. "Anke is not loyal."

"What if I promised she won't?"

"What promise? She fired you."

"You don't know Anke anymore," Mari said.

Sigrid surprised Mari by linking their arms. Mari recoiled at being so close to her, and her dense, spicy Chanel perfume, but she could no longer stand. With a scorpion sting of fear, she realized she hadn't drunk too much. Sigrid did this. Just like she did whatever she did to the other writer. Now Sigrid led her outside, her head lolling on her neck. The cold air helped. But she was too far gone. Mari's eyes closed. Her mind was afraid, but her body felt wrapped in gauze.

"Step down," Sigrid instructed.

Like two separate animals, her mind fought while her body was docile as a child. Mari obliged. Her boots filled with warm water. Her eyes flew open. Sigrid had led her onto the top step of Dante's pool. The water danced with shadows in the low light. Mari fell through time, back to the night Mal died. He was small for a man, and on that night, he'd also been drugged, and suicidal. Sigrid had been young, strong, ruthless. Yes, it was easy to understand how it had happened. Mari whimpered.

"You are certain you are so smart. You think you see everything. Now I believe you see reality. We are eight miles from town. The cell signal is very bad. But there is a house phone. If we call now, the ambulance will arrive to pump your stomach. It is embarrassing for you, to have taken barbiturates and champagne for your nerves on the flight. But you live. Or you are one more accidental drowning. One more casualty. One more writer who goes off the rails. Jack is good. Dante is good. The band is good. We go on. Enjoy our lives. Make money. You do not."

Sigrid forced Mari to step down again, up to her ankles.

"It's not like you can just"—Mari put all of her effort into getting out these few words—"have another accidental drowning, lose another writer, and no one suspects."

"It is rock 'n' roll," Sigrid said. "At the most rarefied level, where only the few can go. Accidents happen all the time. Especially to the weak. Who can't keep their heads together. Who do not belong here. Like Mal. Like the first writer. Like you. The story writes itself. You are inexperienced, under too much pressure. You are scared, you overindulge, you die."

It sounded plausible, even to Mari. Sigrid gripped Mari's arm and continued talking, fast and hot, with the intensity of someone who had not been free to speak before.

"You, of all people, should understand, Mari. Always have to earn your place. Always have to be useful. Not beautiful. Not charming. Not talented. You must do whatever it takes to be invited to stay. Don't you dare judge me for something you would do yourself, in a heartbeat. And now, you are how old? Thirty-five? Forty? Think how tired you are. Now, imagine to be seventy. You have given away your whole life. You have nowhere. I am being more than fair, because Dante likes you, because now he has said he will write with no one but you. Your talent as a ghost could save you. But you will have to play by my rules. It is time to decide."

Mari's eyes were slits, but she understood Sigrid as she hadn't before. There was nothing else for Sigrid—this was her whole life, had been for a long time. Mari comprehended everything, slow as her brain was working. If Mal had dumped Anke, she and Sigrid were both out. Through Anke's influence, Sigrid had been put in charge of Mal's estate. She had gotten the will signed. Then he fired her. Started acting crazy. Threatened her. The life insurance would be null if he committed suicide. So, she had made it look accidental, providing Anke with money, igniting the spark between Anke and Dante, securing Anke's position with the band and therefore her own. Much more valuable than money to someone with nowhere else to go.

Sigrid made her focus, her fingernails like knives against Mari's skin.

"Times have changed, Sigrid," Mari said. "Crimes are much easier to detect. I was in Axel's room—I saw the documents. I saw Mal's note. I know he didn't just have a meltdown."

"So you have broken and entered into this room that is not yours, and yet you have no papers, no proof," Sigrid said. "I have lots of friends in the police, from all these years, being a fixer for the band, as you want to label me. My friend in the police department in Las Vegas would want to question you—I mean, how else would you get an important job like this? Your résumé is not so good. This friend, he called me late last night. Told me about a young woman he booked. Assault. Theft. *Solicitation.* You see, I had asked him to run a check on Dante's writer, before we hired her. And he noticed this young woman has the same last name as Dante's ghost. He knows this could be very embarrassing for Dante, for the band."

"Vivienne? But she didn't hurt anyone. She got thrown out of a car by her date."

"Maybe you are not so good at learning the truth after all," Sigrid said. "When I bail her out this morning, which, let me say, not just anyone can do on a Sunday, I told her what her story is. If she wants to keep from hurting you. If she wants to make it all go away. This is not her first arrest for solicitation, as you must have known. She could have done real time."

Of course, how else did she think V got by? She didn't want to see it, so she didn't look.

"Oh," Mari said, all her clever words used up.

Mari's sleepy mind drifted to Anke, alone, smoking, holding a vigil for her drowned men; Vivienne, alone, in the back of a police car the night before, all her pretty survival tools smashed and ruined; Mari, right here and now, alone, about to lose it all. But she hadn't lost yet.

"Do you know what most prostitutes go down for?" Mari forced her voice to be steady. "Tax evasion. I wrote a book with an escort, and I'm sure her accountant can help V get ahead of any financial liability she might face. What's more concerning is your suggestion of local law enforcement corruption. When V goes before the judge to clear all this up, I'm sure he'll want to know just how she got bailed out on a Sunday and by whom—" Her eyes closed like mousetraps.

SIXTEENTH:
LISTEN

There is one aspect of ghostwriting you can't fake, and you can't learn. You either have it or you don't. This is the capacity to listen like your life depends on it. Such next-level ability to focus on others can't be taught because it's usually honed while surviving trauma. You see, there's something about fame that changes most people. Even while surrounded by love and adoration, they can sniff out those who might betray them by caring more about something else. A ghost never will. There you have it, the ingredients for a fruitful collaboration: The codependent, type A ghost idolizes the star, no matter how she behaves, for as long as it takes. Offer a client this level of self-abnegation, and you've got the job. Only problem is most people can't. It's unnatural, uncomfortable, probably unhealthy. But not for a true ghost. For a true ghost, it's fuel.

First, there was blackness and shattering pain—a sharp hammering within her head, like someone had taken an axe to the inside of her skull. There was the taste of plastic and bile. The burn at the back of her throat like she had swallowed a lit cigarette. She couldn't breathe. Couldn't swallow. She groaned, pushed out, hit something soft on something hard: an arm.

"Relax, Mari," a male voice said. "There is a tube down your throat.

We had to get everything out of you. When I pull, it will feel weird, maybe hurt. But it will be over fast."

Before he had finished warning her, he was removing the tube. Mari tried to roll onto her side, curl into a ball, away from the prying light, the feeling of being watched, of being ashamed.

"Don't move, pet," Dante said.

Even with her eyes closed, his voice was his.

"Your blood pressure is very low," the EMT said. "We've started an IV with fluids. You're going to have the headache to end all head-aches tomorrow. But you'll live."

The full horror of her last moments with Sigrid flashed back to Mari, and her eyes popped open. She remembered: Vivienne. She had let V in, and it had been her undoing. Or it had saved her. As scuzzed as her brain was, Mari tried to anticipate Sigrid's next move.

"We couldn't get an ambulance out here," the EMT said. "So, we came in my truck. We recommend you get admitted, just for the night, to be monitored."

"I don't have health insurance," Mari said.

"Fucking America," Dante said. "Bloody hell. They sail across the Atlantic and turn into a bunch of savages. Mari, if it would feel safer, I'll take care of it. Just say the word, luv."

Mari pictured the sterile room, the smell of bleach, the sound of a canned laugh track from a TV down the hall, the loneliness of lying there without anyone knowing, or caring, or being on their way to visit. She caught Dante's smoke-shop scent, felt his Zen calm, even under these radical circumstances. Mari didn't want to leave his side. She had managed to hold on to this fucking job. She had managed to hold on to her life. She was going to stay until the end, whatever it would bring. Without opening her eyes, she shook her head: *No.*

Mari was trying to sit up amid the soft cushions of the kitchen's window seat. Dante had deposited her there with a mug of strong tea—her hand was shaking, but she forced down a few sips. She was already embarrassed, and she was trying to conjure her wits. Two housekeepers rushed to and fro, peeling potatoes, icing mineral water, pulling everything together with well-practiced synchronicity. Mari latched onto more bits of the scene as her focus began to return.

Fiona was basting an enormous rack of lamb, in a gorgeous copper roasting pan. Fiona's persimmon silk blouse was unsplattered and sliding off her shoulder in an alluring way. She was barefoot and expertly dodging three dogs and her nine-year-old son—Basel—who was debuting his new penny whistle tune for his dad's departure. The room smelled of hot fat and peppery rosemary, and Joni Mitchell was singing about a free man in Paris. Mari felt the nettle sting of tears. Some of it was the trauma of what she'd been through, and her shame at having Dante see her that wrecked, even if had been Sigrid's doing, not her own; he didn't know that, and she couldn't explain it to him. Mostly, though, it was the ache of wanting.

She had coveted many things as a ghost, usually the surprising luxury items—the LV flip-flops, the Hermès sweatpants, the Montblanc pen on the desk of a client who wrote in emojis. This was different. This was a whole life she'd never had a chance for, first because of her dad's inability to hold it together and keep his concert-promotions gig, which had been his entrée to this world. And then because of what had been required of her to survive, lashing herself to her computer. Then she thought of Anke, sixty miles away. She had lived more than most, and still, she had ended up alone. But that wasn't true, was it? She had her own fortress, a devoted son, an ex who sent flowers to acknowledge a book that could embarrass him. No one was immune to the diminishment of age—except for maybe the band—but it meant something, daring to create in your lifetime, not just a mountain of books but a home, a clan, a life.

Mari forced herself to smile, even if she couldn't quite muster engaged, amused, or included. Dante's two daughters from his second marriage were telling Fiona the story of their photo shoot in the desert that day for *Vogue*. One had a kaftan line; the other made hand-poured, chakra-clearing candles. They were so gorgeous, and intimidating, but the truth was, they seemed nice. All of Dante's kids did. Mari felt even more left out, like she had some defect in her DNA, her dad's hungry blood in her veins, that had made all of this impossible for her. At least Sigrid was leaving her alone, under the guise of taking care of some last-minute tour details, Mari figured. But it was weird that she hadn't shown her face once since Mari had been revived.

Dante radiated goodwill down the table, adorned with eucalyptus branches, pomegranates, and off-white beeswax candles. Mari was unsure what to do when Dante lifted his hands. With a twinkle in his eye, Dante turned to Mari, who had been seated on his left.

"You probably weren't expecting this from an old hippie Neanderthal like me, but I always say grace when we're together as a family," he said.

As everyone joined hands, Mari nodded, very aware of holding Dante Ashcombe's hand.

"Thank you, first and foremost, to my lovely, blushing bride, Fiona," he began, "for preparing this beautiful feast, and for putting up with me. Thank you to my children for being here tonight to break bread with me before I embark on the road. It is a solace to these old bones. Thank you to my right hand, Sigrid, who keeps the spaceships running on time. And to my left hand, Mari, who has been trusted with the greatest asset of all—my story, my legacy. Thank you, always, to the powers that be for the grace in our lives, and the food before us. May we all go forward from this table in good health, especially those of us who have had a blustery evening."

Dante squeezed Mari's hand. His last words managed to seem like a kind gesture, not a joke or judgment. Mari was mortified to feel a single tear trickle down and streak her makeup. With both hands clasped by those on either side of her, she couldn't do anything about it. So, she let it be. When she turned to Dante to acknowledge his mention, he seemed touched. She figured it was far from the worst he had seen of her. She was desperate to ask about Sigrid, who was absent from the dinner table, but she decided to follow his lead and lean into the festivities.

Then, before he could make her think he was a different person than she had come to know, instead of saying "Amen," Dante called out a robust "Salut!"

It was quite the finale for Dante's memoir—dogs running in and out, chewing lamb bones under the table, Dante and Fiona laughing as they finished each other's sentences, young Basel performing his triumphant concert as the sticky toffee pudding was served.

Mari felt like a corpse. All she wanted to do was lie down, even though she should force herself to scratch out a few notes before she forgot the details, which would make the book all the more vivid. But the group seemed determined to sit and talk over sherries. Mari's teapot had been refilled, and she was coming back to the world.

"The bonfire!" Dante called out.

Everyone stood and began to search for their wraps. Mari shook her head to clear it. She stumbled, caught herself. The others were across the room, helping Basel into his suede jacket, with fringe, of course. Only Dante noticed. Not that he seemed to mind. Her "accidental" overdose had been attributed to Dionysian abandon, and it had seemed to make him like her more. But she didn't think she could force herself to stay awake by a bonfire, and she still had an intense meeting with Anke in the morning. She had been worrying over her options, and her best plan seemed to be asking Anke if she could stay over, to be available first thing. The thought of writing seemed impossible, but nothing that had happened tonight had extended her deadlines.

"Dante," she said, her voice croaky. He waved the others ahead and bent to hear her. "I appreciate your hospitality, but I've had quite a night. Anke expects me to meet with her tomorrow. Could your driver please take me to Palm Springs?"

He gave her a long look, reading between the lines, although she wasn't sure how much.

"This is a good plan, Little Marie," he said. "I'll ride with you."

"No, no, I couldn't take you away—"

"I insist," he said. "Let's go and explain to Fiona."

Gathering all her reserves of strength, Mari made her most gallant possible exit, thanking Fiona for dinner, saying good night to the children. Finally, she surveyed the whole circle, afraid, but looking for Sigrid. Mari hoped she would never have to see her again, but she felt more unsettled by her absence, unsure if she should tell Dante what had happened. Meanwhile, Dante was kissing his wife's mouth and explaining he would accompany Mari back to the Palm Springs airport so they could have a final hour together for his book.

"Don't work too hard, my darling," Fiona said.

"Don't fall asleep before I get back," he replied, growling in her direction.

Mari had to yank herself away from the happy family and the fire, back into the silent house. But she was the ghost who always had more work to do. Dante stopped off in the kitchen. He trickled four Advil into Mari's palm, handed her a bottle of water, then held the door for her.

Mari felt so woozy, she had to close her eyes against the fast-food neon as they got stuck at traffic lights in Yucca Valley, on their way to Palm Springs. The inside of the Escalade was like a rocking cradle. She was swaddled in a butter-soft cashmere blanket and didn't want the ride to end. She had survived, but for what? The thought of going back to her thirteen-year-old Honda sedan with the sun-rotted seats and the grimy windows, driving to Trader Joe's for deadline treats, chaining herself to her computer in a cheap Airbnb, made her want to cry. And she did.

Next to her, Dante shifted. His presence had a comforting weight, like he'd keep the coyotes at bay. He was a good dad. It must be nice for his kids. She could feel him turning toward her in the darkness. Now that they were traveling down Highway 62, back onto the flat plains where Palm Springs nestled against the mountains, few headlights illuminated his face.

"Don't cry, Little Marie," he said. "You just overindulged is all. I've been there—you know I have. Nothing to be ashamed of, is it?"

She chewed on his words for a long time. She was bone-tired but mostly sober. She had been so confident in Vegas, even back at his house. She had been wrong. Sigrid had let her be, maybe because of Dante's belief in her, maybe because she wasn't as much of a real threat as the first writer, Axel, had been, but she was in over her head. The right thing was to admit it.

"It was foolish of me to think I could write your memoir when I have so little experience. Your book will be read for generations. You need a writer who is stronger than I am."

In the darkness, Mari heard Dante flip open his lighter. Leaning forward into its glow, he looked his age—older, even—but also beatific. He cracked his window and exhaled through it.

"Why am I writing this book?"

"Well, celebrities write books for three reasons: money, acclaim, or for a comeback or branding pivot—it's one of the surefire ways to get on morning TV."

"Do you think I give a rat's tit about drinking coffee with some poor old gal they've got Botoxed to the high heavens? Why am *I* writing this book? Not *celebrities*. Me."

Mari studied what she could of his profile, rising to meet his question, which demanded the use of her skills and put her back on solid ground. She considered what she had learned of Dante—not the facts and figures, but the essence of who he was, which she was now more fluent in than Fiona, Sigrid, or Anke. She had always presented that being a ghostwriter was only a job, and she did it for money, access, and praise. She had pretended her unconditional love was an act, a trick she used to gain deeper intimacy. But the truth was, in rare cases like this, she underwent the alchemy of understanding and did become them. It was a gift she treasured. She knew Dante better than he knew himself, and like a mother, she felt deep tenderness toward him.

"No one knows you. Jack can't be bothered. Your fans want the pirate Dante of their workaday fantasy. Maybe your wife and kids even see the caricature. Sigrid knows you, but you pay her. The one person who ever came close was Anke. You gave her to Jack, afraid if you didn't, you would lose the band, lose everything. You sold out your love. You've spent decades looking for that feeling again. But it's not something you can buy. Or will. Or conjure. You would like to be known again by one person before you die. In the process of writing this book, you've been surprised to find that I do know you. But really, you're talking to Anke. To try to apologize, maybe explain. If millions of other people get to know you, too, well, all right."

Dante was silent, and Mari wondered if, after everything, this would be the moment when she had gone too far. But she was too weary to act anymore.

"Do you have your little doodad?" he asked, not sounding the least offended.

Soon her recorder's red light was visible, glowing, an echo to his cigarette ember.

"Was it your dad or your mom?" he asked.

"My dad." She didn't have to know what he was asking to know the answer.

"Me, too. I know my memory is shit, but the stuff from when I was little, it seems to get more vivid. My dad, he was fickle, like the weather in April. To get even the tiniest drop of goodwill out of him, you had to listen like the dickens. It was the one way to avoid getting hit. It was the way, maybe, just maybe, once or twice a year, when you least expected, to connect—to be allowed to light his smoke or bring him a fresh can of lager, to be the recipient of a song or a joke. It's brutal to live like that as a kid—kids are supposed to just *be*, not always *try* to be. But when you grow up, and you know how to listen like that, it's a superpower. A sixth sense."

"My dad drank anything that was on the house," she said. "His thing was casinos. Cards. Horses. Gambling. I saw him every few years, and when I did, it was clear he didn't understand why he was there—what was the spread on spending time with a kid? There was none. No profit. No gain. So, what's the point? I tried to listen for just the right thing to say, to be perfect. I developed my perception into my superpower. And now my dad is the only person who remains immune to my skills."

"You're writing my book, Mari. Don't sell Anke out. Or me. But I want you to use your superpower to write what you see, speak from my heart. Tell the truth, like you just had the courage to do. I don't do no. As you are aware. And these really are the Last Days of the Midnight Ramblers. I suppose we carried the day over poor old Syd, but we're not immortal, none of us."

"I respect that, but it wouldn't be fair."

"What's fair to you? Where are you in all this? My book could make you. Don't you think it's time for you to be made, for your life to get a dollop easier?"

No, the little voice inside Mari said. That was the problem and the solution. It was never her time. Which was why she was so good at her job. Which was why she was trying to make the leap to a new life now. But it didn't come easy to her. These were the moments in a person's destiny when they either took the risk and thrived—or wilted and failed. She was on the cusp.

"I was lucky, the way it happened to me," he said. "I mean, international rock star at nineteen, pretty much the definition of blessed, innit? But also, I wasn't old enough to be scared, or to understand what was happening, or how it could all go away anytime. It's harder when we get older. We've seen more bad shit. We know more."

"Yeah," she said.

"You know the best thing about living your life behind a mask?"

"Behind it, you're free."

"Righto. People envy me because I'm rich. It's all they know to dream. They think I'm smoking joints for breakfast, swimming in my infinity pool, snogging my brains out."

"Aren't you?"

They laughed.

"I jest," she said. "I've seen the twelve-hour workdays. The band practices that go past midnight. The press calls snuck in between the meetings, recording sessions, and songwriting."

"I'm not complaining. I could do less. But it keeps the blood pumping. And while I'm doing all this, and dancing for the nice people, I'm free. Everyone stopped thinking to look behind the mask, years ago. Back here, I can observe. Feel. Think. Read. Love. Give someone a chance because I know she deserves it."

Mari had been so consumed with the illusion that she was controlling everything, she had forgotten the others around her might actually get to know her behind her own mask, maybe even be moved to do something on her behalf. For once, the surprise was the good kind.

"Thank you," she said.

"Turn off your doodad," he said. "This is not for the book. We never speak of it again."

She thought about pretending to hit stop, hiding the red light with her thumb, but she was in too deep to consider only herself anymore. She nodded, even though he couldn't see it.

"We must do what we can to help Anke," he said.

"That's why I came to Vegas, but I don't even know if she'll let me be her writer."

"Let me tell you something, luv," he said, giving her hand an affectionate tap. "No one *let* me and Jack and Mal be rock stars. No one will let you do nothing, neither. You are Anke's writer, just as you are my writer. I know it's unconventional. But who's going to say no to me?"

"Anke?"

He snorted with laughter, and she joined in, relieved.

"Under normal circumstances," he said. "But there is too much at stake. In many ways her book is even more important than mine—and it takes a lot for me to play second fiddle, you know. Truth is, I used to suspect her. I'd lie awake at night and wonder if I'd been caught in the web of a black widow. But that was when she was just a fantasy I'd had for a long time. Then I got to know her. She never did anything for a farthing in her life. Anke acted, only, out of love. Even those Mandrax, that was love. If you could have seen Mal, it was horrible, like something out of Dante's *Inferno*, his brilliant mind an instrument of torture. I think, in a way, he was begging her to end it all. But that is poetry, not something most people would understand, unless it is written just so, and Anke can make peace with it. She can be very stubborn. We must help her."

"I agree. But will she let—"

"Tsk-tsk, try again."

"She will let me."

"Yes, and you must trust that when she does, you will find the right words. I do."

"And Sigrid?" she asked.

"Called the EMT for you and waited for them to arrive, even

though it almost caused her to miss her flight from Palm Springs to LA, in order to fly back to Germany."

"But your tour—"

"Her mother is dying. She must be there."

"Dante, I know what she did," Mari said.

"Do you, Little Marie? When we have spoken of the fixer, we have talked of what they do for those of us on top, to keep us at that level. We haven't talked about how they also work on behalf of those who can't handle it at the top, who need an exit fashioned for them."

"Sure, those who can't handle it because she poisoned their minds, maybe worse."

"Mal's mind was poisoned. Axel's mind was poisoned. Sigrid's mind was poisoned, after a fashion. Yours was not," Dante said. "Not everyone belongs at the top. They may end up there briefly, but for some, it doesn't last."

"That's pretty cynical. And you're flattering me."

"I'm respecting you enough to tell you the truth, which I think you already know."

"Are you sure you know the whole truth about Sigrid?"

"After how she behaved with Axel, we had decided it was time for her to retire," Dante said. "Don't you dare quote me: but we're all too old for this. The plan had been put into place by management, but she was going to stay in the States long enough to help us launch the tour. I never thought you were in danger, or I wouldn't have let her get so close to you. Tonight, it became clear she wasn't going to go quietly, and so, she needed to go—immediately."

"And what of the truth Anke writes in her book?"

"That is Anke's book. Anke's truth."

"Really?"

"I trust you, Little Marie. We will talk more of this as you are writing, when Axel has come home from rehab and seen his daughter. He will get a tribute in my book. Would you really see Sigrid in prison?

For doing her job well? Let her be. It's not even an early retirement. She's seventy. But she has been made to leave the road, and so, she is paying in her way."

"Retirement is worse than death for her," Mari said.

"Yes, you and Sigrid understand each other." Dante grinned. "She always liked you. And I have always understood why."

Mari flushed with emotion. It was almost too much. But she found she could bear it, just.

SEVENTEENTH:
SAFEGUARD

*Being a skilled ghost means being good, not just at writing, but also at
managing people and their confessions. Sometimes it means being a fixer—
getting ahead of a potentially damaging revelation and massaging or delet-
ing it. At first, you feel guilty, as if you are thwarting the public record. But
it doesn't take long for you to see the logic at play. A memoir isn't meant to
be a litany of every sordid act ever committed; it is meant to have an arc
that can inspire as much as entertain. Sometimes too much badness will
ruin the potential of its gift.*

Twenty minutes later, as the Escalade pulled into Anke's driveway,
illuminating the giant *A* on the gate, Mari started to laugh. She
was shattered, barely sober, a little unhinged.

"What's the punch line, luv?"

"I assumed the *A* was for 'Anke,' but of course it's for 'Ashcombe.'
Dante Ashcombe."

"I bought this house first, but when I got the place in JT, I never came
here. Too many polo shirts. I like my desert a little wilder. But it was
good for Anke. And for Ody when he was a wee lad. I always told her
to spread out, build herself a yoga studio, put in a proper pool, but she
liked that little cement box. You can take the girl out of Germany—"

The driver exited the car and pushed open the gate. It was clear he had done this before.

"When was the last time you were here?"

"When Anke came out to work on her book, I brought her some flowers."

"Those flowers arrived in the middle of the night—I was here then. I didn't even know."

"Not everything is for you to know, Little Marie."

"But I know now."

"Because you have earned my trust. My wife would not understand. With wives, they are always worried about sex with other women. No matter how many times I tell her I would never. Not at this age. Not when I know how good I have it. Still, it's the ember of her fear. I would not do anything to feed that fire. Anke and I have a cup of tea, talk about Ody, that is all."

"What do you say about Ody?"

"Even though he is almost fifty years old, he is our child. We have hopes and dreams for him. We have memories of his whole life. There is plenty to say."

The car pulled up in front of the house. Anke stood outside, wrapped in her pale pink cashmere throw. She was so beautiful you found yourself discovering it all over again, every time you saw her. But she was leaning on her cane. Mari was surprised, thinking she would have been too vain. Rimbaud sat at her feet. Anke stepped forward to receive two kisses from Dante.

Mari stood back shyly. This was the first time she had seen Anke since the intimacy of their weekend together, since Anke had doubted her integrity and prose enough to fire her. She didn't know how much Anke was aware of what she had been doing, or how much she approved. She wanted to feel galvanized by Dante's belief in her, but mostly she felt exhausted.

"Magdalena, what has happened to you?" Anke said, examining her ghost.

"Mari tied one on a bit at my place, but she's all right," Dante said.

Mari hated the implication she had been unprofessional, but she took it.

Anke and Dante talked in low voices as Anke led them back to her private lounge. As she watched Dante open the door, and slow his pace to match Anke's, Mari saw them for what they were: not lovers. But friends. Parents. And twin flames. The kind of true love that endured.

Mari realized this could work out, as she had written it in her mind, and she would still never know all the shadowed corners in this story. Or all the feelings behind the deeds, both dark and heroic. Even with everything she had learned, the books would tell a partial truth. To stay on the inside, she must agree to keep the secrets, as the others had done; not doing so was the only misstep that could cause her to be ejected, as the first writer, Axel, had been.

Dante sat across from Anke, where Mari normally perched— apparently it was his spot, too. Mari sank into a velvet-covered barrel chair, a mohair blanket on her lap.

"I can't stay long," Dante said. "Fiona thinks I'm dropping Mari off at the airport. It is our last night at home before a very long tour."

"Our last night, too," Anke said, her voice shadowed with something Mari couldn't read.

"I couldn't not see you," Dante said.

Anke smiled, accepting his acknowledgment of her import in his life, using her power for good. Patted the couch for Rimbaud.

"Ja, you should go to Fiona," Anke said. "Just one cup of tea."

"Always got time for that," he said, smiling with his eyes.

A silence fell as Anke removed the basket containing her special blend of herbs from the teapot, poured out the fragrant liquid. She placed a few dried figs and almonds on the saucer of a cup. Handing it to Dante, she indicated he should give it to Mari. He obliged. After the day she'd had, it felt wonderful to be cared for like this. The china rattled a little in her hands. Mari forced herself to sit up, pull herself together, for whatever this moment was.

Dante returned to his seat and received his cup. Mari had spent so much time over the past few days with their younger selves, analyzing their motives and their love. But being with them now, she found they just made sense.

"While the three of us are together—" Dante began.

"Don't ruin the moment by talking too much," Anke said.

He laughed. "For once, it is not my usual folderol. This is important."

"Ja, okay," Anke said.

"Should I get out my recorder?" Mari asked.

"For this conversation, no," Dante said.

Mari nodded that she understood.

"Anke, you are hiring Mari to write your book?" Dante said.

Mari was too exhausted to feel nervous—she was relieved to finally know, either way.

"I am not decided. She has been very helpful to me of late. But. She is erratic."

Anke still had more power over Mari than she would have liked, and she blushed.

"She is very loyal, and sometimes that causes her to be overextended, but she is excellent at her job. And a good girl. You are hiring Mari to write your book?"

"Ja, okay then."

A bead of sweat trickled down Mari's armpit. She held very, very still.

"I have hired Mari to write my book," he said. "She has my blessing to do both, if she has yours."

"You are lucky to have her. Dante, your book proposal, I must say—" Anke made a sound like spitting.

Dante laughed, not seeming at all surprised. "Well, Sigrid wrote most of it, so—"

"I could tell. I do not know why you refuse to listen—"

Mari felt the longing to confess all, but she didn't know enough yet to risk it.

"Mari is writing my book, so you will be happy with what is in it and what is not."

"We will see," Anke said.

The reminder of the two books she must complete made Mari slack with weariness.

"There is one thing upon which we all must agree," Dante said, looking from one woman to the other. "Ody is my son. Do you understand? He is my boy. End of story."

Anke bit her lip, nodded. Tears threatened to overflow her eyes, but she did not allow them to fall. Mari knew all too well why this restraint was important to Anke. She had been given cars, diamonds, sailboats, songs, houses, even a son. But it was still hard for her to receive.

Dante drained the last of his tea, clattered the cup into its saucer. He reached into the inner pocket of his leather jacket and pulled out a sheaf of folded papers. He placed them in Anke's grasp. For a long moment, they were connected by the document.

"It is only what is yours," he said. "This house. It belongs to you. It belongs to Ody. I should have made it official years ago. I think my pride got in the way of my better instincts—it was the last thing I held over you, the final bit of control. I'm sorry."

"Oh, Dante," she said. "Danke."

Anke dropped the deed without a glance, took his hand in her own, laced her fingers through his. Pulling it up to her face, she pressed her cheek against his skin.

Mari gave them space for their goodbye, which was longer and more tender than she would have expected. But she could now see, whether it made sense to anyone else or not, they had both figured out how to make their lives and their loves work for themselves. Dante turned to Mari. Just thinking about saying goodbye to him made her throat feel tight. She forced a smile, to show him how much she appreciated his loyalty, his kindness, and his belief in her.

"Take care, Little Marie," he said. "We will speak again soon."

She laughed with relief, feeling the weekend's tension break, and leaned up for him to kiss her cheeks. After Dante showed himself out, Anke pulled her wrap tight and looked at Mari.

"I take it you have met Sigrid," she said. "It is written all over you."

Mari nodded. "Sigrid plays a dangerous game. She'll do anything."

"Ja, you and Sigrid are much the same."

Mari rebelled against the thought—stealing a journal and threatening a writer felt worlds apart. But Mari knew Anke was right; she understood that level of vulnerability, and even if she would never commit murder, she would do a lot worse than she'd thought possible before this job. Clearly she was in no state to handle the delicacy this conversation required—not tonight.

"You have survived," Anke continued. "You are more gifted than I think. This is why I will hire you again. If you are this courageous in your life, you can be this courageous on the page."

Mari awoke at the sound of a faint rustling. By the time she had felt for her glasses, and managed to sit up, the room was empty, silent. Her head throbbed. She was surprised to find herself back in Anke's guest bed. Clutching her forehead against the pain, she remembered everything, the anxiety, the champagne, the pool, the truce, the hushed conversations, the two ghosting jobs.

She wanted nothing more than to sleep. But when she looked at her phone, it was three p.m. Anke had already let her rest far beyond their meeting time of eleven a.m.

Forcing herself to move through her headache, she sat up and walked to the desk, where someone had placed a tray. With a bottle of cold Gerolsteiner, a glass with a lemon wedge, four Advil, a teapot, almond milk, a plate with dark brown peasant bread, ham, and cheese. Having managed to get down a little food, and been revived by a hot shower, Mari sat still.

She was unsure how to proceed. The kindness Anke had shown her, and the intimacy with Dante she had let her witness, made Mari feel like she had finally earned her trust. But Mari knew this was a tender moment. She still had much to prove.

She texted Anke: "Thank you for letting me sleep. I am ready to work, whenever."

Fifteen minutes later, she got her response: "Yes."

Armed with her laptop and her recorder, Mari stepped out into the corridor. Ody was sitting there with his long legs splayed, deep in his phone.

"Hey, ghost," he said.

"Hey, prodigal son. When do you leave for tour?"

"A few hours," he said. "I hope I didn't wake you when I brought in your tray. I'm garbage at all that domestic stuff. But Anke let the help go. There's no one left but us. Listen—"

His phone buzzed, and his eyes dropped to it.

"Anke," he said. "Wondering where we are."

"I'm ready when you are," Mari said. Her instinct told her to avoid his need, and to focus on her own. She was already serving two masters. To add a third would feel like self-induced schizophrenia.

He stepped close to her. "You could have grabbed the money from Dante's book and run," he said. "I respect that you're taking on Anke as well. I don't think you would be here if you didn't care."

"But—"

"Don't let Anke pervert your intentions. She acts on impulse. She—" He paused, searching for words.

"Her impulses seem to have been right more than not," Mari said.

"But as you know, she is not well. There was supposed to be a surgery for her hip, but they found something in her blood, so now they say she could not survive. The pain grows every day, consuming her from within. She has been given morphine. She—she—she is not well."

"I'm so sorry, Ody," Mari said.

"She is proud. But it drains her—more and more. She says she can't stand it."

"But she won't go to the hospital."

"She won't go anywhere. But she won't stay." His voice cracked.

Finally, Mari could read the tension between Anke and Ody. Anke was planning to end her life. Soon. But now that she was up against the finale, she was afraid—of being forgotten, of being misunderstood. Mari hated the thought of a world without Anke. But she had become so entwined with her that, whatever Anke desired, she found she must champion it as her own cause.

"Anke wants a legacy, which I will give her, and with that in place, she has lived the arc of her life. There is an end to her fear, her suffering. You would deny her that peace?"

"This isn't about me," he said.

"No, it's not." She began walking toward Anke's room.

"She's not Anke to me," he said. "She's my mother, and I can't bear to lose her. We could still have more time. She is so stubborn. But maybe you can help me change her mind."

Mari heard the heartbreak in his voice, understood why so many mountains had been moved to get him out on the band's world tour, under the wing of his father, away from this house. Anke had a plan all her own. The thought of never seeing her again made Mari's chest feel tight. She wanted to turn around and be his friend. But it wasn't time for that, not yet.

Mari knocked, but there was no response. Ody was close behind her, and he pushed open the door. Mari stepped forward. They were like two children, both wanting to get to Mom first. The room was empty. He opened the door leading to Anke's bedchamber.

The long, jewel-colored drapes let in diffuse light, keeping the space dim. It was even more intimate than her lounge—everything curated, beautiful, precious.

Anke sat up in bed, an IV coiling down and into her arm. Rimbaud was nestled by her.

"You are looking better today, Magdalena," she said.

"I feel much better. Thank you. I am ready to work."

Mari knew not to be the first to acknowledge Anke's illness, or the weakness it implied.

Anke paused as Rimbaud stood, turned in a circle three times, then settled in closer. She winced at even this faint pressure on her hip, but she did not move him. Mari drew nearer to Anke, daring to sit on the edge of her bed and take her hand. Up close, Anke smelled like Fracas.

"You hold all the cards, Anke, as you always have," Mari said. "Sigrid isn't a threat anymore. We've made a truce. She'll go her way, and we'll go ours. Dante gave you his blessing and his word. You are free to have your day, to tell your story."

"If you have made a truce with Sigrid, then we cannot tell my story," Anke said.

Mari bit the inside of her lip. Anke was right. Mari was the one who'd hamstrung them. Then she thought about how they'd all needed to bend and contort themselves, to avoid the truth for the past fifty years. She didn't want to live like that, no matter what honesty cost her and V.

"I'm sorry, Anke," Mari said. "Sigrid blackmailed me. It has to do with my sister, Vivienne. I promised her that we wouldn't write what she did to Mal."

"Ja, that is Sigrid. But I would not write it even if we could. Who can blame her? I abandon her, as does everyone else in her life. Even when we are together in Los Angeles, I am caught up in my own drama. I am vain and a coward. I am not a good friend."

"But you were so young. You were—"

Mari became aware of Ody, seated in the chair next to his mother.

"You had everything to lose. And Mal, maybe he was already lost."

"He was lost, but as long as he was alive, there was still hope."

"Yes, hope for you, Anke. But not for Mal. He left a note. Sigrid can't prevent us from revealing this—it was for you. Or maybe for Nancy. But he was trying to communicate that he had reached the end."

"What note?" As Mari pulled it up on her phone, Anke slid on her glasses.

"Maybe he felt the least he could do was say, 'Sorry.'"

Anke surprised Mari by clutching the top of her hand.

"Ja, I'm sorry," Anke said. "I never saw it that way, but before Mal leaves my room, he stops and lets Syd go on without him. He turns and says, 'I'm sorry, Anke.' I say, 'Fuck you and your sorries, you sick bastard.' And he goes. But I thought it was for Nancy, for pushing me."

Mari nodded her head, not saying anything, letting Anke piece together her memory and its implications for herself, allowing her the space to forgive herself—or not.

"Nancy, she tells you about this note?" Anke asked.

"Nancy signed a document, from the band's lawyers, saying she would never speak."

"The music business is the devil's work." Anke made her spitting sound.

"Nancy has not betrayed her agreement. But the note came to be in my possession. As long as I do not say how, it is ours to use. You didn't kill him, Anke. Maybe he took your Quaaludes without knowing it, but he would have taken them gladly, and more. Everyone in the band knows it. By this section of the book, the reader will know it, too. We will reveal the truth of his mental state at this time."

Anke sighed, leaning back into her pillows.

"Okay, we will use the note. And the Mandrax. That is all I know. After, Mal left my room. I do not hear anything more until Nancy is running through the house, screaming Mal has died."

Mari wanted to ask if she was lying for herself or for Sigrid. But she understood now that once you asked a question, whether or not it was answered, you couldn't take it back. And yet Mari was starting to realize she was going to have to ask herself the hard questions, if she didn't want to end up as unable to hear the truth as her clients could sometimes be.

"We won't let this one night define you, I promise," Mari said. "Tell me how you reinvented yourself and your life began anew. Tell me how you want people to know you. I will work like I am your own army of ghosts."

Ody leaned toward his mother, smiling. "Mari can stay here with you, while I'm away on tour, to help you with your book and to make sure you're comfortable," he said. "We'll explain everything to the publisher, get an extension of your deadline."

Anke reached her other hand to Ody but didn't acknowledge his words. Instead, she spoke to Mari: "After today, when I am gone, you will stay here, and you will handle everything?"

"I will handle everything, just as you would."

"And you will be a friend to Ody? Yes, you will be his dear friend, his best friend."

Mari nodded because her chest was too clenched to speak. She had been so sure Anke had no vision, but it was Mari whose goals had been small. She had been worried about a writing job, a little money. By fighting hard to earn her place, she had been given so much more.

Six hours later, Anke had finished her tale. For the last thirty minutes, when she visibly tired and began to wind down, Ody vented his tense energy into his texts, as if forcing them into the ether.

"If you need to leave for the airport, my darling, you should go," Anke said. "I understand the band cannot wait. It is okay. I know you love me. As I love you."

Mari was surprised by the tenderness in Anke's voice, which she didn't often show when Mari was in the room. Ody seemed to hear it, too, because he smiled at his mother, although the rest of his body was barbed with anxiety.

"I'm happy to be here with you," he said. "We have time yet. Mari will stay with you, and I can have Rosenda come back tomorrow."

Anke shook her head with a gentle no, turned to Mari, who was stretching her wrists.

"I think that is all, then," Anke said.

Mari scanned her mind. She couldn't think of any questions important enough for her to press Anke, who looked exhausted and wan, and had been taking frequent sips of a dark, strong-smelling tea. Next to it on the nightstand were four vials of morphine. The number was not lost on Mari. No matter what Mari had uncovered, no one could absolve Anke but herself.

"Thank you," Mari said, bowing to her. "I'll leave you two alone."

"Mari, you will stay," Anke said. "Odin, come here and kiss your mother."

He stood, frozen, and shook his head. He knew and hated what she was asking of him, to give her the grace of a warm goodbye, even though he was furious at her for her choice.

"Komm her, Mäuschen," Anke said.

He took a breath, so deep and shuddery Mari traced its length from across the room. Slowly, he walked to his mother's side, let her take his hands in hers. He bowed his head. Anke began to speak to him in German.

When Anke stopped talking, tears were streaking Ody's face. He had always seemed like a perfect dutiful son and assistant who had put aside his own musical career to be of service to his parents. But here at his mother's side, he was a little boy full of feelings. He didn't cover his face or avoid the moment, difficult as it was. She could see both Anke and Dante in him.

"Now, please leave me alone with Mari," Anke said. "She will take care of everything, be my voice on the page and in the world. You can trust her. You can rely on her."

Again, he shook his head, even more vehemently, squeezed his mother's hand.

"Odin, it's time. I put it off, for you, for as long as I could. Please, let me go. It hurts too much, and it will hurt more every day. Let me have my dignity and do it my way."

Finally, he nodded, kissed her hand, again seeming so much like Dante, in his body, his movements, his casual focus. "I love you, Mutti," he said. His eyes down, he left.

Mari joined Ody outside Anke's room, twenty minutes later, shutting the door with a soft, firm click. Ody was pacing, smoking, which she had never seen him do. She almost didn't recognize him. He leapt forward, grasping the knob. Mari put her own hand on his, removed it.

"No," she said. "She's fallen asleep. Rimbaud is with her. It's how she wanted it."

"I have to be at the airport forty minutes ago," he said. "You shouldn't be here."

"You heard Anke. Please, trust me. Anke does. Dante does."

"You think you can come in here, learn our lives in a few weeks, and tell us our stories?" He looked like he wanted to hit her, and she didn't blame him—she knew it was his grief acting on him.

"I'm so sorry for your loss, Ody," she said.

She studied him, his handsome face, the elegant length of him, wondering what he did and didn't know about his parents, the lives they had led before he was born. Well, she would let him have as many illusions as she could. So much of Anke's subterfuge was for him, after all.

"Ody, as you heard, it is Anke's desire that she lives to see the publication of her book."

"But—" he said, his voice hopeful.

Mari shook her head, letting him know it was too late.

"She wishes to live in public, which is what I can do for her. It's already done, exactly as Anke planned. Please, try to be at peace. Let me take care of the details—for Anke, for you."

"I'm trying to protect her, to be a good son."

"You are a good son. Anke knows it. Dante knows it. Now it's time to prove it. You said you would help me."

"Yes, but how?"

"It was Anke's desire that she lives—in public—to see the publication of her book," Mari repeated herself. "It's the only way to be sure we control the story, and with it, Anke's legacy."

Ody looked at her for a long moment, and then a dawning realization arrived, and it was clear on his face; he might not like what his mother had orchestrated, but he accepted it.

"Fine," he said. "But I'm doing this for her. Not for you. Or for Dad."

She nodded. Before she could stop him, or get in his way, he burst through the door into Anke's room. Mari hesitated, decided to give him the privacy of this moment at least, since Anke had enforced how everything else would go, right up until her end.

When he emerged, he held his hand to shield his eyes so Mari couldn't see his face, but tears were everywhere. She wrapped him up in a big hug and held him until his sobs stopped. "I have to go," he whispered. "Stay here as long you need. I'll text you from the road."

She nodded, walked him out, accepted his kisses on her cheeks, locked the gate from the inside.

Mari felt self-conscious as the workers stole glances at her in Anke's pink silk kimono. The crew had arrived just before seven a.m., as the sky was blooming with color, to check the outline of the new pool before pouring its shell. Looking down at her hands, she noticed the sand crusting her fingernails, hid them behind her back. But she didn't go inside. After all, this was what she had agreed to do, for Anke, to wear her clothes, to take care of her house, and to maintain her voice and legacy. She had to accept all that came with it, didn't she? As she had learned from Anke and Dante, the mask one wore was its own expression of selfhood. Mari was still new to believing she could pull it off, as they always had, but she was gaining confidence.

The foreman had said she didn't need to be there. Concrete was loud, and ugly, and kicked up particles of dust. They had agreed on the dimensions Mari had requested, and the new pool's relation to the house before he'd had his guys excavate the shape the day before.

But it seemed disrespectful not to be there, not to watch the changing of the guard, as the old plunge pool that had been put in by the original owners in the '20s was replaced by something deeper and more permanent. And to say goodbye to Anke one last time.

The truck backed up to the hole. Shouts bounced around the yard. For a moment Mari got caught up in the propulsive excitement of something being built, work being done well, and she forgot. But as the metric tons of liquid concrete filled the giant gash in the earth, and obscured it from sight forever, she remembered. Every moment she had spent in this house with Anke. Everything she had risked. Everything she had agreed to. The edges of her vision blackened, the iron maiden of anxiety making it hard to breathe. She wanted to be here, yet couldn't stand it.

She prepared the tray for the workers, as Anke would have, with Heath ceramic mugs, cloth napkins, sliced fruit, and cheese. Then she left them to it and set herself up, alone in the house, Rimbaud at her feet, ready to write the ending.

EIGHTEENTH:
CARE

Deadline time is different. Some trifling detail takes a whole day's labor. And yet it must be attended to with particular care—a single sensitive scene within the whole writhing story that has to be rewritten again and again. Plus, it's hard for clients to remember which Christmas was which, and how old they were in the years between big events. They often get their timelines wrong, and fact-checking dates can take hours. That's why endurance is crucial, and yet, whenever you are with your client, it must be made to look effortless, so as not to scare them off.

The weeks inched by, the days and nights becoming indistinguishable, because of the necessity of sitting for all those hours, choosing and placing and polishing each of the 75,000 words that went into constructing a book. Even with frequent bribes of caffeine, sugar, and masturbation—anything to bear the monotony—many long dull spells were endured. Of course there were dazzles of inspiration, connecting two important moments in the story or finding the perfect turn of phrase. She could become enamored of a passage and read it aloud again and again, like the intoxication of the first days in bed with a new lover, until she forced herself to move onto the next section, which was rough, unwieldy, and held no pleasure.

Ody checked in daily by text. One night he was in Paris. The next, Milan. He had his own tedious spells to fill—the downtime between sound check and the show, the early-morning bus calls for runs of dates when it made more sense to drive than fly. But there were also many diversions—strolling through the Uffizi during a morning off, racing the Autobahn on a rented motorcycle. Having no news of her own to report, Mari replied with pictures of the desert sky at dawn when she was riding an all-nighter. Or the cluster of glasses near her laptop, containing mineral water, coffee, red wine, and kombucha, fronted by a plate of fresh figs and dusty roasted almonds. Sometimes, in a burst of confidence, she sent him an excerpt, a bit of dialogue that made either of his parents dance to life on the page, or a funny story he maybe hadn't heard before. If he had a reaction to seeing the familiar china and linens, if he'd noticed them at all, or to being introduced to his family as the world was about to know them, he didn't say. But he kept writing to her, day after day, even just a quick hello, and she always wrote back. Their correspondence was its own insight into the question of how loyal, to her and her cause, he would be, and also a way for them both to process all they were missing and anxious about.

It often felt like the clocks had stopped, like she was running in place and would never get anywhere. Although she was lonely and would not have wanted anyone to witness her long, intimate conversations with Rimbaud. Although she was sometimes shattered by deep grief and self-doubt, desperate for anyone she could talk to about it all, to ask if she had done the right thing. She was still good at forcing herself to sit, maybe better than ever, because of all that was at stake now. And so, time did equal pages. She finished Dante's book three days before their deadline so he could read it and give his approval before she sent it in to their editor.

Sitting at her computer, drinking a small glass of mezcal, she thought of how far she had come. Izzy had been promoted to fill Sigrid's position. During the emails they exchanged, Mari did not have to look deeper for subtext, as she always had with Sigrid. She could just do her job. It was a relief. And yet she was proud of what she had learned about herself from her time near Sigrid. She had hoped Anke's book would be a ladder, and yes, she had climbed it after all.

There were edits of Anke's book as well. Mari pretended to confer with Anke, regarding specific scenes and moments when something might be written differently. Occasionally, she asked Ody. But she mostly answered the questions herself from her own existing notes, or the map of Anke's life and psyche that was now imprinted within Mari, as surely as her own.

Ody extended his dates on the road, agreeing to sit in for all of their tour, as if he did not want to come home. They played Los Angeles, but no one thought to invite Mari. Or maybe they thought against it. Ody made no effort to see her. She wasn't surprised. Being a ghost could be like being that lover you did the crazy sex stuff with, or fought the nastiest—once you split up, you couldn't stand to be in the same room together. It was too intimate. At first, she followed the band's social media and press coverage, marveling at her closeness with Dante, how well she knew these legends in ways that few others did. She told herself it was "research," and since she was thinking about the band twelve hours a day, it felt like part of the overall Ramblers blur.

Several times, she picked up her phone to text Vivienne, but Mari was scared, unsure whether to tell her that she knew the full story of Vegas, and who she really was. It made her sad that V had been forced to pick up the wreckage once again and stuff it deep inside. So she could go on with the business of surviving. Mari was even more afraid to maybe learn she wasn't, that time was operating in a different way for V. And that, maybe, the months spent placating and titillating an unkind man in Chicago were much longer than the months spent stretching sore muscles and eating too many vegan chocolate chip cookies while on deadline for two high-paying, high-profile books.

So, she put down her phone and told herself that she and V had made an agreement. She still had a few months.

In early March, both books went to the printer—first Dante's, and then Anke's. Several days passed, without a single email pinging her in-box with a last-minute question or proof. Mari endured inevitable moments of doubt—while shampooing her hair, she recalled Dante's hilarious run-in with a kangaroo from a 1975 tour stop in Sydney. As she walked Rimbaud, she parsed her descriptions of Mal for anywhere she had been histrionic or unfair.

It wasn't long before she didn't think about either book so much. She even began to regard them with fondness. It was as if an experiential amnesia had set in, like the kind she had read about that allowed women to forget childbirth's agony in order to go through it again. She was as proud as any new mother who had endured a gruesome and extended labor. She had been stuck in a situation where there was no choice but to keep moving forward, even when she had thought it would break her, maybe kill her. Through her determination and, yes, her unconditional love, she had found depths she hadn't been aware of, and she had come through.

August 7, 2019. The fiftieth anniversary of Mal's death. Onstage at the Hollywood Bowl, the band paused, six songs into their set. Jack retreated to the drum riser, sipped from a glass bottle of water, toweled off his tousled hair in a sexy, relaxed way. Dante pushed pedals with his designer work boot, tuning his guitar, squinting against the smoke from his cigarette. Ody bounced on his brown suede moccasins, drank an Amstel Light with restraint.

As if on cue, they circled up, the drummer leaning down from behind his kit, and bowed their heads together. At the group's center, Jack spoke into his mic:

"We could not go a moment further without acknowledging it was fifty years ago, today, that we stood on this very stage and mourned

a man without whom this band would not exist—the brilliant, maddening, maddeningly brilliant Mal. In his honor, we're going to play a
song we don't normally do. Of the many bang-up tunes he wrote, it's
always been our favorite, and we'd like to dedicate it to his memory,
with all our love."

Ody leaned back to strum a few simple folksy chords on his acoustic
guitar. Dante smiled at him, appearing blissed out by the music, and
the feeling that never grew old, of playing with his boy, his son. Dante
threw out a few thunderbolts of slide guitar, as if from on high. The
drummer set the tempo with floor tom, then added a shimmer of snare.
The music was taking shape, but it was still subdued enough for Jack to
talk over it.

"Although Mal was twenty-four when he passed out of this world,
he was an old soul. He did a lot of living in his short time here. We
will always be grateful for the passion, the frisson, he brought to the
group, without which we would not be quite the same as we are."

Mari rolled her eyes. She was sipping iced tea with fresh mint,
watching the live feed of the show on the wall-mounted flat-screen TV.

"Half-truths are like chili peppers, Jack," she said. "A little goes a
long way."

Standing to refill her glass, she turned up the volume. The TV was
wired into the house speakers, and the song thrummed through the
rooms. It was as if the band were there with her, inside her life, even
though only Rimbaud was present.

She danced a little, in front of the couch, the new pale pink kaftan
she'd ordered for herself silky on her bare skin, the makeup she'd put
on that morning—because it felt like a special occasion—making her
look like she was attending a party.

The song stuttered through three false outros, hit a fast stop. Dante
stepped up to the mic.

"For this next number, I'd like to introduce our special guest, whom
we've been lucky enough to have out with us for this tour: my son Ody."

As fans cheered, Ody sauntered up, leaned toward his dad, and echoed his moves.

Mari smiled. Seeing them together would never not make her happy and proud. The ding of an email sounded from her laptop, which was open on the coffee table. She turned down the volume, grabbed her computer. Rimbaud hopped up next to her, settling in, as he did now.

The email, addressed to Anke Berben, was from their publisher. Not their editor, but their editor's boss's boss, and the subject line read "CONGRATULATIONS!!"

> *Dear Anke,*
>
> *Please accept heartfelt congratulations and best wishes, from your entire team, in recognition of the remarkable feat of your second week at the top of the NYT Bestseller list. We appreciate your great courage and sincerity in the writing of your wonderful book, and we value all you have done and continue to do to promote it. We are with you!*

As when doing press for Anke, Mari had found it best not to overthink her tone or the substance of her correspondence. There was a certain in-between state she could reach where she was channeling what was needed. She replied quickly. Hit send.

Trailing her eyes down her in-box, she sighed. A half dozen email interviews were waiting for Anke, and since she had managed to push for all the promotion to be done electronically, she couldn't be stingy with her attention to this portion of Anke's plan.

It had never occurred to her that having a better, more beautiful life, in which she was able to indulge herself, would make it harder to do the things she didn't feel like doing. But her many years of deadlines, always met because there had been no safety net, had been like time in the army. The old discipline was coiled within her, and Mari could unleash it at will.

Her iced tea kicked in, and she banged out replies. Each was as warm and aloof and funny and oddly syntaxed as Anke on her best day. The concert played in the background. When Mari had responded to everything that needed immediate attention, she put her bare feet up on the coffee table. Leaning back into the throw pillows, breathing the room's cedar scent, she watched the band finish its second encore. They stood at the lip of the stage, arms around each other, and bowed as one. The crowd went mad with appreciation, and she thought about how it felt for these men to belong a little bit to her, in a way even their most ardent fans would never know. There was an art to access, to really getting to know someone, and only certain people had mastered it like she had. Because of this, she had been rewarded with these gifts.

She had pulled off both books, received her payments, paid off her debt, and taken Ezra's advice not to rush into her next ghosting job, waiting to see what these bestsellers did for her demand. And now she allowed herself to relax into the rhythms of the house. In the morning, she woke without an alarm for her meditation, sun salutations, and a swim. She drank tea with a light breakfast in the garden. When being away from her computer made her feel adrift, she went into Anke's lounge, closed her eyes, and grabbed a book. She was learning about mythology, poetry, design, fine art. In the evening, when it was cooler, she worked in the garden, walked Rimbaud, took a final swim as the sun set. When she stretched out in the water now, she wasn't lonely. She had the feeling of peace that came with belonging inside her own life. She felt like Anke was there with her, showing her how it was done.

Now it was time for her to share. It had been five months—she didn't have everything in place yet, but she wasn't going to break her promise. She scrolled through her contacts. Feeling generous, she launched a FaceTime connection, even though she hated live video. To her surprise, V picked up on the second ring. If she was still in Chicago, it was late there. Vivienne was beautiful, as always, but she had become so skinny it was draining her looks. Dark fabric hung behind her, pressed against the top of her hair from all sides. "Hi," Vivienne whispered.

"Where are you?" Mari asked.

"Somewhere I can talk. Where are you?"

"Palm Springs. Why can't you talk somewhere normal? Are you okay?"

"Okay-ish."

Mari was already longing backward, for the languid peace and quiet of the paradise she had occupied for the past months. But she knew she needed something new, even if it wasn't exactly what she wanted. Trading one isolation for another wasn't good.

"I have a place," Mari said. "It doesn't really belong to me, but we can always stay here, for as long as we need, while I make arrangements for the place that will."

"Thank you," V said.

Mari didn't allow any snarky comments inside her head, just smiled with real warmth.

They made quick and efficient plans for V to get out. When they'd finished, she hung up. The band was playing its final encore. Mari walked through the house, with seventeen thousand people cheering in her ears. She luxuriated in the pleasures of the space, running her hands over antique tables and cashmere throws, pausing at the window to ponder the exquisite view.

Rimbaud click-clacked behind her on the Spanish tile floor. She had been pent up in the air-conditioning, working all day, just like in her old life, and she couldn't stand it anymore. Only now she had a better choice, and she would enjoy it. Already stripping, she strode into the baking heat, her feet light on the hot concrete, before diving naked into the water.

As she flew through the cool blue liquid, gliding the length of the pool, she heard Anke's voice, in their final moments together, after Anke had sent Ody out of the room.

"There is one truth we still need to discuss," Anke had said, petting Rimbaud. "I think you should know what is in my secret heart, in order to become me on the page. I would never take Dante and Ody away from each other. I am happy they are together. Mal *was* Ody's father. But I didn't kill him, even though Ody could only benefit if he died. For years, I punished myself because I felt responsible for Sigrid, like I had created the monster she was. I let the guilt eat me whole. But as I have told my story, I have made peace with my intentions. I brought Sigrid to LA to try to help her. I did not know what Sigrid would go on to do. The question of her guilt is between her and Mal and the universe. All I ever try to do is protect my son. Mal's estate continues to go through me, to Ody, for as long as it can—do you understand?"

"Of course," Mari said. "Anke, if I may—"

"Ja, Magdalena," Anke said. Her eyes were still bright.

"There are many ways to be a father," Mari said. "And Dante, he's really good. So maybe he has too many kids by too many women, and he spent a little too much, and he can't take care of Ody in that way. But when Dante looks at all of his kids, he makes them the center of the world. It's the kind of gaze that makes a person feel seen. It's the best gift you could have given your son."

These were people who loved deeply, and with loyalty that could endure all the tests of fame, money, and time. They had allowed Mari inside, made her feel like one of them. Even Sigrid had left a space for her. This was why she had risked everything to be here, to protect Anke and Ody, to seal away the past in her book, and in Dante's book, forever. She lifted Anke's hand into her lap. "Don't think about it anymore," Mari said. "You have earned your peace."

"Thank you, Magdalena. You are a better version of myself."

"Thank *you*, Anke. It has been my honor."

Closing her eyes, and smiling like a little girl, Anke tilted her head up for Mari to kiss her cheeks. As Mari's lips touched the papery skin and felt the warmth of Anke's blood close to the surface, she was filled with a mother's fierce loyalty, the deep and complete acceptance of unconditional love. Mari stroked Anke's hair on her pillow. Anke's smile lingered as she nodded. She had chosen all the words she needed to say, and now she was silent.

Anke's eyes fluttered closed, her breathing slowed.

"I'm here," Mari said. "I will always be here."

Mari had spent hundreds of hours with the young Jack and Dante, writing about the summer of '69. When she watched them onstage together, late in the summer of '19, she saw them as their former selves, lithe and beautiful, crackling with fresh notoriety, opulence, and power.

Backstage, in the greenroom, Mari sipped champagne as she waited for Dante to emerge from his post-show massage. Izzy was chatting up the select music journalists who warranted VIP access. It was a relief to no longer need Sigrid's blessing, to have earned an undeniable place here, and to feel the confidence of not just knowing how to fit in but also how to enjoy herself.

Mari edged over to the bar to refresh her champagne just as Dante entered. "Little Marie, it's grand to see you," he said. "You really did it after all. A number one *New York Times* bestseller is no small thing. Not to mention the many stars you have lassoed for our dear Anke. You must come to JT. Stay for the whole weekend. You're invited anytime."

He put his hand on Mari's shoulder with goodwill.

"Dante, you're looking fierce," Mari said, accepting his lips on each cheek.

"Don't blow smoke. I look like a skeleton in a Punch-and-Judy bit, but I'm still dancing."

He bent his knees and did a little move she recognized from the show. She laughed. But he wasn't smiling. He had summoned her from her new house in Mérida to their concert at a legacy rock festival at the Hard Rock Cafe in Cancun. She had been surprised at first, and then uneasy. But she had been careful, every step. She had never lost her courage. She had bested Sigrid. Now she had to face whatever this was.

Dante gave her a long, hard look, something he was exceedingly good at. She felt like she was being reprimanded by her dad—well, a real dad. She doubled down, stood taller.

"I meant what I said during our drive to Palm Springs, Marie," Dante said. "It's time to think about you. Even ghosts deserve a little happiness. Don't be a stranger. It's too lonely."

At first, she felt uncomfortable, like she was in trouble, but then she forced herself to reassess—being a part of any kind of clan meant accountability. It was nice.

As much as Anke had given her, her absence had been required to unlock her gifts, leaving Mari as alone as she'd ever been. In a few hours in the desert, Dante had shown her how to be a family, and he had allowed her to feel like she belonged to his. Lying to him had been the hardest part of the whole charade. Maybe a deep secret part of her had known this moment was approaching, because tucked inside her purse was Anke's favorite pink silk scarf. Inside were the four empty morphine vials.

When he first received the fabric in his hand, Dante recognized it as Anke's, and his face defaulted to its boyish grin, thinking a game was afoot. As he was opening the folds, now it was Mari who pulled them back into a private corner. When he saw the parcel's contents, his face crumpled. He turned to the wall, shuddered.

"I never left her," Mari said.

"If that's true, she was lucky until the end. I don't know if I could have stood it."

"You would have. For Anke."

"Yes, for Anke." He leaned down, kissed each of Mari's cheeks, his eyes wet.

Ody appeared beside them, in his silent way.

"Are you all right, Pop?" he asked.

"You knew?" Dante replied.

Ody looked away, nodding his head.

"I'm afraid I need time to metabolize this information," Dante said. "Little Marie, be well. Visit us soon. Ody, I think I'd like to take dinner in my room. I will see you then."

Ody nodded again, now turning to smile at his father. The two men hugged. Mari and Ody both watched Dante as he disappeared into his private dressing room, waving off those who tried to grab him on the way. Once he was gone, they stood awkwardly, a little too close together, not making eye contact. Unsure what to say or how to be. It was easier by text.

"Are you holding up?" She broke the silence.

"No? Yes? For now, I suppose. I don't know about when tour ends, which it has to, eventually. How about you?"

"I don't know—the same? It varies, day to day. But mostly, I feel okay."

"You don't have to do this forever," Ody said. "It was too much for Anke to ask of you."

"It was what Anke wanted, and she took care of almost everything ahead of time, even left a forged death certificate, dated 2021. I'm happy to keep it up until then. It wouldn't really make sense after that anyhow. Press for a new book lasts a few months. Then the paperback will stir up a bit of new attention. After that, there won't be much for me to do."

"Thank you, Mari," he said. "We'll figure it out."

"You will continue to receive the publishing from Mal's estate for that time, and also all the royalties from the book. After that, you will have her estate."

"And I'll be free to tour with my band. She never liked me to be away. But how will we do it when the time comes?"

"I'll write up a press release," Mari said. "It will say Dante, you, and myself, we had a private ceremony. The body was cremated."

He winced at the last word but nodded.

"But for now, Anke lives on," she said.

"Just so you know, I consider the Palm Springs house yours, too. You should feel free to use it as much as you like, anytime. I can't imagine setting foot there again."

"When you're ready, let me know," Mari said. "I'll fly up and meet you. It's all waiting for you, just the way she arranged it, as if she's in the next room. She feels very close."

"It's different for you, she was my mother."

"Yes. But also, it's different for me. I have been her."

"Let's not talk about that here. We did what she asked us. For now, that's enough."

"Thank you. I couldn't have done it without you."

"Well, we did it," he said, dodging her kindness, or maybe the guilt by association. But he didn't seem angry. Or if he was, it was just one feeling of many, like the complex web of family, of love—the ways we are bound to each other, by blood, by affinity, by need. He stepped closer, seemed about to reach for her hand. Mari inhaled jaggedly, feeling potential blossom.

Izzy zipped up. "Ody, the journalist from Telemundo has some questions for the band. Come with me now, please."

Mari was surprised by how sorry she was to see him walk away, but she had no doubt that Ody would be in her life forever—there would be time for whatever was meant to be. That was the best part of what she had gained through osmosis from Anke—a belief in herself that fed a deep belief in the universe and, in turn, made her feel safe in her life, even during the in-betweens.

Grateful for everything she had been allowed to keep, Mari walked out of the room, still finishing her glass of champagne. It was possible—and fun—to live like a rock star. For starters, just decide not to give a fuck about the small stuff. As Mari closed the green-room door behind her, her phone buzzed in her purse. Ody had texted: "Thank you."

Mari left as she had come in, through the hotel's private celebrity entrance, projecting that she belonged and feeling more like she did than ever before. But, also like Anke, she was sure there were more interesting adventures for her out there in the world—beyond the velvet rope was freedom and the surprising opportunities of a life that had yet to be written.

As Mari waited for the valet to pull up her car, she turned and surveyed the scene. It felt vulgar and overbright: sunburned tourists wearing tequila-brand sombreros, drinking foot-long margaritas. But that was okay. She had done what she had come to do—the rest of the day, the month, her life belonged to her now, and she was no longer alone. Vivienne stood up from a nearby table, where she'd been having a drink while Mari wrapped up her business inside.

Vivienne joined Mari under the hotel's awning. "Are we happy?"

"We're happy," Mari said. The valet pulled up Mari's vintage Land Cruiser. She tipped him well as he exited the vehicle. Between the seats was the copy of Anke's book she had brought along, and then not given to Dante, feeling too much like she was showing him her report card. It was always hard to reconcile the finished book, an inert object, with all the passion and endurance and leaps of faith that had gone into creating it—not to mention the love. She tossed it over her shoulder, and it landed in the backseat.

Vivienne climbed into the car. Mari put her foot on the accelerator and drove away, toward their new home in the jungle, toward their new take on family, toward messy, joyous life.

ACKNOWLEDGMENTS

Bottomless thanks to my agent, Kirby Kim, who has helped me to navigate the worlds of publishing and celebrity for more than a decade with style, wit, and steadiness. Not only did you give me the idea for this book but you made it so much better with your advice and edits. Thank you to Eloy Bleifuss for excellent notes on this novel and infinite help on all fronts over the years. Thanks, also, to everyone at Janklow & Nesbit for taking care of business for me. And thank you to Jasmine Lake for excellent insights and help in bringing the Ramblers to the screen.

Zack Wagman, for being that rare, perfect blend of extremely smart and very funny and kind (sorry about all those adverbs). I may have already published a lot of books, but you were the editor who made me a debut novelist, and who helped to make that novel so much better with your wisdom and trust. Also, thank you to Maxine Charles, Bob Miller, Megan Lynch, Malati Chavali, Marlena Bittner, Nancy Trypuc, Claire McLaughlin, Katherine Turro, Elishia Merricks, Maria Snelling, Amber Cortes, Helen Laser, Samantha Edelson, Audrey Iorio, and everyone at Flatiron and Macmillan Audio for taking a chance on my first novel and supporting me to make it as undeniable as it could be. I can't wait to do it again!

Dave Litman, for designing the rock 'n' roll book cover of my dreams.

Crystal Patriarche and the entire BookSparks team for their expertise and support in the launching of this book.

Writers who read early and multiple drafts, talked me down off ledges, and inspired me with your own brilliance: Meg Howrey, Sarah Langan, J. Ryan Stradal, Chris Terry, Mel Toltz, Erin Almond, Steph Cha, Alex Segura, Rob Hart, Katie Gutierrez, Katrina Woznicki, David Sedaris, and a very special mention to Cathy Elcik, who has read more drafts of everything I've written and given me more pep talks than anyone could reasonably expect—I'm both lucky and grateful. And writers who supported me with advice, laughs, and the inspiration of your own work: Steffie Nelson, Caroline Ryder, Valerie Palmer, Laura Feinstein, Giuliana Mayo, Janet Fitch, David Francis, Brad Listi, Jodi Wille, Elizabeth Barker, Edan Lepucki, Julia Ingalls, Ivy Pochoda, Jim Ruland, Matthew Witten, Sara Sligar, Kate White, Regina Robertson, Laura Warrell, Christine Sneed, Holly West, Curtis Ippolito.

Jen Bergstrom, Carrie Thornton, Lisa Sharkey, Matt Harper, Farrin Jacobs, Kate Dresser, Leah Trouwborst, Jeremie Ruby Strauss, Brant Rumble, Jan Miller, Lacy Lynch, Shannon Marven, Dabney Rice, Nena Madonia Oshman, Nicole Tourtelot, Marc Gerald, Belle Zwerdling, Katey Sagal, and all my many amazing clients, for making my years as a ghostwriter so interesting, inspiring, and fun.

Russ, Bonnie, and Amber Tamblyn (as well as David Dunton and everyone on our team at Blackstone Publishing) for being an adoptive creative family and letting me sneak away from our collaboration on Russ's book to meet my deadlines for this novel.

Friends who were early readers and helped me with my foreign accents (all missteps are mine): Meredith Drake Reitan, Tiemo Mehner. Friends who gave me advice, about the legal ins and outs of the music business and legacy rock estates: David Lessoff; and Dante's gear: Imaad Wasif.

Friends who supported and inspired me during the many, many, many years it took me to become a debut novelist, including: Beth Cleary, Rebecca Berman, Brett Frenzel, Deanna DeVries, Malin Akerman, Kate Micucci, Jess Schmidt, Sam Barbera, Jodi Jackson, Iwalani Kaluhiokalani, Arrica Rose, Heather Crist, Brooke Delaney, Kathleen Whitaker, JoJo Sweiven, Fil Ruting, Amy Hoffecker, Patrick Brennan, Apryl Lundsten, Andrea Bowers, Sabra Embury, Chris Wallenberg, Amy Wallenberg, Marissa Nadler, Freyja Bardell, Cynthia Carlson, Sarah McCabe, Elissa Scrafano, Joshua Grange, Laurel Stearns, and Piper Ferguson.

Richard Stein, with love and gratitude, for supporting me and this book with love, advice, inspiration, and many delicious meals.

James Reed, for buoying me with treats, laughs, pep talks, playlists, strong coffee, and Dolly memes.

My family, for believing in me when I declared I was going to be a writer at age sixteen and for giving me so much love and support along the way, and especially my mom, for giving me my love of books, and whom I love to talk novels with more than anyone else in the world.

ABOUT THE AUTHOR

SARAH TOMLINSON, a former music journalist, has been a ghostwriter since 2008, penning more than twenty books, including five *New York Times* bestsellers. In 2015, she published the father-daughter memoir *Good Girl*. She wrote *The Last Days of the Midnight Ramblers*, her first novel, in between assignments for a who's who of celebrity clients.